THE DEMON STRAIN

DEMON HUNTER BOOK TWO

KERRY ADCOCK

Published in the United States by Wolfpack Publishing, Las Vegas

CKN Christian Publishing
An Imprint of Wolfpack Publishing
5130 S. Fort Apache Road 215-380
Las Vegas, NV 89148

cknchristianpublishing.com

Paperback ISBN 978-1-63977-941-3
eBook ISBN 978-1-63977-109-7
LCCN 2022933123

THE DEMON STRAIN

CHAPTER ONE

Obersalzberg
Southern Bavaria
The Republic of Germany, 1930

ON A BEAUTIFUL SPRING evening an expensive and exclusive black Horch 670 Sport Cabriolet's 12-cylinder engine purred as it cruised quietly through the picturesque Bavarian countryside near Obersalzberg, a mountainside retreat situated above the small city of Berchtesgaden. The seventy-five-mile drive from Munich had been uneventful as the chauffer pulled up in front of a small chalet named, *Haus Wachenfeld*, exited, and opened the door for a beautiful young blonde woman.

Frieda Getman stepped out and politely nodded to the driver. Frieda was a well-known actress in Europe during pre-World War II, who had performed on stage in Berlin, London, Paris, New York, and Los Angeles. She'd also starred in several motion pictures and was well thought of in all the important social circles. She wore an elegant blue dress that was snug in all the right places and matched her blue eyes. Her blonde hair was medium length and curled up at the ends.

As Frieda approached the front door it was opened by the house-keeper, a fortyish woman, who smiled slightly and ushered her inside. Frieda noticed that the entry hall was decorated with cactus plants in blue, green, and yellow Italian pots called *majolica*.

"*Guten abend*, I am Fraulein Getman," she said.

"I am Angela," the woman replied. "Please follow me." The housekeeper, Angela, turned and led Frieda down the hall to the main living area. The room was nicely but modestly furnished and had a fire burning in the fireplace which gave the room a warm glow.

"This is such a wonderful place," mentioned Frieda as she took in the small chalet. "Does Herr Wolf own it?"

Angela shook her head. "*Nein*, he rents it from the widow Frau Winter. Please sit and Herr Wolf will be in shortly."

"*Danke*," said Frieda. She sat down on the couch, opened her purse, and took out a cigarette.

"*Bitte*, Fraulein Getman," Angela said anxiously, "No one is allowed to smoke inside." She pointed to a small balcony. "You may step outside and smoke if you wish."

Frieda nodded but put the cigarette back in the pack and sat back to wait. Her thoughts drifted back to a few months ago when she'd met Herr Wolf. She'd been introduced to him through a mutual friend and found him intriguing even though he was not what she would've called handsome. After several parties and events, they became friendlier culminating in her invitation to the chalet for dinner. Her mutual friend mentioned that Herr Wolf was interested in politics and had even written a book whose title she couldn't remember. If it wasn't a movie or acting script Frieda didn't read it. She hadn't noticed that a young woman had stepped into the room, nor did she know how long the woman had been standing there until she spoke.

"Are you the actress Frieda Getman, from the movies?" asked the woman quietly.

Frieda turned at the sound of the woman's voice. "Why, yes, are you Herr Wolf's daughter?"

The young woman smiled briefly but shook her head. "*Nein*, he is my uncle. I am Geli." She had dark hair and wore a plain pleated skirt with a white blouse. Geli struck Frieda as more of a child than a grown woman. "I'm taking voice lessons."

"That's wonderful," replied Frieda with a smile. "I hope you'll keep them up and someday I'll be honored to go to your performances."

The woman nodded but had a dour look which made Frieda feel unwelcome.

A door opened, then closed, and Frieda turned as a man entered the room. He was five foot eight, about a hundred and eighty pounds with dark black hair and a mustache. "*Guten abend*, Fraulein Getman," he said with a smile.

Frieda came to her feet and extended her hand. "*Danke*, Herr Wolf, it's a pleasure to see you again, but please call me Frieda."

Herr Wolf took her hand gently but firmly. "It's my pleasure, Frieda. I see you've met my niece, Geli. Come, let us eat. Angela has made us a marvelous meal."

As they turned to leave the room Frieda smelled a strange odor, like ashes and rotten eggs. She glanced over at the fireplace thinking maybe something was burning in the fire, but it appeared undisturbed. Frieda was escorted into a dining room full of modest furniture. "Your chalet is very comfortable."

Herr Wolf shrugged and frowned. "It's not big enough or nice enough. I hope to purchase it from Frau Winter when my book becomes a success."

"I heard that you wrote a book, but I'm afraid I'm not much of a reader. I prefer the performing arts."

"Of course," he said with a slight smile, but Frieda detected a moment of disappointment in his eyes.

Dinner went pleasantly but Frieda did find it odd that no meat was served, only vegetable dishes but she remained polite. It was rude to insult a host's food choices. Through dinner Frieda talked about her next movie plans and Herr Wolf said how that was helping the economy but that Germany was suffering at the hands of the allies that had defeated Germany in World War I. Frieda noticed how intense and focused his eyes became when he spoke about the Fatherland and how he felt Germany was being mistreated. Geli added some small talk but remained quiet through dinner, and Frieda felt somehow it was because of her.

Dinner had taken longer than she had anticipated so Frieda had to cut the time short as she had to return to Munich. Herr Wolf walked Frieda to the door where her chauffeur stood just outside with the car door open.

"It was a wonderful dinner, Herr Wolf," exclaimed Frieda.

"We must do this again," he replied. "I'll call on you again and set up another time."

Frieda smiled, waved and climbed into the Horch Cabriolet. The car turned and drove off towards Munich. Herr Wolf closed the door and walked back to the other side of the chalet.

Geli stood and looked out of a side window at the retreating taillights of Frieda's car. "I don't like her," she said to herself then turned and headed down the hall but stopped when she smelled that same awful smell again. *Ashes and something rotten*. She waved a hand towel around in the air and vowed to put more flowers in a vase to cover whatever was making that smell.

————

Monument Valley,
Northern Arizona
U.S.A., Present Day

TOM PARKER, a thirty-year-old computer programmer from California and an experienced hiker smiled at his wife as the couple climbed over a low rise. Amy, a professor at UCLA and equally experienced hiker stared into the glowing sunset. The Parkers loved the natural beauty of northern Arizona and had hiked through the rugged Monument Valley many times. The massive valley, called Tse' Bii' Ndzisgaii by the Navajo, encompasses over 91,000 acres and is some of nature's most beautiful country. They sat down on the worn red siltstone which made up the majority of the rock in the area and watched the sunset spectacle in red, gold, pink, and dark blue. They sat for awhile and watched the sun dip below the horizon.

They'd brought enough gear, water, and supplies to last them for several days. They preferred to hike back into the more secluded areas away from the usual tourist sites and were currently somewhere between Mitchell Mesa and Mystery Valley. They scouted around for a good camping site and Tom found a nice ledge up against a tall rock formation to block the wind.

In short order they had their small tent set up. Tom heated their dinner on a small fire downwind and away from their tent. Afterward they sat near the dying fire enjoying the sounds of the desert night. The fire had died down to coals and Tom went to pour sand over it when he heard a strange raspy hissing sound. He hesitated and cocked his head toward the sound. "Did you hear that?"

Amy was bent down gathering up their gear. "No, what was it?"

Tom shook his head. "I don't know but it was strange." He shrugged and poured more sand on the fire when he heard it again. He turned to his wife in the dark.

"I heard it this time," said Amy. She looked around but it was too dark to see anything. "What do you suppose it is?"

Tom shook his head. "I don't know."

They heard the sound again only this time it was accompanied by the sound of claws scratching on rock.

"What do you think now?" asked Amy in a whisper.

"I don't know, but it's definitely some type of large animal." Tom slowly slipped over to where Amy was sitting and squatted down beside her. He picked up a small hatchet that they used to cut up wood. They heard the sound again. A flapping sound followed by a screech from overhead that sounded neither human nor animal. Both Parkers jumped at the sound and Tom pushed Amy back against the rock wall. "Stay put."

Amy reached out and grabbed his shirt. "No," she whispered. "Stay here."

Tom patted her arm and stepped away from the wall. "Whatever you are, go on, scat," he yelled. Tom hoped that if it was an animal the sound of a human voice would scare it off but instead a large form dropped out of the sky. Tom yelled at the thing to get away, but the dark form answered back with high and low pitch screeches. The creature moved closer while it continued to screech at Tom who backed away and swung the hatchet back and forth yelling, "Get away."

The creature knocked Tom to the ground as Amy's eyes widened in fright. She grabbed a flashlight and shined it on the two struggling forms but before Amy could see much more than a huge dark form with wings it blotted out the stars as it took off holding Tom by the shoulder. The abnormality turned, looked at her with one glowing yellow eye, and screeched.

Tom cursed, yelled, swung, and chopped at the thing as it flew off into the dark. Amy sat for a few moments staring into the dark where they'd disappeared. She then heard a distant screech which jolted her to her feet, and she ran into darkness with no idea of which way to run.

CHAPTER TWO

Hotel Adlon
Berlin
Republic of Germany, 1932

FRIEDA SAT on the couch in her luxurious suite at the famous Adlon Hotel near the Brandenburg Gate and stared out of the window at the city lights reflecting off the rain. She'd finished a performance earlier for several of the local diplomats and was tired. She sat by the window dressed in a silver-colored satin evening gown with matching shoes.

Even though Frieda's performance had been a success she was still disturbed after reading in the paper that Geli had committed suicide in an apartment rented by Herr Wolf in Munich. Frieda had met Geli several more times and each time the woman seemed unhappy. Since Geli's death she'd seen Herr Wolf less and less which made Frieda think about how she felt about Herr Wolf. She knew that he'd been dating other women but felt that she was the most important and the rest were just for his amusement.

Whenever she went to his chalet to visit, she had the strange feeling that someone was always watching so she was glad he was in

Berlin on business and was coming to see her. Whenever she mentioned that strange feeling to Herr Wolf, he said he never noticed.

There was a soft knock on the door, a key turned in the lock, and Herr Wolf entered the room. He removed his coat and laid it on a chair nearby. Frieda thought about how much he'd changed from the first time she'd met him until now. He seemed to have aged ten years as he came and sat down on the couch.

"I'm sorry to hear about Geli. She seemed like such a wonderful young woman," said Frieda.

"*Danke*, she was a unique girl," answered Herr Wolf.

Frieda decided to try to brighten the mood. "So, I hear that you're running for Chancellor?"

At the mention of the next election Herr Wolf seemed to perk up. "When I win the election, I'll change Germany for the better."

Since Frieda's first visit to Herr Wolf's chalet, he'd become more popular with the public especially after his book, *Mein Kampf*, had become successful. He'd worked even harder and elevated himself to a status where he felt he could lead Germany back to its previous glory. They sat and talked of the election and of Frieda's performance tonight.

"So, Adolf, I've always wondered why they call you Wolf since that's not your formal name?" asked Frieda changing the subject.

Adolf looked at her with those intense penetrating eyes and smiled. "Adolf means 'Noble Wolf'."

They had room service deliver a fabulous vegetarian meal, and after dinner Frieda quietly turned out the lights.

J Double T Ranch
Sutton County, Texas
Present Day

THE MORNING SUN shone bright over the vast west Texas land. The air was clear and crisp with just a slight chill of early fall. From atop a nearby hill a lone rider sat tall in the saddle and watched a small herd of cattle moving slowly below. He wore a short crowned black Stetson hat covered in dust, a gray work shirt, jeans, rider's chinks commonly called half-chaps, and spurs. He watched as another rider kept the herd moving towards a nearby watering hole. A cow-dog that looked more wolf than dog ran around the herd barking and keeping them in line. The lone rider rested his forearm on the saddle horn, titled his hat back, and smiled. *How things change and how things stay the same.*

His memory drifted back over the last couple of years when the rider, Jacob Taft, an ex-Army Major turned cattle rancher moved out to west Texas to live a life of peace and solitude. He'd bought a small ranch at an auction when the elderly owner died and since then he'd worked hard and built a small herd of cattle.

His life started going in the direction Jake wanted, or so he thought, until everything changed when a little more than a year ago, he received a totally unexpected visitor in the form of a heavenly being commonly known as an angel. Jake initially didn't believe it was true and it took a while for the heavenly host to convince him that it was all real. Since then, Jake had learned and experienced so much so quickly when the angel subsequently sent Jake on a quest to stop a group of demons planning a terrorist attack on the United States. "Angels and demons," said Jake out loud and chuckled which received a snort from his horse, Buck, so Jake reached down and patted his favorite horse.

Now back at his ranch he worked his cattle as if nothing had changed. He shook his head in amazement, jiggled the reins, and rode down the hill to help move the cattle. It was hard, dusty work but he enjoyed every minute of it. Jake was the sole owner and until recently he was the only one working the ranch. Fortunately, his small herd had grown faster than anticipated so a month ago he'd hired an old wrangler named Roy to help. The cattle settled down to grazing and drinking from a watering hole nearby. Silently the two riders turned and rode the half mile or so to a cluster of buildings that Jake called home.

The homestead consisted of a main house, a barn, and a large corral. The single-story rock and wood house was over a hundred years old and had been restored to its original state except for a few modern amenities like plumbing, air conditioning, and electricity. It was actually two separate buildings connected by a porch that went the entire length of both buildings. One building held the living room, kitchen, and dining room while the other building held two bedrooms. A silver Ford Taurus was parked in front as the two rode up.

"Looks like Miss Ellie's here," said Roy, a fiftyish, short, thin man with a handlebar mustache and a quick smile. "I hope she made lunch; I'm starving."

Jake frowned. "Yep, but she brought Pam and a reporter with her."

"A news reporter?"

"Yup, he's from some magazine called the *Christian Digest*. They're going to help pay for Ellie's new church building but only if I give him an interview. I said no but finally gave up and agreed to it."

They both dismounted in the shade of a large oak tree which shaded part of the house and part of the corral. They stripped the saddles from their mounts.

"I'll water and cool them off while you go see...the reporter," said Roy with a wink and a grin.

Jake winced at the mention of the reporter. He pulled his Winchester 30.30 from the saddle sleeve and walked towards the house. The half-wolf half-dog came trotting up and followed Jake. About four years earlier the dog, Roscoe, had wandered up onto Jake's front porch as a pup. Roscoe decided he liked it and stayed. Since then, he had become a hard-working cow-dog as well as fought demons along side Jake, saved him and Ellie more than once, and had the scars to prove it.

At the sound of his spurs jingling, a petite, attractive dark-haired woman came to the kitchen door. Her long hair was tied up in a bun giving her a professional business look. She wore a dark blue shirt, black slacks, and modest shoes. She waved and stepped out on the porch. The dog came up, wagged his tail, and sat down next to her.

She looked down and scratched him behind his ear. "Hello, Roscoe," she said with a smile and looked up at the tall broad-shouldered Jake. "Well, look who Roscoe dragged up."

"Ellie, you're going to spoil him like that," Jake growled.

Ellie stood on her tip toes and kissed the six-foot-four cowboy lightly on the lips. "Worse than I'm spoiling you?"

Jake smiled. "Aren't pastors supposed to be doing church things like visiting the sick, or the needy?"

"And you're the neediest I know," she said with a smirk.

"Can you two love birds take that someplace else?" said a voice from the nearby rocking chair.

Jake and Ellie looked over at a man sitting in the rocking chair. He was an older man with a bushy mustache and lamb chop sideburns. His clothes were out of style about a hundred years ago. He wore a broad cloth shirt, brown pants stuffed down inside old worn-out boots. He looked normal but yet he had a greenish blue hue to his whole body. His name is Ned Parker. He's what most people call a ghost but prefers to be called a disembodied spirit. He's the original owner of the land and even though he died many years ago he loved the place so much he stayed.

"You're just jealous," joked Ellie with a wink.

Ned just smiled and lit up his pipe. Even though Jake could see Ned all the time, no one else could see him unless he decided to appear to them and allow them to see him. Since he'd grown accustomed to them and liked Ellie and Roy, he allowed them to see him.

Ellie grabbed his arm and led him inside the kitchen. "We've fixed lunch and I wanted to see how Roy was working out."

A short, thin, young man with well groomed dark hair and large round glasses wearing a conservative brown suit waited inside. He stuck out his hand. "Good afternoon, Mr. Taft, my name's Albert Simpson."

Jake removed his hat, hung it on a hook on the wall, and shook hands with the young man. A blonde woman who had just placed plates and cups on the table turned and smiled brightly. "Hello, Jake."

"Pam," said Jake flatly.

Pamela Martin was a perky blonde in her mid-thirties, head-strong, and never afraid to give her opinion. She owned the local newspaper called the Shady Oak Gazette, the local coffee shop, and had been the driving force in the creation of the Shady Oak Community Church where Ellie was the pastor. Pam was also Ellie's best friend.

Jake went over to the sink and washed his hands. "Mr. Simpson, I want you to know from the start that I'm not in favor of this interview. I'm only doing it to help Ellie's church."

Ellie smiled and patted Jake's shoulder. "Jake doesn't like talking about himself, so you'll have to prod him."

Pam snickered.

Jake frowned and looked at Ellie. "Whose side are you on?"

"I'll finish getting lunch ready while you get ready for your interview," Ellie said with a grin.

While Albert set up a laptop computer on the kitchen table along with a tape recorder, Jake watched Ellie work and was still amazed at how lucky he was. She came into his life shortly before the whole demon problem came up. Jake had sought out her advice about it and even though she was a full-time pastor she'd accompanied him while he tracked down the demons that were trying to change human history. Their relationship had bloomed and now they were engaged to marry. Jake sat down at the table and looked over at Albert. "So, Mr. Simpson, where do you hail from?"

Albert smiled brightly. "Please, call me Al. I'm a graduate of Christian Evangelical College, from upper Ohio. I studied journalism and was trying to make my way in the Christian journalism world. I thought this might help."

Pam sat a large plate of sandwiches on the table and the two women sat down. Ellie said a quick prayer and they all dug in.

"How's Roy working out?" asked Pam.

"Roy's a hand," replied Jake. "He's punched cows from Texas to Montana and knows more about cattle and stock than I'll ever know. He's working out fine."

"Good," said Ellie. "He seems like a nice man."

As if on cue, Roy clomped up the steps and into the kitchen. He removed his hat. "Howdy, Miss Ellie."

Ellie smiled. "You're right on time, Roy, sit down."

"Yes, Ma'am, and it's good to see you too, Miss Pamela."

Pam smiled. "Roy, when are you going to just call me Pam?"

Roy shook his head. "It just wouldn't be right Miss Pamela, but maybe some day." Roy washed his hands at the sink, sat in an empty chair, and grabbed a sandwich. "So how are things going with your church? I heard they have the frame up on the new building?"

Ellie nodded. "Yes, the building's going fine but I'm not sure if it's all good."

Roy, mouth full of food, looked up at her puzzled.

"Since this whole demon thing came to light, we've been overwhelmed with people coming to the church," explained Ellie. "Some came to gawk as sightseers while some came because they thought they could get some extra special spiritual enlightenment. Then we had the usual cult members, UFO believers, and other weirdos."

"That doesn't include all the news media that camped out thinking that they'd get something," added Jake. "I had to put a lock on my gate for the first time to keep them off the ranch."

"Some even climbed past the barbed wire fence and tried to come in," said Ellie. "Fortunately, over the last few months it's dwindled down to almost nothing now. We still get the occasion fanatic or news person, but I just send them to see Pam."

Al pushed his glasses up on his nose. "Even though we've all been taught about demons and Satan, it's still hard to imagine that these demon creatures really exist."

Jake nodded. "Oh, they exist alright. I was skeptical at first, but it didn't take long before I believed."

"So, all of you can see these creatures?"

"No, not all the time," Ellie answered with a shake of her head. "Jake is the only one who can see them all the time and of course Roscoe. For some reason animals are always able to see or at least sense them."

"And they don't look human?" asked Al as he typed notes on his laptop.

Jake nodded his head with a mouth full of food, so Ellie answered. "I suppose they looked human or what we think angels would look like at the beginning but over time they just became twisted and misshaped because of their evil. They do have the ability to temporarily change their appearance to look human."

Jake continued. "It's taken a while for me to get used to seeing them all the time. Sometimes it reminds me of some alien planet."

Al glanced around.

"There aren't any around here," said Jake with a chuckle. "I can see them but apparently they stay invisible to everyone else."

"But wouldn't you still bump into them?"

Ellie smiled. "We don't completely understand it all, but they seem to remain physically transparent and only solidify when they want or need to do something physical."

"And that's when things turn ugly," said Pam with a frown. "That's when all the shooting, screaming, and running starts."

"So, when did all this start? When did this angel appear to you two?" asked Al.

"He appeared to Jake first," corrected Ellie.

"I was in the barn putting up some hay when he appeared," explained Jake. "I grabbed a shotgun and ordered him off the property."

"You pointed a gun at an angel?" interrupted Al.

Jake wiped his mouth with a napkin. "I didn't think he was an angel at first. He didn't look like what everyone thinks an angel would look like."

"What did he look like?"

Jake raised an eyebrow and looked at the young journalist. "He reminded me of one of those WWF wrestlers."

Ellie laughed. "Malachy's about seven, almost eight feet tall. His skin's golden bronze in color and his pupils are like flames. He wears all white and usually carries a huge golden sword."

"But that didn't make you believe him right away?"

"Nope, it didn't," said Jake. "I thought it was some sort of costumed prank or trick but after he disarmed me without any effort I began to wonder."

"Why would that make you start to believe?" asked Al.

"I used to be in the military," said Jake bluntly.

Ellie smiled. "Jake is being modest. He was a highly decorated member of an elite military unit."

Jake frowned. "I was in…well most of the missions were highly classified so don't put that in the magazine article. After Malachy left, I got to thinking and went to see Ellie. Even though we had only met she's the only person I could think of to talk to about it. She convinced me to wait and see, then sure enough, Malachy came back several days later."

"What did he say?"

"He said the world's totally screwed up."

"That's Jake's short version," Ellie explained with a smirk. "What Malachy said was that our world's changing and not always for the better. Wars, famine, and terrorism are at an all-time high and as we all know the world economy is suffering.

"In the United States our morals and God's laws are being replaced by demands for total freedom of the individual. The freedoms good men fought and died for in the past have been turned into doing whatever you want by saying it's a personal right. Violence is everywhere. It's in our homes, our streets, our schools, our cities, and our music. Religions of all types are growing everywhere and Satan along with his demons are taking advantage of this. Satanism and the occult are now a protected religion, so it appears he's no longer satisfied with being subtle to try to gain ground."

Roy had been listening intently. "So, what about this Mala-chee angel feller', have you seen him lately?"

"I haven't seen Malachy for several months," answered Jake. "Maybe that's the end of it."

"I wish it was, but I have a feeling it's not," said Ellie with a shake of her head.

———

**The _Berghof_,
Southern Bavaria**

The Republic of Germany, 1936

FRIEDA WAS a little confused after she'd received a note from Adolf that he needed to see her at once but was thrilled at the chance to see him again as she patted her lower abdomen. She had a surprise for him.

Since he'd become Chancellor of Germany in 1933, she had been careful to avoid going directly to what used to be his chalet because of the publicity it had gotten. Getting this note to meet him at the chalet was an unusual request. He'd purchased the chalet, renamed it *Berghof,* and made numerous renovations. The chalet had been enlarged with more rooms and a large terrace was built onto the exterior. A large picture window that could be raised and lowered was built in and a small movie theatre had also been added. The chalet was nicer, more modern, but had lost its small cozy charm.

A light snow fell as her car pulled in front and Frieda was met by an unfamiliar housekeeper who, without a word, led her to what was now called the "Great Hall". The original room had been enlarged, was covered with expensive pine wood, and the old fireplace had been replaced by an even larger one made of red marble. It no longer had the warm comfortable atmosphere it did years ago. Frieda sat in one of the expensive antique chairs that the building was now furnished with and after a few moments a blonde woman entered the room.

"Fraulein Getman," said the woman coldly.

Frieda smiled and appraised the young woman. She reminded Frieda of herself, as she was attractive with the same body shape and features as Frieda with one exception; the woman had a scar on the side of her neck. Frieda then remembered seeing the woman sitting in the VIP section when Hitler became Chancellor.

"I am Fraulein Braun," said the woman politely.

Frieda smiled. "You must be Adolf's secretary."

Fraulein Braun smiled condescendingly. "Fraulein, I am not the *Fuhrer's* secretary."

Frieda knew that Adolf had other women but... "How nice to

meet you, and how may I help you?" Despite the cold reception Frieda was trying to be pleasant, for now.

"This visit is to inform you that you will no longer see the *Fuhrer*," said Fraulein Braun coldly.

The Fuhrer? Frieda knew that Adolf had started using the name *Fuhrer* since he became Chancellor. She started to have a bad feeling about this meeting and looked around for Adolf's head housekeeper. "Where's Angela?"

"She no longer works here," said Fraulein Braun rudely.

"But she was Adolf's sister."

"Half sister," corrected Fraulein Braun. "And from now on you will not call the *Fuhrer* by his first name."

Frieda jumped to her feet. "Who do you think you are telling me what I can say and not say? Where's Adolf?"

"He's not here. He's in Berlin on business."

It then dawned on Frieda what was going on. "You sent the note. You sent for me to try to scare me off, well it won't work. I'll call Adolf as soon as I get back to Munich. Better yet, I will see him in Berlin when I return home."

Two uniformed guards quietly entered the room.

Fraulein Braun stared coldly at Frieda. "Angela has been banished from here and you are too. I know that you have family. I would hate for them to have an unfortunate accident."

"Are you threatening me?" screamed Frieda. "Do you know who I am?"

"Yes," said Fraulein Braun. "You're an actress tramp, now get out."

Frieda stepped forward and raised her hand to slap Fraulein Braun but one of the guards grabbed her.

"Goodbye, Fraulein Getman," said Fraulein Braun as she motioned to the guards. "Throw her out."

Frieda was roughly escorted out to her car and waiting chauffer. While driving back to Munich Frieda cried and held her stomach, knowing that the little life growing inside her now would never know his or her father.

CHAPTER THREE

State Highway 191
20 miles north of Chinle, Arizona
Present Day

NAVAJO TRIBAL POLICE Sergeant Robert Greymountain started his day as he normally did on patrol looking for any signs of burglaries, graffiti or other criminal activity done overnight and when satisfied there was none he headed for a quick breakfast. He'd almost made it to the diner when the department's dispatcher, Gladys, informed him that a woman had been found wandering up Highway 163 west of Mitchell Mesa. *Some tourist got lost again,* he thought as he turned his utility police vehicle around.

About forty-five minutes later, he pulled up to two cars parked on the side of the highway. The occupants were all out of their cars and huddled around a woman who was sitting on the ground. One of the men approached him as he stepped out of his truck.

"We found her walking down the road and she looked like she needed help," said the middle-aged man wearing a Hawaiian shirt and tan shorts.

"Has she said why she's out here?" asked Sgt. Greymountain.

The man shook his head. "Nothing that makes sense, she just keeps saying that a monster grabbed her husband and flew away."

Sgt. Greymountain raised an eyebrow and looked at the woman. She was sitting on the ground holding a water bottle given to her by one of the stopped travelers. She was coated in dirt and minor scratches.

"Must be the heat got to her," said the tourist.

"Must be," said Sgt. Greymountain with a nod. "Thanks for the help."

"No problem. We're headed to the Grand Canyon." The man wandered off, gathered his family, and left.

Sgt. Greymountain walked over to the woman and squatted down next to her. An elderly woman from the other car wetted down a rag and gave it to the woman to wipe her face.

"She looks like she's walked a long way through the brush," commented the elderly woman.

Sgt. Greymountain nodded. "How are you feeling?" he asked the young woman.

The woman was drinking water from the bottle. She'd accepted the wet rag and wiped her face.

"Can you tell me what's going on?" he asked.

The woman sat and stared into the distance for a minute but didn't answer.

"Can you tell me your name?"

She looked at him. "Amy."

"Well, Amy," said Sgt. Greymountain softly. "I'm Sgt. Greymountain of the Navajo Tribal Police Department. You're safe now but I need to know what happened."

Amy turned and looked at the middle-aged Navajo dressed in a khaki colored uniform. Her eyes began to tear up. "My husband is missing. He was…was…taken by a monster."

"A monster?"

"Yes, or something." Amy shook her head. "It all happened so fast."

Sgt. Greymountain put his hand on her shoulder. "It's okay. We'll find him. Where were you at?"

Amy looked around but seemed confused. "I'm not sure."

"Yes, you do. Calm down and think. Were you camping at one of the campgrounds?"

"No, we hiked out into the wild. Tom and I like to rough it. We were...near the mesa." Her eyes lit up. "Yes, yes, we were near Mitchell Mesa, on the west side."

"Okay, good," said Sgt. Greymountain softly. "Do you need any medical assistance?"

Amy shook her head. "I just want to find Tom."

"Let's get you into the truck and we'll see if we can find him."

Sgt. Greymountain helped Amy into the police vehicle, took the elderly woman's name and thanked her for her help. He climbed into the police SUV and drove south towards Mitchell Mesa. After obtaining Amy's information and her husband's, he radioed in and asked for more assistance in looking for the missing man.

Thirty minutes later, Sgt. Greymountain stopped on the side of the road. "Are you sure this is where you came out?" he asked Amy.

"Yes, yes, I remember that rock formation," she said and pointed to a small group of rocks.

"Good, it's a start." Sgt. Greymountain reached for his radio and notified the other officers where to meet.

Within a few minutes, several more police vehicles arrived occupied by Navajo police. Sgt. Greymountain climbed out of the SUV and gathered them around. He gave them a description of Tom Parker and where he was last known to be.

"Do you think something jumped him?" asked Officer George Simmons, a young Navajo officer.

"I don't know but it's obvious that something happened. She said something or someone grabbed her husband and flew away."

"Flew away?" asked Officer Kevin Flowers, another Navajo officer.

Sgt. Greymountain shrugged. "That's what the woman said. I don't know what she saw but let's check as much as we can before we call in more search and rescue help."

"Do you think she's crazy?" Officer Flowers asked.

"Let's hope not, Kevin," answered Sgt. Greymountain with a

smirk. "I ran a check, and she does have a husband named Tom. Gladys said she checked the roster back at headquarters and it shows that they both paid park fees so until we know different, we go on the idea that he's out there and possibly in trouble."

All the officers nodded and broke up to start tracking back toward the mesa. Sgt. Greymountain walked back to the truck where Amy waited.

"Did they find him?" she asked anxiously.

He shook his head. "No, not yet, but we'll start here and work back. I'll take you back to the office where you can wait and then..."

"No," interrupted Amy. "I want to help look."

"I don't think that would be wise. We don't know how long it will take or what we might find."

"You mean find him dead?"

Sgt. Greymountain nodded solemnly.

"I don't care, I want to help look."

The Navajo sergeant looked around, thought for a second or two, and kicked some dirt with the toe of his boot. "Okay but stay with me or one of the other officers. I don't need you going off by yourself and then we have to look for you too."

Amy nodded and Sgt. Greymountain gathered some extra water bottles, first aid kit, and other emergency supplies which he placed in a tan department issued backpack they used for such occasions. They started back across the desert towards the mesa. An hour later, they came to the campsite. Sgt. Greymountain had Amy stay back as he scouted around for tracks but only found the footprints of Pam and Tom coming in and hers running out. He also located a spot where there appeared to have been a struggle. He scratched his head.

"What? What did you find?" asked Amy.

"Nothing and that's the problem," answered Sgt. Greymountain. "There are no footprints of your husband leaving, just this area where you said they fought."

"I told you, the thing grabbed him and flew off."

"Did the thing say anything?"

"It was just screeching like a wild animal."

Officer Simmons walked up from the other direction.

"Did you see any tracks over there?" Sgt. Greymountain asked.

"No, Sarge, nothing over here."

Sgt. Greymountain walked back to Amy. "Which way did you say you saw your husband carried off?"

Amy pointed northeast. "As best I can remember it took Tom off in that direction but it was dark so it could have swung around and gone any direction."

Sgt. Greymountain nodded in understanding and looked at Officer Simmons. "George, it's beginning to look like we need a helicopter, some dogs and more help."

It was mid-afternoon before more than a hundred search and rescue personnel arrived and began combing the area. The search helicopter had already arrived and was in the air looking for any sign of the missing man. Three K-9 handlers with their search dogs arrived and were briefed by Sgt. Greymountain. They took their bloodhounds to the spot where the struggle occurred but as soon as the dogs got close, they began barking, whining, and shying away from the spot.

"What's wrong with them?" asked Sgt. Greymountain.

One of the dog handlers, an older man named Bill, shook his head. "I don't know. It's like they're afraid of the smell."

"Of the missing man?"

"No, of something else. Whatever he got mixed up with is upsetting the dogs. They don't want to track. I've never seen this before."

"How strange," mumbled Sgt. Greymountain.

"We'll let them cast in a larger area but back from the scene to see if I can get something." The group led their dogs back several feet and let them wander the area for Tom's scent.

The Navajo sergeant walked around looking for any sign of what might have happened. He turned and looked up at the sky then out towards the higher points of the mesa. "Amy," he said, "can you try and think about what this thing looked like?"

Amy stared at the spot where Tom had fought with the unknown assailant. She shivered and wrapped her arms around herself even in the warm weather. "It was about the same size as Tom I think but it had large wings. It had a yellow eye."

"A yellow eye?" interrupted Sgt. Greymountain.

"Yes, I only saw one," replied Amy as she shivered again and looked away. "That's all I remember."

"That's fine." Sgt. Greymountain looked towards the high points of the mesa. He picked up his radio. "Charlie, this is Greymountain."

A voice responded from his radio. "Go ahead, Sergeant."

"Can you fly a parallel line with the edge of the mesa? If this thing is some sort of large bird, then it might have a nest or something up along the edge."

The radio sounded again. "10-4, I'll see if there's anything."

Sgt. Greymountain watched as the rescue helicopter banked and headed to the rim of the mesa and started flying a path parallel to the mesa.

Amy stepped up beside him. "Do you think he might be up there in the rocks?"

Sgt. Greymountain nodded. "It stands to reason that if the thing is birdlike then it might have a nest or a place to live up high, not down on the ground."

They watched the helicopter fly up and back along the rim of the mesa. After twenty minutes of making several passes it was obvious that nothing was up there. Sgt. Greymountain glanced at Amy and shook his head. Bill came up and said that they were unsuccessful in getting a scent. Sgt. Greymountain thanked him, and the three K-9 searchers left with their dogs. Sgt. Greymountain glanced over and saw Amy standing by the tent with her head down, sobbing.

"I'm sorry. We'll keep looking but there are thousands of acres out there."

Amy looked up at him with tear filled eyes. "I know, I just can't help but think about him out there hurt and needing help."

Sgt. Greymountain sadly nodded in agreement. "He could be anywhere out there, and it could take months to search and without any idea of where to start we may never find him. I'll have one of the officers take you back to town."

They walked back on the trail towards the road when Sgt. Grey-mountain's radio squelched.

"Sergeant, this is Charlie. I saw a flash of sunlight on something. I'm swinging around to check it out. I'll let you know in a second."

Amy's eyes widened at the news, but Sgt. Greymountain shook his head. "It could be anything. People leave stuff out here all the time. We find clothes, boxes, cans, lids, hubcaps, all kinds of junk."

Charlie, a retired military helicopter pilot, often gave up his time to volunteer for search and rescue. He knew that most of these turn out badly, but he was willing to give it a chance. He flew the helicopter closer to the wall of the mesa looking for any sign of life. The flash of reflected light again struck the cockpit and appeared to come from a crack in the wall about seventy feet down from the rim. Charlie swung the helicopter around and came in headfirst as close as he dared to the wall. At first, he couldn't see anything but then an arm came out of the shadow of the crevice and waved a piece of cloth frantically.

Sgt. Greymountain and Amy had walked back up to the campsite. Several of the searchers came along after they had seen the helicopter narrow down to one area of the mesa.

Charlie's voice suddenly came over their radios. "Sergeant, I have someone up here. I can't tell who it is but I'm being flagged down. It could be our missing man."

A cheer erupted from the small group surrounding Sgt. Greymountain.

"Thanks, Charlie," said the Navajo Sergeant. "Can you swing around and get a basket?"

"I copy that," said Charlie. "It looks like you can rappel down the side and reach him from the rim too." He switched his radio over the external speaker. "This is search and rescue. We have people coming to your location. Stay where you are, and we'll have help to you shortly. I'm going to leave for a few minutes and retrieve a basket to get you down."

The arm waved back in acknowledgment. Charlie swung the helicopter around and flew to the highway and landed on the road. The personnel there attached the basket to the bottom and loaded up two of the rescuers trained in rappelling. Within minutes, Charlie dropped the two off at the rim and hovered just off the mesa's rim. The two professionals anchored their lines and quickly rappelled down the side.

One of the men, Jim, went down the side of mesa and looked for the crack which held the missing person but after dropping sixty feet he couldn't see anything. He radioed Charlie. "I can't see where he is?"

"Move about twenty feet or so to your left," answered Charlie.

Jim crabbed his way around the rocks until he could see a form wedged into the crevice. He drew in close and saw it was a man. "Are you badly hurt?"

The man leaned out and shook his head. "I don't think so but my shoulder hurts."

"My name's Jim. What's yours?"

"Tom."

Sgt. Greymountain, Amy, and several of the searchers were huddle around the radio listening. Upon hearing that it was Tom, Amy started crying and a female searcher wrapped her arms around her while she wept.

Jim grabbed the sides of the crevice and worked his way inside. He saw that Tom sat on a small ledge just inside. He was bruised and covered in dried blood from several large scratches and gashes.

"How did you get up here?"

Tom made a grim smile. "You wouldn't believe me if I told you. Can I get off this mountain now?"

Another rescuer rappelled over and guided Charlie over so he could grab the basket. After a few minutes, they had Tom strapped into the horizontal basket and he was lifted away. The helicopter dipped and swooped towards the road. "Sergeant, I'll drop him off at the road and then come pick up his wife," radioed Charlie.

Sgt. Greymountain acknowledged him and turned to Amy.

She smiled brightly. "Thank you so much, Sergeant Greymountain." Amy grabbed him and hugged him tightly. "You saved my husband."

Sgt. Greymountain felt awkward and blushed. "We were lucky." His radio suddenly squawked.

"Sarge, this is Flowers. We found something that I think you should see."

"10-4," said the sergeant. "I'll meet with you as soon as I get Mrs. Parker back to the road."

Fifteen minutes later, Amy was dropped off at the highway and ran to her husband who was being treated by medical personnel in the back of an ambulance. She bent down, kissed him several times, and then looked him over. He had numerous bandages on his arms and legs from his injuries. All the questions could be answered later; right now, she was just happy to have her husband back safely.

"Are you okay?" she asked.

Tom smiled. "I am now. Are you okay?"

Amy started crying again. "I'm not the one who was carried off by a flying monster. You're the one that's injured."

"I'll be fine with a little rest." Tom frowned. "It wasn't a bird but I'm not sure what it was. It was like a nightmare."

Amy hugged him. "It's all over now. You're safe."

———

SGT. GREYMOUNTAIN WALKED over three quarters of a mile to where Officer Flowers and a couple of rescue people waited. "What did you find?"

Officer Flowers motioned for him to follow, and they climbed over a section of the red colored rock. On the back side of the rock Sgt. Greymountain saw a large corpse of something on the open rock. In the still air he smelled rotting flesh. It was crumpled up in a pile except for a large wing that was spread out to one side. The other wing was folded up under it.

"What is it? A *chindi*?" Officer Flowers asked nervously.

"I have no idea," said Sgt. Greymountain with a roll of his eyes. *Chindi* is the Navajo word for devil. He stepped up for a closer look. Parts of the thing were almost completely decayed while parts of it were still intact. It looked to him like a human, but some parts were bird like. The face looked humanoid, but it was hard to tell with the amount of decomposition. He also noticed that there were not flies or other pests around the corpse.

"Could this be the thing that grabbed the hiker last night?" asked Officer Flowers.

"From the amount of decay, it had to have been here for days, so I doubt it," answered Sgt. Greymountain. "We need an expert to look at this."

"What do we do with it for now? This is bad medicine."

Sgt. Greymountain wiped the sweat from his forehead. "Photograph it and then bring the basket back. We'll fly this thing back to headquarters and let Doc Sammons look at it."

Officer Flowers hesitated. "Do we have to touch it?"

"I doubt this *chindi* will bother you, it's obviously dead," replied Sgt. Greymountain with a frown.

"It's still bad medicine; real bad medicine."

———

SEVERAL HOURS LATER, a Land Rover pulled up to the park headquarters and an elderly man climbed out then went inside where Sgt. Greymountain waved him inside one of the offices.

"Good afternoon, Sergeant," said Dr. Thomas Sammons with a smile. "I got your call and while I don't mind helping, I don't know why you called me." Doctor Sammons was one of the local physicians that the Navajo people used. He was in his late sixties, short, and slightly rotund. He had retired from a successful practice in New Jersey but always wanted to live in the west, so he moved to Arizona. He'd planned to oil paint and watch sunsets but after seeing the shortage of medical staff in the area he felt the need to help.

Sgt. Greymountain shook the doctor's hand. "Doc, I called you because you're the doctor with the most experience and if you can't help us, you'd know who to call. We were just going to send it to the medical examiner's office in Flagstaff, but I wanted you to see it first."

Dr Sammons nodded. "I'll do what I can. Now where's the corpse?"

Sgt. Greymountain led the doctor back to a freezer in the back of the building. They didn't have a morgue, so they'd placed the thing in one of the large freezers used to store animal meat. The sergeant opened the freezer and stood back. Doctor Sammons looked the thing over for a minute or so.

"What is that smell?" asked the doctor.

"I think its sulfur."

"Help me get it out," said the doctor,

Sgt. Greymountain called another officer who reluctantly helped them lift the corpse out and onto the floor. Doctor Sammons looked, bent down, and turned the now partially frozen thing over. He poked and prodded it, then stood up and rubbed his chin.

"What is it, Doc?" asked Sgt. Greymountain.

"I've never seen anything like this but if it's what I've read about you'd better call the FBI."

————

Berlin
The Republic of Germany, 1945

THE WAR HAD GONE BADLY for Germany and the allies were closing in on Berlin from all sides. Frieda had heard a radio broadcast from the BBC, the British Broadcasting Corporation that a few days earlier the Red Army had raided the *Fuhrerbunker* and that Hitler was dead.

She sat in her apartment in Berlin with no electricity, no running water, and little food. As the war had taken its toll on Germany, Frieda transferred most of her money to a Swiss bank account to protect it. That left her little to keep for herself and her nine-year-old daughter living in semi-comfortable conditions. When the Russians encircled Berlin, the electricity went out and soon the water was cut off. Without electricity she could no longer listen to Germany's Reich Broadcasting Corporation or the BBC for updates on what was going on so she could only assume it was for the worse.

For days Frieda heard bombs exploding and gunfire everywhere and knew it was only a matter of time before it would make its way to her. Her press agent encouraged her to leave Germany months ago when it appeared that the war was turning and the Third Reich was collapsing, but Frieda refused to leave. She wanted to remain as close to Hitler as she could even though she had not been able to see or speak to him.

Frieda sat at the table by candlelight but was unable to see out of the apartment windows. The windows in the building and most others too had been boarded over to keep in any light to avoid being detected by bombing raids. It had never occurred to her that Germany might lose the war, and she had no idea what to do or where to go. She covered her face with her hands and let her tears flow then was startled by a soft touch. She looked down at the smiling face of her daughter, Priska.

"Why are you crying, Mama," asked the bright-eyed dark-haired girl.

Frieda wiped her tears away and tried to smile back. "I'm just tired and worried about what we're going to do. I want you to be safe."

Priska cocked her head slightly. "But we are safe, Mama. My friendly kitty, Herr Degen says everything is going to be fine."

A kitty named Degen? thought Frieda. She stared at her daughter as if not understanding. "Who is Herr Degen? Where did you meet him?"

"My friend, Herr Degen, comes to my room to help keep me safe. He came today and said we need to go to a better hiding place."

Frieda was surprised and afraid. She got up, took Priska's hand, and walked towards her bedroom. "Show me your friend, Herr Degen, please, dear."

"Sure, Mama," said Priska. "He's big and strong and can fly too."

Frieda stopped at Priska's door and pushed it open slightly. The first thing she smelled was ashes and rotten eggs which immediately reminded her of the smell at Hitler's chalet years ago. Even though she had a strange overwhelming feel of dread, she forced herself to step inside the child's bedroom. At the sight of the thing Frieda's whole body shook with fear and her knees weakened. The thing was a seven-foot-tall tiger-like creature, covered in fur with huge wings. He stood on two cat legs, but his hands were almost human-like with long curved claws. His face was that of a Bengal tiger with huge, sharp teeth, and his eyes glowed yellow.

Priska patted her mother's hand. "It's okay, Mama, this is my kitty friend, Herr Degen."

The monster smiled showing razor sharp teeth. "*Guten abend*, Fraulein Getman, I am Lord Degen."

Frieda didn't know whether to faint or run. Before she could do either, Priska pulled her hand, and she allowed the child to lead her over to the bed where she sat down. Priska walked over to Degen and took a furry, clawed hand in her tiny hand.

"Herr Degen says he can take us somewhere safe," said Priska as she smiled and looked up into the demon's yellow eyes.

"You will hurry and pack," said Degen. "Hitler and that fool woman Braun are dead. You two are now my only hope. Get what you can together and be ready to leave."

Frieda sat and stared, not sure whether to believe what she was seeing, so Degen stepped forward and leaned down into Frieda's face. The stench of decaying flesh and sulfur almost made Frieda faint. "Do you want your daughter to live, or do you want her to die at the hands of the Russians?"

At the mention of Priska dying, Frieda stood up. "I will get our things together." She went out into the hall, pulled a suitcase from a closet, and filled it with some traveling clothes. When she retuned to Priska's room to get her clothes, Degen was gone. "Where is he?" asked Frieda.

Priska was putting a small coat on her doll and answered without looking up. "Herr Degen had to leave to prepare our way. He said some men will come in a few minutes to help us."

Frieda wasn't sure what was going to happen but if it kept Priska alive and safe, she would risk it. After loading Priska's clothes in a smaller bag, she sat down on the bed next to her. "How long have you known Herr Degen?"

Priska thought for a moment. "I can't remember, Mama. He's always been here for me. He tells me stories after you fall asleep and gets me a drink when I was thirsty. He even told me about the *Furhrer*.

Frieda's eyes widened. "What did he tell you about the *Fuhrer?*"

Priska kept fiddling with her dolls coat while she chatted. "Oh, he said that he was a very important man and that someday he will be important to me when I grow up."

Before she could ask another question there was a knock at the door. Frieda crept to the door and carefully opened it a few inches. Three SS troops dressed in black uniforms stood at the door.

"Fraulein Getman?" asked one of the men. "Lord Degen sent us to take you to safety."

Frieda got Priska from the bedroom and together they followed the three SS troops down the hall.

CHAPTER FOUR

Federal Bureau of Investigation
Office of Deputy Director of Paranormal Activities
935 Pennsylvania Avenue Northwest
Washington, D.C.
Present Day

DEPUTY DIRECTOR OSCAR RUIZ sat at his office and read through the latest reports. He still hadn't completely adjusted to being promoted to deputy director after Deputy Director Sullens was killed by demons last year. The door opened and Agent Stephanie Williams walked in carrying a file.

"Not more paperwork," groaned Deputy Director Ruiz.

Agent Williams smiled. "C'mon, Oscar, don't tell me you hate your job already?"

"I just didn't know there would be so much paperwork."

"Well, here's more for the pile." The five-foot-seven, blonde, veteran FBI agent had been Deputy Director Ruiz's partner after Agent Kimbell was killed in a gun battle with assassins. She'd gone on to help stop a horde of demons from trying to take over Washington D.C.

"What is it this time, aliens from Mars or a creature from the Black Lagoon?" After Deputy Director Ruiz had been promoted, he was assigned to oversee a newly created section of the FBI that investigated paranormal or demonic occurrences. Some of the agents have nicknamed them *The X-files* or *The Men in Black* from the popular movie and television show years ago.

"This is a call from Arizona. They say they have a creature in their freezer that they want one of us to look at," explained Agent Williams as she handed it to him.

Deputy Director Ruiz raised an eyebrow. "They say they have a real specimen?"

"That's what it says," answered Agent Williams as she plopped down in a chair in front of Ruiz's desk.

"The last call we got was some hunter that found a rotted grizzly bear carcass with some hide still attached. I wish we could get rid of that hot line and end half of these fake calls."

Agent Williams shook her head. "I don't know, Oscar, this one didn't come in through the hot line, it was sent in through normal law enforcement channels. A Navajo police sergeant out there had a doctor look at it and told him to call. They enclosed photos of it too."

Deputy Director Ruiz opened the file and began reading. After a few minutes, he flipped through the series of photos before laying them down. He sat back and rubbed his chin. "They have a man that was attacked by this thing, and it flew away with him?"

Agent Williams nodded. "It appears that it grabbed him and took off carrying him, but he was able to stab it enough that it dropped him. He crawled into a crack in the rock wall and hid. They think the thing died later from the stab wounds. That's the only part I'm not sure about." She subconsciously reached up and touched two long vertical scars on the side of her face. A demon had clawed her during an attack while she and Deputy Director Ruiz drove down a Washington D.C. freeway. "We both know that Jake Taft is the only one that can kill demons."

Deputy Director Ruiz leaned forward, opened the file again, and looked at the photos. "It sounds like another hoax, but from the police report and photos something happened out there. I'll call

Jake and see what he thinks. We may have to go out there and see."

Agent Williams stood up and headed for the door. "You mean I might have to go out there. You're stuck behind that desk."

"Don't remind me."

City of Magdeburg
Allied Occupied Germany
70 miles west of Berlin, 1946

IT WAS JUST after three a.m., cloudy, damp, and cold at an isolated area just outside of Magdeburg, Germany. Two young Soviet officers stood in the light drizzle and guarded a flatbed truck nearby that had several wooden crates underneath a tarp. The entire area was under construction and a concrete foundation was scheduled to be poured in the morning for a new building going up.

"This is ridiculous," said Junior Lieutenant Kuzenka as he rubbed his hands together to keep warm. "We are officers. They should have *Gefreiters* guarding these crates."

"*Da*, I agree," answered an equally miserable and cold Lieutenant Fedul who kept his hands stuffed in his pockets and stamped his feet to keep warm. "This could even be done by privates, not us."

Lieutenant Fedul was a tall blond-haired Russian who had fought bravely in World War II which had ended six moths ago, and since then been part of the Soviet occupational forces in this section of Germany.

Junior Lieutenant Kuzenka, a dark haired, short, stocky Russian of Mongolian descent pointed towards a staff car parked nearby. "We freeze in the dark while they sit in the comfort of their car."

"Probably drinking Vodka and smoking cigars," added Lieutenant Fedul.

At their comments the staff car doors opened, and two Soviet officers climbed out and walked towards them. The two young officers snapped to attention and saluted.

"At ease," said an older gruff voiced colonel.

The two young men relaxed. The second Soviet officer stood behind the colonel. His collar rank showed him to be a general, but he kept his head down which made it difficult for them to see his face in the dim light. Lieutenant Kuzenka glanced at the other lieutenant who just shrugged slightly.

The colonel stepped forward. "Comrades, men, your country needs your assistance but also your secrecy."

The two men stood up straight. "Of course, Colonel Evastfy, we are at your service," replied Lieutenant Fedul.

"*Da*, of course, sir, for Russia," said Junior Lieutenant Kuzenka.

"Good," said Colonel Evastfy with a smile. "I need you two to bury these five crates tonight so they can be covered by concrete in the morning."

Lieutenant Kuzenka's mouth dropped open and Junior Lieutenant Fedul stared dumbly. "You want us to dig and bury these crates tonight, in the dark, in the cold, sir?"

Colonel Evastfy nodded. "*Da*, it is imperative that it is done tonight. You would be doing a great service to your country and to the world." Colonel Evastfy stepped even closer to them. "And it's an order."

The two young men snapped to attention. The general turned and walked back to the staff car while Colonel Evastfy watched the two men dig into the ground. They soon were sweating despite the cold and removed their uniform jackets. A large hole was dug out and the two tired lieutenants trudged over to the flat bed truck. They pulled back the tarp and exposed five crates that measured two feet by four feet and one smaller wooden box about the size of a shoe box. What struck them wasn't the size or shape of the crates but the smell.

"What's that stench?" asked Junior Lieutenant Kuzenka.

Lieutenant Fedul rubbed his nose. "It smells like burned flesh."

They both turned to the colonel who merely nodded and pointed to the large hole. The two men then lifted each crate and placed it in the hole while trying not to inhale too much of the stench. Once they had all five of the crates in the hole they stepped back from the smell.

"Now, cover it up," ordered Colonel Evastfy.

The two men didn't need any more urging and covered the rotting stench. They leaned on their shovels afterward as the Soviet colonel inspected the site.

"Good job, comrades."

Lieutenant Fedul wiped the sweat from his face with a handkerchief. "Colonel Evastfy, now that they have been buried can we know…"

"*Nyet,*" snapped Colonel Evastfy. "The less you know the better off you are. Just know you have done Russia a service. Now, clean up so we can leave this place."

The lieutenants scraped off the mud as much as they could from their boots and put their uniform jackets back on. They followed the colonel back to the flatbed truck.

Lieutenant Fedul pointed at the box left on the truck. "What about this small box, sir?"

"I'll take care of it," answered Colonel Evastfy.

The staff car door opened, and the unidentified general exited the car and approached. The two lieutenants turned and saluted the general. He looked at the two lieutenants from under the brim of his uniform cap. "You have done well, thank you." He nodded to Colonel Evastfy.

The colonel who was standing behind the two Russian officers raised a gun and abruptly shot both in the back of head. Their bodies crumpled to the ground next to the truck. The general looked down at the bodies. "Send their bodies back home with full military honors. I'll send the families a letter saying they died in battle against a few German army holdouts."

"As you wish, General Prokosha."

The general reached up and removed the box from the flatbed truck, turned and walked back to the staff car. The car then drove off into the darkness. Colonel Denis Evastfy loaded the two bodies on the flatbed, covered them with the tarp, climbed into the cab and drove away.

———

Shady Oak Community Church
2203 E. Hollis Street
Shady Oak, Texas
Present Day

ELLIE SAT in the office section of the temporary buildings that made up her church. She heard construction vehicles and men's hammering outside as the basic structure of their new church was beginning to take shape. She put down her coffee cup and looked out of the window. It was thrilling that the small church had grown and was building a permanent home, but at the same time she was apprehensive about what the future brought. Ellie was the pastor of the church but also engaged to Jake. Since he was given the ability to see demons all the time and kill them it had brought the responsibility of helping whenever and wherever he was needed. He'd been overwhelmed by calls and requests from every cult or group about exorcisms, UFOs, or ghost hunting. She had a feeling that he'd be needed in the future and her place was with him, but she also felt her place was at her church. She just hoped that she didn't have to someday choose. Her thoughts were disturbed by the sound of her phone ringing.

"Good morning, Shady Oak Community Church, Ellie speaking."

"Good morning, Ellie, this is Oscar Ruiz."

Ellie smiled to herself at the sound of his voice as it had been a while since she'd seen him. While working as an FBI field agent, Ruiz had helped Jake rescue her from a group of demons that had kidnapped her from her hotel in Washington D.C. "So how are things in the FBI, Oscar? Are you having fun being in charge?"

Deputy Director Ruiz groaned. "No, I'm not used to desk duty yet. Lately I wish I was still a field agent."

Ellie laughed. "C'mon now, it can't be that bad yet."

"It can be a beating," he complained with a chuckle. "The reason I called is I can't get a hold of Jake. I've called several times, but I can't get through. Is everything alright?"

"Yes, everything's fine," answered Ellie with a laugh. "Jake's probably out working the cattle. He doesn't carry his phone with him."

Deputy Director Ruiz snickered. "That sounds like Jake. He was born 100 years too late."

"That's the truth. I'll try to get a message to him. He's supposed to come into town tonight for dinner. What's up?"

Deputy Director Ruiz sat back in his chair. "I received a report from Arizona that I wanted to talk to Jake about."

"What kind of report?"

"It's from the Navajo police. They found what they think might be a demon and they have it frozen in a meat freezer."

Ellie raised an eyebrow. "That sounds strange. They decompose so rapidly. There's no way they could have found one, transported it, and froze it before it completely decayed."

"That's what I thought too. I have some photos too that I thought Jake might look at."

"Send them to my email address and I'll show them to Jake."

"When is that man going to get a computer or fax?"

Ellie laughed again and shook her head. "I wouldn't hold your breath. He sees computers and cellphones as an unneeded luxury where we see it as a necessity."

"Have him call me after he sees the photos, please."

Ellie told him that she would and hung up the phone. After Jake rescued the president's daughter and subsequently saved the president's life during a congressional hearing in Washington D.C., the president reinstated Jake's military commission as a major in the U.S. Army. Jake was put on loan to the FBI and since then Jake's been helping the FBI off and on as a sort of consulting demonologist. Ellie wasn't sure that was a good thing as it meant taking more time away from his ranch and from her.

A frozen demon?

CHAPTER FIVE

Government Storage Compound
City of Buzlanovo
12 miles southwest of Moscow, Russia

ON THE OUTSKIRTS of the small Russian town of Buzlanovo, is an old worn-down warehouse long overdue for repair. It's one of several storage warehouses left over from the cold war. The fence around the compound was rusted and worn but kept out the average wanderer. Each building is an archive of items long since unwanted and unneeded. A single security guard sat in a lone guard shack at the entrance. The guard's small motor scooter sat against the outside wall.

Yuri Osipushka sipped his coffee. He glanced out of one dirty window at the upcoming darkness and shifted his overweight bulk around in his chair. His day was almost over, and he was glad to be going home. He showed up everyday, sat in the shack, and drank his coffee mixed with a little Vodka until it's time to go home. For the last fifteen years he'd never had a visitor. The lock on the gate had never been opened that he could remember. Osipushka worked there ever since the local factory shut down and in the town of only

17,000, he was lucky to land a job at all. He collected his small pay from the government once a month and put food on the table for his wife.

Yuri took another sip of his drink when movement from across the compound caught his eye. He blinked and shook his head. *Too much Vodka in the coffee,* thought Yuri. He lifted his cup again when he saw another blur of movement. He stared out the window for a minute or so and this time he saw a shape near one of the old warehouses. Yuri slowly heaved himself up from his chair, opened the small door, and stuck his head out. "Hey, get away from there," he yelled.

There was more movement and Yuri heard metal scraping on metal. He shook his head in disgust. *Must be juveniles trying to steal old junk,* he thought. Yuri grabbed his flashlight and waddled through the weeds towards one of the warehouses where the noise came from. He came upon an open door to warehouse number four. The lock had been pried off and cast aside. There was a smell around the door that he couldn't quite identify, a burnt smell. Yuri looked inside at the pitch-black darkness of the warehouse. He shined his light inside and illuminated row after row of dust covered boxes and crates stacked on metal shelves or on top of each other. He'd never been inside any of the warehouses and had no idea what was kept inside.

"This is security, you had better come out now," he yelled. When no one answered he stepped inside and walked down the middle aisle shining his flashlight all around. The farther in, the worse the smell was. He'd made it to the end of the long aisle when he heard a crash from another aisle. He whipped his light to the left. "Who's there?" he demanded. He started to sweat. *No one's supposed to be in here,* thought Yuri. His job was to sit in the guard shack, not look around in a dark warehouse. He heard a scratching sound and something moving around. The sound of a door being opened was heard and then he felt a cool breeze. *Something must be refrigerated in here,* thought Yuri. He turned and saw two glowing yellow eyes staring back at him. Yuri froze. From the direction of the yellow eyes came a deep hissing sound. Yuri backed away slowly at first then turned and ran as fast as his obese body could carry him. He heard the sound of something moving behind him, but he didn't stop. Yuri bolted out of the door and stumbled through the weeds towards his guard shack with only one thought in mind, *Call for help*. He reached the guard shack and threw the door open. Yuri had never used the phone the entire time he'd worked there but he grabbed the phone receiver off the wall and dialed. The phone line was dead. It either had been cut or had never worked. He dropped the phone and turned to the door to flee but stopped in his tracks. A pair of yellow eyes stared back at him. Yuri tried to scream but it was cut off as a clawed hand sliced across his face and throat.

————

J Double T Ranch
Sutton County, Texas

JAKE AND ROY finished the day's work on the ranch. Roy had driven the truck out to repair a section of broken fence while Jake checked the area for strays. He loved ranch work because it gave him the personal satisfaction of doing it himself and building something for the future. It also was a reason to avoid Al. The young journalist was nice, but Jake loathed revealing his personal life.

Jake rode into the barn followed by Roscoe. He stripped off the saddle and brushed down Buck. He was loading hay and feed into the stall when he heard Roy drive up in the truck. A minute or so later, Roy stuck his head in the barn.

"You still goin' to town tonight?"

"Yeah," said Jake. "I'm meeting Ellie for dinner."

"Isn't that young magazine feller going to be there too?"

Jake frowned. "Yeah, thanks for reminding me."

"So, stay here."

"No, I promised Ellie I'd do the interviews. The magazine is helping to pay for her church building so I don't want to disappoint her."

"And you're leaving poor ol' me out here to fend for myself?"

"Roscoe can keep you company."

Roy snickered and headed back to the house. "C'mon, Roscoe, let's go find us something eat. Those two love birds will starve us to death if we don't."

Jake chuckled and shook his head.

Forty-five minutes later, Jake drove onto Highway 8 in his red Ford pickup which looked brown from a thick coating of west Texas dust. Jake figured he'd have to wash the truck before he and Ellie got married. On the way into town, he thought about the phone message that Deputy Director Ruiz had left him on his cellphone. He'd checked the phone when he came in, and thought about calling him back but decided he'd talk to Ellie about it first. *A frozen demon corpse?* It didn't make sense. Jake knew that as soon as a demon dies the corpse decays at an incredible rate and in less than an hour it could be dust.

It was past dusk, and lights were coming on in Shady Oaks as he passed the old, rusted water tower. It was a common west Texas town. It consisted of the usual small-town businesses —a grocery store, feed store, Dairy Queen fast food restaurant, a "home cooking" type restaurant, churches, elementary, junior, and senior high school.

Jake turned off onto a side street and saw a portable church building. A small sign stood out front advertised the church, Shady Oak Community Church, Ellie Thompson, Pastor. The church's new building was under construction in a lot next to it. He saw cars in the parking lot and several church members stood outside talking. As he turned into the parking lot his headlights crossed the construction area. Out of the corner of his eye he caught sight of something. He looked back and saw two forms bent down next to one of the support beams of the new building. One was stocky, hairy, brown colored with dark spots and a face that resembled a boar hog. The other was a taller sleeker, insect looking thing about the color of sand. *Demons.* The taller one watched as the boar-like demon worked near the base of one of the support beams.

Sabotage! Jake whipped the steering wheel hard to the left and floored it, racing across the parking lot towards the two demons.

MIDWEEK CHURCH SERVICES had just finished, and people were milling around outside the building. Ellie, Pam, and Al were standing at the front of the portable building talking when they saw Jake pull in.

"There's Jake now," said Ellie. "We're going to grab a bite to eat; do you want to come along?"

"No," said Pam with a shake of her head. "I have to head over to the newspaper and help get tomorrow's issue ready."

They watched as Jake suddenly swerved towards the building under construction.

"What in the world?" commented Ellie.

"Does he normally drive like that?" asked Al.

"No, but with Jake nothing's normal," Pam answered dryly.

Jake's truck suddenly skidded to a stop.

"What's he doing?" asked Al.

As if in answer to his question Jake jumped from the truck and pulled his Mossberg 20-gauge pump shotgun from the gun rack behind the seat. He raised the shotgun to his shoulder and fired in the direction of the building under construction. A muffled shriek came from the area of one of the support beams. The trio looked into the dim light and saw for the first time a form suddenly appear and fall to the ground. Jake pumped another round into the shotgun and fired again. A winged form suddenly appeared in the sky above the construction site. Several church members joined Ellie, Pam, and Al as the creature flew around towards them. They immediately saw the glowing yellow eyes as it dove at them. People scattered in all directions except for Al who stood frozen as the creature swooped straight at him. Just as the creature reached them, Ellie jerked the young man to the ground out of reach. The demon flew by over them and as soon as the thing safely cleared the crowd another shot rang out, then another. The hellish thing finally fell to the ground. Jake ran over to the group of people and helped Ellie to her feet. "Are you alright?"

"Yes, I think so," said Ellie.

They all slowly got to their feet, looked around, and it appeared no one was hurt. They followed Jake over to the church building under construction and found the hog-like demon crumpled up next to the support beam. The thing was dead and started rapidly decaying so the smell of death and rotting flesh was immediate.

"I hate that smell," remarked Pam.

Despite his initial fear Al snapped off pictures of the demon in rapid succession. "What is that smell?"

"Sulfur," said Ellie.

"Do they always smell like that?"

"Nope, sometimes it's worse," said Jake.

The small group then walked over to the other demon and noticed that it was still alive as it squirmed to try to get up. Jake pointed his shotgun at the thing while Al's camera clicked pictures.

"What were you planning to do?" demanded Jake.

The tan colored demon hissed at him. It had a large chest wound from the shotgun slug and its wings were crumpled up underneath it.

"What were you doing to my church?" Ellie asked.

The demon cackled and then coughed, spitting up blood and red foam. "It's too late."

"What do you mean?"

Before the thing could finish, it coughed, rolled over and died.

"What do you think it meant?" asked Ellie.

Jake shook his head. "I don't know. I guess we'll never know now."

"It talked," said Al. "It actually spoke words." He turned to Jake. "Do you always shoot first and ask questions later?"

Jake frowned. They walked back to the construction area where Mr. Tillon was examining the beam with a flashlight. They saw that the demons had cut into the support beam in several locations. The cuts were small but over time it would have weakened the structure and eventually the building would have collapsed.

Al snapped more pictures. "This is more than I could have hoped for, real demons."

"We'll have to check all the support beams for damage," Mr.

Tillon explained. "The beams will have to be replaced which will put our construction time back weeks."

"At least we found out before something horrible happened," said Ellie.

"You're right. Our new building will have to wait," answered Mr. Tillon.

Jake was standing off to the side while they talked about what to do about the damage, when to call the construction company, and if the insurance would pay for any of the damages when suddenly Ned Parker appeared. "Jake, you need to come quick, those devil heathens are trying to destroy the ranch. Hurry."

He turned quickly and sprinted towards his truck.

"Jake, where're you going?" Ellie asked.

"Ned says demons are at the ranch," he yelled as he climbed inside and started up the truck. He raced out of the parking lot towards home.

"Ned? Who is Ned?" Pam asked as she looked around.

"I'll tell you later, c'mon," answered Ellie as she ran towards the parked cars.

"Let's take mine, it's closer," yelled Pam.

The three piled into her blue Ford Explorer, and a minute later they were racing to catch up to Jake. Fifteen minutes later, they crested a rise in the road and saw a red glow in the vicinity of Jake's ranch. Pam's Ford Explorer headlights lit up the dust in the air where Jake had turned onto the dirt road leading to his ranch. Pam whipped the Explorer onto the road, flew through the gate, and under the sign which said J Double T Ranch. Dust swirled behind them in the dark as they sped down the dirt road towards the ranch house. As they came over the small hill that hid the ranch house from the road, they saw the flames. The barn was completely engulfed. Most of the corral and holding pens were knocked down and some of the fencing was on fire. Part of the house's front porch had been burned and collapsed but it appeared the rest of the house was still intact. They saw that Jake had already stopped in front of the house. They saw him run to the front door with his shotgun in hand and burst inside. Pam's Ford Explorer skidded to a halt in the dirt, and they all climbed out. Al started taking pictures of everything.

Jake came out of the house a minute later and looked around.

"Roy?" asked Ellie.

Jake shook his head. "No one's inside."

"Look over there," Pam said and pointed at the corral area.

Most of the fencing was down. Roy's horse was dead, and the carcass was headless. They found the head impaled on one of the fence posts.

Al's face turned pale.

"Roy," yelled Jake.

They all began yelling Roy's name.

"You three stay together and look around but be careful," Jake said. "Demons might still be around."

They spread out calling Roy's name while Jake made a high-pitched whistle that he used to call Roscoe. They continued calling for Roy as they searched the ranch house area. The barn had collapsed and was now just a pile of burning lumber, a large bonfire. They gathered back at his truck.

"Where could they have gone?" asked Ellie.

"I just hope they weren't in the barn," Al commented.

Ned Parker yelled from around the corner of the house, "They went this way." He pointed west into the dark.

"Who is that man and where did he come from?" asked Pam wide eyed.

"That's Ned," Ellie answered hurriedly.

"But how did he get here?"

"He lives here. He's a ghost," replied Ellie as she followed Jake past the house.

"Oh of course he is," said Pam sarcastically.

Jake had already run well ahead of them into the darkness. As they tried to follow the direction, he'd gone, Ellie said, "I hear a dog barking. It must be Roscoe." After a few minutes, they all heard the dog barking. They climbed up the embankment of a small wash and saw a large pecan tree in the moonlight with several figures under the tree, one being the barking Roscoe. They approached and saw

Jake bent down next to a man sitting up against the tree. There was a much larger man kneeling also. Roscoe ran out to meet them. "Good boy, Roscoe," Ellie said and rubbed his fur.

They ran up to the three men. The large man stood up as they approached. He was a giant of a man, over seven feet tall, dressed all in white with a huge golden sword and even in the dark they could see the concern on his face.

"Roy's hurt but not seriously," said the angel, Malachy.

"What happened?" asked Jake.

Roy spoke up first. "Roscoe and I were eating dinner when I heard the horses start snorting and carrying on. I grabbed a rifle and went out to see what varmint had come up. I'd never seen anything like it. There were ten or fifteen of those demon critters around the barn and pens."

"They broke through our defenses," said Malachy. "We had a protective ring around your ranch in case they wanted to take revenge for what happened in Washington D.C. There hadn't been any activity in months."

"You mean angels have been guarding this ranch for months?" asked Roy.

Malachy nodded. "We let our guard down."

"It's not your fault," said Ellie.

"I fired a shot in the air to scare those heathens away," explained Roy. "They all just cackled at me and set fire to the barn. I fired at a few of them, but nothing happened. I remembered what Miss Ellie said about Jake being the only one that can kill those things, so Roscoe and I lit outta there."

Ned had appeared and added, "I tried to stop them, but they just laughed too and ran right through me."

Roy looked over at Ned. "I don't remember seeing you back at the house."

"He's Ned Parker, the original owner of the ranch," explained Jake.

"But that would mean that he's…"

"Dead," replied Jake. "He's a ghost."

"I prefer disembodied spirit," Ned added.

Roy shook his head. "Why am I not surprised? With all these stinking demons and giant angels running around, why not add a ghost, I mean disembodied spirit?"

"We were able to rally and drove them away from the ranch house," interjected Malachy. "They managed to burn some of the porch, but we put it out."

"Roscoe and I ran this way to hopefully get away from them," explained Roy. "A few followed us and attacked me. They got me in the leg and shoulder. Roscoe fought 'em off while I crawled up the hill and under the tree. The strange thing was they charged at me but kept their distance. I knew I couldn't hurt 'em but I shot at 'em just to make myself feel better. Roscoe stood his ground. They kept jumping at me but didn't come any closer. Roscoe kept 'em at bay until your big friend arrived."

"Can you walk?" asked Jake.

Roy nodded and Jake helped him to his feet. Roy gingerly stood on his injured leg.

"I'm not going to be of much help for a few days," explained Roy.

"I think you've earned a little vacation," said Jake was a tight smile.

"I just don't know why they didn't attack me. It was like they couldn't come any closer."

"You're on sacred ground," answered Malachy.

They stared at Malachy who pointed to a small stone marker on the ground. It had the name *Mobak* inscribed on it.

"Of course," said Ellie. "It's Mobak's grave which made this ground holy. The demons couldn't come on sacred ground, like a cemetery."

"But Mobak was a demon?" said Pam.

"Yes," said Malachy. "But he died saving you which still makes it sacred ground."

"I'm just glad it was there," said Roy with a grin.

Ellie looked around. "Where's Al?"

Jake motioned over his shoulder with his thumb. "He's back over there. He fainted."

Pam and Ellie stepped over, bent down, and helped Al up to a sitting position.

Jake turned to Malachy. "What's going on? Why did they suddenly start up after so many months of doing nothing?"

Malachy shook his head. "I don't know. They're on the move though. We haven't gotten any information yet about what or why but I'm afraid they have something planned. Be careful."

"I will, thanks for the help." Jake shook the big angel's hand.

"And thanks for stepping in and helping me," added Roy. "I never would've believed you existed until I seen it myself."

"Someone once said blessed are those that haven't seen and yet believe," said Malachy with a grin and then disappeared.

"What? ...what did I miss?" said Al suddenly as the Pam and Ellie helped him to his feet. "I walked up and then saw...oh my, I saw a huge man...an angel? I froze and everything went black."

"You fainted," said Pam dryly.

Ellie held one of Al's arms to help keep him steady. "Don't feel bad. The prophet Daniel fainted when he saw an angel too."

"Who is that man and why does he look bluish?" asked Al pointing at Ned.

"That's Ned, and I'll explain later," said Ellie.

Jake rolled his eyes. "C'mon, let's get back to the house. Roy needs medical attention, and we need to start figuring out what this is all about."

CHAPTER SIX

Gooseneck State Park
State Highway 316
Southeastern Utah

THE SUN HAD SET over the beautiful, rugged canyon area. Four young men had been hiking all day around the San Juan River and located a spot near the river to set up camp. After enjoying their campfire meal, the men sat around and talked about football and women. Once a month they got together and went hiking over the weekend.

Todd, a tall, dark haired young man walked to the river and retrieved several six packs of beer from the water. He'd placed it there earlier to keep it cool.

"You're the man, Todd," said Jeff, a short stocky blond haired young man.

"I thought we might need some extra refreshment."

"Did you carry them all this way?" asked Mike, Jeff's brother.

"Yep, it'll be worth it."

Todd passed the beers around. Jeff kicked another piece of wood into the fire. "Man, it doesn't get any better than this."

"Yes, it could," responded Mike. "Belinda could be here."

The group burst into laughter.

"You're dreaming, dude, she's out of your league," said Dan, the fourth one of the group.

"Uh huh, and only because you struck out with her," answered Mike. "She's needing a real man."

The comment resulted in more laughter from the group.

SNAP

"Did you hear that?" asked Jeff.

"Nope," replied Mike.

"Maybe its Belinda coming to make your dreams come true," said Dan.

Todd turned to the darkness beyond the campfire. "Hey, dude, come on in. We got another beer. We can share."

They listened but there was no further sound.

"I guess he wasn't thirsty," said Todd.

Over the slight breeze came the smell of something rank, like rotting eggs and something else.

"Oh, man, what's that smell?" asked Jeff.

"Mike, I told you if you have to go, do it away from camp," said Todd.

"Funny man," said Mike.

Dan stood up and looked around. "I didn't smell anything when we first arrived."

One of them was about to make another comment about Belinda when a low growl from the nearby rock formation cut it short.

"What was that?" asked Jeff.

Before anyone could answer, a dark form appeared at the edge of the campsite and all four men stared in horror. At first glance it appeared to be a black bear...on steroids. It was three times the normal size with abnormally large teeth. Parts of its fur and skin had rotted or burned away showing the tendons and muscles. One normal shaped eye stared at them while the other glowed yellow.

Dan was standing closest to the thing and before he could even move, it swiped at him with a huge claw that ripped half of Dan's face loose from his skull. Dan screamed and fell back into the dirt as the skin on one side of his face flapped back and forth spraying the area with blood. Todd grabbed a piece of burning wood from the fire and swung it at the beast. The monster roared and knocked Todd to the ground. The others watched in horror as the behemoth stepped forward, opened it mouth, and engulfed Todd's entire head. It clamped down and crushed Todd's skull like an egg. Jeff jumped to his feet and dove into the river in terror while Mike ran up a dirt path towards the hiking trail. The creature dropped Todd's corpse and lunged towards Mike. Jeff swam farther into the water as a horrid scream brought his attention back to the riverbank. The last thing he saw was the huge thing dragging his brother's corpse away into the darkness as the river swept him downstream.

J Double T Ranch
Sutton County, Texas

THE COUNTY AMBULANCE service took Roy to Pecos to treat his injuries. Besides some cuts and claw marks that needed stitches, they felt he was going to be fine, but the hospital was going to keep him overnight for observation. Jake sat on the porch of his ranch and surveyed the damage. He removed his hat and shook his head. Ellie, Pam, and Al stood next to Pam's truck while Ned was quietly sitting in his rocking chair on the porch smoking his pipe.

"We can stay if you need us to," said Pam. "Are you sure he'll be alright?"

"Yeah," answered Ellie. "I'll have him drive me back."

"A real ghost and an angel, all in one night," said Al wide eyed. "This story is going to be awesome."

Pam and Al drove off into the night. Ellie walked over and sat down on the steps next to Jake. She leaned over and laid her head on his shoulder. "Everything will be alright," she said. Jake didn't say anything, so Ellie put her arm around Jake's broad shoulders. "I know one thing; our life together will never be boring."

Jake turned and looked at her. He chuckled at first then burst out laughing. He hugged her and kissed her. "You're amazing, you know that."

"Just what a woman wants to hear."

"I never liked that barn there anyway," Ned said with a grin.

They both looked back at the former living ranch owner and laughed.

"Do you have any idea of where to go from here? Those demons are up to something."

Jake looked around. "I don't know." At that moment his cell phone jingled and the number on the screen showed it was from Deputy Director Ruiz. "Evening, Oscar."

On the other end Deputy Director Ruiz immediately detected the stress in Jake's voice. "What's going on? What's happened there?"

"Oh, just the usual, demons tried to sabotage Ellie's new church building, demons attacked my ranch, injured my ranch hand, killed a horse, burned my barn, and ran off the cattle."

Deputy Director Ruiz sighed. "I'm sorry and this might make it worse. I just received word that a man was fished out of a river somewhere near a small city named Mexican Hat in southern Utah, babbling about something attacking his camping site. From what he told the local authorities they think three were killed. The lone survivor escaped by swimming down the river. It's too dangerous to try to hike down in the dark so when the sun comes up, the sheriff's deputies are going to go investigate. I'm going to send Agent Williams out to Arizona first then on to Utah. I'd like for you to go too."

Jake looked around at what was left of his ranch and sighed. "I'll drive to El Paso and catch a flight in a day or so. I have to salvage what's left here first."

"I need you there as soon as possible. I'll have transportation at your ranch tomorrow evening to take you there."

"That's too soon, Oscar."

"I'm sorry but I need you there."

Jake groaned. "I'll be ready." Jake hung up and turned to Ellie. "I think we got our answer as to what to do next."

Federal Bureau of Investigation
Office of Deputy Director of Paranormal Activities
935 Pennsylvania Avenue Northwest
Washington, D.C.

DEPUTY DIRECTOR RUIZ hung up the phone and rubbed his tired eyes. He hated pressuring Jake into this considering what had just happened to his ranch, but he needed his expertise. Agent Williams had entered the office while he was on the phone and sat in a chair on the other side of the desk. He looked up at her. "Sorry to get you out here so late but it's important."

"No problem, it was an excuse to get out of a boring date anyway."

"There's been another attack."

Agent Williams raised an eyebrow. "Where?"

"It was near a city called Mexican Hat in southern Utah." Deputy Director Ruiz pushed a file across the desk to her.

She picked up the folder and scanned the report. "It's vague, too early to know for sure. Could it have been a regular bear and the beer making him exaggerate?"

Deputy Director Ruiz shrugged. "I thought about that myself but it's too much of a coincidence, that's why I don't want to dismiss it. I need you to look at this frozen thing first and then up to Utah. Jake Taft is going to meet you in Arizona."

Agent Williams got to her feet and turned to leave. "Do you think they're related attacks?"

Deputy Director Ruiz shrugged. "I don't know. That's what I want you to find out...and..." said Deputy Director Ruiz cautiously.

Agent Williams frowned.

"I'm assigning you a new partner."

"Oscar, no, I..."

Deputy Director Ruiz held up his hand. "I know you don't like partners and only put up with me temporarily, but I need someone to watch your back."

Agent Williams sighed. "I hope he's not a smoker."

"If he is," Deputy Director Ruiz replied with a smile, "I'm sure you'll break him of it. His name is Terrell Pyle." He handed Agent Williams a file folder. "Here's his file. Try not to hurt him."

———

Government Storage Compound
City of Buzlanovo
12 miles southwest of Moscow, Russia

VIKTOR GORDYA SAT in his cramped government car and looked once again at the map in his lap, at the intersection of two small roads. He'd driven from Moscow to Buzlanovo after receiving a call from one of his superiors about a dead guard. Viktor didn't understand how the death of a guard at a forgotten warehouse could possibly be important to him. He had more cases on his desk than he had time and wasn't happy about being called out here about a routine death of a security guard.

He turned left and drove a quarter of a mile down the road until he saw the gate of the warehouse. A police vehicle was parked at the gate along with a white van. He parked behind the police vehicle, unfolded his six-foot three-inch frame from the little car, and walked towards the guard shack.

A young Buzlanovo police officer watched the tall blond-haired man wearing a long black ankle length leather coat approach. The large man's walk reminded the officer of a large and deadly predator. He swallowed hard. "Are you the man they sent from Moscow?"

Gordya nodded and showed him his ID and badge, that of an agent for the FSB, the Federalnaya Shuzhba Bezopasnosti, also known as Federal Security Service, the new version of the old Communist KGB.

"So why did you make a great deal of trouble and have me sent out here?" demanded Gordya.

The young officer shook his head. "I assure you I didn't ask for anyone from the FSB. I simply called the number I found in the guard shack, told them that someone broke into one of the warehouses, and that I found the guard dead. I was called back by someone from the FSB and was told to stand by and not touch anything. About an hour later, that white van showed up. The driver's been taking pictures but not talking."

Gordya looked at the van and frowned. "How did you find out about the death?"

"We received a frantic call from the guard's wife. When he didn't come home last night, she came out here this morning and found him."

"Where is she?"

"She had to go back home to call so my partner is sitting with her at her home."

Gordya sighed. He'd hoped he could wrap this up and head back to Moscow by mid-morning. "Very well, let me see what this is about?"

They walked over to the guard shack and saw that a gray tarp had been thrown over the body of the guard. Gordya looked inside and raised an eyebrow as the walls and windows inside the shack were covered in blood splatter. The inside of the shack had a strange smell, like a chemical…maybe sulfur. He reached down and started to lift the tarp, but the police officer grabbed his arm.

"Don't…"

Gordya glanced up at him with cold ice blue eyes and saw the pale face of the young officer staring at him.

"I covered him as soon as I found him," explained the officer, "after I vomited."

Viktor jerked his arm away. "Then go wait by your car."

The police officer nodded and walked back to his car and lit up a cigarette. Gordya turned and pulled away the tarp to reveal what was left of Yuri Osipushka. After instinctively glancing away he forced himself to look back and saw that Osipushka was in three large pieces scattered on the floor. His head was tilted to one side. His eyes were open, staring wide, and his mouth was gaped open in a death scream. The guard's skull was peeled back, and his brain was gone. His right arm and part of his left leg were missing. His torso was ripped open and most of his internal organs were gone. There were large claw marks all over his body. He noticed that there were no flies or insects flying around. The body had been there all night and into the morning but had not drawn any insects yet. *What could have done something like this?* Gordya jerked the tarp back over the corpse and stepped into the compound yard. He walked through the weed covered area to the warehouse. A man in a white jumpsuit walked out carrying a camera. The man was short with thick glasses.

Gordya showed him his badge. "Who are you?"

The man smiled showing crooked stained teeth and flashed a military ID card. "Sergeant Sokolof, I am with the Department of Military Intelligence."

Gordya looked surprised. "Why is the military involved in the death of a security guard at a worthless warehouse in the middle of nowhere?"

The man smiled again which irritated Gordya. "It's not the death of an insignificant guard but what may have been stolen."

"What was taken?"

"I'm still checking the records. Some of them are fifty or more years old. When I find out I'll put it in my report to the intelligence command and you can go through proper channels to get a copy."

Gordya gritted his teeth. He was being stonewalled, and walked back to the guard shack. The Russian police officer strolled over to him.

"What do you think did this?" he asked indicating the corpse of the security guard.

Gordya just shrugged. "I don't know."

"Could it have been wolves? They sometimes come out of the woods looking for food. Maybe they attacked him and ripped him to shreds like that."

"Wolves don't break into warehouses and steal."

The officer nodded. "*Da,* you are right."

"When is the truck coming for the guard's body?"

The young officer shrugged. "I was told that someone would come for the body and not to ask questions."

Gordya was furious. He'd been called out of bed to drive out to the isolated location only to be stonewalled by military intelligence. He walked away from the officer and pulled out his cell phone. He dialed a number and a male on the other end answered. *"Da."*

"This is Gordya. I am out at the warehouse near Buzlanovo on this dead security guard. M.I. is here and they're tight lipped about everything. This is unacceptable for my investigation."

The voice on the phone hesitated. "One moment."

Gordya ran his fingers through his short blond hair in frustration. After five minutes of waiting on the phone, the voice came back. "Cooperate with them." The voice then hung up.

Gordya slammed his phone shut. *This whole thing stunk of politics.* He stood and waited until Sergeant Sokolof came back to his van and loaded his camera and a few small sacks into the back of van. When he turned around Gordya was standing behind him.

"What did you find out was stolen?" demanded Gordya.

Sergeant Sokolof glanced up at the tall blond FSB agent. "Nothing, I found nothing."

He turned to shut the van door when Gordya grabbed him from behind and slammed his head into the door frame, knocking his glasses off. The sergeant fell to the ground and grabbed his head which began to bleed from a gash in his head. Gordya jerked the little man to his feet and pushed him back against the side of the van.

"Don't lie to me," he growled. "What was stolen?"

Sergeant Sokolof sneered at him. "You will answer for this. You've assaulted a member of the military."

Gordya grabbed the man's white jumpsuit and slammed him into the van again. "I won't ask you again. I might make it look like you were tragically attacked by whatever killed this guard."

"Are you threatening me?" demanded Sergeant Sokolof but in a weaker voice.

"Not if you tell me what I want to know."

"I don't know."

"Liar. They might never find all of your body parts."

Sergeant Sokolof looked into the hard blue eyes of someone he realized you didn't bluff. "I'm telling the truth. I called my superiors and told them the box number that was missing. It was in a refrigerated section of the warehouse. They told me the job was finished and to keep my mouth shut or else."

Gordya released the sergeant who then grabbed a rag from his pocket and held it over the gash on his head. Sergeant Sokolof picked up his glasses while the blood leaked down onto his white jumpsuit.

"What kind of box?" asked Gordya.

Sergeant Sokolof glanced around as if someone might be watching. "I don't know but from the looks of the space where it sat it was about the size of a large shoe box," he whispered.

"That's it?"

The sergeant nodded. *"Da,* I read them the inventory number from the sequence and location in the warehouse. The box had been frozen, and I'd guess from the numbers was very old, perhaps fifty or sixty years old. That's all I know."

Gordya turned and walked back to his car. *Why would anyone brutally kill a security guard and break into a warehouse and only take a small old box?* He turned his car around and headed back to Moscow. In his rear-view mirror, he saw Sergeant Sokolof yelling at the young police officer and pointing at Gordya's car. The officer just shrugged as if to say he didn't see anything.

———

J Double T Ranch
Sutton County, Texas

THE SUN ROSE on Jake's land making it look more like a war zone than a ranch. The barn was a pile of smoldering wood, one half of the porch to the ranch was on the ground, and the other half was hanging loose. Most of the fencing to the corral was down and he had a horse carcass to bury. Roy was on his way back from Pecos but would not be a help for several days. The more he saw damaged, the more his anger burned. He hadn't asked for this, but he was going to make sure someone or rather, something, paid for it.

He backed his pickup around to where the horse carcass was and tied a rope to the hind legs. He tossed the head into the bed. He would drag it far enough away and bury it. Roscoe stood on the open tailgate, apparently supervising everything.

"You could help," snapped Jake.

Roscoe barked and looked off to the east. Jake looked over and saw a huge cloud of dust coming his way. *Now what?* He stepped around and pulled his shotgun from the front seat of the truck. Within a few minutes he saw a line of pickup trucks and cars in a convoy pulling onto his ranch. He recognized Ellie's Ford Taurus and Pam's Ford Explorer but the rest he didn't know. Several of the trucks had trailers full of lumber and building supplies. The small army pulled up and parked around the ranch house. Ellie climbed out of her car with a big grin on her face.

"Ellie, what's this all about?" demanded Jake.

Ellie continued to smile as George Tillon walked by, already pointing to the barn and the corral.

"Will someone tell me what's going on," Jake growled.

"They've come to help," replied Ellie. "Last night Pam called George and told him what had happened out here. George called Bill Wade who called Jim Stanford. The more people that found out, the more wanted to help. They all knew you were too stubborn to ask for help so they just showed up."

"I can't pay for all this?" stammered Jake. "I, I, I can't let ya'll do this."

Pam walked up. "Everyone chipped in to pay for the lumber and no one would take a dime from you considering everything you've done to help us. We're going to have an old-time barn raising."

Jake stood and stared at the people as they unloaded lumber and began working on the porch. He shook his head. He knew Ellie's church couldn't be bought or threatened so he did what he knew he should and pitched in to help.

In no time the framework for a new barn was being constructed in a different spot, the broken posts were removed from the corral and new ones put in. With help the carcass was loaded into the truck bed and several men took it to bury it. The burned part of the porch was torn down and the remaining section was repaired.

At lunch time several more vehicles showed up loaded with food and drinks for the workers. Roy showed up in one of the vehicles carrying desserts. He limped and was sore but looked fit. Some of the older single women from the church seemed to take an extra interest in Roy, and the more interest they showed the more he limped. *That scoundrel,* thought Jake with a chuckle. They took a break to eat, rest, and talk.

"So, where's Al?" asked Jake while he balanced a paper plate on his lap. "I would've thought he'd be chomping at the bit to be here."

"He's still at the motel. I didn't let him know about it," said Pam. She motioned to the group of people scattered around the ranch eating, laughing, and talking. "These people didn't come out here to have their picture taken for some magazine. They came out here because they care."

Jake nodded in agreement.

While they were eating, they noticed that Buck, Jake's horse, came trotting up followed by two other horses. A couple of the men from the other ranches offered to help round up Jake's herd. As long as the fences weren't torn down, they should be easy to find.

By the end of the day, the frame and most of the barn's roof was on. The crowd loaded up their tools but promised to be back tomorrow to finish. Jake thanked as many of them as he could before they left. They were good people who could be counted on, and Jake could never repay them but knew they would never accept anything in return. Roy was sitting in the rocking chair on the porch softly snoring. His ordeal had worn him out more than he let on. Ned was in the other rocking chair smoking his pipe. Roscoe was asleep between them on the porch and opened an eye as Jake stepped inside the kitchen. Ellie and Pam were making dinner.

"You're not going back to town?" asked Jake.

"No, we're fixing dinner so we can leave with you tonight," answered Ellie.

"Count me in too," added Pam. "I wouldn't miss it for the world."

Jake put his hands on his hips. "This isn't a vacation. I'm going out there to look at a corpse of some sort and look for a creature that killed three men."

"I know," said Ellie. "Now, wash up so we can eat before they show up. Our bags are in the car."

Pam just smiled. "Where she goes, I go. Give up, Taft."

Jake threw his hands up and stomped off to the bathroom to clean up while mumbling something about being outnumbered. The two women giggled.

After dinner Jake pulled the suitcases out of Ellie's car and sat them on the porch. "Are you sure you want to go? This may be a wild goose chase, or it could get dangerous real fast."

"Do you think you can get rid of me that easily? Mr. Tillon and I have a standing agreement. When you get a call, he'll take over until we get back, no questions asked."

Jake laughed and shook his head. He'd learned better than to try to talk them out of going. Ellie and Pam had been through thick and thin with him. The two women had impersonated prostitutes to gain entry to a demon lord's lair, fought off a demon in a hotel room in Virginia, and stood by him while he fought for their lives against a horde of demons in the basement of the Jefferson Memorial. "What about Pam's magazine boy?" asked Jake.

"You got lucky. Al's staying here. Pam will call him later."

"And I'll look after things here until you get back," added Roy from his seat in the rocking chair. Ned just nodded.

Before Jake could respond they heard a low thumping sound. He stepped off the porch and saw a dark shape headed in their direction. The helicopter flew in low over the house and landed about fifty yards away. All Jake could see were the flashing lights on the aircraft. A man climbed out of the copilot's seat and approached. "Major Taft?"

Jake nodded. They grabbed their bags, and with Roscoe tagging along they followed the man to the helicopter. Jake noticed that it was a small twin turbine Agusta A 109 light utility copter that had no markings and was painted black.

Covert.

Pam and Roscoe climbed inside while Ellie looked questionably at Jake when he handed a large coffee thermos bottle to the copilot who took it without question. Once inside, the helicopter lifted into the air and headed northwest. The inside of the cabin was covered in soft, tan leather and quite comfortable. Roscoe and Pam found seats across from them and settled down.

"What was that all about?" asked Ellie.

"What?"

"The thermos?"

"An experiment," answered Jake.

"What kind of experiment?"

"I called Oscar earlier and asked him to try to look into something for me. I'll explain later."

They all sat back and soon fell asleep to the drone of the engines.

————

Le Club Bar
207 Hougang Street 21
Moscow, Russia

VIKTOR GORDYA SAT at a local bar nursing his drink. It had been a miserable day. After coming back from Buzlanovo, he'd tried to make a few contacts on other cases but was unsuccessful, so he left early and headed to one of his favorite bars. He was on his second cognac when his cellphone rang. He answered it, listened for a moment, and hung up. His day had just gotten worse, so he paid for his drinks, walked outside into the late evening air, and headed to his car. *What does First Deputy Director Kondrasha want?*

Thirty minutes later, Gordya sat outside the first deputy director's office in a hardback wooden chair. He assumed his summons was a result of the assault on that worthless Sergeant Sokolof. He thought about what twist he was going to put on it to avoid being sent to a remote station in Siberia when the secretary's intercom buzzed. The middle-aged woman simply nodded to him. Gordya stepped into the office, stood, and waited.

First Deputy Director Kondrasha was in his late fifties, stocky build, with bushy eyebrows and bald. Gordya had heard rumors about First Deputy Director Kondrasha. He was tough, unsympathetic, and ruthless if need be. Most high-ranking officials had offices that resembled a five-star hotel with plush furnishings, but this first deputy director kept his office in stark contrast. He sat behind a large wooden desk with hardback wooden chairs, no pictures, no rugs, and no personal items.

"Sit," said First Deputy Director Kondrasha.

Gordya sat in one of the chairs in front of the desk. He noticed that his knees were higher than normal, indicating that the legs of the chair were shorter, making him sit lower than the first deputy director. *A power play to make me feel inferior* thought Gordya. The first deputy director sat and read through some papers from a red colored file. *Top Secret*. Viktor sat without interruption. *This is bad*. Gordya knew that you weren't called to see the second in command of the FSB, the leading political force in Russia, for tea or a pat on the back. *This was very bad*.

After what seemed like an eternity the first deputy director put the file down and looked up at Gordya from underneath his bushy eyebrows.

"Why did you strike Sergeant Sokolof?" he asked in a deep hollow voice.

Viktor thought about all the scenarios he'd concocted while driving over to the office, but he knew none would hold up. "Sir, I struck him because he wouldn't tell me what he knew."

First Deputy Director Kondrasha sat back in his chair and folded his hands on his lap. "Did he tell you?"

"He said he didn't know what was stolen, just that it was a small box."

"Did you believe him?"

"Yes."

First Deputy Director Kondrasha nodded. He reached into the folder, pulled out a piece of paper, and tossed it across the desk to Gordya who picked it up and read it. Viktor frowned. "Is this real?"

"*Da*," growled First Deputy Director Kondrasha. "As of right now, only a hand full of people know of this."

Viktor placed the paper back on the desk. First Deputy Director Kondrasha picked it up and placed it back in the file. He leaned forward and placed his elbows on the table. "I want you to find it and bring it back to me, no one else, just me. Is that understood?"

"Yes, First Deputy Director."

The deputy director picked up another folder and handed it to him. "This might aid you in your mission. You're wasting time."

Viktor abruptly got to his feet and left the office. Once he reached his car he sat behind the wheel and opened the folder. It was the autopsy report on Yuri Osipushka. He read through the gruesome details of the man's death. *What a horrific death.* He made a mental note of the claw marks that didn't look routine. *None of it looked routine.* It reminded him of something he'd read several months back. It was a newspaper story from America.

Viktor Gordya started his car, pulled out into traffic, and headed towards his apartment. He was already contemplating his plan of action. He wasn't sure why or how, but he knew somehow that the death of an overweight security guard and theft of a seemingly insignificant box from an old broken-down warehouse was tied to one man. Jacob Travis Taft.

CHAPTER SEVEN

FBI Headquarters
935 Pennsylvania Avenue Northwest
Washington D.C.

AS THE SUN set over the nation's capital, Agent Williams pulled in front of the FBI building and saw a tall, athletic looking Black man standing by the front door holding an overnight bag.

Pyle. She'd read his file. He was 30 years old and unmarried. He'd played professional football briefly as a wide receiver before joining the FBI. He'd been assigned to mundane routine assignments and had a few minor commendations. She stopped and the man approached the car. He tossed his bag in the backseat and climbed in the front.

"I'm Agent Terrell Pyle."

"I'm Williams." She put the car in drive and pulled away from the curb. "Why are you here?"

Agent Pyle turned and looked at her with raised eyebrows. "I'm here to go with you to Arizona."

"I know that, but why did you ask to be in this unit? No one volunteers for this duty. They call us the 'MIB for demons'."

Agent Pyle smiled. "I've been assigned to forsaken places investigating stuff like minor forgery, thefts of cows, and bad counterfeiting. I saw the opportunity to do something different, so I volunteered."

Agent Williams frowned. "Did they tell you the last couple of agents that worked with me ended up dead?"

"Yes."

"Do you have any children? Engaged?"

"No."

"Good, no grieving children or widow."

Agent Pyle looked over at the female agent. She was attractive but in a hard way even with the two scars that ran vertically down the side of her face. He'd heard she was tough, blunt, no nonsense and that working with her was the same as having your wisdom teeth pulled without anesthesia. "So, these things actually exist?"

"Yes."

"So, these monsters actually attacked you and that's how you got cut, I mean clawed?"

Agent Williams cracked a slight grin and nodded. "When Oscar was my temporary partner after his partner had been killed, we were attacked by demons on the freeway. We didn't know what they were then."

"Then this Taft guy showed up?"

"Yep, it was pure luck that he just happened to be going the same way. One of the monsters had peeled the top of the car back and was about to rip me to shreds when Taft showed up. That's how I got these scars. You still want to do this?"

Agent Pyle sat quietly for a moment and then nodded. "Yes, and you're wrong. They call this unit 'The Ghoul Squad'."

Agent Williams laughed. "It figures."

———

Arizona State Highway 160
South of Kayenta, Arizona

THE HEADLIGHTS of a shiny black BMW lit up the road south of Kayenta on Highway 160. The young, blonde-haired woman driving ignored the quickly fading sunset and slowed down to a paved road that cut off to the left. She was in the Black Mesa area of Arizona, known for its dark lines of coal that have been mined for years.

She pulled up to a guard shack next to the gate. The property was surrounded by an eight-foot-high fence that went miles in either direction. She rolled the window down as a security guard approached the car, nodded to the woman, and punched in a code on a box mounted on a pole. The electric gate opened, and she drove through, followed the winding road up through the beautiful pinion and juniper trees that covered countryside as it switched back and forth through the property until she came into view of a large estate. The buildings were set back against the side of the rocks and blended nicely. She drove up to a circle drive, stopped, and was met by a man who took the car and drove off to park it in a separate parking garage.

The woman entered the large adobe style house, but once inside, the decor took a drastically different direction. The wood was dark oak mixed with pine. The carved columns and banisters were of Bavarian and German style. Paintings on the wall were of Germany, especially Bavaria.

The young woman's high heels echoed as she walked down a marbled hallway passing walls covered with German tapestries depicting hunting scenes. She stopped at a set of heavy wooden doors and knocked. A female voice called for her to enter. She stepped into a large library filled with books from floor to ceiling. There were no windows in the library and only a few lamps lit the room. A slim figure sat in a wheelchair by one of the lamps. At the sound of the young woman's approach the woman in the wheelchair turned. She was old with worn, wrinkled skin and thinning white hair.

"Ah, my child, it is good to see you again," she said.

The young woman approached and hugged her gently. "*Gross-mutter*, it is good to see you too. It has been too long."

"Much too long, Gerda."

The woman named Gerda blushed slightly. *"Danke, Grossmutter.* You're looking well. How was your flight?"

The old woman waved her hand in the air. "It was bumpy and loud. I hate coming to this dry horrid country. The airport's small and those people are disgusting. What do you call them? Savages? Redskins? Indians? How do you stand coming to this place?"

"To be politically correct they are called Native Americans and I find it bearable only because I know that it won't be forever."

"Ya, ya," said the old woman. "So how are our plans going?"

Gerda frowned and shook her head. "It's slow and tedious. The work is not going as we had expected."

"Ya, I would imagine not. The rock is hard to dig, and we must be careful. It takes time."

"But *Grossmutter,* time is not on your side."

The old woman laughed which caused a fit of coughing. She held a delicate handkerchief over her mouth. Gerda reached over and handed her a glass of water that sat on the end table.

"Danke, child." The old woman drank carefully. "I know that I'm old and may never see the complete end. I wish that your dearest mother, Priska, was still alive and could be here too but all I want is to live long enough to see this part finished."

"You will, you will."

The old woman sat her glass down. "I heard that there have been some problems here at the lab too."

"Who told you there were problems?" asked Gerda with a frown.

"I did," answered a deep scratchy voice.

Gerda detected the smell of sulfur, rotting flesh, and fur just before she looked up and saw a seven-foot tall, muscular form step out from one of the deep shadows of the library.

Lord Degen.

"Why did you have to tell her anything? We have everything under control," snapped Gerda.

A furry and clawed hand suddenly grasped Gerda around the throat. "Remember your place, woman. You may be important elsewhere but to me you're nothing."

The old woman interrupted. "Now, my dear Degen. I'm sure Gerda didn't mean any harm. She's of the *Fuhrer's* lineage after all."

Degen released Gerda, stepped all the way into the light, and even though Gerda had seen him for many years she still hated the sight of him. He held a staff made from human bones and tied together in places with strips of tanned human skin. Degen reached over and put a clawed hand on the old woman's shoulder. "She won't be if she doesn't learn to curb her tongue."

The old woman reached up and patted the furry hand. "Now, dear, Gerda is a little headstrong, but she knows her place."

"She'd better."

"So, what is the problem here?" asked the old woman.

Gerda glowered at Degen but smiled when she looked back at the woman in the wheelchair. "Nothing that would concern you, just some of our workers don't last as long as we had hoped, and we have to keep reproducing more."

"So, we just need to make more," growled Degen.

"It's not like breeding rabbits," responded Gerda. "Some of the donors don't always survive the first time. Some of the embryo eat their way out of the womb and kill the donor."

"Get more donors."

"Getting donors are not as easy as it sounds. We have to be careful not to take too many from one city or it will draw suspicions."

"Aren't these homeless people, street people, prostitutes, or hitch-hikers?" asked the old woman.

"Yes, *Grossmutter*," answered Gerda softly. "We still have to be careful not to draw attention."

"We don't want excuses," roared Degen. "We want results. Maybe I should take over this project."

"Now, Degen, my love," said the old woman, "Decapitated or dismembered workers will do us no good. They're not easily obtained so we have to be patient."

"I've been waiting too long for my plans to come about, and I'm becoming impatient. So is Lord Satan."

The old woman reached up and began stroking the fur on the

demon's arm. "I know. It's been a long time for me too. It's not like the old days. We have to be more patient."

Gerda went and stood beside her grandmother. "I do have some good news."

The old woman smiled but Degen simply stared with yellow eyes. Gerda picked up a phone off the end table, dialed a number and said, "Send her up." Gerda hung up and looked down at her grandmother. "Even though some of our tests have not been successful we've been making progress."

A minute later, the door opened and a petite, feminine creature walked in. The old woman and Degen stared for a moment. Gerda smiled.

"This is number 10191," announced Gerda.

The creature was five-foot-six inches tall, 120 pounds, and looked like a typical young woman except one eye was yellow while the other was blue, and she had no body hair.

Degen walked slowly around the creature numbered 10191, examining her carefully. "She's nearly perfect," he said.

Gerda continued to smile. "Yes, she is. Some particular DNA takes better than others. She's remarkably intelligent too."

Degen snarled. "I could care less how smart she is. What I'm concerned with are we capable of breeding more? Will this genetic line be good enough to produce Hitler?"

"We hope she will be one of many that we will work with to keep perfecting our tests to achieve our goal."

"And if the DNA sample from Russia is too degraded, we can use Gerda's to fill in the gaps," added the elderly woman.

Gerda nodded and turned to 10191. "Return to your area downstairs."

The creature 10191 silently exited the room. Degen looked pleased at the progress, so Gerda thought it was a good time to drop the really bad news. "There was an unfortunate incident however."

The old woman looked up while Degen growled.

"We had an escape from the dig site. We've located the digger and will retrieve it, but the other is still loose. We'll capture it before too long."

"How did that happen?" demanded Degen.

Gerda glared back at Degen. "The more violent ones had been transferred to the dig to be used by the guards to control the diggers. As I said these creatures aren't stupid, the digger slipped by one of the guards, let the violent one loose, and then escaped. The guards tried to stop it, but it managed to get away."

"What is it?" asked Degen.

"A hybrid-bear."

"What happened to the guards? Were they punished for their stupidity?"

"It killed the guards."

"Good," snapped Degen. "It will serve as a reminder to the other guards not to be sloppy. Where is the digger?"

"It's dead. It was killed by a hiker in area to the east of us near Monument Valley."

"It came all the way back here?" growled Degen. "Why would it come back here?"

Gerda shrugged. "The scientists think it's coming back to where it was born. Apparently so is the hybrid. We're making arrangements to get it back."

Degen snorted. "I don't trust your incompetent thugs. I'll see that the digger is recovered. Why haven't they captured or killed the other?"

Gerda nervously flipped her hair with her hand. "My men have tried to track it but it's difficult on the rocky terrain. They've shot it, sprayed it with acid, but so far, it's eluded us. We will apprehend it."

The devil beast turned, went out through the wooden doors into the hallway before turning back. "Make it happen and soon." Degen disappeared down the hall, his claws clicking on the marble floor.

The old woman looked up at Gerda. "Please excuse Lord Degen. He had grand plans many years ago but failed. He's been trying to rebuild his reputation with his majesty, Lord Lucifer. This may be his last chance and he's becoming anxious."

Gerda sneered in Degen's direction. "I don't trust him."

The old woman smiled. "You just have to get to know him. When it's all completed it will be different. The world will be different."

Airborne over the Midwest
USA

THE COMMERCIAL AIRCRAFT settled at its cruising altitude and most of the passengers were asleep. Agent Williams dozed while Agent Pyle read the file for the tenth time.

"So, they think this thing is real?" asked Agent Pyle.

"That's what they said," answered Agent Williams without opening her eyes. "I'm not sure I believe it."

"Why?"

Agent Williams opened her eyes and looked over at Agent Pyle. "Well, demons decompose at an incredible rate. They can easily be down to skeletons in an hour and to dust in two. The warm air of Arizona would have accelerated the decomposition so there's no way they could have frozen one fast enough."

"So, what is this thing?"

Agent Williams shrugged. "That's what we're supposed to find out."

"Do all demons look alike?"

"No. Each one looks different. They come in every shape, size, and color. Some appear to be more animal or insect than human. I guess it depends on how it changed over thousands and thousands of years. Taft's angel friend told him that since demons were kicked out of heaven, they've been changing into what they are now."

"So how do we know if it's a demon or not?"

Agent Williams frowned at him. "I would hope you would be able to tell by looking at them and they all smell like sulfur and ashes in their normal state. The problem is some can transform themselves to look like humans for a short time but when they do you can't smell their normal stench."

"And we can't kill them?"

Agent Williams nodded. "That's correct. Only Jake Taft can kill them. Taft's two female friends blew one up though. She said that it lost two limbs and a wing so it seems if we use enough firepower we can crippled or disabled them but not kill. It healed over with only half of its body left. I imagine if we could crush or disintegrate one enough there wouldn't be enough left to really harm us but that's only speculation."

Agent Pyle looked confused. "But if we can't kill them then how did that hiker kill this one?"

Agent Williams raised an eyebrow. "Our job is to find out."

Apparently not all the passengers were asleep. A bald, elderly man in the seat in front of Agent Williams turned slowly around and stared wide eyed at the two agents. It was obvious that he'd overheard them.

"Can I help you?" asked Agent Williams sarcastically.

The man turned back around.

Agent Pyle snickered.

————

Shady Oaks Community Church
2203 E. Hollis Street
Shady Oaks, Texas

A DUSTY RED Dodge Charger pulled up in front of the Shady Oaks Community Church. A tall man wearing an ankle length black leather coat climbed out of the car and stretched. *What a desolate area,* he thought. He looked around and saw several workmen at a building under construction. He walked up the steps of the portable building that was the church and stepped inside. It was a large room with chairs that could be moved around making it a multipurpose building. He went to an open door and saw a young woman behind a desk who looked up when he entered. "Hi, I'm Janet, how can I help you?"

"I am looking for a Miss Thompson," said the man with a strange accent.

Janet Pearston was the cheerful and bubbly part time secretary for the small church. She was puzzled by the man's accent. "Pastor Thompson isn't here right now. Can I help you?"

The man smiled. "I'm trying to locate her friend, Jacob Taft."

At the sound of voices Mr. Tillon came out of an adjacent room. "Good morning, I'm George Tillon. I'm the associate pastor. Maybe I can help you?"

The man shook his hand. "I'm trying to locate a friend of mine. His name is Jacob Taft."

Since the events over the last year or so the church had been contacted by many people claiming to be Jake's friend or relative wanting to see or talk to Jake. Ellie and Mr. Tillon had been vigilant at keeping Jake buffered from them. "He's not here right now. I can take a message if you would like me to?"

"I see you're building a new church across the parking lot," commented the man.

"Why, yes, we are. Everything was going fine until some demons sabotaged it and now we have to replace some support beams."

The man raised an eyebrow. "Demons?"

"Yep, sometimes it's hard to believe but they were trying to slow down our progress, but we'll get it done. They attacked Jake's ranch too." Mr. Tillon winced when he realized that he'd mentioned that Jake had a ranch. He didn't want to give out too much information.

"I came all the way from Moscow to speak to Mr. Taft," explained the man. "It's very important that I speak with him as soon as possible."

"Jake and Ellie have gone away for a few days on some business. I can take your number and when I get a hold of them, I can give them your number."

"Can you call him right now?" The man was obviously getting irritated with these people.

"I'm busy right now but I'll call him as soon as I get a chance. Just leave your number with Janet and I'll call them in a bit."

The man's jaws clenched but he smiled. "Thank you." He leaned over the desk and wrote a number on a piece of paper then gave it to Janet. He went out, got in his car, and left while Mr. Tillon watched him leave.

"What a strange man," said Janet.

And dangerous, thought Mr. Tillon.

Viktor Gordya drove a few blocks away, turned up an alley, and parked. He opened a small briefcase and removed an earpiece. He attached it to a small recorder. When he'd written his number down and handed it to Janet, he subtly attached a small listening device to the underside of her phone. Viktor now sat back and listened. He was sure the man would call Jake right away.

CHAPTER EIGHT

Navajo Tribal Police Department
Route 7
Chinle, Arizona

NAVAJO TRIBAL POLICE Sergeant Robert Greymountain sat at his desk when he heard the thumping of a helicopter. He got up and looked out the window at the approaching black helicopter. *No markings? How strange.* He walked out back as the small helicopter landed at the far end of the parking lot. He watched a tall cowboy climb out and help two women out with their luggage. A dog that appeared to be half-wolf jumped out also. As soon as they were clear the helicopter took off and disappeared over the horizon. He walked up to them. "I'm Sergeant Greymountain. Welcome to Arizona."

The tall, broad-shouldered cowboy smiled and extended his hand. "I'm Jake Taft. This is Ellie Thompson and Pamela Martin."

Sergeant Greymountain turned to the two attractive young women. "It's a pleasure." He glanced down at the dog. "And this is one of your colleagues?"

Jake laughed. "This is Roscoe."

Sergeant Greymountain rubbed the dog's ears, then look up at them. "You're not the FBI?"

"Ellie and I help the FBI from time to time, and Pam is her friend," said Jake with a smile.

"Yes, I remember Agent Williams saying something about an army major and his civilian friend might be coming. He didn't say anything about another woman though."

"She just comes along to annoy me," said Jake sarcastically.

Pam frowned. "He's rude. I'm Ellie's friend. I come along to help keep Jake out of trouble."

A cowboy, two women and a wolf dog. Realization suddenly came to him. "You're the demon killer?" said Sergeant Greymountain.

"I've been called that," grumbled Jake. He didn't like being called that, but the news media had tagged him with it, and it stuck.

Sergeant Greymountain studied them now with more interest. "Agent Williams called earlier to say she and another agent would be here within the hour. You're welcome to come in and get some coffee while we wait for them."

They followed Sgt. Greymountain into the building and helped themselves to the fresh brewed coffee. Jake's cellphone rang, and he immediately answered when he saw that it was Ellie's church number. "This is Jake."

"Jake, this is George Tillon."

"Morning, George. Do you need to talk to Ellie? She's right here."

"No, I wanted to give you a heads up. A man came by this morning looking for you."

Jake rolled his eyes. "Not another reporter?"

"This man was no reporter, Jake. He said he was from Moscow, Russia."

Jake stiffened. "What's his name?"

There was silence on the phone.

"George?"

"I'm sorry, Jake. I was just thinking. I never got his name. He said he was a friend and it was very important. He wanted me to call you right then."

Jake frowned. "What did he look like?"

Ellie noticed the subtle change in Jake and walked over by him.

"He was a tall man with blond hair, blue eyes, and rough look-ing," explained Mr. Tillon.

"Did you tell him where we were?"

"No, of course not, is there anything we should be aware of?"

Jake rubbed his chin. "No, and don't worry, he won't be back."

"And by the way, they've just about got everything cleaned up at your ranch. The barn will be finished soon. Have you looked at the thing yet?"

"No, not yet we're waiting on the FBI to get here. If you need us today and can't reach us, you can contact the Navajo Police Depart-ment. After that we'll be heading up to a town called Mexican Hat up in Utah."

"Got it, be careful."

Jake hung up.

"What's wrong?" asked Ellie.

"Nothing."

Ellie placed both fists on her hips and stared up at him. "Jacob Taft don't try that with me. First it was that thermos bottle and now this. What's going on?"

"Ok," said Jake as he held up his hands in surrender. "George said they'll be finished at the ranch soon and then a Russian man showed up at the church looking for me. That's all."

Ellie nodded and smiled. "Well, that's great news about the barn." Her pretty face then went from a smile to a serious look. "Now, who is this Russian man?"

Jake's eyes narrowed and he glanced off into the distance. "A ghost from my past."

"A good ghost or bad ghost?"

"I don't know. If he's who I think he is, his name is Viktor Gordya. I worked with him on several joint operations years ago. He used to be KGB. I don't know what he does now."

Ellie's eyes widened. "KGB?"

"KGB?" repeated Pam from across the room. "Who?"

"A ghost from Jake's past?" said Ellie.

"A KGB ghost is looking for Jake?" asked Pam as she walked over to them.

Ellie sighed. "No, no, I'll explain later." She turned back to Jake. "What should we do?"

"Nothing right now," said Jake with a shrug. "Except keep our eyes open."

"For a Russian ghost?" asked Pam.

Jake frowned and walked off to get more coffee. Sergeant Greymountain announced that a car had pulled into the parking lot occupied by a woman and man. Jake looked out the window and saw Agent Williams and a Black man climb out of a car and walked towards the building.

"They're the FBI agents," Jake said.

A moment later, the two FBI agents entered the building and spotted them.

"Morning, Agent Williams," said Jake.

Ellie and Pam hugged her. "It's good to see you, Stephanie," they both said.

Agent Williams introduced Agent Pyle. Sergeant Greymountain introduced himself and pointed to the coffee pot. "Do you want to get some coffee now or see the guest of honor first?"

"I've had so much coffee on the drive out here I won't sleep for three days," said Agent Pyle.

"Let's see the corpse," said Agent Williams bluntly.

As they turned to go out the door a man stood quietly in the doorway. He was a Native American, in his late sixties or early seventies, long braided gray hair, white shirt, blue jeans, worn boots, and carried a walking staff.

"Grandfather," said Sergeant Greymountain with a smile. "We didn't know you were here. Welcome."

The old man smiled and nodded. "I am Elijah Greymountain." He extended his hand towards Ellie and Pam. "I'm this worthless, slow working, police sergeant's elder."

The two women laughed and shook his hand. "I think your grandson's a nice man," said Ellie.

Elijah Greymountain laughed back. "He's a fine grandson but if I tell him that he'll get a big head."

Jake stepped forward and shook his hand too. "I'm Jake Taft."

The elder Greymountain took a quick appraisal of Jake. "Ah, you're the one that fights the evil demon spirits? I've heard about you."

Jake nodded. Agents Williams and Pyle introduced themselves to the Native American elder.

"So, Grandfather, what can I do for you," asked Sergeant Greymountain.

"I've come to see the frozen monster, of course."

Sergeant Greymountain raised both eyebrows in surprise. "How did you know about that?"

Elijah Greymountain gave his grandson a sly smile. "I have my sources. I saw the unmarked helicopter land and then when that car pulled up, I knew it had to be about this thing you have here." He then extended each elbow to Ellie and Pam who took his arms. "Now, Grandson, while I escort these lovely women you can lead us to this creature of evil."

Sergeant Greymountain shook his head and smiled. "Everyone, come this way."

They all trooped outside and around the corner to the back of the building where the freezer was kept. Jake suddenly froze and Roscoe growled.

"What's wrong?" asked Agent Williams.

Jake jerked his head towards the roof's edge.

"What do you see?" asked Ellie.

Jake was looking off into the distance. "A small demon just flew off. Now, why would it be sitting up there..." He turned and looked at Sgt. Greymountain. "The freezer."

They all ran down the length of the building to the small storage room. Inside was the large freezer. The lock was still intact, but the lid had been ripped off. It was empty. Sgt. Greymountain cursed and kicked the side of the freezer. Elijah Greymountain looked at Jake. "It looks as if your adversaries didn't want it found."

Jake grunted and nodded.

Sgt. Greymountain grabbed his radio. "Gladys, this is Greymountain. When was this freezer checked last?"

Gladys came back on the air a moment later. "The dispatch log showed that Officer Flowers checked it an hour ago. What's wrong?"

"Someone broke into it and stole the corpse," he snapped.

Officer Flowers was out on patrol and overheard the conversation on the radio. "Sarge, I checked it last, and it was locked up tighter than a drum."

"10-4, it's not your fault. Can you come see if you can get some fingerprints off the freezer? Maybe we can identify the thieves."

"On my way," said Officer Flowers.

"Sergeant, I don't think you're going to find any fingerprints," commented Agent Williams. "Demons don't have fingerprints."

Sergeant Greymountain frowned but nodded in agreement. "I have to try. The chief's going to have my hide for this."

Elijah Greymountain put his hand on his grandson's shoulder. "The chief will understand. If you'd posted a guard, they would've killed the guard."

"Yes, or maybe not," said Sergeant Greymountain. "I still feel like a back water cop who let the main evidence slip away."

"Sergeant," said Agent Williams, "I quickly learned that in dealing with demons nothing's for sure. Don't sweat it. We still have the photos that might help. We're planning on going to Utah to visit a man that was reportedly attacked. It may be linked, and I hope they can shed light on this."

"And we still have a creature loose up there to find," added Agent Pyle.

"Now, since that's settled," said the elder Greymountain trying to brighten the mood, "I'm hungry, let's go have breakfast. Will you all be my guests?"

They all agreed and walked back to the front while Sergeant Greymountain remained behind and stared at the freezer. "I got a bad feeling about this," he said to himself.

After breakfast, Jake rented a Chevrolet Tahoe and followed the two FBI agents to Shiprock, New Mexico. Tom Parker was recovering at the Northern Navajo Medical Center. The 55-bed facility was the largest medical facility serving that area and the Navajo Nation. They pulled up in front and parked.

Once inside they asked at the information desk and were sent to room 35 where they found Tom Parker. He was sitting up in his hospital bed while his wife, Amy, sat nearby.

Agent Williams stepped forward and showed him her official identification then pointed at the others. "I'm Special Agent Williams with the FBI. This is FBI Special Agent Pyle, Major Taft and his two associates, Ellie Thompson and Pamela Martin."

Tom Parker smiled and motioned for them to come in. He was bruised, bandaged and stitched up. Tom looked carefully at Jake. "Aren't you the guy I read about in the papers? You know about these things?"

"I'm only beginning to learn. Looks like you had a run in with one yourself," answered Jake.

"I'll survive," said Tom. "But it took a lot of stitches to put me back together. So do you think it was some sort of devil that attacked me?"

"Is that why the FBI's here?" asked Amy.

"Yes, we're here to look into the attack," replied Agent Williams. "We need to determine if it was demonic. What can you tell us about the thing?"

"It was dark, so it was hard to see it, but the Navajo police have it frozen and stored somewhere," said Tom.

No one answered.

Tom frowned, "What happened?"

Agent Williams sighed. "The storage freezer was broken into, and the corpse was stolen."

Tom frowned and looked over at Amy. "Someone is trying to cover something up."

"That's what we think too."

Amy looked up at Agent Williams. "What can we do to help?"

Agent Williams sat down on the edge of the window and took out a notepad while Agent Pyle turned on a voice recorder. "We need you to tell us everything you can think of. We need to know what you saw, what you heard, and even what you smelled."

Tom explained in detail what happened the night he was attacked and carried off. Amy held his hand tight while he went through the entire story. When he was finished, Amy had tears in her eyes.

"We appreciate you telling us," said Agent Pyle. "Every detail might be important."

"You said it had one yellow eye," asked Jake, "and not two?"

Tom nodded. "Yes, it only had one yellow eye. The other one wasn't. Why?"

Jake looked over at Ellie. "It could be important. I've never seen a demon with one normal eye and one yellow eye."

"It kept squawking at me the whole time."

"Maybe it wasn't a demon and that's why Tom was able to kill it," said Agent Pyle.

"Maybe," said Jake. "But then what was it and why did demons steal the body?"

"We don't know for sure that demons stole the corpse," interrupted Agent Williams. "You just saw one nearby."

"True, but this leaves us with more questions than answers," said Jake.

"What if this is some sort of half breed?" asked Pam.

They all looked at the young woman.

Jake turned to Ellie. "Is that possible?"

Ellie thought about it for a minute. "I don't know. I'd have to do some research."

The group left the Parkers and walked out to the vehicles where Roscoe greeted them with a bark. When they were on the road headed towards the Arizona border, Jake noticed Ellie was deep in thought.

"A nickel for your thoughts?" asked Jake.

Ellie put her finger to her lips in thought. "I was just trying to recall any Biblical instances where demons and humans intermingled. I need to do some research but if I'm right it's not going to be good."

———

Private Estate
Highway 160
South of Kayenta, Arizona

GERDA WOKE early in the morning at the estate. She dressed in jogging clothes and went outside where she breathed in the cool morning air. She felt good about the way the experiments were going despite Degen's complaining. She hated the furry tiger-like fiend and the way he talked down to her. As soon as their plans were completed, she would be able to separate herself from his control. She couldn't see how her grandmother had tolerated Degen all these years but for now she had to endure his glare and bad temper. She turned onto a jogging trail and ran the two-mile route. When she returned to the house her grandmother was sitting in the den in her wheelchair.

"*Guten morgan, Grossmutter,*" she said.

"Ah, Gerda, *guten morgan,*" answered the woman. "How are you this morning?"

"I'm good. Why are you up this early?"

The old woman laughed. "At my age I need very little sleep. There will be time for that later. I am having breakfast; will you join me?"

"Of course, *Grossmutter.*" Gerda turned and pushed the elder woman in the wheelchair down the hall and into the dining room. She stopped at the doorway when she detected a familiar stench and saw Degen sitting at the table.

"*Guten morgan*, my dearest," said the old woman.

Degen grunted. He sat at the far end of the table eating something that Gerda didn't recognize. The other settings had eggs, bacon, toast, and coffee. Gerda wheeled her grandmother up to a spot, and then sat down across from her.

"You're eating early this morning, my love," commented the old woman.

"Infant creatures are best eaten fresh," answered Degen.

Gerda had begun to fill her plate with eggs but stopped. "You're joking."

Degen chuckled deeply. "No, human, this is one of the experiments that went badly. No need to waste good infant meat."

Gerda slammed her fork down and got to her feet. "Excuse me, *Grossmutter*, but I've lost my appetite. I have things to do today." Gerda turned and stomped out of the room.

The old woman began eating her breakfast. "Degen dear, why do you torment her so?"

Degen looked up at her with his yellow eyes." I do because she's a spoiled human that needs to learn her place in this plan."

"But she's my grandchild."

"Then, Priska, you had better teach her."

"Yes, dear."

"We recovered the dead escapee from the human's police freezer."

Priska smiled. "That is good news."

Degen shook his snout. "No, one of my spies, Sarba, stayed behind after they removed the carcass and saw that a group of people had arrived."

"Why is that bad?"

"Besides two ignorant Indians there was a tall cowboy, a dark-haired woman, a black man, and two blonde women along with a wolf dog. It's most likely this Jacob Taft, his preacher woman friend, that newspaper woman, and probably two law enforcement agents."

"What did they say?"

Degen growled. "That coward Sarba flew away when he saw them, so we don't know for sure it was them."

"Can you ask lord prince Zardren? After all this part of the world is his territory?"

"That idiot," snapped Degen. "Last I heard he was trying to find a way to get to Taft's ranch, but several legions of hosts have a protective ring around it. I think Lord Satan gave him that position just to watch him fail and show how inept he really is. Besides, he doesn't know I'm here and I want to keep it that way."

"What if it's Taft and his friends?"

"I'll have them killed. Nothing is going to disturb my plans this time."

CHAPTER NINE

City of Mexican Hat
San Juan County, Utah

THE SUN HAD SET hours ago when the two vehicles parked in front of the Knotted Pine Lodge in Mexican Hat on Highway 163. The town of only a few hundred or so residents offered a few motels and the Knotted Pine Lodge which had been built for visitors to the thousand-foot sandstone cliffs at the edge of Cedar Mesa, Gooseneck State Park, and the deep canyons of the San Juan River. A phone call earlier to the San Juan County Sheriff's office had informed Agent Williams that after the survivor had been fished out, he had been brought to the Bluff Medical Clinic in Bluff, Utah just east of Mexican Hat.

The Knotted Pine Lodge was a clean, rustic, one story hotel built of logs. The main building held the lobby, restaurant, and rooms attached on one end. The rest of the rooms were smaller cabins scattered around the property.

They unloaded their suitcases from the car, checked in at the hotel, and received their keys to their cabins. Jake and Agent Pyle shared a room while Ellie, Pam, and Agent Williams shared another.

They dumped their luggage in the rooms and Roscoe promptly took over one of the beds to settle in for the evening. Jake and Ellie walked over to one of the wooden benches nearby while Pam and the two FBI agents headed to the hotel restaurant for a late meal.

"Have you ever been to this area?" asked Ellie.

"Nope," answered Jake as they sat arm in arm. "I'm sure it's beautiful, more so in the daylight, but I'd enjoy it more if we weren't here on business."

After a few minutes, they walked into the hotel lobby and Ellie noticed Jake kept checking behind them.

"What's wrong?" asked Ellie.

"We're being followed."

As they passed the lobby bathrooms, Jake grabbed Ellie and pulled her into the men's bathroom. "Jake," she cried out.

"Shhh" said Jake. He shoved her into a stall and backed up against the bathroom wall.

Ellie remained quiet. She'd learned long ago to trust Jake's actions no matter how odd they might be. A long minute later the door to the bathroom came open and a figure stood in the doorway. Jake's fist shot out and punched the person in the face, grabbed him by the shirt and slammed him to the floor. He pulled his fist back to hit the stalker again when he saw who it was.

"Al, what the..." asked Jake.

Ellie heard Jake say Al's name and stepped out of the stall. About that time an elderly Chinese man opened the bathroom door and looked at the big cowboy straddled over a young man whose nose was bloody and glasses askew with a woman standing by a stall. He turned pale and quietly closed the door and left.

Ellie reached down and helped Al to his feet. "Jake, you hit him?"

Jake backed up. "I...I thought he was a...a..."

Ellie grabbed some paper towels and ran them under the cold water.

"I thind yu bwoke my nobe," said Al as Ellie pressed the wet paper towels to his nose.

"He didn't mean to hit you," said Ellie.

"Yes, I did. I just didn't know it was you. What are you doing here?"

"I cuwant wabe any wonger so I cabe hew."

"What did he say?" asked Jake.

"I think he said he couldn't wait any longer and came here."

Al nodded.

"Why?" demanded Jake.

"Let's get out of the men's restroom first and deal with it later," said Ellie.

The three walked out of the men's room and past a group of Chinese tourists. The older man was chattering in Chinese and pointing at them.

"He slipped on some soap," said Jake with a shy smile.

Once outside they found a bench and sat down. Al's nose had stopped bleeding. He checked his glasses and found they were bent but not broken.

"Now, how did you get here?" asked Ellie politely.

"How did you find us?" demanded Jake irritably.

Al touched his nose gingerly. "Janet told me where you were. I couldn't just sit there and wait so I took a flight to Flagstaff, then a bus up this morning. I just waited until I saw you."

"You could've been seriously injured sneaking around like that," said Ellie. "Why were you secretly following us?"

"I thought if you knew I was here you'd get mad and not finish the interview."

"You got that right," snapped Jake.

"Now, Jake," said Ellie. "Al, that was foolish. You should've just told us you were here. We wouldn't be mad."

"Yes, we would've," growled Jake.

Ellie rolled her eyes. "Do you need us to take you to the hospital?"

"Any hospital or medical clinic's miles away," grumbled Jake.

Al shook his head. "No, I think I'll be fine."

"Good, then he can go back to Texas," said Jake.

"He might as well stay here since he made the trip," suggested Ellie.

Jake frowned. "Then call Pam and tell her to babysit him."

"Let's get Al back to the cabins and put some ice on his nose," said Ellie.

The three walked back towards their rooms and were met by the other three.

"Al, what're you doing here?" exclaimed Pam.

"Who's this?" asked Agent Williams.

"He's Al Simpson, a journalist," explained Pam.

"What happened to him?" asked Agent Pyle.

"Jake hit him," said Ellie.

"He's a journalist so he probably needed it," said Agent Williams with a smirk. Jake chuckled. They took Al into the men's cabin while Ellie went and got ice from the ice machine. While Ellie was gone, Al had explained what his interview was about.

"So, you're writing a story about Jake?" asked Agent Williams.

"Yes," said Al with a nod.

"You're either very brave, or very crazy."

"I'm beginning to think you're right," explained Al. "Since we've met, he's killed two demons that sabotaged Miss Thompson's church, I saw the aftermath of his ranch attacked by demons, I saw a real ghost, and I almost saw an angel."

"Almost?" asked Agent Pyle.

"Al fainted," said Pam sarcastically.

Al decided to try not to explain. Ellie came back and with a bag of ice on his nose he turned to Jake. "Pam said that the frozen demon was stolen, and you think more demons are involved."

"Why don't we just grab a demon and interrogate it?" asked Agent Pyle.

"Demons are not all knowing. They're creations too, just like we are," explained Ellie. "One may not know what others are doing."

"They're just uglier and meaner," added Agent Williams.

Jake shrugged. "I agree, but as a last resort we might have to try even though I doubt they'd be willing to tell the truth."

———

AFTER A LATE DINNER Jake and Ellie walked back down to the cabins. Agent Williams had called Deputy Director Ruiz and gave him the updates while Agent Pyle typed their updates into a laptop. Jake and Agent Pyle said goodnight and went next door to their cabin. Al was watching TV while Roscoe dozed on the bed. They began getting ready for bed.

"Where am I going to sleep?" asked Al.

"In your motel room," answered Jake.

Al looked down at the floor. "I didn't have time to make reservations. I don't have a room."

Jake went to the closet, pulled down an extra blanket and pillow from the upper shelf, and tossed it at Al. "You can have the chair or the floor. It's your choice."

"Why does the dog get to sleep on the bed?"

"You move him."

Al stepped over to the edge of the bed. Roscoe opened one eye and growled.

"The chair will be fine," said Al.

———

10 miles Southwest of Mexican Hat
San Juan County, Utah

SHARON AND BOB HALL were driving up a small road and late for their motel reservations. "If you'd not taken so many photos back at the Grand Canyon we'd be there by now," complained Sharon.

"We may never be back this way for years, so I didn't want to miss anything," explained Bob.

The Halls had taken some time off to travel around the United States. They were planning to end up in Denver before flying back.

"Are you sure you're on the right road?" asked Sharon.

"Yes, Sharon," snapped Bob.

"Well, you've never been good with maps."

"I got us this far."

"And where is this exactly, the middle of nowhere?"

"We'll be in Colorado in a few minutes," argued Bob.

Bob was a salesman for a furniture store and Sharon was a librarian for the county library back in Mississippi.

"This doesn't look like a main road," whined Sharon.

"Since we were so late leaving, I took this road. I think it's a short cut," said Bob through gritted teeth.

"Why didn't you rent a GPS with the car?"

Bob rolled his eyes. "I was trying to save us some money. How many roads can there be out here?"

After a few minutes of driving in the darkness Sharon couldn't wait any longer. "Bob, turn this thing around and head back. You're lost and won't admit it."

"Yes, Sharon."

Bob slowed the SUV down and made a u-turn in the road. The back right wheel went off the road and spun. The SUV slid sideways.

"You idiot, what're you doing?"

"I'm trying to turn around. Now be quiet."

Bob was able to get the SUV turned around and headed back the other way.

"Well, that's the worse driving I've ever seen," said Sharon.

Bob turned his head and looked at his wife. "Will you just..."

His words were cut off by Sharon's scream as she pointed ahead. Bob looked back quickly as the headlights of his truck lit up a giant bear hunkered down in the road. The thing stood on two feet and roared at the SUV. Bob thought at first it was a mirage then swerved to the right to avoid the beast causing the SUV to fly off the road. The vehicle nosed off into the ditch, bounced up and struck a large boulder. The airbags deployed sending a cloud of white powder into the air. Bob and Sharon sat stunned for a moment before looking at each other.

"Are you alright?" asked Bob.

"You moron, you could have gotten us killed," yelled Sharon.

"Just call for help on your phone," snapped Bob.

Sharon dug around and found her purse while Bob tried to open the driver's door.

"My door's stuck," he explained.

The hood and both fenders of the Dodge Durango were crumpled and pinned both doors closed. Steam hissed from a ruptured radiator.

Sharon dialed 911. "The car rental insurance is not going to cover this, and now my cell phone is out of range."

"Just keep trying. I'll climb out through one of the back doors." Bob climbed back over the center console. As he did, he noticed a set of eyes looking through the rear window. One was a normal bear eye, but the other was glowing yellow.

"What the..." Bob looked back at Sharon who had turned to see what he was talking about when the creature suddenly came around to the front and climbed upon the crumpled hood. Sharon spun back around and was face to face with the beast through the cracked windshield. The huge monstrosity snarled at her, showing sharp teeth. Sharon screamed and threw herself towards the back of the vehicle and ended up in Bob's lap in the back seat.

"Use your phone, hurry," cried Bob.

Sharon tried to dial, but her trembling hands dropped the phone. She reached down, grabbed the cellphone off the floorboard, and tried to dial again about the time the windshield was swept away by a huge claw. The thing peeled back the top of the SUV like aluminum foil and crawled into the SUV with both terrified occupants.

CHAPTER TEN

Bluff Medical Clinic
190 N. 3ʳᵈ Street E.
Bluff, Utah

THE NEXT MORNING, the group arrived at the Bluff Medical Clinic in Bluff, Utah. The city was not much bigger than Mexican Hat, but it did have a small clinic. They trouped inside where Agent Williams identified herself to the young woman at the desk and they were shown to a side office where a tall, well tanned sheriff's deputy welcomed them.

"Good afternoon, I'm Deputy Will Bridges."

Agent Williams introduced the group to him. Deputy Bridges appeared to be in his late thirties, broad shouldered, with short cut dark hair and brown eyes. Agent Williams looked him over more than once while he shook hands with the rest of the small group.

"I was told that you're here about the attack?"

They all nodded. "Any idea what it was that attacked them?" asked Agent Pyle.

"We don't know exactly. The tracks we found were bear but huge, much too big for a regular black bear."

"A grizzly bear maybe?" asked Jake.

"We don't know for sure what it was, but it did some awful damage. We went down and surveyed the scene and it's nothing like I've ever seen. The two bodies we found were almost completely eaten."

"I thought there were three dead?" asked Agent Williams.

"We are assuming from what the witness said but we still haven't found the third body."

"Any idea where the creature went?" asked Jake.

Deputy Bridges shook his head. "The tracks led back west. We tried to use dogs to track it, but they just whined and shied away. I got the call from headquarters that told me the FBI were on their way, so we decided to wait until your group got here to track the thing down. If it is just a black bear, we can handle it, but if it's something else we may need all the help we can get."

"I agree," said Agent Williams. "Where's the survivor?"

"He's in the exam room to the left. The kid's been through a lot. He stayed in the water for hours the other night, terrified to come out until some locals fished him out. It's a miracle he didn't die from hypothermia." Deputy Bridges pulled a notebook from his pocket. "His name is Jeffrey Trendall, a local from Hatch. That's a city just up the road. I got a formal statement from him that I can make a copy for you."

The deputy escorted them down to the room and knocked. A female voice from the other side asked who it was, and Deputy Bridges identified himself. The door opened and a stocky female nurse let them enter.

"Jeff, these people are with the FBI," explained Deputy Bridges. "They want to talk to you about what happened."

Jeff was wrapped in a blanket sitting in a chair. His blond hair was a mess, his eyes were bloodshot, and he was bruised from head to toe from being bumped into rocks while in the river.

Agent Williams stepped forward. "Jeff, I'm Special Agent Williams and this is Special Agent Pyle. We're from the FBI." She also introduced Jake, Ellie, and Pam.

Jeff just nodded with empty and sunken eyes. It was obvious he hadn't slept.

"I know this must be horrible and we're sorry for your loss, but we need to know what happened," asked Agent Pyle.

Jeff looked at them for a moment. He looked down at the floor and started rocking back and forth. Agent Pyle removed a small digital tape recorder from his jacket pocket and turned it on.

"You were camping?" asked Agent Williams.

Jeff nodded.

"You were with your brother Mike?"

Jeff nodded and continued to rock.

"What happened out there, Jeff? We really need to know."

Jeff didn't respond for over two minutes but finally told them the story in bits and pieces. He sounded remote, displaced from it, and when he finished, he continued to stare at the floor while rocking back and forth. Agent Williams glanced at Agent Pyle who nodded indicating that he'd successfully taped it.

They all thanked him and headed to the door. Jeff looked up. "Ma'am, I was told that you're a preacher, right?"

Ellie nodded. "I'm a pastor of a church."

"Why did God do this?" he asked.

"Jeff," said Ellie softly. "God didn't do this; we think a demon did."

"So, what're you going to do?"

"We're going to hunt it down and kill it," said Jake.

Jeff stared for moment at Ellie and Jake, nodded, and then went back to rocking. They quietly shut the door and left.

"That poor boy is going to need a lot of counseling," said Ellie as they walked back down the hall.

Jake could see the tears in her eyes. "If he'll ever recover," he added.

"What do you think?" asked Agent Williams.

"It does sound like some sort of demonic creature," said Jake.

Al had been quietly taking notes and knew not to interrupt while they had interviewed the young man. "It never occurred to me that demons could kill so many people."

"How do you figure it to be some demon thing?" asked Deputy Bridges. He didn't believe in such things.

"From Jeff's account and from your description of how the dogs acted earlier, I'd say it was demonic of some sort."

"How are we going to track it down?" asked Agent Pyle.

"Hopefully we can run it down on foot with Roscoe's help but if not, we'll use mules or horses," explained Jake.

As they walked to the car in the cool and crisp air Deputy Bridges's cellphone rang. He answered it, listened for a moment, and stopped in his tracks. He was plainly unhappy by the sour look on his face.

"What's happened?" asked Agent Williams.

Deputy Bridges took off his hat and spit on the ground. "There's been another attack. This time it was a couple of tourists. Their vehicle was peeled back, and they were...eaten."

"When?" asked Jake.

"Where?" asked Agent Williams.

"It occurred last night southwest of Mexican Hat on a side road."

———

ALMOST TWO HOURS LATER, they pulled off the road behind several San Juan County vehicles parked on the side of the small road. The Dodge Durango was in a ditch, and they immediately noticed the top of the SUV had been peeled back. Two sheriff deputies stood just behind it. Another Ford Suburban was parked across the road which appeared to be some sort of crime scene and command post for them. San Juan County Sergeant Coleman approached the group and Deputy Bridges introduced them all.

"It isn't a pretty sight," explained Sergeant Coleman while he rubbed his jaw. "Whatever this thing is it ripped those people to pieces. They never had a chance."

"Let's take a look," said Agent Williams.

Jake looked over at Ellie and Pam. "We'll wait here," said Ellie.

The group trooped over to the Durango. Jake noticed that Al had followed them. "Are you sure you want to see this?"

Al nodded confidently. "I'm sure I've seen worse in horror movies."

Jake shook his head. Since the top of the Durango had been ripped back it allowed easy access to the interior. What they saw inside was beyond Al's worst horror movie. The inside of the SUV was coated in blood and gore. The woman, Sharon, had been dragged halfway up into the front seat as if the creature was trying to get her out but gave up. Her left arm and part of her torso was gone. Half of her head was missing, and she resembled a china doll that had been dropped and broken. The man, Bob, or what was left of him was still in the back seat. He sat there like he was patiently waiting except the top half of him was gone. Part of his spinal cord and lower ribs protruded from the lower torso. The group stood and stared at the gruesome scene. Al made gurgling noises.

Agent Williams pointed away from the vehicle. "Go over there; don't throw up in the crime scene."

While Al regurgitated his lunch on the ground, the others spoke with the deputies who'd been working the scene.

"Looks like it wasn't in a hurry to get away," commented one of the deputies. "It's strange that there are no insects flying around the gore. It was the same at the other scene; no insects."

Jake nodded. "That helps to confirm that this thing is part demon. Insects stay away from any corpse that demons have been at."

"It headed east," said a middle-aged deputy named Bothman.

"Yep," said Deputy Bridges, "directly towards civilization."

Jake nodded. "More people."

"More victims."

"What does your department want to do?" asked Agent Williams.

"Sergeant Coleman's on the phone now with Lieutenant Beggett who's going to brief the sheriff," explained Deputy Bridges. "The logical thing would be to warn everyone but that may cause a panic. The hunters would come out of the woodwork looking for this thing and we'd be falling over each other or worse, shooting at each other thinking it was the creature."

Ellie and Pam overheard the discussion and walked up to the

group. They tried not to look at the Durango. "We can't just let people go around without some type of warning," said Ellie.

Deputy Bridges nodded. "I know, but we need to decide how to protect them without causing a major panic."

"How many officers do you have?" asked Agent Williams.

"Not enough. We must cover this whole county which includes all of these small towns. That's not nearly enough to cover this area."

"We have to do something," urged Ellie.

"I know," said Jake grimly.

Private Estate, Highway 160
South of Kayenta, Arizona

PRISKA SAT in her wheelchair and read after calling home to Germany. Her reading was interrupted by a familiar smell, and she smiled as she looked up to see Degen standing nearby. She could tell he was irritated by the way his tail was twitching back and forth. "Ah, Degen, my dear. How are you?"

Degen grunted. Priska put the book down on her lap and sighed heavily. "What's wrong?"

"The cowboy and his friends are in Utah," snarled Degen. "They're helping the local authorities track down our runaway." His claws dug into the wooden floor as he paced back and forth. "Those accursed humans will ruin everything if I don't do something to stop them."

"I'm afraid they will." Priska rolled her wheelchair over to the phone and picked it up.

"No," said Degen. "I will have them dealt with."

Priska replaced the phone.

"Turelka," yelled Degen.

A short, thick, slug-like demon appeared from the hallway.

"Yes, you're most disgusting putrid lord," answered Turelka.

"I want you to find that cowboy Taft and his friends...and kill them. They're in that town called Mexican Hat. Our runaway killed some humans near there and so the cowboy is snooping around with two FBI agents, his two women friends and several local law enforcement deputies."

"Yes, most horrid lord."

Degen stopped pacing and thought for a moment. "Don't attack them together or we'll draw too much attention. Watch them and when they're separate then kill them."

"What if the FBI agents or the deputies interfere?"

"Kill them too."

––––––

Knotted Pine Lodge
101 E. Highway 163
Mexican Hat, Utah

JAKE, the two FBI agents, Sergeant Coleman, and Deputy Bridges went to discuss the possibility of the creature coming into town, so Ellie, Pam, and Al went back to the lodge and sat outside under the large wooden hotel patio for a quick dinner. The air was cool, and the sky was turning a beautiful shade of reds, blues, and yellows as the sun set.

"This is incredible country," said Al as he pushed his partially finished hamburger off to the side. After what he'd seen earlier, he didn't have much of an appetite.

Ellie smiled and nodded. "I know what you mean. I came from Pennsylvania. As soon as I saw the wide-open spaces and big blue sky of the west, I knew I was hooked."

Al turned on his laptop, took his camera, and attached a cord to it. "I took some photos of the area and thought it would go well with my article. So, Malachy finally convinced Jake to hunt down these demons?" he asked as he typed on his keyboard.

"Yes, and we were lucky too," said Ellie. "Right after that a demon attacked our church."

Al looked wide eyed at Ellie. "A demon attacked you in church?"

"Not during a service," explained Ellie. "Pam and I had just returned from Pecos with a used piano for the church when that monster showed up."

"And his two pets," added Pam.

"Pets?" asked Al.

"They were huge lizard creatures," explained Ellie. "They tore the church doors down while Pam and I were cleaning the old piano. We called for help and hid behind the piano while the creatures tore it apart trying to get to us."

"We held them off until George Tillon came and tried to kill them," added Pam.

"Held them off?" said Ellie sarcastically. "All we had were the broken legs of the piano bench."

Pam smiled. "Hey, we used what we had available."

Ellie rolled her eyes. "George arrived and shot the fiends and that's when we found out we can't kill them. He shot them several times with a shotgun, but their wounds healed almost instantly. One of the lizards attacked George, and we thought we were goners, but Jake arrived. He shot and killed one of the lizards but then the demon attacked Jake."

"What did this demon look like?"

Ellie sat her tea glass down and thought for a second. "The thing was horribly ugly. It was part lizard and human. Its head resembled a huge horned toad, his torso was human, but the lower half was lizard."

"And of course, it stunk like sulfur and ashes," said Pam with a frown.

"What happened to the lizard that attacked George Tillon?" asked Al.

"Malachy showed up," said Ellie. "He killed it."

"And Mr. Tillon?"

"He ended up with a dislocated shoulder and a few scratches."

"Thank God that Malachy showed up."

Ellie nodded. "I still don't understand why angels show up at certain times but not other."

Al stopped typing. "Do you have any idea how angels appear or disappear?"

Ellie shook her head. "No, not for sure and it's only a guess but it seems angels have the ability to step between our world and the heavenly realm."

"I read somewhere that scientists believe there are several dimensions of reality," added Pam.

"I've heard that too," agreed Ellie. "I just don't know where heaven fits into it all and it's a mystery we may never understand. Now, getting back to your article; Malachy then told us to head to Florida."

Al nodded as he typed. "The article I read from the *Washington Post* said in Florida you tracked down a demon covered in insects?"

"I read that article too," said Ellie with a frown. "It wasn't very positive. It insinuated that it wasn't even a demon and that they still don't exist."

"A lot of people still refuse to believe they exist," added Pam.

"Since the story came out the world's had a couple of major hurricanes, an earthquake, grass fires, riots, murders, and who knows what else. People believe there's more to fear from what they can see than from demons that they can't see or refuse to see."

"So how did you know where to go in Florida?" asked Al while the waitress removed their plates from the table.

"Pam did some research and found where people were being attacked in the Ocala National Forest," explained Ellie. "We put two and two together, so Jake staked out a spot in the woods close to where the other attacks took place. It was near a campsite of a family who was camping during spring break. The demon attacked the family inside their camper."

"And Jake shot it inside the camper?"

"No," said Ellie. "Jake chased it outside."

"Then I hit it with the suburban," added Pam proudly.

Both of Al's eyebrows raised in surprise. "You did what?"

"Yep, I hit that thing as hard and fast as I could. I knocked it clear across the road."

"We had handheld radios so we could talk to Jake," explained Ellie. "For our safety he made Pam and I park a half a mile away. We heard the commotion and came to help. She hit the monster and then Jake killed it."

"Wow, I bet that was exciting," said Al.

"It was after that when we began to see a pattern that these monsters were killing people that worked for Martech Laboratories along with random killings to cover up their main intentions. You see, the husband of the family in the trailer, Theodore Helms, is Vice President of Martech Labs."

"What part did Martech Labs play in this?"

"Martech Labs did research for diseases."

Al looked up from his laptop. "I'm confused."

Ellie smiled and patted Al's arm. "I know it is. We were confused at first too. Hasan Ghazi was a demon that transformed to look human and had built a large trucking and helicopter manufacturing corporation. His plan, after kidnapping the president's daughter and using her as a hostage was to dump micro-toxins over Washington D.C. resulting in millions of people becoming ill and die. This would have caused a major disruption in our government and during the confusion Ghazi planned to take over. Martech Labs would have been one of the few laboratories that could have found an anti-toxin. Without the anti-toxins, millions of lives would have been lost and his plan might have worked."

"So, he was eliminating the competition before he even started?"

"Exactly."

"And that's when you tried to warn them?"

Ellie nodded solemnly. "We tried to warn Mr. Farnswarth."

"I read that he was president of Martech Labs. He and his wife were found dead in their home."

"Yes," said Ellie sadly. "We went to his home, but two demons had already killed him and his wife before we could warn them." Ellie's thoughts drifted back to finding Mr. Farnswarth dead in his den with one arm ripped from his body and a gaping hole in his chest. They found Mrs. Farnswarth dead in the upstairs bedroom with her head cracked open like an egg. She shivered when she remembered seeing a demon calmly eating the dead woman's brain before Jake killed it.

"How did you find out it was Ghazi behind it all?" asked Al.

"It took a while for us to figure it out. Just by luck one of the demons at the Farnswarth's house got cocky and mentioned Jackson. We thought at first that it was referring to a person, but we figured out there was another Martech lab in Jackson, Mississippi so we went there. When we got there Jake convinced a demon to give us some information in exchange for its life and it told us to go to New Orleans."

"So, what happened to the demon that gave you the information?"

"Jake killed it," said Pam sarcastically.

"Oh," said Al. "Does Jake always do that?"

"Most of the time."

"So, what was in New Orleans?" asked Al.

"A place called Hell's Corner," said Ellie with a sigh. "It was an area just outside of New Orleans that had never been rebuilt after hurricane Katrina. It was a section of run-down buildings that housed brothels, drug houses, and other low establishments. The local parish deputies were too understaffed to really put a dent in it. The local demon lord is Tarnac who lives in an old southern mansion. He told us about Ghazi."

"How did you get inside? Wouldn't they recognize you?" asked Al like a kid sitting at a campfire listening to a scary story. Ellie suddenly blushed and didn't answer.

Pam giggled. "Jake came up with a plan. Ellie and I dressed up like prostitutes and we waltzed in with Mobak as a guide."

"Mobak? Isn't he the demon buried at Jake's ranch?"

Ellie immediately spoke up. "Yes, he was a small gray demon that Jake captured to use as a guide. He'd been abused by the larger ones. He led us to Tarnac in exchange for Jake letting him go."

"Sounds like these demons were very helpful."

"Not really," said Ellie. "As soon as we left Tarnac's mansion he sent his horde of demons after us. Jake killed as many as he could, and we were lucky to get away in one piece."

"What happened to Mobak?"

"Surprising, at the last moment Mobak tried to help us but was fatally injured. After he died, Malachy buried him near that tree where we found Roy the other night. We put the small headstone there later." Ellie quickly glanced over at Pam as she knew that Pam had grown fond of the little demon during the short time that they'd been around him. Pam's face remained passive.

"Is Tarnac still there?"

Ellie shrugged. "We don't know. We've never been back. I heard that it's been raided by law enforcement but how do they catch something they can't see?"

"Good point," murmured Al. "So do you really think that these creatures here could be some sort of half-breed or hybrid?"

Ellie pushed a loose strand of hair behind her ear while she sipped her tea. "I've been doing some research. The scriptures talk about a group called "Nephilium" in the sixth chapter of Genesis. They intermixed with humans and had children. They became very evil and wicked and helped lead to the downfall of man and the ultimate destruction of mankind through the flood."

"What are Nephilium?" asked Pam.

"Some scholars think they were just large men or giants, but some think they were fallen angels, or what we call demons. They would have looked more human back then before they developed into the ugly creatures that they are now."

Al shook he head. "So you're saying that demons, before they became hideous monsters, had human wives that gave birth to half-human and half-demon?"

"That's one interpretation," said Ellie. "As a result, they became so wicked that God decided to destroy mankind by a great flood. That became the story of Noah and the ark."

Pam put her fork down. "Then they might be trying to do it again?"

Ellie shrugged. "I don't know."

Al stopped typing. "What if it's true and they're successful?"

Ellie glanced at Al with a worried look. "They would be faster, bigger, and stronger than humans and it could bring the end of the world as we know it."

Al took off his glasses and rubbed his eyes. His nose still hurt from being hit by Jake. "Could this be for real?"

Ellie wrapped her arms around herself as if she suddenly got chilled. "I'm afraid so, Al. I didn't think the world had gotten to this point. If it is, it may be the start of it all."

Al put his glasses back on and noticed something in the distance. He squinted into the dusk. "Ellie, how big are the birds in this area?" Ellie didn't hear him, so Al tapped her on the arm and pointed to the sky. Ellie looked up and saw two distinct large shapes flying in their direction. "Oh, dear God no," she gasped. She turned to Pam. "We have to get inside, now."

Pam turned and saw the shapes flying towards the lodge. She jumped up and grabbed Al. "Move it. Get inside." As Pam pulled him towards the door, he reached for his laptop. "Leave it," snapped Pam.

Once inside they ran down the hall and around the corner. Ellie peeked back as two demons landed on the hotel patio. One was tall and bright yellow, with a pointed snout while the other was a large purple one with small brown spiked horns protruding from his arms and legs. The purple one looked at the laptop while the other looked around.

"Why can we see them?" whispered Al.

"Like we said they solidify when they plan to do something physical," whispered Ellie.

"And that usually means doing something physically bad to someone," whispered Pam.

"What are they looking for?" asked Al.

"I think they're looking for us?"

Ellie looked at Pam. "What about the waitress? She'll be coming to check on us in a minute. We can't let her walk out there."

"If they're looking for us, maybe they'll leave her alone."

Both women turned and stared at Al.

"Probably not?" he said sadly.

The demons sniffed the air and looked around. The purple one made grunting, clicking, and squeaking sounds like dolphin or whale sounds.

"What's it doing?" asked Al.

"It's talking to the other one," answered Pam.

"But they speak English. I heard the one at your church."

Ellie shook her head. "They can speak whatever language they want but they seem to use this to talk to each other."

One demon walked out of sight. The large purple demon appeared to be in charge, turned, and looked in the open door that led into the hotel. Ellie and Al jerked back.

"Do you think it saw us?" whispered Al.

"I don't know. We need to warn the waitress and find a place to hide," said Ellie.

"Our room?"

"No, that's the first place they'll look."

Ellie led the way down the hall and around the corner into the lobby of the interior dining area. Fortunately, there were no other patrons in the restaurant. The waitress, a young college age woman named Debbie, approached them.

"Is everything alright? Do you need your check?" she asked with a raised eyebrow seeing three people hunkered down behind a table. Ellie was about to answer when she saw one of the creatures walk around the corner towards the interior of the restaurant. They grabbed the young waitress and shoved her behind one of the tables.

"What are yo…"

Pam clamped a hand over Debbie's mouth and whispered in her ear. "There are two huge ugly things outside that want to kill us. Shhhhhhh."

Debbie's eyes widened, she nodded, and Pam took her hand away. The tablecloths hid them temporarily from the monster's view. Debbie sniffed the air. "Rotten eggs?" she whispered.

"Demons," whispered Ellie.

Debbie's face went pale.

"We need to call for help," said Pam.

"Cellphone?"

"No time," said Ellie. She turned to Debbie. "Do you have a panic alarm?"

Debbie pointed behind her. "It's at the desk in the main lobby."

Ellie knew that they couldn't stay there for long. Someone might walk in, or the two hellions will eventually find them. She thought for a second while the brute stood in the doorway of the patio and looked around the restaurant. "Where can we hide?"

"There's a storage room just to the left," explained Debbie.

Ellie looked around. If they kept the tables between them and the demon, they might make it to the door. "Stay down and move towards the door. Follow Debbie to the storage closet. I'll call for help from there."

The four moved as quietly as possible away from the table towards the door, trying to stay out of sight. Once in the hallway they stood up. Debbie motioned for them to follow her. Pam grabbed her arm. "Where is the alarm?"

Debbie pointed down the hall. "It's down and to the left, at the desk under the counter."

Pam nodded and started to move but Ellie stopped her. "No," said Ellie. "Stay with us."

"Nope," said Pam. "Y'all get into the storage room, and I'll call the cavalry." She pulled away and darted across the doorway and down the hall.

Ellie shook her head in frustration but followed Debbie down the hallway to a door. They ducked inside and Al jammed a mop against the doorknob.

"That won't keep them out," said Ellie.

"I know but it made me feel better."

Ellie looked around for anything that they might use as a weapon. There was broom, a bucket, a vacuum cleaner, and numerous cleaning supplies. Ellie took a bottle of bleach down and unscrewed the cap. They waited in the dark trying not to make a sound. Minutes that seemed like hours ticked by.

"Do you think Pam made it?" asked Al.

Ellie glared at him.

———

AFTER ROUNDING THE CORNER, Pam saw the large main desk in the lobby, but no one was there. The desk clerk had stepped away, so she ran behind it and looked for the panic button. She saw a white button attached to the underside of the desk and pushed it. She pushed it again and again and again. She now had to find a place to hide and saw a large empty bottom shelf in the main counter and crawled in as best she could. *It'll have to do.* She thanked God for having a small frame and none too soon as she heard the scraping of claws on the floor as a demon came into the lobby.

————

WITH THE SAN Juan Sheriff's office located in up in Monticello, Utah, there was no office in Mexican Hat, so Jake, San Juan Lieutenant Bill Beggett, Sergeant Coleman, Deputy Bridges, and Agents Williams and Pyle sat in a small café.

"So, Will, what you're telling me is that a deranged creature that might be half demon is loose just outside the city?"

Deputy Bridges nodded. "I know it sounds out of this world, sir, but I have five deaths to prove it."

Lieutenant Beggett was in his fifties, retired from the military, and had been looking for a quiet county to work as a law enforcement officer. This was not what he had in mind. "Forgive me if I'm not completely convinced that this is real. Are you sure it's not just an injured or sick bear that can't hunt on its own, so it went for easier human prey?"

"No, sir," said Jake. "You saw that this thing peeled back the top of a Durango like it was nothing and ripped a couple to shreds. A sick bear couldn't do that."

Lieutenant Beggett frowned. "I agree, but to think it's some kind of devil from hell is almost unbelievable." He was about to make another comment when their radios squawked.

"Attentions all units, anyone in the Knotted Pine Lodge in Mexican Hat area, the panic alarm has been activated. Whoever it was pushed it five times."

"10-4, we'll go take a look," answered Lieutenant Beggett before he turned to the group. "Isn't that where you're staying?"

"Yeah," said Jake who had already jumped to his feet. "Ellie and Pam are there." As they all rushed out to their cars, Jake called Ellie on her cellphone.

———

THE THREE STAYED AS quiet as they could in the storage room. Ellie was about to open her cellphone to dial Jake's number when they heard claws on the wooden floor and leathery wings against the wall. Al and Debbie looked wide eyed at Ellie. Her heart was pounding, and she just knew the demons could hear it. The sound came right up to the door and stopped, but then moved on down the hall. Ellie didn't realize that she was holding her breath and let it out slowly. Al looked relieved and smiled just as Ellie's cellphone rang and she pushed the button to stop it from ringing. The storage door was suddenly ripped off the hinges.

"Surprise," screeched the yellow devil.

Al jumped back against the shelves which caused bottles and cleaning supplies to rain down on them. Debbie screamed as loud as she could.

———

PAM COULD SMELL the sulfur and ash as the demon lurked around the lobby. *It must have seen me come in here,* thought Pam. She knew it was just a matter of time before it found her when she heard a toilet flush. *Oh, no, the desk clerk.* She heard a door open down the hall and the sound of footsteps coming closer. Pam knew the creature would kill the desk clerk as soon as he came into the room. She knew she had to do something to distract the demon but before she could even move a horrible scream echoed from down the hall. *The storage room?*

———

ELLIE SQUEEZED the bottle of bleach into the demon's face. She knew it wouldn't hurt it but perhaps it might distract it long enough for them to run. She grabbed Debbie by the hand and jerked her into the hallway. The purple creature must have heard them and ran towards them from the desk lobby area. Ellie, Debbie, and Al turned to run the other way towards the restaurant, but the yellow brute was already out of the storage room and blocked their escape. It tilted its head back and laughed. The purple demon smiled with a wicked grin. *Trapped.*

JAKE DIALED ELLIE'S PHONE, she answered, but all he heard was a blood curdling scream before the phone went dead. The others also heard the scream coming from the phone as they reached their vehicles, threw themselves into their cars, and sped out of the parking lot hoping they weren't too late.

AL FAINTED.

Debbie screamed.

Ellie's knees shook and she tried not to let her voice tremble. "What do you want?"

The purple demon chuckled. "Why, you are interfering human, we don't want anything from you. We've come to kill you."

Ellie was terrified but had faced demons before and refused to give in. "You know who I am. Jake Taft is on his way and if you hurt us, he'll hunt you down and destroy you."

The large purple demon's yellow eyes narrowed, and he shook his head. "Your friend can't help you now. We'll deal with him when we're done with you." The behemoth reached out and grabbed Ellie by the throat. "So, as for you..."

"Comrade, let the woman go."

The purple devil turned and stared at a tall, blond man with ice blue eyes, wearing a full length, black leather coat.

"Idiot human," growled the purple hellion. "This is none of your affair but when I'm finished with them, I'll kill you too."

A gun seemed to appear out of nowhere in the man's hand and he calmly shot the demon three times in the head. The shock of rounds knocked the demon back and caused him to release Ellie. She coughed, tried to breathe, then grabbed Debbie and ran back towards the restaurant. The other demon leapt over the purple one on the floor and charged the man who shot it as well. The impact of the bullets knocked it down but to the man's shock and horror the wounds healed over almost immediately. Without hesitation he turned, ran down the hall behind Ellie and Debbie, and out onto the open-air patio with the demons in hot pursuit.

"Run," snapped the man. "I'll hold them off."

"No," said Ellie as she pulled his sleeve. "You can't kill them."

"*Da*, I noticed that, so we need to run faster."

They ran down the steps leading from the patio to the parking lot as the yellow wasp-like demon was within reach of them. The man spun and kicked it in the chest which knocked it down. He swung at the purple one, but the beast blocked the blow and hit him which sent the man to the ground. The archfiend jumped on the man's back, grabbed his hair, and pulled his head back exposing his neck. The purple freak smiled showing his jagged teeth. "I'm going to bleed you out and let you watch while I kill the women slowly."

The darkness was lit up by headlights, the sound of police sirens, and screeching of tires. The man strained against his captor, but the demon held him tight. He looked up into the degenerate's yellow eyes and spat at him which only resulted in the demon roaring with laughter.

"FBI, freeze," yelled Agent Pyle.

The demon didn't even look up as it put one sharp pointed claw to Viktor's throat. "Say goodbye to your friends," joked the brute.

A large hole suddenly appeared in the demon's forehead followed by the sharp report of a Colt .45 handgun. The other demon watched in horror as his purple cohort collapsed and immediately began to decompose. The wasp-like demon spun around and leapt into the air.

Jake fired at it before it disappeared through the trees. Ellie was flushed and breathing hard as she ran to Jake.

"Are you alright?" asked Jake.

Ellie nodded. "Yes, thank God you got here in time."

"How many are here?"

"Just two that I know of."

Agents Williams and Pyle along with the San Juan Sergeant and Lieutenant rushed inside the lodge to check for sure. Debbie sat down on the kerb and cried while Deputy Bridges softly talked to her. Pam appeared at the patio's door followed by the male desk clerk who looked totally confused.

"I heard all the shooting, so I knew Jake had to be here," she said. "Oh, and by the way Jake, I'm alright too."

Jake frowned and Ellie grinned in relief. "Well, Pam, I'm glad you're okay but where's Al?"

Pam shrugged. "He was with you last time I saw him."

Agent Pyle came out escorting Al. "I found him passed out on the floor."

Al sat down next to Debbie. "I thought I was going to die right there."

Debbie turned and stared at Al. "Do ya' think?" she said sarcastically.

"I wonder why they didn't kill the journalist?" asked Agent Pyle offhand.

"I don't think they were after Al. I think they were after Pam and me," said Ellie. "They might have been successful if it hadn't been for this man," said Ellie pointing to the tall blond man. "He saved our lives."

The man had recovered, brushed dirt off his jacket, and stood next to one of the deputies staring down at the dead purple creature. Jake walked over and put a hand on the man's shoulder. "You're a long way from Russia, my friend, but I'm glad you were here."

The man turned, made a rare smile, and hugged Jake in a huge bear hug. "Jacob, it is good to see you again. I'm glad I was able to help you and your friends." His face became serious again. "I wish this was just a visit but I'm here on business that may involve you. We need to talk."

Jake nodded. "As soon as we get this mess cleaned up, we can have dinner and talk." He motioned towards Pam and Ellie. "Ladies, this is Viktor Gordya."

"This is the KGB ghost?" asked Pam wide eyed.

Viktor raised an eyebrow. "A ghost?"

"Never mind," said Jake. "I'll explain later. Where are you staying?"

Viktor motioned with his head to the lodge. "I'm in room 12."

Lieutenant Beggett and Sergeant Coleman approached and eyed the big Russian suspiciously. Jake introduced Viktor to them and explained that he had come to talk to Jake about some business and was just lucky to be in the area. That seemed to temporarily satisfy the deputies. "I need all of you to meet back inside and give some statements about what happened," said Lieutenant Beggett. He turned to Deputy Bridges. "Call Jess and tell him to get the camera and crime scene kit so we can process these things before they get any worse. These things already stink."

———

IT WAS NOW LATE NIGHT, and after making his written statement Jake stood in the hotel entryway drinking coffee when Lieutenant Beggett came out. "We're just about done with Miss Thompson," he said.

Jake nodded and sipped his coffee. Lieutenant Beggett sighed and looked around. "This is a great area to live," he commented. "We have normal crime but nothing major and certainly nothing like this. I've been a Christian all my life but never really believed in devils and monsters until now." He glanced over at Jake. "Do you think this bear demon creature will come into town?"

"I don't know, sir," said Jake after thinking for a moment. "If the thing can find enough food it may stay out, but if not..."

"And that means people?"

Jake shrugged. "Possibly."

Lieutenant Beggett went over and sat down on a wooden bench. "I was told that you're ex-military?"

"Yes, sir, Army."

Lieutenant Beggett nodded. "I was Navy for 24 years. When I retired, I said I'd move as far away from large bodies of water as I could."

Jake chuckled.

"We're going to brief the entire department and try to increase patrols. I've spoken with the sheriff, and we agreed not issuing a public announcement yet. I've also informed the highway patrol but I'm hoping you and the FBI can hunt this thing down before it comes to that."

"And what if we can't?"

Lieutenant Beggett shook his head. "I guess we'll deal with that if it happens."

Jake stared up at the mountains to the west. "The river and the canyons will hopefully keep the thing from coming in too close."

The lieutenant nodded. "We can only hope but if it gets hungry enough nothing's going to stop it."

Before Jake could comment, Ellie and Pam walked out and joined the two men. "They're just about finished with Al. He didn't remember much," explained Ellie.

Jake chuckled. "That boy faints at pretty much everything."

"I'm just glad they didn't think to kill him after he passed out."

"What about this Gordya character? Is he legit?" asked Lieutenant Beggett. "I never worked with any Russians. Your FBI friends were not happy with him showing up unannounced. Agent Williams is suspicious of his intentions."

"Viktor definitely walks to the beat of a different drummer," said Jake with a smirk. "Since the collapse of communism, we worked together when I was assigned to the embassy on a few joint covert operations several years ago. He's straight to the point, loyal, but deadly. He's a great man to have on your side and someone you don't want as an enemy."

"And he's in my county, shooting monsters in a hotel," commented the lieutenant. "I know he has some sort of diplomatic exemption but if he hadn't helped your lady friends, I'd have him sent back to Russia."

Jake nodded. "I understand, sir. He said something about important business to discuss with me. I don't know what it is but if he came all this way it must be important."

Lieutenant Beggett stood and adjusted his gun belt. "That might be so, but if he starts anything else I'll ship him to I.C.E. in Salt Lake City so fast he won't know what happened." With that said, he walked back inside. Jake stood and stared out at the mountains. *What's this creature doing out here? Why here? Where did it come from? Why is Viktor here? Why this area? Why now?* Ellie came and slipped her arm around his. "What's bothering you?"

Jake looked down at his beautiful wife-to-be, "Everything, there are so many questions and I don't have any answers."

Ellie squeezed his arm. "It's not all on your shoulders, Jake. We're all in this together. We'll get it sorted out."

"There are so many things bothering me. I haven't seen but a handful of demons lurking about. It seems that they're purposely staying away. Why? If no one can see these things, then why are they hiding? I haven't heard from Malachy which bothers me. If there's something up, I would've thought he'd let me know."

"Who knows with angels?" said Ellie with a smile. "They have their own agenda, and they work differently than we do. I'm sure he'll let us know when he can or when he's supposed to. The population here is so small in this area maybe these demons just don't want to be here or maybe these devils are hiding not to draw attention. It's perplexing but we'll get it worked out."

Jake reached out and wrapped his arms around Ellie. "Now, how did I get lucky to have such a wonderful woman to keep me grounded?"

Ellie laughed and kissed him. "I guess you're just blessed."

Pam rolled her eyes. "Oh, please."

Ellie wrinkled her nose and grinned.

CHAPTER ELEVEN

Private Estate
Highway 160
South of Kayenta, Arizona

"TURELKA," bellowed Degen as he sat in a large, overstuffed chair in one of the elaborately decorated bedrooms on the estate. The room smelled too clean, too fresh, and too much light came in through the windows. He'd have to have the workers quit cleaning the room.

The short, thick, slug-like demon named Turelka came into the room. "Yes, your most hideousness?" he said as he bowed down.

"Don't flatter me, you worthless excuse; have they returned from exterminating that cowboy and his cursed friends?"

The slug-like monster hesitated, and his slow response was answered when Degen kicked the demon in the side.

"Answer me," growled Degen.

Turelka coughed and rubbed his side. "Yes, your most repulsive lord, one of them returned a few moments ago."

"Only one, what happened to the other one?" Degen stood and threw his arms up in the air. "Don't tell me they didn't accomplish this simple task? Bring whichever useless bag of bones survived in here... NOW!"

Turelka slinked out of the room and returned a few moments later with the yellowish demon that had survived the failed attack. The fiend was obviously shaken knowing that he'd failed and immediately threw himself face down on the floor in front of Degen in a show of absolute submission. "What happened?" snarled Degen.

The demon raised his head to answer when Degen grabbed him by one of his wings and threw him across the room into the wall. A painting of a German farm scene fell off the wall. The creature slowly recovered and stayed on his knees. "Please, most atrocious master. I simply followed Maulin to the lodge where the human women were. It was all so simple until another human interrupted."

Degen grabbed the smaller beast by the throat and held him off the ground. "Why did you attack them all together, especially when the cowboy was there?"

The fiend coughed, gagged, and answered Degen in clicks and squeaks.

"If it wasn't the cowboy, who was it then?" yelled Degen. Even though demons did not require air to breathe it could become deadly if Degen maintained his grasp. Finally, Degen released the smaller hellion who fell to the floor in a heap. The demon rubbed his neck. "Lord Degen, he was just a human with a foreign accent."

Degen whirled around causing the demon to duck down. "What kind of accent?"

"Russian."

"What did this Russian do?"

The brute felt that he'd regained some stature with Degen. "He ambushed us and shot the two of us. We were stopped momentarily but long enough for them to run outside. When we chased them outside, the law enforcement humans arrived along with the cowboy who shot Maulin. I knew that our attack was compromised so I felt coming back to report it was best."

Degen went and sat back down in his chair. "You're a liar. You ran because you're a coward." He scratched his fur with one claw.

"Very well, go to the site of our current operation and tell Hammer to give you a task."

The demon nodded as he backed away. "Thank you, your most wretchedness."

After the dejected creature left, Degen looked at Turelka. "Make sure he never comes out. I can't tolerate failure."

Turelka bowed and hurried away. Degen sat and clicked his teeth together in thought. *A Russian?*

FBI Headquarters
Office of Deputy Director of Paranormal Activities
935 Pennsylvania Avenue Northwest
Washington D.C.

DEPUTY DIRECTOR RUIZ was about to leave for the evening when his cellphone rang.

"Oscar, this is Williams."

By the tone of her voice, he knew something had gone wrong. "What's happened?"

"There's been an attack here by two of those devil monsters. While we were talking to the sheriff's department personnel here two of them attacked Taft's two female friends. Everyone's fine except for a few nerves being frayed but it was fatal for one creature."

Deputy Director Ruiz's heart skipped a beat. "They attacked Ellie and her friend, Pam?" he asked as he sat back down behind his desk and started taking notes.

"Yes, they flew in and tried to kill Miss Thompson, Miss Martin, and some newspaper guy. There was a waitress here too, but she'll be fine." Agent Williams continued and gave him a run down on what happened and ended it with the information about Viktor.

"A Russian FSB agent?" asked Deputy Director Ruiz as if he hadn't heard it right.

"Yes, an FSB agent. His name's Viktor Gordya and he came

looking for Jake. He said he had something important to talk to him about," explained Agent Williams.

Deputy Director Ruiz ran his hand through his salt and pepper hair. *A Russian Agent?* "I'll have the CIA run a check on him. In the meantime, find out what he's doing there and don't trust him."

"Me, trust a man?" said Agent Williams. "Perish the thought. I'll get Pyle to email you a complete run down and it will be in your email box by morning."

"That'll be fine and be careful. This thing is getting more twisted every day." Ruiz hung up, sat and stared at the desktop in thought. *An attack on Jake's ranch, a stolen frozen demon, monsters eating people, demons trying to kill Jake and his people, and a Russian. Could it get any worse?* Deputy Director Ruiz picked up his office phone and dialed the FBI lab. When a lab tech answered, he asked for Dr. Crammer. A few moments later, an elderly man answered. "This is Crammer. What can I do for you, Oscar?"

"How is our little experiment going, Doc?"

"Good, our firearms experts have been able to create the round but without anything to test it on we don't know if it'll work."

"Thanks, doc, send me a box of the ammo over." Deputy Director Ruiz hung up. *I have a bad feeling we'll be testing them soon.*

———————

2 Miles Northwest
Mexican Hat, Utah

THE CREATURE WAS CROUCHED near a huge boulder that overlooked the San Juan River and the city of Mexican Hat. The monstrosity was hungry again, but no matter how much it ate, it still hungered. It had been temporarily eased after it ate most of the two humans during the attack on the Dodge Durango, but the hunger came back too soon. It killed a cow but now the hunger came back more intense than before. It was always kept fed in the cavern with unwanted or worn-out diggers but now it had to find its own prey. It also suffered from the pain inflicted by the group of humans that had chased it when it escaped. It'd seen the dark clothed men again later when they worked their way through the valley. They'd tried to kill the creature without luck and even used acid but so far it survived and eluded them. The abnormal creature hated them, feared them, and wanted to be as far from them as possible.

It was too tired to work its way down the steep side, so it padded back towards the east hoping there were home sites that held easier meals. The desert didn't yield much in the way of food or homes but luckily after a few minutes the creature saw a home with lights on inside and heard voices coming from inside. It sniffed the air and took in the aroma of cooked meat which made its stomach growl. It crept slowly up to the back of the modular house, stood at the edge of the wooden patio deck, and looked through the back glass patio door. A small child about two years old waddled by but caught sight of the creature. She stopped, stood at the patio door, and stared at the deformed bear.

"Teddy, Teddy," said the toddler. She reached up and tried to open to sliding glass door. The creature stepped up the steps of the wooden deck towards the door. As it approached the glass door, the child's mother walked by and stopped to see what the girl was looking at.

"What do you see, Catey?" asked the woman.

The child banged on the glass. "Teddy, Momma, teddy."

The woman looked up, instantly took in the creature, and screamed. The bear hesitated for a second at the sound of the scream which saved their lives. The family's two hunting dogs were asleep around the corner under the trailer and downwind, but at the sound of the scream came lunging around the corner. The bear sensed their approach and instinctively turned towards the two dogs. Both dogs barked and growled at the thing while it roared a warning. In the meantime, the husband grabbed his hunting rifle, pointed it out of the kitchen window, and fired. The blast hit the creature in the side and knocked it backward off the deck. The thing roared and rolled over to gain its footing as the two hunting dogs bounded down the steps in hot pursuit. The man threw open the glass door and fired another shot at the bear but missed. The creature turned and ran into the darkness followed by the two dogs.

"Anne, call the sheriff," yelled the man. "Tell 'em we have a rabid grizzly bear up here."

———

Knotted Pine Lodge
101 E. Highway 163
Mexican Hat, Utah

AFTER A LATE DINNER the group went to their respective rooms to get some rest knowing that it would be early morning when they'd start the job of tracking down the creature.

Viktor wanted to meet with Jake alone even though Agent Williams had major misgivings about it. Jake assured her that everything would be fine so soon both men sat at a wooden table just outside in the cool night air.

"So, Jacob, I hear you've become quite the celebrity?" asked Viktor with a slight smirk.

Jake frowned and shook his head. "I'm just doing my job."

"And what actually is your job?"

"When I'm not working on my ranch, I'm helping out the FBI."

Viktor raised a blond eyebrow briefly. "This can't be the wild and wooly Jacob Taft I know, the one-man army that wreaked havoc in Southeast Asia and saved me from a band of mercenaries in Khuzestan?"

Jake blushed and shuffled his feet. "Times and things change."

Viktor sat back and stared at Jake for a few moments. "So, your Christian God gave you the ability to see these demons? Your lady friend said that only you can kill them too?"

Jake shrugged and nodded. "I know it sounds crazy but that's what happened."

"Da, I wouldn't have believed it if I hadn't seen it earlier myself."

Jake went on to tell Viktor about how Malachy appeared to him and everything that transpired since then. At the end of the story

Viktor shook his head. "I read all that in the newspapers but I'm still not sure what to believe."

"So why are you here?" asked Jake bluntly.

Viktor looked up and off into the darkness. "There was a burglary at an old warehouse in a small town outside of Moscow. A box was taken."

It was Jake's turn to sit back and stare. "You came all this way about a stolen box from an old warehouse?"

Viktor nodded sadly. "*Da*, and the security guard was killed. He was attacked and ripped to shreds."

"Could it have been an animal or someone trying to cover something up?" asked Jake.

Viktor shook his head. "*Nyet*, my friend, the first thing that I noticed was the strong smell of sulfur and ashes. It made we wonder why those substances would be involved."

"Maybe someone planted the chemicals there to trick you?"

"Maybe, but then I noticed something odd about the insects."

Jake frowned. "There were no insects, maggots, or flies."

Viktor nodded.

"So, what's in the box that's so important to a demon?"

Viktor sat back and thought for a moment. "We've been through many tight spots before, my old friend," Viktor hesitated another moment. "What I tell you must remain between us for the time being."

Jake rubbed his jaw and nodded.

"Someone or something removed the only remaining bones of Adolf Hitler from cold storage."

Jake stared at his Russian for a heartbeat or two. If it had been anyone else, he would have thought it was a joke, but the big man's face was stone cold sober. "Ok...so what do some old bones have to do with me?"

Viktor leaned forward. "It was logical to start with you since you seem to be the demon expert. Any idea why?"

Jake leaned back in his chair and looked up at the starry night sky in thought. "I don't know but if demons are involved it's going to be bad." At that moment, Jake's cellphone rang, and he saw that it was the sheriff's department. He answered, listened for a moment, and his face tensed. He hung up, got up and looked down a Viktor. "This will have to wait. That was from the sheriff's office. Our creature just tried to attack a family near here."

They headed towards the two cabins that their group occupied. "You wake Agent Pyle and I'll get Agent Williams."

Viktor nodded, walked over, and knocked on the room door where Jake and Agent Pyle were staying. Jake stepped over to the women's room but before he could knock, Agent Williams jerked the door open.

"I thought you might already be asleep," said Jake.

"Not while you're sitting out there with that Russian," she grumbled. "I don't trust him; so what's wrong?"

"There's been another attack," said Jake.

"Give me two minutes." Agent Williams turned back inside and in less than two minutes she came back out. Viktor and a sleepy Agent Pyle approached. "There was another attack?" asked Agent Pyle.

Jake nodded as a San Juan County deputy drove up. A young deputy rolled his window down. "Are you the FBI people?"

"Yes," answered Agent Williams. "We'll follow you."

County Road 215
San Juan County, Utah

AFTER FOLLOWING the deputy on a winding county road through the dark countryside they finally arrived at the modular home where the bear had been spotted. There were a couple of sheriff department vehicles but also a large group of men milling around in various types of hunting attire. Trucks, Jeeps and four wheelers were parked everywhere.

Deputy Bridges approached their car as they parked and got out. "Evening, folks, welcome to the circus."

"Who are all these people?" asked Agent Pyle.

"They're local hunters, townspeople, and gawkers. News travels fast and before we even arrived, several of them were already here. More of them have been coming ever since."

Jake shook his head. "Deputy, it's not safe for them to be here. They don't know what they're up against. I don't want anyone hurt unnecessarily."

"I know, and the sheriff's on his way but I'll do what I can for now," said Deputy Bridges. He walked over to the nearest pickup and climbed up in the back. "I need everyone's attention." The large group gathered around the truck. "I know that all of you are here to help track this animal down, but I want to warn you not to."

The group began mumbling and grumbling. Deputy Bridges didn't like the way it was going. It wouldn't take much to turn ugly. "Now, I know that you want this thing dead as much as I do but we have experts here from the government that can handle it."

"The government? What can they do that we can't do?" yelled a man from the crowd. The rest of the crowd chimed in.

"Look everyone," yelled Deputy Bridges. "It's not going to help arguing. I appreciate your willingness to help but this can be done with only a few of us."

Another San Juan County patrol vehicle arrived and parked. A balding, tall thin man in his sixties climbed out and walked up to the group.

"Evening, Sheriff," said several of the men from the group.

"Sheriff Jefferson," yelled a man dressed in hunting clothes. "Your deputy says we can't go hunt down this rabid bear."

San Juan Sheriff Ronald Jefferson smiled and climbed up into the bed of the truck next to Deputy Bridges. "First, I don't want anyone going out there in the dark and getting hurt. We don't know where this thing went or where it came from so I don't need anyone running off into the dark, but I do need to set up a perimeter." The sheriff then pointed eastward. "I want all of ya'll to set up a line that stretches north and south to keep this animal from getting by. Put your backs to the river and keep each other in sight and if you see anything then yell out." The sheriff turned to one of the deputies. "Deputy Bothman will help get everyone set up."

By then all the men were nodding in agreement and slapping each other on the back.

"But do not, I repeat, do not shoot at anything if you don't know what it is," added Sheriff Jefferson.

While Deputy Bothman began organizing the group and getting them dispersed, Sheriff Jefferson climbed down from the bed of the pickup. Agent Williams shook the sheriff's hand and introduced the group.

"Sheriff, are you sure it's a good idea to keep these men out here?" asked Agent Pyle.

The sheriff nodded. "These are all good men who mean well. I'm sure this thing is long gone by now and after a few hours of waiting in the dark with nothing to do most will go home."

Jake looked off into the darkness. *I hope so*, he thought, *for their sake.*

"So, what do we do now?" asked Agent Pyle.

"We wait," said Agent Williams. "If it doesn't show back up, we'll hunt it down when the sun comes up. I'll call Oscar and give him the update."

Unfortunately, this posse of men didn't know that the creature was just out of sight hunched down in the grass, watching the men spread out. It had tried to head back the way it came but the other group of men in dark clothing was working their way straight at it. The creature was trapped between two groups of armed men and there's nothing more dangerous than an injured, cornered, trapped wild animal.

AS THE HOURS ticked by the large group of men dwindled down as the excitement wore off. Most men had gone back home to get some sleep before going to work in the morning. It had become increasingly difficult for the ones on the perimeter to keep each other in sight. The property owners, Anne, and Jim Barnes kept everyone supplied with coffee and snacks as a means of thanks for their efforts.

Agent Pyle and Williams sat on the deck at the back of the house and took turns napping while the other watched. Viktor and Jake had taken the place of some of the men who left to keep the perimeter as safe as possible. Jake watched the darkness for the creature, hoping to see its yellow eye before it got too close. His mind kept trying to put some of the pieces together. *First, there was the attack on Ellie's church, my ranch, an attack by a flying creature in northern Arizona and several attacks here. Are they related or just random demon activity? And is Hitler's bones related?* Jake shook his head. All he wanted to do was build a ranch and have a quiet life, not chase after demons and monsters. His thoughts were broken when one of the men on the perimeter yelled out that he'd spotted something. The sheriff, who'd been leaning over the hood of his truck looking at a map of the area, yelled towards them, "Everyone on the perimeter stay put."

Agent Williams and Pyle approached the sheriff and together they walked a hundred yards south to an outcropping of rock where a young hunter dressed in hunting camouflage clothing was pointing into the dark. "Sheriff, I saw something, I swear," he said.

"Are you sure, Jimmy?" asked the sheriff.

Jimmy nodded. "I saw a dark form moving around just past that group of rocks."

The group shined their flashlights into the darkness, but nothing moved. After several minutes of watching, the sheriff turned back towards the house. "If you see something again, give a yell. It might have been anything, Jimmy." As the sheriff and the FBI agents walked off, Jimmy mumbled and cursed about no one believing him. They had to pass Jake on the way back. "Did he see anything?" he asked.

Agent Williams shrugged. "He said he saw something, but we didn't."

"It might have been a raccoon, lizard, or anything," added the sheriff. "Jimmy's a young kid who could be seeing monsters everywhere."

Jimmy turned to the man that was stationed to his right. "Hey, Ted, I know the difference between a lizard and a bear. I saw something. I swear."

"Sure, kid," said the man called Ted.

Jimmy frowned and turned back towards the dark desert. "I know I saw something." He settled back down to watch when he heard a cough. Jimmy turned towards Ted again. "Did you hear that? Ted?" When Ted didn't answer, Jimmy got up and walked over to where Ted sat against a rock. "Ted, didn't you hear that noise? I don't want to yell out again or they'll think I'm an idiot." When Ted didn't answer Jimmy nudged Ted, who slumped over to the ground. "What the…," said Jimmy. He shined his flashlight on Ted's face and saw a small round hole in his forehead as a trickle of blood ran down across Ted's nose. Jimmy screamed as he stumbled back, tripped, and fell back on the ground. Sheriff Jefferson and the FBI agents stopped and turned. "What did he see now?" asked the sheriff.

"I'll go check and see what scared him this time," volunteered Deputy Bothman. The deputy walked several steps when he caught sight of several dark shapes slipping out of the darkness. "Sheriff, you might want to see th…" Deputy Bothman's words were caught short when he noticed a red dot on the front of his uniform shirt followed by a short cough that slammed him to the ground. Everyone was momentarily frozen as the sight of Bothman falling.

Silencers thought Agent Williams. "Gunfire," she yelled. "Everybody, get down."

One of the hunters turned towards Agent Williams. "What are you talking about? I didn't hear a gunshot. We're looking for a mangy bear." His answer was a slug that tore into his right shoulder and knocked him down. The rest of the men guarding the perimeter scattered for cover as several more red dots searched the area for victims. Jake dove to the ground and crawled beside a boulder.

"How many do you count, Jacob?" whispered Viktor from behind a large rock.

"Maybe six," whispered Jake.

Several more muted shots ricocheted off rocks encouraged them all to stay down. One hunter fired back which only brought more silenced rounds in his direction. *These men are hunters and businessmen, not trained military troops*, thought Jake. *They're no match for whoever is out there.*

"We need a distraction," whispered Viktor.

As if on cue a large form lumbered out of the dark and climbed up on the hood of a sheriff department vehicle. The bear roared and bellowed at the overhead police lights. The oversized thing swiped at the overhead blue and red lights while Sheriff Jefferson hunkered down beside the vehicle and looked up into the enraged stare of the creature. He fired several shots up into the deformed bear's chest and to the sheriff's relief it annoyed the thing enough that it jumped down to the ground. The deformed bear turned back towards the line of men guarding the perimeter and bellowed out another warning. Jake decided that the creature was the more dangerous problem and fired several more shots into the thing until the slide locked back on his Colt .45 and while he reloaded, Viktor continued to pour round after round into the creature as it snarled and growled in defiance. Agent Williams stepped around the front of one of the sheriff's departments vehicle and yelled at Agent Pyle over the sound of the gunfire. "Take care of the active shooters and we'll take the monster."

Agent Pyle nodded and kept firing in the direction of the unknown men who seemed to have faded into the darkness. He yelled for the local men to cease fire and turned his attention to the creature. It had crumpled to the ground and lay motionless.

At a few moments to make sure they weren't going to take any more fire from the unknown attackers, Jake and Viktor approached the bear and noticed that it was still alive. It apparently didn't have the strength to lift its head but still growled deep within its massive chest. With weapons trained on it, Jake bent down and carefully examined it. He noticed that it did in fact have one normal bear eye and one yellow glowing demon eye. Jake turned to one of the men armed with a hunting rifle. "Lend me that rifle?"

"With pleasure," said the local man and handed the rifle to Jake.

Jake took careful aim and shot the repulsive beast in the head.

"It doesn't look rabid," said one of the local men. "It looks deformed...like some sort of monster."

Sheriff Jefferson turned to Deputy Bridges. "Take a few men, check on our wounded, and see if those attackers are dead or alive. And for God's sake, be careful. I don't want any more people getting hurt." He turned back towards the dead creature. Parts of the thing were already starting to rapidly decompose. "That's not possible."

Jake squatted down and examined the thing before looking up at the sheriff. "Just like the ones earlier in town they decompose at an incredible rate. The odd thing about this one is only part of it is. It's not completely demonic."

"Just like the bird thing in Arizona," added Agent Pyle.

"Looks like somebody's playing Dr. Frankenstein," commented Sheriff Jefferson dryly.

Agent Williams frowned and cursed. "Yeah, someone's definitely experimenting."

Jake stood up and nodded solemnly. "I agree and if we don't find out soon, we may have more of these things roaming around."

Sheriff Jefferson shook his head. "I don't need any more of this, creatures running around, unknown assailants shooting at us; we need to get to the bottom of this fast."

"I agree," said Agent Williams. "Those men didn't just show up by coincidence, they were hunting this thing, but why?"

"For sport?" asked Agent Pyle.

"*Nyet,*" said Viktor with a shake of his head. "Whoever did this have an extensive laboratory and resources. I wouldn't think they'd create one simply for sport."

"Either way, whoever did this needs to be stopped," growled Sheriff Jefferson. "I can't have more of this is my county." The sheriff turned to a couple of men standing nearby. "Anthony, get what's left of this thing loaded up and over to the vet's office."

CHAPTER TWELVE

Knotted Pine Lodge
101 E. Highway 163
Mexican Hat, Utah

THE MELEE from the night before had resulted in four deaths. A local man named Ted Davidson was killed along with three of the unknown assailants. Deputy Bothman and several civilians were recovering from gunshot wounds, but none seemed life threatening. The dead attackers were stuffed into the Bluff Medical Clinic's small freezer awaiting autopsies.

Jake, Viktor, and several FBI agents sat at a conference table inside the lodge drinking coffee. It had been a long night of collecting bodies, taking photos, writing statements, and they were all exhausted. Sheriff Jefferson entered the room carrying a large binder. "Have any of you gotten any sleep?" he asked.

They all shook their heads.

"Any news on the identity of the three men?" asked Agent Pyle.

Sheriff Jefferson shook his head. "No, Lieutenant Beggett is handling the processing."

"Good, and as soon as we get their prints, we'll email them back to Washington and run them through our systems. Maybe something will show."

Jake rubbed his tired eyes. "If I was to guess, I'd say they were hired mercenaries."

"I agree," said Agent Williams. "They were too well armed and had expensive equipment that not every local gun store has."

"So why were they hunting it? And where did they come from?" thought Agent Pyle out loud.

Viktor had been leaning back in his chair sipping coffee. "Look at it this way, comrades, they weren't hunting it for pleasure and were more than willing to kill to get it which makes it very important to them."

"That makes sense that they'd want it back at any cost after experimenting with animal and demon DNA," said Jake. "But why was it running around the countryside, risking being seen?"

"Maybe it escaped?" said Agent Pyle off handed.

"I think you hit it on the head, Terrell," said Agent Williams.

Jake sat and stared at the ceiling. "So, someone's experimenting on animals, it escapes risking exposing them, so they have to kill it or bring it back. That makes perfect sense."

The rest of the group nodded in agreement.

"But who's doing the experimenting?" asked Agent Pyle.

"And since we have the animal and three of their dead people, I would imagine whoever these people are they are not going to be happy about it," said Viktor.

Agent Williams sneered. "You just had to rain on the parade, didn't you?"

————

Monument Valley
Arizona

ELIJAH GREYMOUNTAIN WANDERED along the rim of the mesa and had been doing so all morning looking for any sign of where the large bird monster might have nested but so far came up empty. He'd started where the injured white man had been found and worked his way back and forth along the edge. *There must be something here*, thought the elderly Native American. The creature had stayed somewhere but there were thousands of niches and cracks where the thing could have lived.

The morning was cool, but the sun soon heated the rock, and Greymountain broke out in a sweat. *I'm getting too old for this.* He sat down on a boulder to rest and catch his breath. Looking out into the distance he thought how beautiful this strange and barren land was.

A pleasant breeze blew up cooling him and he breathed in the crisp clean air... *What was that?* He sniffed again and caught a scent of something strange. He remembered the same smell coming from the refrigerator at the police department where the strange corpse had been kept. *Sulfur?* He knew there weren't any geysers or volcanic activity in the area, so he got to his feet and carefully looked around. He worked his way down to the edge of the mesa and on the ground, he found a single black feather. He picked it up. It felt odd as if...he lifted the feather to his nose and sniffed. The smell caused him to jerk his head away. Greymountain scouted around and found more of the black feathers. They seemed to collect around a crack in the rim. He crawled to the edge, lay on his stomach, looked out over the edge, and saw a dark opening below and to his right. Greymountain sat up and carefully slid feet first over the edge and dropped down onto the edge of the dark opening. He stared into a cave that led back into the darkness. Shrugging off any thought of going back for assistance, the Native American pulled a cigarette lighter from his pocket that he kept for lighting his pipe and flicked it on. The small lighter lit up a small portion of the cave. Greymountain stepped carefully into the cave which reeked of ashes, sulfur, decomposing flesh, and sweat. He had to stoop slightly as he walked back into the cave. It only receded 25 feet before coming to a dead end. The floor was littered with bones and carcasses of small desert animals that the creature must have eaten. *Nothing here of any help*, thought Greymountain, *and time to go home and take a long hot bath.*

As he turned to leave, the dim light bounced off the cave wall and illuminated something. Greymountain held the lighter up closer and saw what appeared to be a crude painting of sorts. He examined the wall but couldn't make any sense of it. There were depictions of strange looking creatures of all sizes and shapes. They seemed to be unhappy and were being driven by a task master with a whip. *How bizarre?* The figures seemed to be digging around stalagmites or cave formations. *Where are they digging? A cave? This painting looks to have been done recently. Could the thing have done this? But why? Was it possible the bird creature had been intelligent enough to make this?* He knew then that he needed to get back and tell his son who could notify someone else, like the FBI.

———

Knotted Pine Lodge
101 E. Highway 163
Mexican Hat, Utah

A MILD COLD front had blown through the southwest, so Jake, Agent Pyle, and Al walked briskly through the cool weather to the lodge restaurant. Ellie, Pam, and Agent Williams were already seated around a circular table. Jake and the two FBI agents had only gotten a few hours of sleep after leaving their meeting with the sheriff, so coffee was ordered all around before they even thought of food.

Ellie was not happy after hearing from Jake that a group of armed men had attacked them last night. After looking over the menu she looked at Jake who was nursing his second hot cup of coffee. He looked worn and tired. "Has the sheriff's office called back on the identity of the men that attacked last night?" she asked.

"No, not yet we hope after the autopsy something will come through today," grumbled Jake.

Agent Williams gave the waitress her order. "As soon as we get the fingerprints this morning during the autopsy Terrell can email the fingerprints to the lab and ask for a rush. Of course, everything in the FBI is a rush so who knows when we'll get anything back."

Al was wide eyed and loaded with questions. "After I heard

about what happened I couldn't wait to talk with all of you about the ordeal. Can I get pictures of the bear? Can I get interviews with some of the men out there? Is this some kind of government cover up?"

Agent Williams rolled her eyes and Agent Pyle chuckled.

"No," snapped Jake. "It's not a government cover up." The coffee had not done anything to help his mood. He was no closer to solving this problem than he was when he left Texas.

"No, you can't talk to the men that were out there," growled Agent Williams. "But if you don't irritate me too much you might be allowed to photograph the beast."

"What time are the autopsies scheduled for?" asked Pam.

"In an hour or so," answered Agent Williams. "I don't expect to find out too much except how they died, and we know that much."

Viktor Gordya approached and sat down at the table, ordered coffee, black without sugar. "Has there been any news on our party crashers from last night?"

Several of them shook their heads. The group's breakfast arrived, and they ate the rest of the meal in relative silence.

FBI Headquarters
Office of Deputy Director of Paranormal Activities
935 Pennsylvania Avenue Northwest
Washington, D.C.

DEPUTY DIRECTOR RUIZ had just finished reading the emails from Agents Williams and Pyle when FBI Director Bill Chisom strolled into the office and sat down in one of the chairs in front of the desk. Director Chisom had been with the FBI for over thirty years and was well respected by his subordinates for fairness and common sense. "Any news from your people out west, Oscar?" he asked.

Deputy Director Ruiz handed Director Chisom a copy of the emailed reports and leaned back in his chair. "It's a case that's only getting worse by the minute. It seems several people have been killed and there's a Russian agent there with them."

Director Chisom straightened in his chair. "A Russian agent?"

Deputy Director Ruiz nodded. "Yes, sir, Agent Williams said that he's a friend of Taft's and that he came to talk to him. I had the CIA run a check on him." Deputy Director Ruiz passed the director a file folder. "He's worked with Taft in the past and as far as his file he seems to be what he says he is."

Director Chisom flipped through the file on Viktor Gordya, nodded, and ran a hand through his crew cut hair. "Is any of this a matter that the president needs to be briefed?"

Deputy Director Ruiz shrugged. "At this point we don't think so but it's too soon to tell. We don't know for sure if it's demonic or terrorism from overseas. If there is a Russian connection, we don't know of one. In the report Agent Williams and Pyle were fired upon by an unknown group of men last night, but we don't know who they are yet."

Director Chisom read through Agent Williams's report. "Keep me posted. Agent Williams seems to have a knack for finding cases that explode into national problems. As of right now, I'll classify it as localized problem and if it turns into something let me know." The director stood up and walked to the door. "Oh, by the way, a Mister Elijah Greymountain called the main number and said he needed to show your agents something back in Arizona. He didn't say what, but he sounded urgent."

After Director Chisom left, Deputy Director Ruiz rubbed his eyes. He hoped that it was just a local problem, but something told him that he was wrong.

Private Estate
Highway 160
South of Kayenta, Arizona

"YOU ARE COMPLETE IDIOTS," roared Degen at the two men dressed in black. "How can you be so incompetent?"

One of the men, a tall, muscular German nicknamed "Snake" from the snake tattooed on his forearm stared back at the demon. "You didn't inform me that we would we meet with armed resistance. We were only looking for one of your monsters, a freak bear."

The tall demon leaned down and roared into the mercenary's face. "You're a professional killer. Those were amateur hunters and small-town law enforcement. How much force could they have put up?"

"The problem would have been resolved if we had been given more information," argued Snake.

"And it never would have been a problem if you had not let the thing escape in the first place," added the other mercenary, a shorter, stocky German named Fritz.

Without taking his eyes off Snake, Degen's arm shot out, grasped Fritz by the throat, and lifted him off the floor. The man kicked and thrashed as Degen squeezed. He then dropped the man on the floor and placed one huge hind foot on the man's chest. The furry devil reached down and grabbed the man's face with a furry clawed hand. Degen forced a clawed finger in each eye socket and squeezed. Fritz kicked and squirmed as Degen shoved his clawed fingers deep into the man's eye sockets. Blood bubbled out of the eye orbits as Fritz screeched. He eventually lost consciousness while Degen shoved his huge fingers as far into the man's brain as he could until he died. Degen then picked him up by his eye sockets and tossed the dead man like a rag doll across the room where he landed in a heap by the door.

Snake was shaken by Degen's ease of killing but refused to back down. "If we had known we could have handled it differently."

"Get out. I will handle this myself."

Snake nodded, spun, and crisply walked out the door. Priska sat off to the side of the room in her wheelchair and watched the event without comment. Degen paced back and forth across the room and ranted about how he was surrounded by morons. Priska quietly rolled her wheelchair across the room, picked up a phone, and spoke into it softly. A few minutes later, two men came and removed Fritz's body. Priska instructed them to give the body to the workers to be used for food. Finally, Degen stomped out of the room which allowed her to breathe a sigh of relief. Degen had vented his anger on something. She was glad it wasn't her.

———

Doctor Edward Lott's Medical Office
523 East Highway 191
Bluff, Utah

DOCTOR EDWARD LOTT entered his office carrying a cup of hot coffee. Besides having a small medical practice, he also performed the occasional autopsy for the county. Four deceased men had been brought in late last night and Doctor Lott had to reschedule some of his morning patients to complete the autopsies. One man was a local from Mexican Hat that the doctor had seen around town, while the others were strangers that the FBI wanted fingerprinted as soon as possible to identify them.

Doctor Lott strolled down to the freezer where the bodies were kept. He'd planned on having all four done before lunch. He came dressed in scrubs for the procedures since it could be messy and tied on a white apron to help keep the blood off. The doctor whistled while he slipped on his rubber gloves, arranged his instruments, turned on his recorder, and began dictating information about one of the dead attackers.

After giving the height, weight, race, and hair color, he smelled a strange odor. *Sulfur.* Doctor Lott bent over and sniffed the corpse. *Now where was that smell coming from?* He suddenly had the feeling he was not alone and spun around only to be face to face with a seven-foot-tall tiger-like creature. Several other smaller strange looking creatures stood behind the larger one and smiled, showing sharp jagged teeth.

———

PAM, Ellie, and Al decided to do some morning shopping while Jake, Viktor, Agents Williams and Pyle followed Deputy Bridges to Doctor Lott's office in Bluff. They parked out front next to the doctor's Range Rover. They found the front door locked so Deputy Bridges knocked.

"He's expecting us, isn't he?" asked Agent Pyle.

Deputy Bridges nodded. "Yeah, but he's probably in the back where he does the autopsies."

The deputy knocked on the door again, but no one answered. Agent Williams stepped up and pounded on the door. "This is the FBI, Doctor Lott, open up."

Deputy Bridges used his cellphone and dialed the doctor's number. They could hear the phone ringing inside and Deputy Bridges looked worried. The others saw the look on the deputy's face, split up, walked around the building, but could not find an unlocked door.

"This definitely isn't normal for Doctor Lott," said Deputy Bridges. "But after everything that's happened lately nothing's normal."

"We need to get inside," said Agent Williams. "Is there anyone else with a key nearby?"

Deputy Bridges pulled out his hand-held radio. "I'll have dispatch call his secretary. She usually opens up." A few minutes later, the sheriff department dispatcher advised Deputy Bridges that she spoke to the doctor's secretary and due to the autopsies, she wasn't supposed to come in until after lunch. She was a twenty-minute drive away.

"Any ideas?" asked the deputy.

"*Da*," said Viktor. He walked over, raised a big foot, and kicked the door in.

"Works for me," said Agent Williams dryly.

The first thing they noticed was the overwhelming smell of sulfur and ash coming from inside the building. Instantly everyone pulled their weapons then allowed Jake to take the lead since he was able to see demons even when they weren't solidified. They entered the building and slowly but as silently as possible worked their way through the building. Nothing was disturbed or misplaced and at the back of the building they found a metal door.

"This is where he does the autopsies," whispered Deputy Bridges.

Agent Williams nodded, reached out carefully, and grabbed the doorknob. She looked over at Jake, nodded, threw the door open, and rushed in expecting to find it full of demons. The room was empty but smelled even more of sulfur, ash, and death.

Ted Davidson's body was still there but the other three were missing. In their place was Doctor Lott, or what was left of him. He was on the metal exam table on his back. He'd been cut open from throat to pelvis and all his internal organs were gone. His skull had been cracked open like an egg and his brain was missing.

On the metal table between the doctor's feet was the tape recorder. Deputy Bridges carefully reached over, hit the rewind button which rewound the tape for a minute or so, and then hit the play button. The doctor's voice came on. They listened while he whistled and gave the first deceased man's height, weight, race, and hair color. There was a pause then the doctor sniffed twice. They heard a shuffle and the sound of the doctor backing into the metal table. "Who are you? What do you want? Why are you wearing those costumes? Why are..." said the doctor but was cut off by the sound of high-pitched clicks and squeaks.

"What's that sound?" asked Deputy Bridges softly.

"Demons," growled Jake. "That's what it sounds like when they talk to each other."

The sound of Doctor Lott's blood-curdling scream sent chills through the group. They heard scraping, clawing and tearing followed by the sound of slurping and chewing. Each person listened to the sickening sound and in their mind's eye could see the devils ripping the doctor open then devouring parts of him. The tape then went silent.

Deputy Bridges reached over and turned off the recorder. Nobody spoke for several seconds as it all sunk in. Agent Pyle sighed in disgust while Agent Williams rubbed her temples with her fingertips. Deputy Bridges pulled his cellphone out and dialed the sheriff's office. Viktor cursed in Russian, and Jake shook his head in frustration.

"They beat us to it again," said Agent Pyle dejectedly.

Jake suddenly turned to Deputy Bridges. "The vet's office, we need to warn them."

Deputy Bridges hung up from calling his lieutenant and dialed Dr. Hodges's veterinarian office but there was no answer. He frantically grabbed his radio and called the dispatcher. "Lois, this is Bridges, I need you to look up Dr. Hodges's pager number and page him immediately. I also need another unit over here to guard this crime scene. I've already called the lieutenant."

The dispatcher acknowledged, "10-4."

Jake headed for the door. "We'll see if we can get to the vet's office before they do."

"I doubt you can get there in time but good luck," said Deputy Bridges with a nod. Jake, Viktor, and the two FBI agents ran to the car and were soon speeding toward Dr. Hodges's office. Agent Williams's cellphone rang; she answered, listened for a minute and hung up. She gave a slight smile of relief. "That was Deputy Bridges. He said Dr. Hodges was still at home, so he was told to stay there."

"At least we won't find another casualty," said Agent Pyle.

Viktor looked over at the young FBI agent. "But what might be waiting for us could be worse."

———

Patsy's Gifts
410 E. Highway 163
Mexican Hat, Utah

THE WEATHER WAS cool and crisp in the city, but the air was clean and fresh. Al, Ellie, and Pam walked down through the small town. They left Roscoe in the car since most shops and stores don't allow dogs inside, especially half wolf dogs. They stepped inside a local souvenir shop and wandered up and down the aisles eyeing souvenirs as well as other locally made odds and ends. Pam looked through a rack of Utah T-shirts while Al browsed the book section.

Ellie picked up a music box made of cedar, opened it, and smelled the fresh wood smell. "I just love the smell," she commented.

Pam lifted two T-shirts with Utah printed in large print on the front. "Should I get the pink one or the light blue one?" she asked. Ellie walked over and looked at the T-shirts. "Get the pink one. It'll match your boots."

Al picked up a candle in the shape of a pinecone and smelled it. "Why would anyone buy a candle that looks like a pinecone when they can get a real one right here in Utah, and besides this one smells like rotten eggs?"

Ellie spun around and Pam dropped the T-shirts. It took a moment for Al to realize what he'd just said. He carefully put the candle down and walked over to the two women. Ellie glanced around the store quickly for anything out of the ordinary. Besides the salesclerk at the rear of the store stocking Native American style blankets there was a young woman with long dark hair wearing a ski jacket standing at the card section looking at postcards of Utah.

"Let's get out of here," whispered Pam.

Ellie nodded and they walked towards the door with Al trailing behind. He was pale and his eyes were wide with apprehension. Ellie abruptly stopped. The path to the door was clear but she did notice that the view in front of the door seemed to waver. Ellie didn't feel right about it and backed up. "Let's sneak out the back," she whispered.

In a blink of an eye the view of the door wavered again, and a huge demon stood where an empty space had been only a moment before. The monstrosity was at least six feet tall with gray-bluish rough skin. It was overly muscular, no nose, a double set of needle-sharp teeth, and two large tusks that curved out and back. Ellie got the impression of a half hippo, half baby elephant without a trunk on steroids with yellow eyes. The demon rested a large axe on its shoulder. Another smaller demon flew from behind the large one. This little demon was only a foot tall with feathered wings and resembled a small winged furry monkey with a long thin birdlike beak lined with sharp teeth. It squeaked, clicked, and chirped in demonic language as it pointed towards the trio.

Ellie turned towards the back of the store. "Hide and try to get out the back way."

Pam and Al didn't need any coaxing and split in different directions. The huge demon roared in delight, as if it was some kind of game, and stomped down the aisle after them swinging the axe back and forth knocking items off the shelves. Ellie ducked down behind a display of novelties while Pam dove under the rack of T-shirts. Al looked around for any place to hide when the monster rounded the end of the aisle. Al hunkered down behind a small stand of belts which the monster knocked aside with one hand. The little demon sat on the top of a nearby display cabinet and cackled. Al looked up from his crouched position at the face of the thing and fainted. The yellow eyes seemed to sparkle with delight, and it roared which caused the shelves to rattle and the front windows to shatter.

The huge fallen angel reached out for the unconscious Al when Pam leapt on its back and shoved one of the 3x large T-shirts over its head temporarily blinding it. The beast swung around at Pam, but she'd dropped to the floor and backed away.

Ellie had sprinted from behind the display towards the rear of the shop when she saw Al had passed out on the floor. Pam grabbed Al by the shoulders and tried to drag him towards the back exit. The overgrown devil roared again, ripped the shirt loose, spun, and swung the axe narrowly missing Pam. The little demonic one screamed and cheered the larger demon on as it picked up a rack of jackets and threw it at Pam and Al. The throw missed them but landed at Pam's feet which caused her to release Al and tumble to the ground. The behemoth smiled, stepped up and lifted the axe up to deliver the death blow. Pam held up her hand as if it would protect them both when Ellie jammed a hiking stick into the beast's right thigh. It roared in pain, grabbed the hiking stick, and pulled it out while Ellie tried to help Pam drag Al to the back of the store. The demon held the bloody hiking stick in one clawed hand, the axe in the other, and lifted both weapons above its head.

Time seemed to freeze as the tip of a golden sword suddenly

protruded from the giant beast's chest. The monstrosity dropped both weapons, tried to grab the tip of the sword, and with a puzzled look fell to its knees as the tip of the sword was removed. It tried to roar but only gurgled as red froth bubbled from its mouth and fell forward with a crash.

Ellie and Pam stared dumbstruck at the now dead demonic thing on the floor and at the small feminine form standing behind it. It was the woman who'd been looking at the postcards earlier except now she looked different. She no longer had on jeans and a ski jacket but was dressed all in white and held a thin golden sword inlaid with gems. She wore a form fitted golden colored vest that was embroidered with ancient lettering and had small slots that held small golden knives and other equally deadly weapons. She had large wings and her hair was still black as night, but her skin was a light tint of gold, and she had the distinct eyes of flames that identified her as…an angel.

The big-eyed winged monkey knew his welcome was over and flew rapidly towards one of the open front windows. In the blink of an eye the angel grabbed a small golden star shaped weapon from one of the slots in her vest and threw it at the demon. The sharp deadly star struck the demon at the base of its skull killing it instantly. It fell into a heap at the door.

"I don't believe it," said Pam wide eyed. "A butt-kicking female angel."

"Pamela, shush…," said Ellie as she turned to the heavenly being. "I'm Ellie and we're so eternally grateful to you for saving us."

The female host smiled. "Praise be to our God. It was my pleasure."

"I'm glad you were in the neighborhood," said Ellie. "Things were getting nasty."

"Yes, yes," added Pam.

"I'm happy to serve. After the attack on you at the lodge, Malachy assigned me to keep an eye on you and it was a good thing," explained the golden-skinned angel.

Ellie smiled. "Tell Malachy thank you. We wondered where he'd been."

The beautiful angel's face frowned, and tiny lightning bolts arched across the whites of her eyes. "The fallen have made several more attempts at getting to your friend Jacob Taft's ranch so we've been busy, and Malachy has been called away."

"Doesn't it ever slow down?" asked Pam as she stared at the rapidly decomposing demons. The smell was started to get nauseating.

The angel shook her head. "Not since the fall."

"May I ask your name?" asked Pam.

"Kiara."

Ellie coughed as the stench of the dead demons started to overwhelm them. "Thank you, Kiara. Do you know what's going on around here?"

Kiara shook her head again. "No, so we must be diligent, alert, and aware of the dangers. I'll be around." With that the angel disappeared.

The two women stared at the open empty space where the angel had stood. Ellie was the first to turn away. "Let's get Al up, find the clerk and make sure she's ok."

They pulled Al to his feet and his eyes fluttered open. They left him leaning against the counter and found the clerk hiding under the blankets she'd been putting away. "Are you hurt?" asked Pam.

The woman shook her head. "No," she answered in a weak voice. "I've never seen anything like that. What are those things?" she asked as she pointed to the decaying forms on the floor.

"Dead demons," answered Pam dryly.

"Patsy's never going to believe this. How am I going to explain all this damage?"

Ellie led her to a chair at the back of store where the smell wasn't as bad and had her sit. "We'll call the sheriff's office for you and the FBI can vouch for what happened. We're just glad you're not hurt."

Pam walked Al back then brought them both glasses of water. The clerk drank a few sips. "Did I really see a golden woman?"

"Yes, you did," explained Ellie.

"What, another angel and I missed it?" exclaimed Al.

Dr. Hodges's Veterinarian Office
213 E 3rd Ave
Mexican Hat, Utah

AGENT WILLIAMS PARKED the rented vehicle a half a block down from the vet's office. Agents Williams and Pyle carefully walked to the door while Jake and Viktor kept an eye on the surrounding area for any unwanted visitors. Agent Williams drew her weapon and nodded to Agent Pyle who had already drawn his semi auto handgun. They noticed the door was ripped off the hinges and she could smell a faint odor of ash and sulfur. "This isn't good," Agent Pyle said off hand.

"Not as subtle as at the doctor's office," Agent Williams added.

Agent Williams motioned with her head for Jake and Viktor to join them. The four carefully entered the building and searched the offices in the front but they were empty. When they arrived at the back where the kennels and cages were, they discovered all the caged animals slaughtered. Kennel doors and cages were torn open. The poor animals inside had been killed violently. Some animals were missing, others had limbs ripped off and thrown around the large room. They checked the back rooms, but the bear corpse was gone.

"Too late, again," said Agent Williams.

Jake put his weapon in the holster and kicked one of the cages in frustration.

"These creatures are clever," said Viktor as he looked around at the carnage. "But why kill these defenseless animals?"

"Because they're scum...they're demons," said Agent Williams angrily. She hated senseless killing.

Jake stomped back into the main office area. "They're taunting us, teasing us. They knew this was our lead to finding out what was going on." Jake's cell phone rang, he answered, and his jaw tightened. "Are you alright? A flying monkey? Another angel? A woman? We'll meet you there! Are you sure?" Jake hung up.

"What is it, my friend?" asked Viktor.

"Ellie, Pam and that reporter kid were attacked in a store," explained Jake.

"What?" snapped Agent Williams. "When? Where?"

"Are they ok?" asked Agent Pyle.

Jake held up a hand to silence them. "She said two demons, a big one and a flying feathered monkey, appeared in a souvenir shop and tried to hurt them but an angel saved them. One of the deputies is there now so she said she'll meet us at the lodge."

They all nodded and headed for the door. Agent Williams pulled out her cellphone. "I'll call Bridges and let him know what we found here."

"Did you say a winged monkey? Like *Wizard of Oz* flying monkey?" asked Agent Pyle.

Jake frowned but didn't answer.

Agent Williams just shook her head.

CHAPTER THIRTEEN

Private Estate
Highway 160
South of Kayenta, Arizona

A YOUNG WOMAN named Sarah awoke to a world that she didn't recognize. She lifted her head which made the world spin. She fell back down until she could focus and found herself in a small ten foot by ten-foot room painted a dull gray. The only light came from the recessed lighting in the ceiling. Sarah slowly sat up on a cheap foam mattress on top of a cot that was her bed. There was a dirty sink and toilet but nothing else. *Did I get arrested last night? Which jail is this?* She tried to remember what happened. She'd met a handsome man in a white van near Tony's Pool Hall in Flagstaff. After getting in they drove towards a motel but after that she couldn't remember anything until now.

She slowly got to her feet, stumbled to the metal door, and looked out through the six-by-six-inch glass window. All she could see through the thick glass were more cells on the other side of a long hallway. The woman shivered.

Sarah dropped out of high school at sixteen and ran away from home to escape her abusive stepfather. Since then, she'd been on her own, living in different places, worked different jobs, and finally ended up as a prostitute working the streets to make ends meet.

She banged on the door and yelled for the jailer to come tell her what she was arrested for, but no one came. *What kind of dumpy jail is this?* She went back and sat on the bed and waited.

She was startled when she heard someone walking down the hall with keys. Sarah realized that she'd fallen back asleep and with no clock she had no idea how long it'd been. The lock on her cell door slid back and a large man in a dark one-piece jumpsuit stood in the doorway.

"Come, now," he ordered.

Sarah walked to the door. "Where am I? What's the charge?"

"Shut up," ordered the guard and shoved her down the hall.

"Hey, I got rights. I'll sue you for civil rights violation."

"Silence," growled the guard again and roughly pushed her.

"Alright, alright, you don't have to be a jerk." She walked in front of him down a long hall painted the same dull gray color past several cell doors. Most were empty but in a few she saw females staring back at her. Their faces were gaunt, and their heads shaved. *What kind of stinking jail shaves women's heads?* The guard opened another sliding metal door and shoved her into a room where a female guard sat at a desk. The room was filled with different types of medical equipment. There was an examination table in the middle of the room and a chair off to one side with straps.

"Hey, what's going on here?" demanded the young woman.

The dark haired, heavy set, pit bull looking female guard was reading something from a clipboard and glanced up at her. "Strip all of your clothes off."

"What? Are you crazy?"

The ugly male guard slapped her across the face. "Silence, strip."

Sarah wiped the blood from her cut lip and removed her clothes. The woman pointed towards a small shower stall. "Shower yourself," ordered the woman. Sarah felt humiliated having to strip naked in the presence of both guards. She turned on the shower, felt the hot water cascade down, as it was nice to take a shower after the rough night she'd gone through. Her small paradise was abruptly halted when the woman guard yelled at her to hurry. After she showered, she stepped out but couldn't find a towel. "Where's a towel?"

The female guard grabbed her arm, shoved her into the chair with straps, and held her while the male guard strapped her down.

"Hey, what's up with this? When do I get arraigned? I want to see the judge, now."

The two guards ignored her. The woman guard removed an electric shaver from a drawer and turned it on.

"Whoa, wait a minute. What are you going to do?" demanded Sarah in a panic.

The male guard grabbed her head in a viselike grip and the female guard started shaving her head.

"What are you doing? Stop. You don't have the right to do this. I want to see my attorney."

After the woman guard shaved off her hair, she removed a syringe from the table. Sarah's eyes widened in terror as the woman jabbed the needle into her arm. Everything began to move slowly and lopsided. She could see them undoing the straps, but her arms and legs felt like lead. They dragged her to an examination table. The last thing she remembered was the female guard looking down at her.

"The donor is ready now," said the guard.

———

Knotted Pine Lodge
101 E. Highway 163
Mexican Hat, Utah

AN HOUR LATER, the group once again sat in the small conference room at the lodge. Jake was elated that Ellie, Pam and Al were not hurt and warned her to take Roscoe with her wherever she went from now on even if store owners didn't like it. Roscoe and animals in general were believed to be able to sense when demons were around.

Sheriff Jefferson, Lieutenant Beggett, and Deputy Bridges sat with the group. The table was covered with crime scene photos and reports. A white board was set up on one side of the room which was also covered with photos with lines connecting them. Agent Pyle had compiled a list of occurrences to help make sense of what might be going on. "This is what we have so far," explained the FBI agent as he pointed to the photos. "A birdlike creature attacked a hiker in Northern Arizona, was killed, and subsequently stolen. A bearlike creature attacked a group of male campers and a middle-aged couple in the SUV here. Am I on track so far?"

Everyone in the group nodded. Agent Williams's cellphone rang so she stepped out to answer it.

Agent Pyle continued. "The bear was killed when it attacked us which tells us that these hybrids can be killed by anyone eventually. The group was then attacked by an unknown group of armed men. One local man and three assailants were subsequently killed. The unidentified bodies were stolen and a doctor in Bluff was murdered. The bear monster's corpse was taken from the vet clinic here as well and all the animals in the clinic were slaughtered. We have no proof that they are related except for the timing and that we believe they're some type of half breed. This tells us that someone is experimenting and trying to clone or breed demonic creatures. That makes six inno- cent citizens; three unknown assailants killed not counting the injured. On the other side, two full demons and two half-bred demons have been killed. I'd say the odds are not slanting our way."

"Thank you, Agent Pyle," said Sheriff Jefferson. He looked over at the others. "I think I can speak for everyone in this area and say that this is totally unacceptable. This is a quiet and peaceful commu- nity, not a war zone. I can't have demons or monsters killing people and destroying stores. We need to find out who these people are and what they are up to, and fast."

Agent Pyle noticed Deputy Bridges had a slight grin. "What's so amusing?" he asked sarcastically.

Deputy Bridges held up a piece of paper. "They may have gotten the bodies and the creature's carcass, but we still have all the gear they wore. I hadn't had a chance to load all of it into the storage room so it's still in the back of the SUV. When I was in the army I was stationed in Germany and remembered seeing those types of assault weapons. They're Heckler and Koch G3 assault rifles. These weapons aren't store bought, and certainly not here in the U.S."

"German Army rifles?" asked Sheriff Jefferson.

Deputy Bridges nodded. "Yes, sir. I can run these through the system and see if they show up."

"Do we have anyone around here with German ties?" asked Sheriff Jefferson.

"I don't recall but I'll do some checking," said Deputy Bridges.

"These men didn't just appear out of nowhere," said the sheriff. "They came from somewhere around here and we need to find out where."

Agent Williams came back in and sat down.

"So while you check any local links to this where do we go from here?" asked Agent Pyle.

"Arizona," said Agent Williams.

"Arizona?" asked Jake.

"Yep," said Agent Williams. "Oscar said that Sgt. Greymountain's father called and said he'd found something interesting."

———

Private Estate
Highway 160
South of Kayenta, Arizona

GERDA ENTERED the dining room and saw Priska already at the large table. She walked over and kissed her grandmother on the cheek. "Good evening, *Grossmutter.*"

Priska patted her granddaughter's hand. "How are you, my dear? Did you have a good day?"

Gerda went and sat down across from her and placed a silk

napkin in her lap. One of the servants brought her a bowl of soup. "Everything is going as planned. The tunnel is progressing along nicely. It won't be long before we reach it."

"That's wonderful. Soon we can notify those in Germany to get ready."

"Yes," answered Gerda with a smile. "And then we can start the process and begin a new world."

Priska smiled and nodded as she ate her soup. The servants brought in the main meal of veal and mushrooms. Both women ate in silence until they heard claws on marble as someone came down the hall. Without speaking Degen entered the dining room and sat down at the end of table, his huge wings tucked in behind him.

Priska looked up and smiled. "Degen dear, what a pleasant surprise. I didn't know you were joining us for dinner."

Degen smiled showing his sharp canine teeth. "I have been pleased with the progress of the tunnel, and my mission to retrieve the corpses was successful. I felt the need to spread some joy."

"That's lovely news," said Priska. "Isn't it, Gerda?"

Gerda merely looked up and nodded. "So, how did your plan to capture the two women go?" Gerda knew that the two demons that had been sent to kidnap the cowboy's two female friends hadn't reported back yet and she'd heard later that they were dead. Because of her hatred of Degen she took every opportunity to dig at him.

Degen looked up at Gerda from under his bushy tiger-like eyebrows. "Why must you try to ruin everything I do, human?"

Gerda gave him her most innocent look. "I just heard that they haven't returned and was wondering."

"Liar," yelled Degen and banged his fist on the table, rattling the dishes. "You know just as I heard that they're dead."

"Dead?" asked the elderly woman. She knew if she didn't say something the two of them would keep going at each other. "How? I thought the demon killer Taft was elsewhere."

Degen growled. "I don't know how those two women keep getting so lucky. Their luck can't hold forever and next time they won't be so fortunate."

"And what do you plan to do with the women when you capture them, my dear?" asked Priska.

Degen finished slurping his soup which he knew disgusted Gerda. "I think I'll use them as a trap for Taft, or maybe I'll use them as donors, or let them play with my pets."

Priska wiped her mouth with her satin napkin. "Are you sure you want to attract that man Taft?"

"I don't care. Soon all my plans will be complete. They can grovel at my feet."

———

Knotted Pine Lodge
101 E. Highway 163
Mexican Hat, Utah

JAKE, Viktor, and Agent Williams loaded their gear into the rental car. Agent Pyle decided to stay to keep working with Deputy Bridges, identifying where the weapons came from. Al, Pam, and Ellie also chose to remain in Mexican Hat since the others were supposed to return in a day or so after talking to the elder Grey-mountain. He had been vague about what he had found but insistent that they come.

Ellie and Pam stood by the car door while Jake loaded his suit-case. Deputy Bridges drove up and honked the horn. He climbed out and walked over to Jake carrying a large package.

"This came for you from Washington. I almost forgot to give it to you," explained the deputy.

Jake took the heavy box from him. He looked at the return address and saw it was from Deputy Director Ruiz. Jake looked up to say thanks, but Deputy Bridges had already turned away and had approached Agent Williams. Jake smiled and placed the box into the trunk and closed it. He turned to Ellie who was quietly watching Agent Williams and Deputy Bridges talk in whispers.

"I think Stephanie has an admirer," she said.

"Yep," answered Jake.

Ellie hugged and kissed him. "Please be careful."

Jake smiled down at her. "Me? You're the one battling demons in the souvenir shop." He then took on a more serious tone. "You need to be careful. We don't have all the pieces together so keep Roscoe close by."

"I will," said Ellie as her eyes misted over.

Jake bent down and rubbed Roscoe's fur. "You take care of her."

Roscoe wagged his tag and licked Jake's hand. Jake stood up and hugged Ellie once more. "See you in a day or so." Jake and Agent Williams climbed into the car that Viktor was driving.

"I'll be careful too, Jake," said Pam sarcastically.

———

Hampton Inn
120 Highway 160
Kayenta, Arizona

AFTER CROSSING INTO ARIZONA, the group pulled into a local motel in the city of Kayenta. With a population of about 4,900 people, Kayenta's located just south of Monument Valley and contained a few hotels and motels for visitors to the area. Williams paid for the rooms, and each went to their room, bone tired. Jake took a quick shower but even after lying in bed for over an hour he couldn't sleep. His mind was trying to unravel the many questions and he was worried about Ellie. He picked up his cellphone and was surprised when it rang in his hand. "I thought you'd be asleep," said Jake.

"I was worried about you," answered Ellie.

Jake chuckled. "I was just going to call you because I was worried about you."

Ellie laughed which made Jake feel better. He loved to hear her laugh.

"Where's Roscoe?" he asked.

"On constant watch," she said.

"He's on the bed snoring isn't he?" asked Jake sarcastically.

Ellie giggled. "I just couldn't go to sleep without hearing from you," said Ellie. "I guess I'm getting spoiled."

"It's fine, I don't mind," said Jake.

After the two talked a few minutes more, Jake hung up and was able to drift off to sleep.

———

THE NEXT MORNING, Jake met Agent Williams and Viktor in the express breakfast area for a quick meal before they headed to meet the two Greymountains. They'd agreed to meet them at the Arizona Highway Patrol office on Adot Road. The Native American police officer leaned up against the door jamb at the entrance when the FBI car pulled into the parking lot. "Welcome back," he said as he shook Jake's and Agent Williams's hand. He took a moment to take in the tall Russian wearing the full-length black leather jacket.

"I am Viktor Gordya, a friend of Jacob," explained Viktor.

Sgt. Greymountain smiled slightly and shook the big Russian's hand. Before anything else could be said, Elijah Greymountain came through the door carrying his walking stick, dressed in the same manner as before, white shirt, jeans, and boots. "Good morning, it's good for you to come all this way."

Jake shook the elder Navajo's hand. "We came because we knew you wouldn't call us unless it's important."

Elijah Greymountain took in the tall Russian at a glance. "*Dabropazhalavat.*"

"*Spasiba,*" answered Viktor. "I didn't know Native Americans spoke Russian?"

"I picked up a little on my travels," said Elijah Greymountain with a smile. "Are you working with the FBI?"

Viktor shook his head. "Nyet, I am here on other business." *This old Indian's more than he lets on*, thought Viktor.

"You're either very brave to be with these people or you haven't encountered any demon spirits yet."

Viktor didn't know if that was an insult or a compliment, so he shrugged. "I have dealt with several already. I am learning quickly."

They all trooped into one of the state patrol offices. "So, what do you have for us?" asked Jake. The elder pointed his staff towards the desert. "I found that creature's nest. There's a wall painting inside that might interest you. I called you because I can't make sense of it."

CHAPTER FOURTEEN

Criminal Investigations Division
Flagstaff Police Department
911 East Sawmill Road
Flagstaff, Arizona

DETECTIVE WARREN BRUTTEN sat at his desk and read through his stack of newly assigned cases. At thirty-seven years old he'd worked patrol for several years, then narcotics, and now in the detective office. He'd logged his new cases onto his computer when his phone rang and was informed from the front desk that a woman wanted to see him.

Detective Brutten walked to the front where a woman waiting impatiently. The five-foot-tall woman was thin, gaunt, used up, with stringy unwashed blonde hair. *Prostitute*, thought Detective Brutten of the woman. She looked vaguely familiar. "Can I help you?" he asked in a bored voice.

The woman jumped at the sound of his voice. "Officer Brutten?"

"Detective Brutten," he corrected. "You look vaguely familiar; do I know you?"

The woman looked around to see if anyone was watching. "You busted me a few years ago for some crack I had on me. I need your help."

Detective Brutten stared at the woman for a moment before he remembered her from a drug bust at the Motel 6 some years back when he was an officer in narcotics. "Your name is...Becky?"

"Beth."

"That's right, Beth, so how can I help you?"

Beth looked up at the six-foot tall, blond, detective. "Three of my friends have been kidnapped."

"I see...kidnapped."

"No, no, I'm serious," said Beth in a panic. "You have to believe me. I'm not crazy. Someone's taken them."

Detective Brutten sighed. "Ok, come on back and you can tell me about it." He led Beth back into the office area and made her sit in a chair next to his desk. Detective Brutten sat in his chair behind his desk, picked up a pen, and tried to look interested. "So, Beth, who kidnapped your friends?"

"I don't know."

Oh this is going to be great, thought Detective Brutten. "So how do you know they were kidnapped if you don't know who?"

Beth tapped her foot nervously and picked at her fingernails which were chewed down to the quick. "They got in a white van and never came back."

"Maybe they got a ride to another city?"

"No, no, none of 'em ever came back. Officer Brutten, you have to find them."

"It's Detective Brutten, and you're telling me that each of your friends got into a van at different times and never came back?"

"Yes, yes, that's what happened."

Detective Brutten scratched his ear in thought. "Is it the same van?"

Beth nodded.

"License plate?"

Beth shook her head.

"What's the description of the van?"

Beth thought for a minute. "It's just a white van without any windows."

"A panel van?"

"Yeah, like a work van of some kind."

"Did these girls get in the van voluntarily or were they forced?" asked the detective as he wrote down the information given by Beth.

Beth shifted her weight in the chair nervously. "Well... yeah... of course... you know... they're working girls, but I'm telling you they never came back. You know, usually they come right back in ten or fifteen minutes."

"What were their names?

"It's Chrisee, TJ, and Sarah."

Detective Brutten rubbed his forehead as he wrote the names down. "I need their full names."

"I don't know their full names, just their street names," answered Beth. "But you got to look for them."

Detective Brutten obtained physicals descriptions of the women from Beth then escorted her back to the front. "I have what you gave me on them. I'll check into it and see what I can find out."

"Thank you, Officer Brutten, thank you, I don't have a cellphone, so I'll call you from a payphone in a few days and see what you found out."

"It's Detective Brutten."

Beth left and Detective Brutten went to his desk and promptly threw the paper in the trash. *Crazy crack head woman.*

Eastern Nevada

DEGEN ARRIVED at a dilapidated building in a deserted area of Nevada. A huge sand colored horned toad demon sat just inside the door and upon Degen's approach, threw itself prostrate on the ground. Without even a glance, Degen stepped on and over the prone demon.

The inside of the building was barren except for a huge hole in the floor that angled down like a ramp into the ground. Degen walked down into a tunnel that led deep underground.

At the bottom the tunnel leveled out into a larger tunnel thirty feet wide by twenty feet high that led off into the darkness. Another demon stood guard at the bottom who also fell to the ground in obedience when Degen approached. Without even acknowledging the prostrate demon, Degen opened his large bat like wings and took flight down the tunnel leaving the prostrated demon behind. Degen passed miles and miles of darkened tunnel that intersected larger caverns that led off in other directions before finally coming to an opening.

It was a temporary staging in a large natural cavern under the eastern Nevada desert. The air smelled of sulfur, ashes, and sweat. Several large vats of disgusting smelling muck used for food sat off to one side. Degen took a deep breath of the stale air mixed with the other pungent odors. *Now this is a pleasant smell*, thought Degen. He'd quickly tired of the clean fresh air from the surface and the tidy mansion where Fraulein Priska and that sassy mouthed Gerda lived. *That will all change soon enough.* He heard digging, cursing, and screeching coming from another tunnel that led off into the dark. Degen smiled and stomped down the tunnel to the source of the noise. The tunnel ended in a sea of workers digging and clawing at the rock. He approached a huge bright red monstrosity with several arms all holding whips and watching the workers. The thing had an almost armor type skin, a huge lobster looking head, and a large scar that ran from the top of its head down across its face making the demon's face seem crooked. One eye was higher than the other and the horns that protruded from the back of its head. It grunted when Degen approached.

"When will we reach it?" asked Degen.

"Soon, lord," said the thing.

"That's not good enough," growled Degen.

"We need more workers, my vile lord."

Degen shook his snout. "We can't afford to take any more donors from the local areas to make more workers."

"When we finally find it, it will be a pleasure to see it used against the humans," commented the monster with a voice as deep as Hades.

"Yes, it will be a glorious day." Degen pointed at the workers. "Now, beat them more, and feed them less. I want it within a few days, or I'll find someone that can." With that said Degen turned and left.

The huge beast frowned and turned back to the hundreds of creatures that were digging into the rock tunnel. The thing raised the whips with all six arms and roared. "Faster, dig, dig faster, or die."

———

East of Highway 163
Monument Valley, Arizona

THE HELICOPTER DROPPED the group off on the top of the mesa several hundred yards from the creature's nest. The two Navajos along with Agent Williams, Jake and Viktor hiked over to the edge where the ledge protruded.

"The nest is in a small cave set back from the ledge," explained Elijah Greymountain. "Be careful dropping down to the ledge. One wrong step or the next one will be a long way down."

Jake went first and dropped down onto the small ledge and immediately his nose twitched from the lingering scent of the half demon mixed with decomposing flesh. He clicked on his flashlight and went inside. Agent Williams and Elijah Greymountain climbed down and followed Jake inside. Viktor and Sgt. Greymountain remained up on the mesa due to the small size of the cave. Jake stepped carefully over small animal skeletons and carcasses while Agent Williams snapped photos of the inside of the cave.

"The drawings are on the wall on the left," pointed out the elder Navajo.

Jake shined his light at the wall which lit up the strange drawings. They studied the wall while Agent Williams took more photos.

"All the paintings are red," commented Agent Williams.

Elijah Greymountain nodded. "I noticed that too, probably dried blood left over from the small animals it killed. It obviously used whatever was available."

Jake squatted down and looked closer as if getting nearer would help make sense of it. "It looks like demons digging in some sort of cave with rock formations just like you explained."

Elijah Greymountain reached up and pointed to a larger demon with many arms holding crooked lines. "I'd say those are whips. The thing's driving them to dig."

Jake rubbed his jaw in thought. "So, demons are making demons or half breed demons dig under protest."

"Forced slavery," added Agent Williams.

Jake glanced over at the Navajo. "Any ideas?"

Elijah Greymountain shook his head, "No, but let's get out of here; this smell's almost unbearable."

"I second that," said Agent Williams as she followed him towards the entrance.

Jake remained for a few minutes staring at the wall. *What would they be digging for or to?*

After climbing back up to the top, Sgt. Greymountain radioed for the helicopter to return to pick them up. While waiting the three explained to Sgt. Greymountain and Viktor what they found in the cave.

"So why would a half demon creature paint pictures in blood on a cave wall?" thought Agent Williams out loud.

Elijah Greymountain spoke up. "Why does anyone paint pictures whether on a cave wall or on a canvas? To tell a story or express their feelings."

"But why paint something that no one would ever see?" asked Viktor.

"Maybe it hoped someone would see it eventually," commented Agent Williams while she checked the digital photos on her camera. "It might be years before someone found this cave though."

Jake opened a bottle of water and took a long drink when he suddenly thought of something. "What if the thing decided to show someone the paintings?"

Elijah Greymountain poked the ground with his staff in thought.

"Are you saying that this bird creature wasn't trying to kill that hiker?"

"The Parkers did say the thing kept screeching at them," said Sgt. Greymountain.

Jake took off his dusty cowboy hat and rubbed his forehead with his forearm. "Maybe it grabbed Parker to take him to the cave and show him."

"And the Parkers mistook it for an attack?" added Agent Williams.

Viktor stared off towards the mountains in the distance in thought. "Do you think it tried to warn them about the digging?"

Sgt. Greymountain sat on one of the large rocks. "Why would a demon warn humans? I thought they hated humans?"

Elijah Greymountain touched his grandson on the shoulder. "But if they're half demon that still means they're part human so maybe it didn't like what was going on?"

As the thumping of the helicopter warned them of its approach Jake shrugged. "It just adds more questions."

———

Knotted Pine Lodge
101 E. Highway 163
Mexican Hat, Utah

AGENT PYLE SAT in the conference room and waited impatiently for the responses on his laptop. Deputy Bridges stood over by a side table and poured a cup of coffee from a small coffee maker that the motel had provided them.

"I wish this thing ran faster," complained Agent Pyle.

Deputy Bridges chuckled. "I'm sorry but our Wi-Fi doesn't seem to run as fast way out here."

"How do you get anything done on time out here?"

"We learn to be patient. Things don't run at a fast pace as the big city." Deputy Bridges sat down in one of the other chairs and propped his feet up on the table. "So how long have you been in this monster hunting unit?"

Agent Pyle chuckled to himself at the new version of their unit's name. "This is my first assignment."

"I heard you played pro ball?"

"Yep, several years back, with the Ravens."

"I see, so how well do you know Agent Williams?" asked Deputy Bridges trying to sound as passive as possible.

"I met her on the way to the airport when we were coming here," explained Agent Pyle. "But I've heard stories."

Deputy Bridges raised an eyebrow. "What kind of stories?"

Agent Pyle tried to hide an amused smile. "Oh, just that she's tough on men. She dates them until she can conquer them, then throws them away like rag dolls."

Deputy Bridges sat motionless for a moment before he noticed the grin Agent Pyle couldn't hide. "Funny."

The laptop beeped. Agent Pyle pulled up the email from the office in Washington. "The weapons don't show to be stolen in the United States, but Interpol hasn't come through. It also says that the only German influence in this area is a company that leases part of the coal mining in the black hills."

Deputy Bridges sat up and came around to look over Agent Pyle's shoulder. "I don't recall any German companies down in that area, but that is across the border in Arizona."

Agent Pyle typed on the laptop for a few moments then pointed to the screen. "The land belongs to the Navajos but the company leasing it is called Wargwolf."

Deputy Bridges shook his head. "Just because some German company is leasing a mining operation in Arizona doesn't mean they had the guns or bred monsters."

"I agree, but I'll ask our analysts in D.C. to look into it anyway," said Agent Pyle.

IT WAS EVENING WHEN JAKE, Viktor, and Agent Williams returned from Arizona. The group went to dinner in the lodge's restaurant while they explained to the others about the discovery of the paintings on the wall of the cave.

Al was wide eyed. "So, you think this half demon bird creature was trying to communicate with the Parkers about something that's going on in this area?"

Jake shook his head. "We aren't saying that as the truth. We are just bouncing ideas around, so don't print that."

Ellie wiped her mouth with a napkin. "Any idea why a group of demons would be digging?"

"Nope, we were hoping that Agent Pyle might have found something related to it."

Agent Pyle put his knife down after cutting his plate of pork chops. "The only possible link to the bear and the German guns was a German company that leases one of the coal mining operations in Arizona."

"Digging for coal?" asked Pam.

"No, I doubt that a group of demons would be digging at the same spot as coal mining," said Agent Williams.

"But demons are invisible so no one would see them," answered Al.

Jake frowned. "The hole they'd make wouldn't be."

"Good Point."

"I've asked our analyst at the bureau to run a check on this company anyway," explained Agent Pyle. "It's just for precaution to cover all our bases."

"And we don't know for sure that the bird demon is even related to the bear one," said Ellie. "It could just be coincidence."

"There are no such things as coincidences in our line of work," said Viktor.

Criminal Investigations Division
Flagstaff Police Department

911 East Sawmill Road
Flagstaff, Arizona

DETECTIVE AMANDA LOWDEN walked by Detective Brutten's desk with a piece of paper. "Hey, Warren, didn't you have a crazy woman come in here the other day saying someone in a van was snatching women off the street?"

Detective Brutten rolled his eyes. "Yeah, what did she do now?"

Detective Lowden shook her head. "It's not her. I got this report that someone was trying to force a woman into a white van near the laundry mat down by the truck stop."

"What was the vehicle description?"

"It says it was a white Ford Econoline work van." Detective Lowden handed him the incident report and walked off. Detective Brutten read through the report. *Could there be a connection?* He knew he'd screwed up because the janitors empty the trash every day. Detective Brutten looked over by the trash can and was thankful he'd missed the trash can when he tossed it away. He picked up the wadded paper containing the names of the three missing women and started running background checks.

———

Wargwolf Private Estate
Highway 160
South of Kayenta, Arizona

PRISKA SAT in her wheelchair in her suite reading by the light of a small table lamp when she heard a soft knock on her door, and a moment later Gerda entered. "Sorry to bother you *Grossmutter*, but I need to talk to you."

Priska placed her book on her lap. "Of course, child, come in."

Gerda came and sat in a straight back chair next to the old woman. "We may have a problem. I've received word from our corporate office that the FBI is looking into our company."

Priska sat for a moment and stared at her gnarled arthritic hands.

"We are so close; do you have any idea how they knew to look into Wargwolf?"

"*Nein*, but this could jeopardize our operation before it's finished."

"What could jeopardize my operation?" said a deep gravelly voice.

Gerda spun around to find Degen standing by the door. "The FBI is looking into our company holdings. I thought you and your goon squad got all the evidence that could lead them to us."

Degen growled low down in his chest and stepped toward Gerda. "I'm sure one of your stupid humans left something behind that led them to us."

"Degen dear, any idea what we should do?" asked Priska. She knew if she didn't intercede, they'd be at it all evening. "How close are we to finishing the dig?"

Degen stopped. His yellow eyes remained on Gerda while he smiled at Priska. "The reason I came in was to inform you that the operation was a success. We have it."

Gerda's smiled brightened. "So, it was there after all that time. Will it still work?"

"Of course, it will still work, ignorant human, we may have to upgrade some of the mechanisms but it's still intact."

Priska sighed and then smiled. "That's wonderful news. Thanks to the Americans' stupidity at leaving it there, it's now our blessing. Now, what do you want to do about the FBI?"

Degen thought for a moment while scratching an itch on his arm with one of his claws. He pulled a small insect from his fur and popped it into his mouth like an M and M candy. "I think I'll set a trap for Taft and his FBI friends that will end their meddling."

"Degen my dearest, might that draw Prince Zardren's attention; after all it is his territory."

"Bah, that moron wouldn't know anything unless someone hit him in the snout with it. My plan will be completed before he even knows what's happening, then Zardren and the rest of the princes of the air can grovel along with what's left of humanity."

———

Crack Canyon
23 miles West of Mexican Hat
San Juan County, Utah

DUE TO THE lack of leads and mounting frustration, Jake explained to Ellie after dinner that he wanted to talk to one of the local demons in the hope that maybe one of them could shed some light on their investigation. He also knew that it was not helpful to talk to demons because telling the truth is nearly impossible for them, but they needed to try anything they could to get a lead.

Knowing that demons hang around drug and narcotic users Deputy Bridges gave them directions to the local drug hang out in the less populated county area. Agents Williams and Pyle, Viktor, and Jake drove down a dirt road to a remote obscure canyon area known to the locals as "crack canyon". Jake told Agent Williams to pull over to the side of the road before they got too close. He climbed out and retrieved a carton from the back of the SUV. It was the box Deputy Director Ruiz had mailed him and inside it was several boxes of ammunition which he split between them.

"I asked Oscar to do a little experiment for me," explained Jake as he opened one of the boxes. "The lab in D.C. made semi-jacketed hollow point rounds embedded with cemetery soil."

Both FBI agents opened their ammo boxes and examined the bullets. "These are bullets with dirt in it?" asked Agent Williams with a frown.

Jake chuckled. "Yes, the bullet's real but the center is embedded with crushed cemetery dust."

"And that helps me how?" asked Agent Pyle.

"We've learned that demons can't touch holy ground which includes cemeteries. Our hope is that it's toxic to them somehow. These rounds may not kill them but if you put enough in them, it may cause them enough pain or trouble to stop them. Oscar had half of the rounds made for your 40s and the other made for my 45."

The two agents began loading their ammo clips with the new rounds. "Has this been tested yet?" asked Agent Williams.

"No," answered Jake reluctantly.

"Great," said Agent Pyle sarcastically. "Let the Black man and the female test the dirty bullets."

Agent Williams smiled while she racked one of the special rounds into her handgun. "You know what always happens in the movies, Terrell, the Black guy is the first one to go."

"I feel so much better now," answered Agent Pyle as he pulled the slide back on his weapon and chambered one of the new bullets.

Jake handed Viktor one of his 45s. "You can use one of mine since the rounds won't fit your Stechkin APS pistol."

Viktor nodded and examined the Colt 45. "I can't believe you still carry these outdated WWII designed relics. Why not get something newer and lighter?"

"I'm still alive," answered Jake.

Agent Williams drove the SUV onto the road and down into "crack canyon". The only two buildings were a dilapidated trailer and a small wooden shack. An old pickup and a dusty Harley motorcycle sat outside.

The group climbed out of the vehicle. The two FBI agents headed toward the trailer while Jake and Viktor walked over to the shack. Jake paused to listen at the door even though he knew that if someone was inside, they would've heard their SUV pull up. Jake reached, turned the doorknob slowly, found it unlocked, so with a glance at Viktor he opened the door and stepped inside. The inside stank of sweat, urine, and who knows what else. The room was illuminated by a single light bulb from a lamp on a side table. Two mattresses were on the floor. A male and female were laying on one of them; the man looked up at Jake and Viktor. "You cops?" asked the pale man with a nose piercing and numerous tattoos.

"Nope," said Jake. "I'm looking for information."

"Dude," said the stringy hair blonde woman with bleeding sores on her arms and face, "we don't know nothin'."

"I'm not looking for it from you," said Jake as he looked around the room for any sign of a demonic creature.

"Who then, man?" asked the tattooed man with the glazed over eyes.

Jake turned and headed out the door followed by Viktor who turned to the two junkies as he closed the door. "We're looking for demons."

"Wow," said the woman. "That's totally cool."

Jake glanced at Viktor who just shook his head in disgust.

———

AGENTS WILLIAMS and Pyle quietly approached the trailer. The door to the trailer was missing and the inside was dark. Agent Williams pulled her small flashlight from her coat pocket and clicked it on while at the same time she pulled her weapon. Agent Pyle followed suit while Agent Williams made a quick look into the trailer, shining her light around the interior before jerking back out. "No one's in the front room," she whispered. Agent Pyle nodded, and they quickly stepped inside the trailer. Agent Williams stepped to the left while Agent Pyle went right, and each shined their lights around the interior of the trailer. The living room held two old couches that were missing bottom cushions and had stuffing coming out of numerous places. A small kitchen table sat in the middle of the adjacent kitchen covered with empty match books, old candles, and small clear baggies used to hold crack cocaine or heroin. A used, moldy refrigerator without a door stood over by the hallway.

Agent Williams pointed towards the rooms on the kitchen end of the trailer. The two agents slowly worked their way down the hallway and checked each room but only found dirty, stained mattresses on the floor. The bathroom did not have any running water, and the toilet and bathtub were overflowing with human feces.

"How can these people live like this?" whispered Agent Pyle.

Agent Williams shrugged and moved on down the hall to the last bedroom. The end room was empty, so the two agents worked their way back to the living room, which was still dark and deathly quiet. They turned down the hall, checked the first room, and the other bathroom which was in the same decrepit condition as the first. The master bedroom was at the end of the hall, but the door was closed so Agent Pyle slowly opened it and they immediately smelled the stench of sulfur, dirt, and ashes. Agent Pyle expected a demon to be waiting but was surprised when nothing jumped out of the dark. He stepped into the room as he shined his light around the room and suddenly felt nothing beneath his left foot. He would've fallen if Agent Williams hadn't grabbed his jacket and pulled him back at the last minute. The two agents shined their lights down and saw that most of the floor was gone and was replaced by a huge hole.

Agent Williams leaned over and shined her light into the large hole approximately ten feet across in a room which was only twelve feet wide. Her light disappeared into the darkness indicating that the bottom was beyond the beam of her light.

Agent Pyle whistled softly. "Wow, that's one deep hole."

Agent Williams snickered and shined her light around the room. The walls were covered in a slimy substance mixed with…blood. "I have a bad feeling about this room."

Agent Pyle nodded. "Nothing here right now though."

As the two agents glanced around the room, they felt a sudden change in the air. A breeze came up from the hole along with a huge list of unbelievable smells. Agent Williams leaned over and shined her light into the hole, but nothing lit up, however a few seconds later she saw a set of eyes…large glowing yellow eyes. "Uh oh," she said.

Agent Pyle leaned over and shined his light into the hole and saw the same set of yellow eyes coming up at them at an alarming rate. "Not good," he added.

"Run," snapped Agent Williams.

Both agents turned and ran through the open doorway just as something large burst from the hole followed by a loud hissing noise. Agent Williams glanced over her shoulder at the end of the hall to see the large set of yellow eyes staring down the hall at her. She turned and fired three rounds at the thing which didn't seem to have any immediate effect…and probably made it mad. Agent Pyle also fired a couple of rounds at the thing as it slammed against the door frame, splintering it into pieces. They then noticed that the rounds had caused the thing's skin to smoke from sizzling flesh wounds. The wounds however didn't slow it down as the behemoth slithered down the hall tearing pieces of the wall loose. It opened its mouth and displayed an ugly set of fangs. By now the two agents realized they were being pursued by some type of huge demonic snake and fled for the door in hopes of escape.

As they reached the living room and turned at an angle towards the door, the creature sped up then slid into the living room. The atrocious snake creature slammed into the kitchen wall due to the confined area while Agent Pyle fired off a couple more rounds.

"Don't waste your rounds in here," yelled Agent Williams. "Just run."

JAKE AND VIKTOR walked to the side of the shack to see if anything was around back when they heard gunfire erupt from inside the trailer. They both grabbed for their weapons and sprinted towards the trailer as Agents Williams and Pyle dashed out the door.

"Snake, snake," yelled Agent Pyle.

"Giant snake," added Agent Williams.

Right behind the two agents a huge brown and black snake rammed the door opening, smashing a huge hole in the trailer as it came through. Jake and Viktor fired their handguns at the reptile.

"The rounds aren't having much effect except making it angry," explained Agent Pyle as he turned away from the door.

The hellish atrocity slithered out of the now wrecked trailer and bowed up to stare down at the humans that were frantically firing at it. Jake fired a couple of rounds into the soft underside of the thing resulting in a high-pitched screech. "Shoot the exposed underbelly; it seems to hurt it more," shouted Jake.

The other three joined in and fired round after round into the underside of the reptile. Fortunately, the bullet wounds caused major injuries that bled as the abomination screeched in pain.

"It's working," exclaimed Agent Williams.

As if to respond to her the creature hissed and spit clear liquid venom at Agent Williams who held up her arm to block the spray. As soon as it hit her sleeve and front of her jacket, the jacket began to smolder.

ACID.

Agent Williams jumped back and jerked on her jacket to get it off. The vile snake lunged toward Agent Williams, but Agent Pyle shoved her to the ground and fired up at the thing. One second Agent Pyle was standing there and the next he was gone.

"The monster's eaten Terrell," growled Agent Williams as she dropped her jacket to the ground.

The remaining three continued to fire, reload and fire in hopes of killing it before Agent Pyle smothered from lack of air. The monster hissed and screeched as it turned toward Viktor. It spat acid venom at him, but he was able to leap safely behind their SUV.

"We've got to stop it," bellowed Jake to the others. "Pyle can't survive much longer in there."

They heard muted gunfire. "Pyle must be shooting it from inside," said Viktor. "Keep it up."

They kept pouring more cemetery rounds into the beast while dodging acid venom, when Jake caught a glance of a figure on top of the trailer wearing all white. Jake dashed out in front of the fiendish snake making it face him. The distraction allowed the white-clad figure to leap onto the back of the monster's head which made the thing twist and turn violently. Like a cowboy at a rodeo the white-clad figure hung on then swung a huge golden sword around and plunged it down into the top of the head of the monstrosity. The snake collapsed immediately to the ground and the heavenly figure known as Malachy climbed off the dead monster.

Agent Williams pointed to the middle of the snake. "Agent Pyle's inside that thing."

Malachy spun around, grabbed his sword, pulled it from the dead reptile and slit the belly of the beast open. Horrid smelling intestines and other unknown organs sloshed out along with Agent Pyle. He was covered in a brown slimy liquid and didn't move for several seconds before he started choking and coughing up brown liquid.

Agent Williams knelt beside him. "Are you ok, Terrell?"

Agent Pyle was on his hands and knees coughing up more brown liquid. "Hell no, I've been eaten by a giant snake. What do you think?"

Agent Williams sighed in relief and glanced up at Jake and Viktor. "He'll be ok."

Agent Pyle slowly got to his feet and glanced around.

Jake turned to Malachy. "Thanks for the help."

Malachy smiled warmly. "I'm glad I was here in time."

Agent Pyle looked up at the giant golden skinned angel. "Okay, am I seeing things or is this guy golden?"

"Why, Terrell, that's the man that saved your butt," said Agent Williams with a grin. "His name's Malachy and he's what most people call an angel."

Agent Pyle froze and stared at Malachy. "You mean angel as in from heaven?"

"Yep," said Jake.

Agent Pyle looked over at Malachy. "Yeah...well, ok...uh, thanks for the help."

Malachy smiled as he slid his golden sword back into the multi-jeweled sheath. "You're welcome." He turned to the others. "I came to tell you about some suspicious demon activity in eastern Nevada near the air force base but we're not sure what they're up to. Be careful and God be with you." The heavenly man then disappeared.

Viktor's only reaction to the heavenly giant was a raised eyebrow.

The two druggies shuffled out of the shack and stared at the decomposing giant snake.

"We heard all the shooting," said the woman. "Wow, man, you killed Plumbob?"

"Plumbob?" asked Viktor.

"Yeah, that's his name."

The man stumbled over and pointed at the trailer. "These really cool looking alien dudes with wings bring women here sometimes and put them in the trailer. I think they're kinda like sacrificing virgins to a god. We heard one say the name Plumbob so we named it that. Why'd you kill it?"

Agent Pyle growled. "It tried to eat me."

"Bummer."

"Plumbob?" said Jake as he rubbed his chin.

"Any idea who or what Plumbob is?" asked Agent Pyle as he peeled off his jacket and tried to scrape off as much goop as he could.

"I'll give the information to Pam," said Jake. "As a newspaper editor she has some contacts and avenues to check. Maybe she can turn up something."

When they approached the SUV, they saw that the paint on the side that had been sprayed by the devil snake was ruined. "I'm glad I took out that extra insurance," remarked Agent Williams dryly.

"We know one thing for sure though," said Jake. "Those rounds will do some damage to a regular size demon. It may just stop a smaller one completely."

As they climbed into the SUV, Agent Williams sniffed the air in Agent Pyle's direction. "Why, Terrell, I think you've discovered a new stench. Do we have to let you ride inside smelling like that?"

"Funny, Stephanie, real funny," muttered Agent Pyle. "Cemetery dirt bullets, a giant demon snake, and she's making jokes."

As the Escalade drove away, a small furry bat-like creature with glowing yellow eyes watched the taillights disappear into the fading darkness then took flight and flew off in the other direction.

———

Knotted Pine Lodge
101 East Highway 163
Mexican Hat, Utah

PAM WAS TYPING on her laptop in their room, and Ellie watched TV while they kept an eye out for the group's return when Roscoe barked as they heard the SUV pull up. They left the room to meet them outside and Pam knocked on Al's door. "They're back."

Al followed them out to the side parking lot where Agent

Williams had parked the Cadillac Escalade. As they approached, they could see by the parking lot lighting that the paint was ruined on one side of the vehicle.

"What happened to the Escalade?" asked Ellie as Jake climbed out of the passenger side.

Jake smiled and rubbed Roscoe's neck. "We had a little run in with a snake."

"A snake did that?" asked Pam.

"A giant demon snake that could spit acid." said Agent Williams who was carrying what was left of her jacket and held it up for them to see the damage.

"A giant demon snake? Acid?" exclaimed Al. "Did you get a picture? Did it talk? What happened to it?"

"It attacked Agent Williams and Agent Pyle. We were fighting it off when Malachy killed it," explained Jake.

"Malachy was there?" asked Al. "What did he say? What did he do? How did he kill the snake?" He kept asking questions faster than anyone could even answer.

Ellie ignored Al and hugged Jake. "What did Malachy tell you?"

"Not too much. He said there's some unusual activity over in Nevada," answered Jake. He turned to Pam. "Can you see what you can find out about someone called Plumbob?"

"Plumbob?" repeated Pam. "I'll see what I can find out."

Agent Pyle came around from the other side of the SUV with Viktor. The slime had dried and was a yellowish-brown crust that covered his clothes. The smell followed.

"Oh, my goodness," said Ellie jokingly. "Terrell, what happened to you?"

"What is that awful smell?" asked Pam as she stepped back to get away from the smell.

"That stupid giant snake swallowed me," grumbled Agent Pyle. "I'm never going to get this smell off me."

Al was ecstatic. "A demon snake swallowed you? Like Jonah and the whale? Can I take a picture?"

Agent Pyle turned and glared at Al. "No, no pictures." He

stomped off towards the room. "I'll be in the shower for the next two hours if anyone needs me."

"And the bullets Oscar sent worked," explained Agent Williams.

Ellie raised an eyebrow. "What bullets?"

"I'll explain later but we may have found a way for the average person to injure or even disable demons."

CHAPTER FIFTEEN

Wargwolf Private Estate
Highway 160
South of Kayenta, Arizona

DEGEN SAT in one of the observation rooms in the sub-basement of the facility. He was watching one of the experiments as it clawed at the walls and howled at the ceiling when a furry bat-like devil flittered into the room and sat on the table next to Degen. It spoke softly into the tiger demon's ear and then flew back out of the room. Degen smiled and clicked his sharp claws together.

The stupid humans took the bait.

He reached over and flipped a switch on a control panel with a single claw. A sudden hiss sounded as a cloud of cyanide gas was sent into the cell killing the experiment in seconds as Degen watched with glee.

———

Knotted Pine Lodge
101 East Highway 163

Mexican Hat, Utah

JAKE HAD JUST FINISHED GETTING DRESSED for breakfast when he heard a soft knock on his door. He opened the door to see his beautiful girlfriend standing with a serious frown.

"Pam wants to see you. It's important."

Jake followed Ellie down the hall to their room. Pam was sitting at the room's round table with her laptop open. She looked up at Jake. "I've been checking into the name Plumbob. You're not going to like this, but the only thing associated with that name is nuclear testing."

"Did you say...nuclear testing?"

"Yep, from 1951 to 1992 the U.S. government tested about 928 nuclear weapons and these tests were conducted in eastern Nevada which is now the Nellis Air Force Base bombing range. They used code names for these tests, and one was called Operation Plumbob."

It took a moment for Jake to soak in the information. "Are you saying that demons are involved in nuclear weapons?"

Pam shrugged and pointed at the screen on the laptop. "I don't know that; all I know is the information that I've got about Plumbob."

Jake felt like he'd just been kicked in the gut. "This is a whole new twist. We need to get everyone together."

———

AFTER BREAKFAST, the group met in the small conference room to go over what they'd learned with the sheriff's department. They all sat around a large oval shaped table.

"A giant snake?" asked a flabbergasted Lieutenant Beggett who sat at the end of the table next to Deputy Bridges. "Here in our county? Eating women?"

Agent Pyle nodded. He felt like he'd scrubbed off several layers of skin to get the smell off. "The damned thing swallowed me and if it hadn't been for a huge angel, I'd be dead."

Deputy Bridges tipped his chair back on two legs with a coffee cup in one hand. "If I hadn't seen those other creatures, I wouldn't have believed it. So, what did you find out?"

Agent Williams sat across the table from the deputy. "The snake didn't tell us anything. It never spoke. What we found out was from two doped up freaks who said they heard one of the demons say the name Plumbob. Jake's angel friend said demons are doing something in eastern Nevada so we're just connecting the dots."

Lieutenant Beggett looked up after writing notes. "So why would they be feeding women to a giant snake?"

"I think they're using the women to breed these half demons," brought up Agent Williams.

"And when they're done with these women, they feed them to the snake?" asked Pam with a shiver.

Agent Williams nodded. "That would be my guess."

"How gruesome," said Al. "So where do you go from here?"

Agent Williams held up her hand for silence and glanced down the table at Viktor. "I think because of national security and the sensitivity of this we need to know where Agent Gordya fits into this before we go any further."

Viktor sat at the other end drinking his morning coffee in silence. He didn't respond immediately to Agent Williams except to set his coffee cup down. His ice blue eyes remained unemotional.

Before Jake could speak up in Viktor's defense, Agent Williams explained. "Jake, I know that you and Viktor go way back. I know that he helped save Ellie and her friends earlier this week but as an agent of our government I must know where Viktor stands in this thing. He's not given us any idea why he's here or what his plans are, so I think we need to hear from him before we go forward with him here."

The room was quiet for a moment before Viktor cleared his throat. He laid his huge hands flat on the table. "*Da*, I have to agree with Agent Williams. She has no reason to trust me. I've told Jake why I'm here but asked him to keep it confidential.

"I would never have believed these creatures existed until I experienced it myself and especially now after what your angel friend explained." He turned to Pam. "I also did some checking with my sources. I would imagine you found out that Plumbob was some sort of nuclear testing from years ago in eastern Nevada." Viktor paused for a moment and took a drink of coffee.

Lieutenant Beggett and Deputy Bridges both looked dumb-founded and turned to look at the others who nodded in agreement.

Viktor continued. "My mission is to obtain a small box that was stolen from a warehouse in Russia. What seemed like an easy task has turned into something much bigger than all of us if this informa-tion is true and implicates what we all think it does." Viktor looked around the room at the others. His face was like granite. "To begin with in 1946 this small box was kept separate from several other larger boxes that were buried near Berlin."

Pam asked the question everyone was thinking. "What was in the boxes?"

"The boxes contained the remains of Adolph Hitler and Eva Braun."

A stunned silence filled the room. Al's mouth dropped open.

"Five crates remained buried there until the 1950s when the KGB secretly dug them up and burned them completely to ash in a secret location in Russia. The small box I'm looking for was placed in a warehouse and it contained several bones belonging only to Hitler. My job is to find that box and return it to Russia."

"But why was the small box separated from the rest of the remains?" asked Ellie.

Viktor shook his head. "I don't know, just that the box had been in the warehouse after the war until it was stolen."

Deputy Bridges leaned forward and put his coffee cup down on the table. "Why do you think a group of demons took it?"

"I don't know that either, but a security guard was killed, literally ripped to pieces during the theft." Viktor looked over at Jake. "I came to talk to Jacob to confirm that it was demonic involvement."

Everyone looked at Jake who nodded.

"When I came here, I didn't know if this was related to your investigation but added to the fact that there may be a German connection in your case makes me believe more that it's all tied together. I just don't know how yet."

The group sat quietly for a few moments as the information soaked in.

"I'll need to inform the deputy director of this addition to the case," explained Agent Williams as she wrote some notes on a pad.

Viktor nodded.

"What would anyone, even demons want with Hitler's bones?" asked Al.

Ellie tapped her pencil on the table in thought. "In some religious sects the bones have a certain power or authority. Some grind the bones to be used as medicines, or aphrodisiacs."

"I don't think demons would need the bones for that, so..." asked Jake.

"They can extract DNA from it, can't they?" asked Deputy Bridges.

Agent Williams sat back in her chair and drummed her fingers on the table. "Yes, I believe so and knowing that an unknown group along with demons are mixing demon and human DNA, so why not Hitler's."

"I hope you're not thinking what I'm thinking," said Deputy Bridges. "These monsters are trying to make another Hitler?"

Jake nodded sadly. "It sure sounds like they are, except they may be trying to make a half demon half human Hitler."

Agent Williams got up from the table with her phone in her hand. "I'll call Oscar immediately and see what he can find out about nuclear testing during Operation Plumbob and that a group of demons may be trying to reincarnate Hitler. This will make his day."

As Agent Williams left the room to make her phone call Jake rubbed his eyes but didn't look up when he spoke. "From here we need to find out where in eastern Nevada these devils are digging, for what, and what it has to do with nuclear testing."

"*Da*, and how it ties to the incidents here," said Viktor.

"I'll check with other agencies," said Deputy Bridges. "If they are experimenting with DNA, where would they get women to use as test subjects?"

"Probably from any of the larger cities like Flagstaff, Phoenix, or Tucson," said Lt. Beggett.

"And we're still waiting on Interpol on the German weapons information," added Agent Pyle.

"It sounds like we get a trip to Nevada," said Jake.

————

FBI Headquarters, Washington, D.C.
Office of Deputy Director of Paranormal Activities
935 Pennsylvania Avenue Northwest
Washington D.C.

A LIGHT RAIN fell in Washington D.C. which did nothing to help the mood of Deputy Director Oscar Ruiz. After hearing from Agent Williams about a potential nuclear involvement he'd made a routine call to the Federal Records Management that supports the National Nuclear Security Administration (NNSA) program. Deputy Director Ruiz's phone rang, and he saw the caller ID showed it to be the FBI director.

"Oscar," said FBI Director Chisom. "Be in the situation room in thirty minutes."

————

TWENTY MINUTES LATER, Deputy Director Ruiz entered the 5,000 square foot White House situation room. He'd never been inside the famous intelligence and crisis room which is more of a small complex with offices, a small kitchen, and room for thirty personnel who monitor world events twenty-four hours a day. Deputy Director Ruiz walked over to a long oval table surrounded by black leather chairs used for meetings. The room was covered in wood panels that held numerous flat panel televisions.

Waiting inside with FBI Director Chisom was Secretary of State Phil Jennings, Chief of staff John Wohlman, Secretary of Defense William Cornelius, Heads of the Joint Chiefs of Staff General Samuel Littlestone, CIA Director Robert Heppell, Homeland Security Chief Sarah Ornelus, and the President of the United States William Campbell.

The group sat at the table and spoke in hushed tones while President Campbell sat at the end and finished a phone conversation. The president had been a senator from Utah before being elected president five years ago. His popularity had skyrocketed after he prevented a biological attack on the nation's capital when Jake Taft saved his daughter who had been kidnapped by the demon Ghazi. He'd won reelection by a landslide after his administration subsequently exposed a conspiracy between an FBI deputy director and a corrupt congressional senator. Since then, the presidency had been mundane, dealing with economic problems, terrorism, and foreign policy until today when a single phone call changed all that.

The fifty-three-year-old president hung up the phone, sighed heavily, and leaned back in his high back chair. "I appreciated everyone coming in such short notice. I just hung up talking with Jonathan Carter, the director of the National Nuclear Security Administration.

"To bring everyone up to date on this, Deputy Director Ruiz received information from two of his field agents in Utah concerning something called Operation Plumbob. A routine check was made by the FBI which came up with a warning flag on the files. We made a call to John over at the NNSA to see why it was flagged, and his news was not heart warming. Operation Plumbob referred to nuclear testing in the 1950s." The president sighed heavily and leaned forward for emphasis. "John is sending me the whole file but in short an undetonated nuclear weapon has been sitting buried in the Nevada desert since the 1950s."

The room remained silent for nearly a minute.

"Mr. President," asked Secretary of Defense Cornelius, "do we have confirmation of this? I can't believe we'd leave a nuclear bomb sitting out in the desert."

"Yes, Will, it was confirmed," replied the president. "John gave it to me in layman's terms. It was part of the Pascal tests in 1957. Normally a 485-foot deep, three foot in diameter shaft was dug and the bomb was placed at the bottom of the shaft. The device would be remotely detonated however one did not explode. Since no one wanted to climb down a 400-foot shaft to see why a nuclear weapon didn't explode, they simply buried the thing and left it alone."

Secretary of State Jennings shook his head. "I can't believe this."

"Mr. President, how does this affect us at this moment?" asked Homeland Security Chief Ornelus. "My guess is someone's found out about this."

The president nodded. "You're correct, Sarah, someone has found out." The president hesitated and shuffled the papers in front of him. "We believe that...demons are trying to obtain the weapon."

No one immediately spoke but a few eyebrows were raised.

"Excuse me, Mr. President, did you say demons?" asked Secretary of Defense Cornelius.

"That's exactly what I said," replied the president sternly. "I know there are still a lot of my peers that are reluctant to believe in such, but the fact is that these things exist. This was proven by that creature Ghazi and later at the congressional hearing when Major Taft killed one. Therefore, we have a unit assigned to monitor these monsters and why I asked Deputy Director Ruiz to attend this meeting. His people are the experts." The president turned to Deputy Director Ruiz. "Oscar, give us an update on what you know."

A trickle of sweat ran down the back of Deputy Director Ruiz. He cleared his throat. "Gentlemen, and Ms. Ornelus, as you know I am responsible for tracking any paranormal or demonic activities." Deputy Director Ruiz quickly gave them a briefing of the occurrences of the last week leading up to the current meeting.

"A Russian agent is involved?" asked Homeland Security Chief Ornelus. "Can he be trusted? What if he's part of the Russian Mafia?"

Deputy Director Ruiz shrugged. "Major Taft vouches for him so until this Agent Gordya does anything otherwise, I suggest we let him stay involved."

The president got up from his chair and walked over to pour himself some coffee. "So, this Agent Gordya thinks the demons have some of Hitler's bones and want to clone him."

"We believe that they want to mix his DNA with demon DNA to create a new half breed Hitler."

"Good god, that's even worse; any idea what this has to do with a nuclear weapon?"

Deputy Director Ruiz looked around the room at the serious faces. "If I was to speculate, I would say if they obtained a nuclear weapon, they'd use it to cause chaos. In some twisted way perhaps, they think a new half demon Hitler will take up where the other left off."

"Mr. President," interjected General Littlestone, "I would suggest the first thing we do is to make sure that weapon is still there and secure it before these things find it. If Deputy Director Ruiz is correct and they are digging now, then we're already behind. I'll put Nellis on full alert and double the patrols, especially in the bombing range."

The President nodded. "Good idea, Sam."

"What is the kiloton of this one?" asked Secretary of State Jennings.

"I was told its almost 2 kilotons."

General Littlestone whistled. "It's not a large one but enough to take out a small city."

"Or do a lot of damage to a major city," remarked CIA Director Heppell.

"I agree, Bob," said the president. "I want you to get with NSA and get some satellite photos of the area to see if there's been any changes in the terrain or any new buildings." The president turned to FBI Director Chisom. "Bill, I want you to give Oscar's people whatever they need."

"Mr. President why are we just leaving this to a small group of people?" asked Homeland Security Chief Ornelus. "With all the resources that we have available we should throw everything we have at them to find this weapon."

"Normally I would agree, Sarah," answered the president. "But this is an unusual situation. We're dealing with intelligent creatures that unfortunately we can't see. If we start a massive investigation, they're bound to get wind of it. For all we know one might be listening right now and we've already compromised their mission."

The group glanced around the room. The president continued. "I feel the smaller the group and the less involved the better chances we have for success. We need to find out where this nuke is, secure it, and make sure it doesn't fall into the wrong hands. We'll quietly give Major Taft and the FBI as much support as we can."

———

AZ Minerals Corporation Airport
7 miles west on County Road 432
Mexican Hat, Utah

AFTER THEY GRABBED A QUICK LUNCH, Jake, Agent Williams, Agent Pyle, and Viktor headed to the AZ Minerals Corporation airport just outside of Mexican Hat. They'd received a call from Deputy Director Ruiz that the president had been briefed on the situation and told that transportation was headed to transport them to Nevada.

Ellie, Pam, and Al stood by while they stacked their gear on the ground. Jake turned and rubbed Roscoe behind his ears. "You take care of everyone." He hugged Ellie. "You be careful while we're gone. We don't have a handle on what's going on and with a nuclear weapon around it could get worse."

Ellie smiled and looked up at Jake. "We will. All we're going to do is hang around here until you find out something. Deputy Bridges will look after us."

"I wish you'd go back home and stay on the ranch until this is over. At least I'd know that you'd be safe."

Ellie reached up and touched his rugged face with her hand. "Now, Jake, you know us better than that. Where you go, I go. Besides we don't how long that would be."

Pam stood off to one side with Al. "Don't worry about us Jake, we'll look after her," she said with a bright smile.

Jake frowned. "That's what I'm afraid of."

The group turned at the sound of the *thump, thump, thump* of propeller blades. A UH-60 Black Hawk helicopter painted in desert camouflage came into view. The two General Electric T700-GE-701C engines whined as the helicopter swung around and landed. Jake noticed that it was armed with two M60 machine guns mounted on each side. One side door opened, and the crew chief waved to them to start boarding.

Viktor and the two FBI agents grabbed their gear, ducked under the spinning blades, and ran to the helicopter. Jake picked up his bags when Ellie grabbed his arm. "I love you, be extra careful," she said teary eyed. Jake looked down at her. "I love you too." He winked and ran to the helicopter. After climbing in and stowing their gear the military helicopter lifted off and turned westward.

Ellie, Pam, and Al turned their backs to the dirt and debris that swirled around as the helicopter took off. Ellie watched the helicopter until it was out of sight. Pam touched her on the shoulder. "C'mon, we need to get back to town. You know Jake, he'll be alright."

Ellie patted Roscoe and walked back to the SUV with her arms wrapped around her, not from the cool temperature but from a sudden feeling of dread that she couldn't shake off.

At the end of the runway a large tan colored rock moved, revealing a yellow set of eyes watching the helicopter fly off and the other group walk back to their SUV. The thing turned and scurried away.

The four new occupants in the rear of the Black Hawk donned their headsets and settled in for the long trip to Nevada while Agent Williams opened her laptop. "According to the satellite maps that Oscar emailed me, we might be able to see something that's out of the ordinary," she explained loudly using her mic.

Agent Pyle spoke up, but no one could hear him. Viktor reached over and flipped the switch on the cord of Pyle's headset. "Oh, thanks," said Agent Pyle slightly embarrassed. "I've never flown in a helicopter before, so how do we expect to see anything if we can't see these creatures?" asked Agent Pyle.

Agent Williams pointed to Jake. "With Jake's help maybe, he can spot something that we can't see."

"Of course," said Agent Pyle. He looked around the interior of the helicopter. "Are these things always this loud?"

The other three nodded and the crew chief just smiled.

"Where are we going to land?" asked Viktor.

Agent Williams turned her laptop around and pointed to an aerial photo. "There's a remote building up near the bombing range where we'll meet the rest of the team that's being deployed to assist us."

"Delta Force? Army Rangers?" asked Agent Pyle.

"Don't know, don't ask."

————

Wargwolf Private Estate
Highway 160
South of Kayenta, Arizona

DEGEN WAS in one the lower levels of the building watching one of their half demons being born when a slug-like demon approached him. "Your most horrible wretchedness, Taft and the FBI agents have left, and they're headed west."

Degen smiled, nodded, and went back to watching the half demon being born. This one looked more human. *We're getting so close now*, thought Degen.

————

Historic Highway 66
Flagstaff, Arizona

OFFICER DAN SARLING drove his patrol car slowly around looking for anything unusual when he noticed a white van stopped around the corner on the side of the road, so he cut off his headlights and cruised up to the corner. He watched as one of the local women leaned in the passenger window and talked to the driver. After a minute, she opened the passenger door, climbed in, and the van drove off. From his experience Officer Sarling knew it was the normal course of business for a prostitute to solicit sex by waving down a car, making the deal, and get in the vehicle. Officer Sarling recognized her as a known prostitute, so he activated his red and blue emergency lights and the van pulled over. He called in the license plate, location of the stop, and then carefully approached the car. He shined his flashlight into the driver side at the White male driver of the van.

"Evening, officer," said the man.

Officer Sarling smiled, identified himself, and asked for his driver's license which the man promptly produced. Officer Sarling shined his light over at the woman. "Hello, Dee, what are you doing in this van?"

Dee, a Native American woman, smiled showing a missing tooth. "Hey, Officer Sarling, I'm just getting a ride from this nice man."

"Uh, huh," answered Officer Sarling sarcastically. He walked back to his patrol car and ran the name which showed him to be from Phoenix, but the van registered from Kayenta, Az. When he was satisfied that man didn't have any warrants he walked back up to the van. "Mister...uh...Schmidt," said Officer Sarling as he gave him his driver's license back. "This woman is a known prostitute. I would imagine that you and she were going to make a deal for some...entertainment?"

"Oh no, sir," said Mr. Schimdt. "I was just giving the young lady a ride to the truck stop. But if you think it's not wise, she can walk."

"Good idea."

Dee frowned, huffed, but got out of the van. The van drove off quickly and Officer Sarling turned to her. "Dee, when are you gonna learn not to get into vehicles with these strange men. You could end up dead."

"I just wanted a ride to the truck stop," answered Dee who then stomped off down the street toward the truck stop. Little did Dee know that Officer Sarling had in fact just saved her life.

CHAPTER SIXTEEN

Remote Command Post (CP)
Nevada National Security Site
65 miles north of Las Vegas, Nevada

NIGHT HAD FALLEN over the Nevada desert. A short, stocky, middle aged man wearing camouflage Army Combat Uniforms or ACUs stood outside an old building watching the night sky. There were no clouds above, so the desert night allowed for a magnificent view of the stars. The building, one out of 1,100 at the site was an old storage building with cracked windows and peeling paint. The Nevada National Security Site previously known as the Nevada Test Site covered approximately 1,360 square miles of rocky, dry, desert, and mountainous terrain. The building had been picked because it was isolated and fit their need for secrecy. The soldier, however, wasn't stargazing but watching for the approaching Black Hawk.

A tall, thirtyish, soldier came out through a side door and joined the man. "Any word yet?" he asked.

The other man nodded. "They're about two minutes out."

The man shook his head. "Colonel, are these people really for real? I mean we've been sent out here to help a major and a group of civilians look for the boogey man?"

Colonel Thomas Price turned to his second in command. "Phil, when I get orders directly from POTUS, I don't question it."

POTUS referred to the President of the United States.

"I understand, sir; I'm just not sure we're needed for this," explained Phil. "But as you ordered the DPVs have arrived and are ready."

Colonel Price nodded. "Let's wait and see what these people have to say. I've been told one of them is a Russian agent."

"For the love of Pete," bellowed Phil. "What're we doing with a Russian agent here?"

"And to make it worse, he's FSB."

Phil spit on the ground in frustration. "How do we know he's not part of the Russian *Mafiya*?"

"We don't."

Before Phil could answer, Colonel Price added, "I feel the same, but orders are orders. Let's keep an eye on him. I don't want him left alone for a minute."

The two men heard the thumping of the Black Hawk before its dark shape came into view. They glanced away from the wash as the helicopter landed. The side door slid back, and the crew chief climbed out followed by the four visitors. They collected their gear as the motors shut down. The four of them walked towards the two men, and Colonel Price was struck how different each one was. The man on the left was tall, wearing a dusty, battered, low crowned cowboy hat, dressed in jeans and western jacket. Next to him was an equally tall blond-haired man wearing a full-length black leather coat. An average height blonde woman walked next to him wearing an FBI jacket. The last of the group was an athletic type, Black male with short hair also wearing an FBI jacket.

The four stopped in front of the two men and dropped their bags. The cowboy stepped forward. "You must be Colonel Price," stated Jake.

Colonel Thomas Price smiled briefly. "You must be Major Taft?"

"Yes, sir, and this is Agent Williams and Pyle from the FBI."

Jake nodded towards Viktor. "This is Agent Gordya from the FSB. He's helping us with this mission."

Colonel Price carefully looked Viktor over then turned to Phil. "This is my second in command, Major Phillip Wilkins."

Major Wilkins nodded to the group then motioned to the side door. "If you'll follow me, we'll get you settled in before our briefing."

Several generators provided electricity for the sparse interior of the old building. Four Hummers and two supply trucks were parked off to one side and at the other end were cots, tables, and gear. In the middle sat several Chenoweth scorpion Desert Patrol Vehicles called DPVs. These were basically armored dune buggies with a 50-caliber machine gun mounted on top of each and a M60 machine gun mounted in the front for the passenger.

Colonel Price pointed over to a room that had once been an office. "We put a cot in there for Agent Williams to give her a little more privacy." He pointed over to a row of cots where a group of rugged looking soldiers sat around. Some played cards, while another listened to music with headphones, while the others lay on cots and rested. None of them even turned at the arrival of the "guests". "This is the rest of the team. I'll let you introduce yourselves. You can stow your gear on the empty cots on the end. Briefing is in fifteen minutes."

———

IN EXACTLY FIFTEEN MINUTES, the entire team sat around two large tables shoved together. An area map was spread out on the table and held down with coffee cups and tape.

Colonel Price started the briefing. "I know that each of you have read the mission file. But to make sure we're all on the same page the information we received directly from the White House was that a two-kiloton nuke is buried out here and has been since the 1950s. Our job's to find its location, make sure no one's taken it, and secure it."

"Excuse me, Colonel," said a muscular soldier with huge,

tattooed arms. "I thought one of the reports said that these alien bugs were digging their way to the weapon."

Colonel Price ignored the reference to aliens. "Correct, O'Rork. We believe these creatures, as Major Taft has described them, are digging their way to the weapon. We need to make sure they don't get it by whatever means. We'll cover by ground using the DPVs and by air using the Black Hawk. If they're out there we'll find them."

"Why not use more resources? We can find it faster?" asked a Black soldier they called Sergeant G.

"We want to keep this as low key as possible. Too much activity would bring questions that we don't want."

"Unless they're using an invisibility force shield," added one of the soldiers resulting in a mass of snickers and chuckles.

"Zip it," snapped Colonel Price. "Major Taft's going to explain to you what we're up against in case we encounter these creatures, so listen up." Colonel Price nodded to Jake at the end of the table.

Jake stood up. "Thank you, Colonel. I know all of you have your doubts but let's clear the air. These creatures exist. I've seen them, fought them, shot them, and killed them." He pointed to Agent Williams. "I'm sure Agent Williams will be glad to tell you about the two demons that attacked her on the freeway near Washington D.C. The scars on her cheek are an everyday reminder of what these things can do."

The entire group turned and looked at Agent Williams who nodded.

"And I'm lucky to be alive after I was swallowed by a giant demon snake the other night," added Agent Pyle.

Jake went on. "We believe they've been breeding half-breed demons to use as slave labor to dig to the weapon. We found one dead in Monument Valley and found its nest where it had painted some pictures on the wall showing them digging."

Agent Williams dug out the photos of the cave and handed them to Jake who passed them around. The men passed the photos around then back to Agent Williams who put them back in her pocket.

"We've also been in southern Utah where six innocent people

were killed by these creatures simply because they were at the wrong place at the wrong time," continued Jake. He reached over, opened a file, and removed a stack of photos. Jake distributed them around the table like he was dealing a deck of cards. "These are the crime scene photos of the attack on these people."

The group of men passed the gruesome photos around resulting in low whistles, frowns, and raised eyebrows.

Jake continued. "Gentlemen, these are real monsters, not something from the movies. They'll kill you without even a second thought; in fact, they may even enjoy killing you just so they can crack your skull open like an egg and eat your brains for dessert.

"These demonic heathens are what we call fallen angels. They hate mankind and will do anything to destroy us. They're usually invisible but we believe that to attack or harm us physically they have to solidify and become visible. That gives us at least a small warning, that and the fact that they smell like burning ash and sulfur." Jake leaned over and placed both hands on the table for emphasis. "And I'm the only one that can see them when they're not visible and the only one who can kill them outright."

"So how do we kill these things?" asked O'Rork.

"Good question," replied Jake. He reached into his pocket and withdrew a single bullet. "This may be the only chance you have to help even the score. This is a specially made bullet from the FBI. The round is normal but has been embedded with crushed cemetery dirt."

"Cemetery dirt?" asked Colonel Price.

Jake nodded. "Yes sir, we've found out that cemetery dirt is toxic to them. We don't know to what extent yet, but we know that it can harm them as it appears to act almost like an acid to them and may even incapacitate them if hit enough times."

"How many times has this been tested?" asked Major Wilkins.

"Only once, when we were attacked by that giant snake Agent Pyle mentioned earlier."

Several team members mumbled and shook their heads.

"I wish that we'd had more time to test them but with the situation as it is we have to go with what we have," explained Jake. "And to make it worse I only have a limited number of these rounds. The

FBI is making as much as they can and will ship them as soon as they're ready."

Major Wilkins spoke up. "So, what you're telling us is that we're looking for demons that we can't see until they attack, and we may or may not be able to kill with only a limited amount of dirt covered firepower?"

Jake solemnly nodded.

"Sounds like a normal day in our world," joked one of the soldiers.

Colonel Price stood up again. "Thank you, Major Taft." The colonel looked around the room at them. "Due to the nature and situation given I'll make this a strictly volunteer mission. No one has to go, and no one will be looked down on by anyone if they refuse." He looked around at each member to make sure they understood.

"I didn't have a date for this weekend anyway," popped off one of the soldiers.

"Who else can say they went on a mission against an army of demons?" said O'Rork.

"Hell, it might be fun to meet my wife's relatives," remarked another. The entire group erupted with laughter.

"Very well, get some rest because we leave at 0730 hours," said Colonel Price.

Knotted Pine Lodge
101 East Highway 163
Mexican Hat, Utah

ELLIE, Pam, and Al were sitting outside on the lodge enjoying the cool evening breeze. Roscoe was lying on the ground next to Ellie's chair. Al was taking photos of the area as usual, while Pam was finishing a tall glass of cola when a San Juan County Sheriff's vehicle pulled up and Deputy Bridges climbed out. He walked over to them carrying a folder. "Evening, folks, I've got some good news."

The three smiled at him. "We can always use good news," said Ellie.

"We got a hit on the German weapons that we took off those attackers. It seems the weapons were sold to a security company named Elite Services out of St. Louis."

"How does that help us?" asked Pam.

Deputy Bridges opened the folder. "It says here that the weapons were sold to Elite Services and they only work for high priced corporations. Guess what company they've worked for in the past?"

"Wargwolf," said Ellie.

Deputy Bridges smiled and nodded.

"I've got a call in to a buddy down that way who works for the county and see if he can find out anything else about them. I'll email your FBI agent friends and let them know." Deputy Bridges got up and left.

"Hmmmmm," thought Ellie. "It's strange that the half birdman was found in Monument Valley near that area."

"And then to have a monster bear in this area that was being followed by a group of men with weapons bought by a German company in that area," added Pam.

"Maybe Jake and the rest of them can figure it out when they get back," said Al.

I just wish Jake was here now, thought Ellie as they headed inside the lodge.

———

Remote Command Post (CP)
Nevada National Security Site
65 miles north of Las Vegas, Nevada

AFTER DONNING DESERT ACUS, heavy Kevlar vests and helmets the team piled into their DPVs.

Agent Williams stared at the armored dune buggy. "If we're looking for demons, why don't we use bigger vehicles like Humvees?"

Sergeant G laughed. "Because we might have to go places off road more than a Humvee can handle. We use these for rapid assault. You'll be fine."

The sun shone brightly on the cool Nevada desert as the five DPVs raced across the ground towards the general area where the nuclear weapon was believed to have been buried. Each DPV had a driver, front passenger armed with the M60, and a rider sitting on a raised platform in back to use the 50 caliber if needed. There weren't any cemetery dust embedded rounds for the 50 caliber or M60, but Colonel Price figured if they encountered them, it could at least keep the devils distracted while the assault rifles and handguns with the special rounds could do some damage.

Agent Williams rode in the front passenger seat while the huge, tattooed soldier nicknamed "Tank" drove. Tank was recovering from the severe chewing out he'd received from her when he'd made the mistake of calling Agent Williams "Little lady" while explaining how to get strapped in. Besides Agent Pyle, the only Black male in the group was Sergeant George Little who everyone just called "Sergeant G". He drove another of the DPVs while above them in the Black Hawk rode Jake and Viktor along with the pilot, copilot, and crew chief.

The small task force had nicknamed themselves the "Demon Killers" or DK for short. Each DPV was equipped with a GPS.

"DK1," radioed Colonel Price from his DPV, "do you see anything?"

"Negative, nothing yet," answered the pilot of the Black Hawk designated as DK1. Jake sat in the main compartment area and gazed out of the side windows with binoculars. Viktor sat on the opposite side and looked out the other windows but knew unless something happened, usually bad, he wouldn't be able to see these fiends.

Forty-five minutes later, the group arrived in the area where the nuke had been left buried. Jake watched as the DPVs circled around the area but couldn't locate an opening of any kind.

"DK2, are they sure this is the spot?" asked Major Wilkins who was designated as DK3.

"Roger, DK3, these are the coordinates given to us by the experts," answered Colonel Price, who was DK2.

"When the experts are sure then I get worried."

"We'll widen our search pattern. Maybe they didn't want to be too obvious that they were digging," said Jake. With that said the Black Hawk banked and swept a larger circle around the area.

"Roger that," answered Colonel Price. "The rest of you start checking less obvious places for a dig site. Maybe the monsters have it covered or camouflaged. They're invisible but a hole in the ground isn't."

Several minutes later, the Black Hawk had widened the search and was well east of the site when Jake noticed a group of demons flying in the distance. Jake turned and started sifting through the surveillance photos of this area.

"What do you see?" asked Viktor.

"Demons," answered Jake as he looked over the pictures and then glanced out the window to confirm what he saw. "About thirty of them came from an area north of here but there isn't anything there of significance except for one of the unused buildings." Jake lifted the binoculars and looked out the window when it dawned on him. He turned and looked at Viktor who must have come to the same conclusion.

"They're using the building as a cover," said Viktor.

"Take us over to that old gray building to the northeast," instructed Jake to the pilot who nodded. "Colonel, we may have found their entry point. There's one of the old unused buildings to the northeast that a large group of demons just left. We're going to check it out."

"We'll use your GPS to pinpoint your position," answered Colonel Price. "O'Rork, stay here and keep an eye on this site while we head towards Taft's position. I don't want to leave this spot unguarded in case it's a diversion."

"Roger, Colonel," answered O'Rork. He pulled over and stopped. "This really sucks," grumbled O'Rork to the other two occupants of the DPV. "They get to go have all the fun and we get to sit and watch dirt blow around." His passenger, a blond, broad shouldered soldier, just shrugged, opened his water bottle, and took a swig.

The Black Hawk helicopter circled the building several times while Jake and Viktor scanned the area. "It looks deserted, but you never know," commented Jake.

Viktor examined the building with his binoculars. "Da, I don't see anything unusual but then again a demon could sit right there, and I wouldn't see it."

"Speaking of demons and monsters," said the crew chief. "Where did those go that you saw earlier?"

Jake swung his binoculars around and scanned the horizon. "I don't know. They were flying just east of us a minute ago."

"Maybe they're behind us and w…"

The helicopter violently tilted as something slammed into the side and the sliding door on the pilot side of the helicopter was suddenly ripped off. An ugly greenish head smiled at them with sharp teeth and yellow eyes.

They all turned towards the beast as it grabbed the crew chief and ripped him out of his seat. The man screamed as he plummeted towards the ground. Jake pulled his .45 caliber handgun and shot the despicable thing between the eyes. "Get us out of here," Jake yelled to the pilot.

The pilot swung the helicopter around and headed west as three more bumps were felt causing the helicopter to drop rapidly. The shell of the Black Hawk was designed to stop small arms fire, so Jake was not able to fire through the sides at the fiends, but it didn't stop the demons from ripping holes into the sides with hellion claws and fiendish weapons. On Viktor's side a dark orange demon had managed to get a leg and arm inside one of the openings, so Viktor shot it with the specially designed rounds and was encouraged when it fell away, twisting, writhing, and screaming.

Since Jake was unable to shoot through the sides, he unhooked his harness and leapt over to the side window where the M60 machine gun was mounted. He opened fire on the group of incoming demons. Since Jake didn't need special ammo, the 7.62 NATO slugs ripped into the demons killing several before they realized the danger and scattered down and under the Black Hawk.

"Look out, Viktor, they're coming under us," bellowed Jake as he fired at a few demons that remained on his side.

"Da, I can see them now," yelled Viktor over the sound of gunfire as he opened up on the monstrosities with his handgun. As the rounds hit their targets the things spun out of the way screaming and twisting in the sky.

"Mayday, mayday, we're under attack," yelled the pilot as he fought the controls to keep the helicopter from crashing to the ground.

Jake continued to pour down a line of fire to keep the abhorrent creatures at bay. The co-pilot yelled a warning as one the demons slammed into the cockpit canopy shattering it. The creature resembled a huge purplish colored condor with armored skin. Once inside the cockpit the fiend pierced the chest of the co-pilot with a long broad sword and bit off the poor man's face in one horrid movement. The pilot put the helicopter nose down to dislodge the beast. Jake fell forward, pulled his .45, and fired into the side of the demon's head spraying blood and demon brain matter on the inside of the cockpit.

"Get us on the ground," growled Jake. "We can't fight them up here."

"I'm working on it," shouted the pilot. He brought the helicopter level and fought the controls in a westward direction back toward the DPVs when suddenly alarm sirens echoed and lights blinked in the cockpit. Smoke began to pour from one of the engines. "They've damaged one of the engines, I'm losing power."

———

COLONEL PRICE and his team spotted the smoke as they raced across to intercept the helicopter. A moment later, the Black Hawk came into view. Smoke poured from the engine compartment. For the first time the team nicknamed "Demon Killers" laid eyes on demons as they clung to the helicopter. Three were hanging onto the bottom while another clung to the side jamming a short sword into the engine compartment obviously causing havoc. Twenty or more flew around and under the helicopter like angry bees.

"Gawd, those things are hideous," said Tank.

"I never would have thought," said the gunner on Agent Williams's DPV.

"You get used to it," replied Agent Williams.

Colonel Price's driver aimed their DPV towards the helicopter. "Quit gawking and see if we can distract a few of them and take some of the heat."

"Roger," snapped Major Wilkins.

"With pleasure," announced another of the gunners.

"DK1, you got several unwanted intruders hanging onto the belly and one on top, do what you can to clear them off," instructed Colonel Price.

A moment later, the ground teams opened up with the 50 caliber and M60 guns which didn't injure any of the demons but did get their attention. Several devils not attached to the helicopter dove right for the group of DPVs.

Agent Williams continued to fire the M60 at the incoming demons. "Ok, get ready, here they come."

———

INSIDE THE BLACK HAWK the pilot fought to keep the helicopter steady. Jake threw open the bottom hatch on the floor and leaned out and under the helicopter into the wind. The three demons turned and looked at Jake in disgust. Jake shot one though the head but could only hit another in the side as it swung to avoid Jake's gunfire. The third abomination swung around and climbed into the open door on Viktor's side. It was a long serpent-like demon with huge fan type ears and two tentacles coming from its nose.

The beast was armed with a scimitar and snarled at Viktor as it climbed inside. Viktor snapped off a shot but only hit it in the torso causing it to shriek. Viktor took careful aim but realized too late that the slide on his gun had locked back indicating that it was empty.

The devil realized it too, smiled, and brought the scimitar around and swung at Viktor's face.

Jake fired twice more at the beast under the helicopter before he was able to kill it. He grabbed the edge of the hatch, pulled himself back upright, and saw Viktor wrestling with the serpent creature. The revolting serpent demon had its tail wrapped around Viktor's ankle with two tentacles protruding from its nose aimed at Viktor. The ends started to glow a bright red which Jake instantly knew was bad. He remembered a demon he'd killed in Jackson, Mississippi, that spewed fire from tentacles in a similar way. He dove across the compartment, grabbed one of the tentacles, and yelled at Viktor, "Get it away from your face."

Viktor had a firm grip on the arm that held the scimitar and grabbed the one tentacle. He jerked the tentacle away just as a strange liquid fire shot out of the two tentacles. Jake jammed his .45 up under the monster's chin and blew the repulsive thing's brains out of the helicopter. The beast went limp, and the liquid flame died off while they tossed the thing out of the open door. They turned back and saw that the interior of the helicopter was now on fire.

————

A LARGE GREEN striped demon with four wings and armed with a huge, curved sword swooped down on Agent Williams's DPV while she fired up at it hoping to bring it down. The gunner on top fired the 50 calibers as the thing flew. The big gun suddenly went quiet, so Agent Williams turned back and saw the soldier's torso slumped over with his head decapitated from his body. Agent Williams changed to her 40 caliber that did have the cemetery rounds. The DPV suddenly swerved right as Tank swung the modified dune buggy around to avoid another demon that swooped down and tried to grab at them.

Agent Pyle and Sergeant G were having their own troubles fighting off two demons that kept dive bombing them as they shot up at the fiends from hell. "I can't get a good shot off," yelled Agent Pyle. Their gunner hunkered down and tried to shoot from a crouched position with the 50 calibers after seeing the other gunner lose his head.

Colonel Price and Major Wilkins were circling and swerving as well to avoid the monsters while firing at them.

"Now that we got their attention, Colonel," hollered Major Wilkins, "what do we do with them?"

Colonel Price glanced back westward and saw the Black Hawk leaving a trail of heavy smoke and flames coming from the interior as the helicopter flew west and out of sight. "It looks like we're on our own now," he quipped. "Head to that ridge to the north and we'll hole up there."

The group turned and made a mad run for a small ridge a quarter of a mile north. "DK2 to CP, we need emergency assistance. We've engaged a group of hostiles and need support immediately. Do you read?"

"Roger, DK2, we've been monitoring your radio traffic," answered a team member back at their temporary command post. "Nellis has scrambled two to intercept. It'll take about ten."

"I don't think we have ten minutes but send them anyway," growled Colonel Price. "O'Rork, get your sorry-can over here, we need some extra ammo."

"I'm already on the way, Colonel, save some for me," answered O'Rork.

"We can't stay airborne. We're going down," yelled the Black Hawk pilot. "...prepare for..." The radio went silent.

Three DPVs reached the relative shelter of the rock ridge and swung their vehicles around as Agent Pyle's and Sergeant G's DPV closed in. When they were within fifteen yards of the ridge a huge, winged demon dropped in front of their DPV. Sergeant G tried to swerve but the left front tire caught the thing's left leg which caused the DPV to cartwheel into the air. The devil brute was also knocked to the ground but quickly gained its feet, roared, and swung a large wide hammer at the DPV with so much force it knocked off the back right axle and tire.

"Give them some cover. Switch to the handguns that have the cemetery rounds. The rifles are only making them angrier!" shouted

Colonel Price. The small team fired into the giant winged devil which only caused it to roar more as each cemetery dust embedded round slammed into it. The revolting thing continued to pound on the inverted DPV with the hammer. Agent Pyle and Sergeant G were shielded from the blows but soon the frame began to crumple.

"Colonel," yelled O'Rork through their radios, "we can't make it to you. We're being attacked by a group of hostile creatures... gunner...Bach...gone...do y..."

Agent Pyle crawled out from the opposite side and tried to help free Sergeant G who was trapped by his harness. The others divided their fire between the damnable fiend with the giant hammer and the others that kept swooping and grabbing at them. Agent Williams suddenly dashed away from her DPV towards Agent Pyle.

"Where's she going?" shouted Colonel Price.

Agent Williams dodged one demon as it flew by then leaped up onto the back of the hellion with the hammer. She grabbed onto one of the huge horns protruding from its head. She jammed her 40-caliber handgun into the creature's ear and fired two shots. The creature threw its head back in agony which dislodged Agent Williams who was able to jump off and roll out of the way. The thing grabbed its head and wailed in pain. Agent Williams ran over to Agent Pyle and finished helping Sergeant G out from under the disabled DPV. While the beast stumbled around and fell to its knees in obvious distress, the three ran back to the others. Tank kept firing at the thing as Sergeant G and the two FBI agents climbed behind their DPV.

"Nice shooting, little lady, I mean, agent," said Tank. "That'll give that thing something to think about."

The three stared at Tank, not sure if he meant to be funny. More demons dropped to the ground and charged as even more swooped and grabbed at the small group. The attackers consisted of demons of all shapes, colors, and sizes armed with long swords, broadswords, scimitars, battle axes, war hammers, pikes, daggers, clubs, and other lethal weapons. As they lumbered directly towards the "Demon Hunters", Colonel Price looked around. "How much ammo have you got left?"

As the heathen devils closed in, they determined they each only had a couple of magazines of ammo each for their handguns.

"I think I know how they would've felt at the Alamo," said Agent Pyle.

A dust cloud rose as the horde pounded closer.

"Let's give 'em hell," shouted Colonel Price.

"Hoooah," yelled Sergeant G.

"Hoooah," yelled Tank.

The elite team opened fire again on the fiends. The ones struck in the head fell to the ground in pain while the rest were slowed by the cemetery rounds but continued to charge towards them.

"Try to aim for the head," bellowed Colonel Price. "It seems to do the most damage."

Major Wilkins fired his remaining rounds at the beasts while three other soldiers emptied their weapons. The rest hopelessly fired at the beasts to no avail as the small arms rounds only caused small annoying wounds on the devils which smoldered from the toxic reaction to the cemetery dust.

A large buffalo shaped demon arrived first, raised a huge scimitar over its head, and bellowed in triumph which quickly turned to shrieks as several large rounds ripped into its side. The brute stumbled and fell to its knees. Another one turned to see where the gunfire came from when the back of its head exploded as several 50 caliber rounds found its target.

The group of soldiers turned just in time to see a lone DPV race over the edge of the ridge as Jake stood and poured 50 caliber rounds into the horde of demons. Viktor was in the front passenger seat firing up at the group of demons still flying around while the driver, O'Rork, shouted obscenities at the demons and fired his handgun.

"It looks like the cavalry arrived just in time," said Major Wilkins.

"About time," said Agent Williams with a smirk.

The remaining demons turned away from the deadly fire and disappeared over the horizon. O'Rork pulled up to the others who cheered, slapped his back, and shook his hand. Colonel Price approached. "What happened?"

"Sorry, Colonel, those monsters hit us on our way over." O'Rork paused. "Jenkins and Bach didn't make it. Those fiends were about to rip me to pieces when Major Taft and his buddy showed up. I was never happier to see a Russian. We got here as fast as we could."

Colonel Price's chiseled face softened, and he nodded. "Bach and Jenkins? They were good men. We lost Collins too. I'm glad you made it when you did though, good job." He turned to Jake. "Where's the helicopter?"

Jake pointed in the direction where the team had last seen it fly over. "We managed to get it down in one piece. The pilot's babysitting until rescue arrives. He said he'd had enough of flesh-eating monsters for one day."

"What about Lieutenant Marshal and Crew Chief Dunham?" asked Major Wilkins.

Jake shook his head solemnly.

Colonel Price's jaw muscles tightened. "Ok, people, load up and let's get this disaster back to the command post."

———

Wargwolf Private Estate
Highway 160
South of Kayenta, Arizona

PRISKA AND GERDA sat at a large wooden table in the den going over a stack of lab results. Priska removed her reading glasses and smiled. "These test results have been remarkable. As soon as the weapon is ready to be shipped, we'll return to the homeland and prepare for the next phase."

"Yes, *Grossmutter*, these latest results have been remarkable," added Gerda. "With this success we can complete the project. Will the Fuhrer be completely himself or will he need to be taught?"

Priska shrugged her thin shoulders. "I don't know. The genetic markers will be there, but I imagine there will be some information and guidance needed. I'm sure Degen will handle that portion."

As if on cue Degen entered the room followed by his stench. The tiger demon seemed to be in good spirits because he was purring which sounded more like growling. "I overheard that the laboratory results have been satisfactory?"

"Why yes, Degen my dear, I think we've gotten to the point where we can start using Adolf's DNA," answered Priska brightly.

Degen grunted in agreement. "As soon as I've finished business here with Taft and his troublemakers we can return."

"Is that venture going well?"

"Yes, the stupid humans are falling for the trap. We led them right to the building and put up a skirmish with the idiots to make sure they knew it was the right location."

Gerda brushed a hand through her blonde hair as she leaned back in her chair. Her back hurt from leaning over the table for hours reading over the reports. "What if they're too afraid to come back?"

Degen glared at her. "They'll come back. Military humans are too proud to not show back up. We killed several of them. They have to come back for revenge or at least to check and see what's going on."

"Have your pets been transferred to the tunnels?" asked Priska.

"They've been placed in cages with the remote locks and the explosive charges have been put in place. The trap is set."

Gerda looked over at the grandmother. "Is all that necessary? Can't we just leave? By the time they found out we'll be long gone with the bomb and out of their reach."

Degen leaned over the table, dug his claws into the wooden table, and roared at Gerda. "Because, you ignorant moronic woman, I don't want to worry about Taft or his people. They have caused me too much time and trouble."

Gerda silently stared back at him, refusing to back down.

"Now, Degen dear," said Priska as she stroked Degen's furry arm. "I'm sure Gerda was just thinking about what might be easiest without causing too much commotion and unnecessary attention. After all we don't want an international problem."

"I don't care about any human's attention; I want this wrapped up and finished before we leave."

"What about Taft's people still back in that disgusting little town?" asked Priska.

Degen sat down in one of the chairs and grinned showing all his razor-sharp teeth. "When Taft is taken care of, we plan to pay them a visit."

CHAPTER SEVENTEEN

Remote Command Post (CP)
Nevada National Security Site
65 miles north of Las Vegas, Nevada

THE ELITE TEAM DESIGNATED "DEMON KILLERS" once again sat around the same two large tables shoved together. After Colonel Price debriefed the team concerning the loss of life and the damage to the vehicles he turned to Jake. "Major Taft, has Washington sent any more special ammunition?"

Jake nodded. "Yes, sir, it will be here later this evening, however it will only be assault rifles and small arms ammo. They're working on a mold for the large calibers."

Colonel Price nodded and frowned.

"As a side note, I received an email from Deputy Bridges," explained Agent Pyle. "It says the weapons those men were using in Mexican Hat were sold to Elite Protective Services and they only work for high priced corporations. One of which is a company called Wargwolf who has a coal business near Kayenta, Arizona."

"That's not far from where the half bird demon grabbed the campers," said Agent Williams.

"And not too far from Mexican Hat area where the monster bear was," added Viktor.

"I also received an email alert from Washington that said the police in Flagstaff ran a plate belonging to a Wargwolf vehicle recently," said Agent Pyle. "I'll have the Flagstaff office contact them and find out why."

"Good, maybe there's something to that," said Jake. "We can check on it when we get back." He turned to Colonel Price. "Pyle, Williams, Gordya, and I met earlier. We appreciate what you and your unit have done to help us, but we agreed that the four of us should be the only ones to enter the tunnel tomorrow to determine if the demons have gotten to the weapon. Your team has paid a deadly cost and I don't want to risk more men without better weapons, ammo, and protection."

Colonel Price rubbed the back of his neck to try and ease his tense muscles. "Thank you Major, I'll take that under advisement."

Major Wilkins spoke up. "Colonel, we could try and coat our explosives with that cemetery dirt."

"Good idea." Colonel Price turned to Sergeant G. "Can you adapt some of our explosives with the stuff?"

Sergeant G smiled. "I'll be glad to give it a try, sir."

Jake frowned. "But, Colonel…"

Colonel Price held up his hand. "Thank you for your concern, Major, but nothing short of heaven or hell could keep us out."

Jake turned, scanned the stern faces of the soldiers around the table and felt a surge of pride at the look of determination in their eyes. "Then let's try to be a little better prepared for them."

———————

AFTER A TRIP TO A LOCAL CEMETERY, Sergeant G and the rest of the team thought of ways to cover their clothes and weapons with cemetery dust. Jake stepped outside while they argued about how to adhere the dirt, and dialed Ellie's cell phone.

Ellie didn't even ask who it was. "I've been worried," she said.

"We ran into a little trouble from some pesky demons, but we located the tunnel," said Jake. He thought it wise not to tell her about the three deaths.

"So, what's the next step?"

Jake heard the tension in her voice. "As soon as we receive another supply of the special rounds, we plan to go in tomorrow morning."

"Another supply? You used up the other ammunition?"

"I said we had a little trouble."

"It sounds to me like you had a small war. Are you sure this is a good idea? Can't you just blow a hole in the ground to see if it's there without going in?"

"That wouldn't work. If the bomb was there, it might bury it deeper and then we'd never know for sure." Jake tried to sound convincing. "All we're going to do is go take a quick look and see if the weapon is still there. If we find them digging, we'll high tail it out and then call in the big guns."

Ellie was silent on the other end.

"Ellie? Honey?" Jake heard a big sigh on the other end.

"Promise me you'll be extra careful. I'm sure they know you're there."

"We'll be careful. Colonel Price and his men are coming up with some other ways to use cemetery dust to keep us all safe."

"Well, he'd better. If anything happens to you, Colonel Price will have to contend with me."

Jake smiled to himself. "I'll warn him. After we check things out tomorrow, we might be able to head back later or the next morning. Is anything going on there?"

"No, I'm just trying to be patient. Deputy Bridges is checking into that German company down in Arizona."

"Yeah, Terrell said there may be a link between this Wargwolf Company and the automatic weapons we confiscated."

"And Pam's bored."

Jake rolled his eyes. "Take Pam shopping or something then. I'll call you tomorrow and let you know what we found out."

"Ok, I love you, be careful."

"I love you too."

After Jake hung up, he stood out in the cool night of the desert and wished that it was going to be as easy as he'd said it was.

———

Criminal Investigations Division
Flagstaff Police Department
911 East Sawmill Road
Flagstaff, Arizona

DETECTIVE BRUTTEN RUBBED HIS EYES. He'd gone through the last six months missing person's reports and eliminated the usual runaways that came back or elderly people that had wandered off and had come to a disturbing conclusion…more women were missing than Beth had said and had not been found. He sat back in his chair, took a sip of his coffee, and looked at the list. According to his count, ten teenagers and fourteen of the local prostitutes were missing not counting the three that Beth told him about. *Twenty-four missing women.*

He sent an email to the dispatch supervisor and asked for BOLO or "Be On the Look Out" for Beth. Detective Brutten wanted to know if she'd seen the van.

———

Remote Command Post (CP)
Nevada National Security Site
65 miles north of Las Vegas, Nevada

AFTER A LIGHT BREAKFAST the group loaded their gear, double checked their weapons, and climbed into the DPVs. Shortly after daylight the small convoy of DPVs left the remote Command Post and sped towards the tunnel.

They were grim faced and tight-lipped knowing what might lie ahead. Communications was kept to a minimum. Even Tank was not his usual male chauvinist self when they stopped within several hundred yards of the old building.

"Do you see anything, Major?" asked Colonel Price.

"No, sir, it appears to be quiet."

"That's what bothers me." Colonel Price turned to Major Wilkins. "Phil, keep an eye on the entrance for us. Watch your back because you only have a few seconds to see these hellions before they attack."

Major Wilkins nodded. "Yes, sir, but with all due respects don't you think I should go and you stay here?"

"Negative," answered Colonel Price. "Sorry, Phil, but I wouldn't send anyone down that hole if I wasn't going myself." He pointed to one side of the building. "Tank, you and Agent Williams take that side while we come from the other side. Listen for any warnings of hostiles from Major Taft."

Tank smiled for the first time. "Yes, sir." He drove their DPV to the left and around the back side of the building. The rest of the group drove up to the opposite side and spread out. Without speaking, the highly trained group carefully worked their way around to the door which was ajar. At Colonel Price's nod O'Rork slid the door open, and the team poured inside ready for anything only to find it empty.

They surrounded the hole that led down into the ground. "The last hole I saw had a giant snake in it," grumbled Agent Pyle.

"The ground slants down and the hole looks big enough for the DPVs," said O'Rork. "Do we walk or ride?"

"We ride," said Colonel Price. "I want Major Taft in the front. He can see them when we can't, and the 50 cal will work when he's using it. So, mount up."

The door to the old storage building was pulled open and each DPV was driven down into the tunnel. When they arrived at the point where the tunnel leveled off, they stopped.

"DK3, can you read us?" asked Colonel Price.

"Loud and clear," answered Major Wilkins. "Don't be a stranger."

"Roger," said Colonel Price. "We're only going to recon and see if the weapon is there."

"Colonel, look at the walls," said Sergeant G as he pointed to the walls of the tunnel. Upon a closer examination they noticed the walls had claw and scratch marks.

"It looks like your theory of using half human demons as slave labor was right, Major Taft," said Colonel Price.

Jake ran his hand over the claw marks. "They made them dig this tunnel with their bare hands...or claws. Sometimes it's not good to be right."

"Alright, let's go see if anyone's home," said Colonel Price. "Major Taft, take the lead."

Since the tunnel was over twenty feet wide, they were able to drive two DPVs side by side with Jake taking the point. They passed through several natural caverns filled with limestone formations on the way and had to slow down to a crawl to maneuver around flowstones and stalagmites of all sizes. Some of the caverns branched off in different dark directions. The only light that penetrated the pitch dark was their headlights.

An hour and several miles later, the team pulled up to a large cavern that held several metal vats near a large vertical stalagmite commonly called a totem pole. Agent Williams and Sergeant G walked over to the empty vats. "They're empty, sir," said the sergeant. "From the stench I'm not sure I want to know what was in them."

Colonel Price looked at his GPS. "According to this the weapon should be two hundred and twenty yards up the tunnel. I don't hear any noise which bothers me." He grabbed his assault rifle and told two team members, Corporals Weatherby and Abbott to stay with the vehicles. The rest of the group spread out and carefully worked their way down the dark demon-created tunnel. The lights attached to their assault rifles bounced off the scratched walls of the tunnel. After only eighty yards they ended abruptly. The tunnel was blocked by rocks.

"Do you think they quit?" asked Agent Pyle.

"Maybe, but I doubt it if they were this close," said Viktor.

"So why did they stop?" asked Tank.

Jake and several others climbed up on the rock pile and examined the walls close to the cave in. "The claw and scratch marks go all the way to the blockage," said Jake.

"It appears the roof caved in here," said Agent Williams. "The question is why?"

"And where did they go?" asked Sergeant G as he shined his flashlight over the rocks and walls.

"If they were still around it would stink of sulfur more than it does," commented Agent Williams as she shined her light around looking for any signs.

Colonel Price turned back towards the vehicles. "I can only smell a faint odor. Let's get out of here. We can bring in some heavy equipment and open this tunnel up, then we'll see if the bomb's there."

They started back to where the two corporals waited when they heard hissing and screeching coming from the entrance. Instantly on guard, they neared the end of the tunnel and detected a stronger odor of sulfur. At the entrance to the cavern, they swung their flashlights around penetrating the darkness and to their shock the two corporals lay on the ground in pools of blood. The two dead soldier's uniforms were smoldering. Their throats had been ripped open, skulls cracked open, and their brains were gone.

"Oh, my gawd," said O'Rork.

"Why are their uniforms smoking like that?" asked Sergeant G as he shined his flashlight around the cavern looking for the assailants.

Jake bent down and examined the unfortunate soldiers. "The creatures must've grabbed their clothes which we covered in cemetery dust and burned the demons. That must have been the noise we heard. They ripped out their throats and knocked their helmets off to get to their skulls."

"The heathen devils attacked the only part of their bodies that wasn't protected," said Tank.

"DK3," growled Colonel Price. "Be careful, we now have two more casualties. Hostiles are nearby."

"Roger, do you need us to head down?" said Major Wilkins.

"Negative but keep a sharp eye out. They ambushed Weatherby

and Abbott. We'll be leaving ASAP. We found the tunnel, but the end was blocked."

"You're too late," said a deep raspy voice from the darkness on the other side of the tunnel.

"Stand by," said Colonel Price.

At the sound of the voice the group quickly took up defensive positions behind the DPVs and nearby rock formations. "This is Colonel Price of the United States Armed Forces, who's there?"

"You won't find the weapon you're looking for," said another voice. "You're too late, you're too late," said several voices in a sick sing song unison followed by fiendish laughter.

Colonel Price looked over at Jake who shook his head indicating that he didn't see anything. "You're trespassing on a U.S. military installation. Give up and no one will get hurt," said Colonel Price.

The answer came in another round of hellish laughter. "Give up, give up, give up," sang the voices in a not so harmonious song.

"Why don't you come out and we'll talk about it," said Colonel Price hoping they would show themselves.

They answered with cackles and catcalls.

"You're making a big mistake attacking a military unit," yelled the colonel.

"You're making a big mistake, you're making a big mistake, you're making a big mistake," sang the devilish voices.

"You'll never get away with this," yelled Colonel Price.

The singing demons didn't respond.

After several moments of silence, Colonel Price turned to the rest of the group. "Mount up, let's get the hell out of here."

Everyone climbed into their DPVs and started up the motors when they heard a snorting sound coming from the other side of the tunnel. Agent Williams turned a spotlight down the tunnel which shined on three huge yellow eyes followed by three large boar hog creatures. These half-breed creature's body sizes were three times the norm putting them at well over fifteen hundred pounds each. They snorted and charged the DPVs.

"Take 'em out," ordered Colonel Price.

The group opened up with assault rifles and 50 caliber weapons which made quick work of the three beasts.

"More experiments gone bad," said Viktor.

"That was easy," announced Agent Pyle.

"Too easy," said Sergeant G.

"I agree," said Colonel Price. "Major Taft, take the lead, move out."

The vehicles pulled into the tunnel and raced towards the entrance as fast as they could. Just as when they came in, they had to slow down at intervals to drive around formations of flowstone and limestone columns. Jake kept an eye out for any unwanted guests, and as they entered a part of the tunnel carved out by demons something caught his eye. He looked back just as a small red light blinked. Jake thought for a second then realized what was going on. *Trap.* "Colonel, we just triggered something," yelled Jake. "My guess is some sort of explosive. We've be set up."

"Everyone, take cover," bellowed Colonel Price as the tunnel was rocked by several explosions which caused dust and smoke to rush down the tunnel.

The DPVs halted and after a few minutes the dust settled enough for their lights to pierce the darkness. "Everyone ok?" asked the colonel, and each member acknowledged they were accounted for.

"They've caved in the tunnel entrance I would imagine," said Viktor. "They have us trapped in here."

"Colonel," called Major Wilkins through their radios. "What's going on down there? We heard explosions."

"We're all ok," replied the colonel. "They caved in the tunnel so we can't get out that way. See if you can find another way in."

"We're on it," answered the major.

Jake shined his flashlight down the tunnel. "Colonel, may I suggest we go back to the nearest natural cavern. It has a larger air pocket and might be a safer area to be in case this tunnel caves in more."

Colonel Price nodded. "I agree. Get these dune buggies turned around and head back to the nearest cavern."

It took precious minutes for the group to get the DPVs turned around in the cramped tunnel and back the other way without a cave in. They entered a large natural cavern ten minutes later and turned the vehicles nose to tail into a crude square for protection amongst the cavern's formations.

"Sergeant G and O'Rork," bellowed Colonel Price, "scout around for another way out or for anything we can use to help protect us until they can send an extraction team."

While Sergeant G and O'Rork scouted both sides of the cavern, Colonel Price radioed the command post and was pleased when they answered.

"We read you, DK2, loud and clear," said the soldier monitoring the radio traffic. "We have your GPS coordinates. We'll start putting together a team and equipment to drill an air hole down to you until we can dig you out."

"We're in a large cavern so we should be fine until you get set up," answered the colonel.

"As long as nothing happens before then," said Tank.

Agent Williams elbowed him in the ribs.

"Major, did you find another way out yet?" asked Colonel Price over the radio.

"No, sir," replied Major Wilkins. "We're still looking."

Sergeant G shined his light around the sides of the cavern and down an empty natural passageway. "Nothing over here, Colonel, but we don't know how far the passage goes."

O'Rork was on the opposite side shining his light around and down another dark natural passageway. He shook his head. "There's nothing over here either, Colonel, except for another dark passageway."

"Alright," grumbled the colonel. "We'll wait here then."

Sergeant G jumped down and walked over to the DPVs. O'Rork stepped down off the ledge near the passageway when a pincer-like arm shot out of the darkness and clamped down on his left upper arm. He yelled and twisted around as a huge brown colored scorpion scurried out of the passageway. The thing was well over five hundred pounds with one yellow glowing eye. Before anyone could react, it raised its stinger tail and impaled O'Rork through the right shoulder.

It lifted him off the ground and slung him across the cavern where he landed next to a tall rock formation.

"Kill it," ordered Colonel Price. The group open fired on the creature as the revolting thing expanded a set of wings and took to the air.

"I didn't know scorpions had wings," yelled Sergeant G over the sound of gunfire.

"They do now," said Agent Pyle as he fired his assault rifle into the thing. "Why do they have to be so big? Can't they be smaller?"

Jake swung the 50 calibers around and poured round after round into the despicable arthropod which brought it down. While Viktor and the FBI agents covered the downed arachnid the rest ran over to O'Rork's crumpled form and carried him back to one of the DPVs.

"He's still alive," said Sergeant G.

"Which one of you is the designated medic?" asked Viktor.

"O'Rork is," said Tank.

Jake grabbed the medical pack off O'Rork's back and Sergeant G crammed gauze and clotting powder into the wound to ebb the flow of blood. "Colonel, he's not going to last long enough for them to dig us out."

"I know," growled the colonel.

"Jacob," said Viktor, "we may have another problem."

CHAPTER EIGHTEEN

Knotted Pine Lodge
101 East Highway 163
Mexican Hat, Utah

PAM, Ellie, Al, along with Lieutenant Beggett sat in the conference room while Deputy Bridges briefed them. "The information I've been able to dig up on Wargwolf Inc. shows it's a company that came into being right after World War II. The company's owned by a woman named Frieda Getman who was a movie star in Germany before the war. She was a big socialite and was seen at times with Hitler before he became Chancellor of Germany."

Pam had been typing notes into her laptop and looked up at the mention of Hitler's name. "She's tied to Hitler?"

Deputy Bridges shrugged a shoulder. "I'm not sure. There's no mention of her after Hitler's rise to power. The bio on her says after the war she created companies that over the years diversified into many different areas like coal, oil, military arms manufacturing, and medical research."

"I'll bet that includes DNA research," said Pam sarcastically.

"Maybe it's just a coincidence?" said Al as he pushed his glasses up on his nose.

"It's too much of a coincidence," said Deputy Bridges.

"I agree," said Ellie. "As soon as Jake calls, I'll give him the update." It was getting later in the day, and she was getting worried since he hadn't called as promised.

"I think this might be the kicker. The serial numbers from the weapons we took from the Elite Protective Service people never show to have been sold anywhere but were manufactured by…"

"Wargwolf," added Pam.

"Correct."

Roscoe was asleep on the floor but suddenly sat up and growled at the door. They all turned towards it when someone knocked softly. Lieutenant Beggett walked over to the door while Roscoe stood and growled at the door.

Ellie looked at Roscoe. "Lieutenant, I don't think you should open that."

The lieutenant hesitated momentarily, which was a fatal mistake as his body suddenly jerked several times as bullets came though the door and riddled his body. Deputy Bridges jumped to his feet and grabbed for his side weapon as two men dressed in dark clothing shoved the door open. Lieutenant Beggett fell dead to the floor as the human assailants armed with assault rifles charged in followed by several demons. One in particular was a seven-foot-tall hairy demon with the head of a bull armed with a large sword.

One of the men turned the assault weapon on Deputy Bridges who was still in the process of drawing his handgun but knew it was too late. In a surprise burst of bravery Al grabbed the assailant's arm which threw off his shot which still hit Deputy Bridges who dropped his handgun and collapsed. The hairy bull demon swung the giant sword and sliced off Al's arm just below the elbow. Al stood in shock for a moment at his missing limb and then slowly slid to the floor.

A green and brown lizard demon with sharp horns protruding from above its eyes like bizarre eyebrows came after Pam but was slowed as Roscoe attacked the thing's leg. The bull demon kicked Roscoe in the side knocking him under the table. Suddenly the heavenly being, Kiara, appeared and sliced through the greenish brown demon killing it instantly as more demons jammed into the small conference room.

The hairy bull demon raised his sword to finish off Al when Ellie leapt onto the demon to try to keep him away. The behemoth simply plucked Ellie off his back and slammed her against the wall. The last thing she saw before everything went dark was Kiara fighting off three more demons while Pam held a chair up trying to keep the other fiends at bay.

———

Remote Command Post (CP)
Nevada National Security Site
65 miles north of Las Vegas, Nevada

VIKTOR POINTED to the passageway where the scorpion beast had entered the cavern and to their horror a dozen smaller versions of the dead one scurried out. These were identical in appearance but smaller, about two to three feet long.

"Oh great, Terrell, you got your wish; smaller ones," said Agent Williams as she fired her assault rifle at the little monsters. The rest followed suit and fired into the abominable arthropods which did stop their advance, but only for a moment. Ten, then twenty, then fifty of the things came pouring out of the passageway.

"Looks like mama scorpion's been busy," remarked Tank.

"We can't stay out here in the open," shouted Colonel Price over the gunfire. He pointed to the other passageway. "Head to that opening and we'll try to set up a defense."

"But, Colonel, what if they're in there too?" asked Sergeant Hamstead, the driver of Jake's DPV.

"We'll have to take that chance, now go...GO!" bellowed Colonel Price.

By then the creatures covered the floor and walls of the far side of the cavern. Sergeant G swung a large backpack onto his shoulder and helped Sergeant Hamstead carry O'Rork towards the passageway. Jake, Viktor, and the rest backed towards the opening, firing in all different directions trying to keep the deadly little degenerates away.

One of them took to the air, zipped over their heads, and landed on Sergeant Hamstead's Kevlar helmet. The cemetery dust covered helmet caused the menace to burn but didn't stop it. It simply took to the air again in flight and drove its stinger under the helmet into the base of his skull, killing the sergeant instantly. When he collapsed, Sergeant G stumbled and fell while trying to hold on to O'Rork. Another two-foot scorpion climbed up Sergeant G's leg and began to burn from the toxic dust. The sergeant kicked the thing away and fired his handgun into it, killing it. Viktor bent down and without hesitation lifted O'Rork onto his shoulders in a typical fireman's carry then headed into the passageway. The rest of the quickly decreasing number of elite team members followed him into the cavern's branch.

They slowly worked their way back into the smaller cavern passageway that at times required them to stoop down due to a low ceiling, dodging large limestone columns and brushing their helmets against small straw like stalactites. The horde of scorpion devils hesitated but followed them into the passageway under a rain of gunfire. As they worked their way down through the maze of cavern formations, Sergeant G would stop for a moment, remove a two-pound bag from his backpack and drop it. Attached to the bag was a remote detonator. After thirty minutes of playing cat and mouse the team hit a dead end, the passageway was blocked. Jake, Sergeant G, Tank, and the FBI agents set up a line of defense, firing at the deformed scorpions. Viktor carried O'Rork to farthest end of the cavern. "Colonel," said Viktor, "he's lost a lot of blood; he needs help soon."

Colonel Price nodded while he radioed the command post but was told that help was on the way but anything big enough to dig them out was still hours away. The colonel rubbed his forehead and cursed. He looked back down the passageway and saw the devils crawling, scurrying, and flying their way. They would run out of ammo long before help arrived.

Viktor made O'Rork as comfortable as possible while Sergeant G grabbed his backpack and removed another two-pound bag. He stepped up next to Jake and pointed down the passageway. "I need you to cover me for a minute. I'm going to try to slow them down."

Jake nodded. Sergeant G ran back down the cavern, opened the bag, poured some dirt on the ground, and swung the bag back and forth in the air to coat the area with the contents of the bag. When the bag was half empty, he dropped the bag and dashed back behind their defensive line. Agent Pyle looked over at him. "Cemetery dirt and explosives," explained Sergeant G. "It should slow them down."

And just as he'd hoped, the little cretins crawled over the holy dirt and screeched when it burned their legs like acid. The army of scorpions halted. Unfortunately, most just flew over as more scorpions pushed forward and knocked the others into the cemetery dirt. Amid the screeches and groans the others flew and scrambled over their smoldering kin.

Sergeant G removed a small handheld device with a small red button. "This will blow the bags."

Colonel Price heard their conversation and had also seen the sergeant dropping the bags along the way. "Go ahead and blow it. Clear a path for us out."

"Give the switch to me," said Jake. "It'll be more effective if I throw the switch."

Sergeant G looked at the colonel who nodded. The sergeant handed the small handheld device to Jake. Colonel Price turned to the others. "Find some cover; we're going to blow these things back to Hades."

Jake waited precious seconds for the others to find cover, while the little atrocities climbed over a bridge of dead scorpions or flew, and pushed the button. Each bag full of cemetery dirt exploded, sending dirt and dust everywhere with a deafening roar. After a few moments, the dust settled, and they all stared back down the passageway. The scorpions within sight were dead, which was great, but they had a new problem. The passageway had collapsed; they were now trapped in a small pocket of the cave.

———

Wargwolf Private Estate
Highway 160
South of Kayenta, Arizona

ELLIE OPENED her eyes to a blurred world but after a moment she focused and realized she was lying on a leather couch in an elegant room filled up with books. She sat up and the world spun which forced her to reach out and steady herself against the arm of the couch.

"You're finally awake," said a female voice with a thick German accent.

Ellie turned and saw an elderly woman in a wheelchair across the room. "Where am I?"

The woman ignored her, picked up a phone, said something in German, and hung up.

"Who are you?" asked Ellie as her memory began to come back. "Where are my friends? What have you done to them?"

The door opened and an attractive blonde woman entered. Without speaking she walked over to a desk and began stuffing papers into a briefcase.

"What's going on?" demanded Ellie. She tried to get to her feet but suddenly a large furry claw forced her down onto the couch. Ellie knew instantly from the stench what it was and looked up at a hideous looking striped tiger-like demon with huge black wings. Even though she'd seen demons several times before, there was something more maleficent about this one.

"Not that it will matter much longer to you but I'm Gerda," said the blonde woman. "This is my grandmother, Priska. That is Degen."

"Priska Getman," said Ellie as she realized who these people were.

Priska smiled along with Gerda. "Ah, so you know who I am?"

Ellie's face reddened in anger. "You can't possibly get away with this. Too many people know about you and your insane plans."

Degen roared with laugher. "Do you think I care that your boyfriend and his little band of heroes know my plans? I trapped him and the other impotents in the tunnel so they could play with my scorpion pets. They're dead by now."

Ellie jumped to her feet. "Liar."

Degen back handed Ellie across the face which knocked her to the ground. Ellie's lip began to bleed as she looked up in defiance at the foul monster. "Where are my friends?"

Degen bent down and glared at Ellie. She could smell the stench of death on his breath. "Your boyfriend's dead, your female friend's dead, and so is your little guardian angel. As for you our lab's prepared to make you a donor for one of our most deadly embryos. They kill the donor when they're born."

Ellie's eyes widened in shock as Degen jerked her up off the ground by her arm. "Enjoy your last few hours...in a cell."

Remote Command Post (CP)
Nevada National Security Site
65 miles north of Las Vegas, Nevada

COLONEL PRICE SHOOK his head in frustration and cursed after hearing from the command post that the large rescue equipment was still forty-five minutes away.

"Colonel, what's your status?" radioed Major Wilkins in a whisper from somewhere above ground.

Colonel Price turned. "How's O'Rork?"

"His breathing's shallow but he's a fighter," said Sergeant G.

"O'Rork's still hanging in there," answered the colonel. "What's the situation up there?"

"We're staged in the area about a half a mile away from your GPS coordinates," replied Major Wilkins. "Our DPV was destroyed by those heathens, so we've found a secluded spot and dug in."

"Stay in cover, there's nothing you can do until help arrives."

"It may not matter," said Agent Williams. "Unless they get here before our air runs out."

"Da," said Viktor. "Try to slow your breathing and talk less to conserve air."

"I agree," said Colonel Price. "Conserve your flashlights. Use glow sticks instead."

"Can it get much worse?" grumbled Sergeant G.

A few minutes later, Tank turned on his flashlight.

"I said save the batteries," growled Colonel Price.

"Sir, I heard something over by the cave in," replied Tank as he shined his light over where the roof had caved in. They all looked and to their horror several of the rocks shook.

"Oh, my gawd," said Tank. "Those things are digging through."

"It just got worse," added Sergeant G.

––––––––––

Wargwolf Private Estate
Highway 160
South of Kayenta, Arizona

ELLIE SAT on a cheap foam mattress on a cot in a faded gray four walled cell, which was ten feet by ten feet. She'd washed her face using the dirty sink and tried to get the sight of Lieutenant Beggett, Deputy Bridges and Al being killed out of her mind. She refused to think about Jake and Pam being dead.

The sound of keys in the cell lock brought her attention back. A man in a dark one-piece jumpsuit ordered her out and told her to walk to the end of the hallway.

"Where are we going?" demanded Ellie.

Without answering, the man shoved her hard down the hallway and as she passed the long row of cells, she noticed women's faces against the thick glass windows staring vacantly. She also noticed that the women's heads were shaved.

At the end of the hallway, they entered a large room filled with medical equipment and an examination table. A chair with straps was off to the left and Ellie suddenly realized where she was. "This is where you do those experiments," she gasped.

An ugly heavy woman in a similar jumpsuit was already waiting, looked Ellie up and down, and turned to the male guard. "She doesn't need a bath, tie her down."

Ellie spun and darted towards the door but was grabbed by the male guard who lifted her off the ground in a bear hug.

"Stop, you can't do this," yelled Ellie as she fought to break away.

The guard lifted her and slammed Ellie onto the examination table knocking the breath out of her. The male guard held her down while the woman strapped her arms. After she was subdued, the female removed a syringe from a tray.

"You can't be serious," said Ellie. "This is inhumane."

The female guard snickered and jabbed the needle into her arm. "Don't worry about shaving her head. She won't survive this one."

———

Remote Command Post (CP)
Nevada National Security Site
65 miles north of Las Vegas, Nevada

"I THOUGHT WE KILLED THEM ALL," growled Sergeant G.

"Obviously not," said Viktor.

"There must have been some that the dust or explosion didn't kill," explained Jake as he checked his weapon to determine how many rounds he had left. He knew there was a chance the creatures would break through before their air ran out.

"Suffocate or killed by deformed monster scorpions," said Tank. "Not my choice of ways to go."

"Everyone," ordered Colonel Price. "Set up a line in case they come through before they can dig us out."

The small group quickly moved around and took up crude defense positions. Agent Pyle's position was slightly to the left behind a rock formation. "Man, I didn't know bats crap some much. There's a lot of bat guano and feathers over here."

Agent Williams rolled her eyes. Tank and Sergeant G chuckled.

Their attention was drawn back to the cave in where several more rocks moved which meant the things were getting closer to digging through.

"At least when they come through so will some air," said Tank.

"Da," said Viktor. "Then they can eat us while we're still alive."

"Killjoy."

Something was bothering Jake. He spun around to Agent Williams. "Do you still have the photos of the cave in Arizona in your pocket?"

"Yes, but what do you w…"

"Just give them to me," interrupted Jake. "I have an idea."

Agent Williams dug the snapshots from her pocket and handed them to him. "I don't know what they'd have to do with scorpions."

Jake shook his head while he thumbed through the photos. "I'm not thinking about scorpions. Bats don't have feathers, birds do, and especially large birds."

"But what would a bird be doing down here?" asked Colonel Price.

"A bird wouldn't but a half human half bird demon would," answered Jake.

"What?" exclaimed Agent Pyle. "You mean this is demon dung. Oh, great."

Agent Williams then realized what Jake was getting at, so she explained. "It was a half human half demon bird that painted scenes in the cave. It must have come this way to escape. There must be another way out."

"That's my thought," said Jake. He pointed to a part of the paintings where a figure appeared to be going towards three vertical lines with a circle. "Look for three vertical columns or anything similar."

Colonel Price stood up and put his Kevlar helmet back on. "Agent Williams and Tank can stay and watch for our unwanted intruders while the rest of you look around for three vertical structures nearby or any kind leading to a possible opening."

The group separated, frantically searched the walls and creases of the cavern for any sign of escape. A couple of rocks tumbled down from the cave in. "Colonel," warned Tank. "We're about to have visitors."

"Here," yelled Agent Pyle. He pointed to a sector of the cavern between three large totem pole shaped columns of limestone. "It's over here by all the guano. There's marks here leading up to these rocks. It looks like there might have been an opening in the ceiling, but it's covered up now."

"Makes sense," said Jake, "The creature probably hid there where Agent Pyle was sitting until it could escape."

"We didn't notice it and the explosions must have closed the opening," said Viktor.

Colonel Price turned towards the group. "Sergeant G, get those explosives. The rest of you get back down there and hold off those ugly insects while we try to blow a hole in this section."

Jake, Viktor, and the rest set up defensive positions while Sergeant G quickly set several explosives that they hoped would open the exit. The two men then took cover down behind a large limestone flow. "Cover," yelled Sergeant G and set off the explosives. The cavern rocked from the explosion and caused several formations to topple and deadly stalactites to fall from the ceiling. Through the dust they saw a beam of light shine down. The group cheered.

"Grab O'Rork, and let's get out of here," yelled Colonel Price. Viktor and Sergeant G lifted the unconscious O'Rork and headed to the now open end. Jake looked up and saw blue sky, but the opening was still almost nine feet above their heads. Jake turned to Agent Williams. "I'll lift you up so you can climb out." Agent Williams nodded. Jake leaned against the wall and made a stirrup for her to step into by interlacing his fingers. He lifted her up and she grabbed the edge of the opening only to be grabbed by two pairs of hands and lifted out. A second later Major Wilkins's smiling face appeared in the opening. "Anybody need a hand?"

"Yes," yelled Colonel Price. "Grab O'Rork when we lift him up."

They lifted the injured corporal up allowing Major Wilkins and another soldier to grab O'Rork's shoulders. They quickly pulled him up and out.

Tank turned back at the sound of rocks falling. "Uh, Colonel, that explosion also opened their hole."

They all looked back at the sight of scorpions pushing and clawing their way through. Jake walked back towards the scorpions, carefully aimed at them to conserve ammo, and shot them. Several more came through and he shot them as well. Agent Pyle, Tank, Agent Williams, and Sergeant G climbed out.

"Sergeant," yelled Jake as he fired at several more. "Where are the rest of the explosives?"

"Down there to your right, Major," answered Sergeant G from outside the hole.

Colonel Price and Jake were the only two left so while Jake shot the revolting demon scorpions, Colonel Price grabbed the bags of explosives. He tossed them down the passageway.

"Climb out, Colonel, and I'll blow it," shouted Jake over the sound of the gunfire.

Colonel Price shook his head. "And leave you down here, not a chance."

"We don't have time to argue, sir," answered Jake.

"You're right." The colonel yelled up at the opening. "Throw me a line."

A long minute later, a rope dropped down. Colonel Price tied it around Jake's waist as he reloaded and kept firing. "Pull the rope when you're ready." He handed Jake the remote detonator and slapped him on the shoulder. The colonel then climbed up the rope to safety.

Jake backed up until he was standing directly under the hole. The flow of scorpions had dwindled down, but several were still coming through the passageway. One of the scorpions flew up and impaled its stinger in Jake's left calf muscle only to be clubbed down with the butt of the assault rifle. Jake gritted his teeth against the pain in his leg as several more scorpions took to the air. Jake jerked on the rope and was lifted quickly up to the ceiling. When Jake reached the opening, he hit the button.

The explosion lifted Jake up and out as dirt, dust, and pieces of cave formations blew out. The ground itself lifted then collapsed down filling in the hole. The group outside were forced back by the blast. Jake sluggishly stood up. His vest and uniform protected him from most of the blast, but he still had numerous cuts from small debris. They stared at the rubble, but no movement was noted.

Major Wilkins spoke up. "Those monsters flew around until you blew a hole in the ground, and they left."

"Do you think we got all those scorpion things?" asked Sgt. G.

Jake nodded his head. "There weren't that many left. I think we finished them off."

A medivac helicopter soon came over the horizon, landed quickly, and loaded O'Rork. They bandaged Jake's leg along with a few of the others' minor injuries. He was thankful that the genetically altered scorpions didn't carry any venom, but the puncture wound still hurt. The medivac lifted off with the critically injured O'Rork while the rest loaded up in a Black Hawk that arrived and headed back to the remote command post.

While in the air, the crew chief tapped Jake's arm and handed him a sheet of paper. Jake read it then crumpled it up.

"What is it?" asked Agent Williams.

"Jacob, what's wrong?" asked Viktor.

Jake's jaw muscles tightened as his fists clenched and unclenched. "They attacked our folks in Mexican Hat. Lieutenant Beggett's dead. Deputy Bridges and Al Simpson were critically injured. Pam and Ellie are missing."

The rest of the flight to the remote command post was in silence.

———

AFTER SEVERAL HOURS of intense debriefing, Jake sat a table drinking coffee with Viktor and Agent Williams. Agent Pyle was heating up a prepackaged meal in the microwave. Colonel Price came in and poured himself a cup of coffee. "Your transportation will be here in about fifteen minutes." He sat down next to Agent Williams. "So, what's your next step?" he asked.

Agent Williams glanced over at Jake before she answered. "We'll head back to Mexican Hat and try to find out what happened there first then go from there."

"I'm sorry to hear about what happened to your people there."

Jake nodded. "Thank you, sir, we'll find them…when we do, someone will pay dearly. Your unit has paid too much already."

Colonel Price nodded solemnly.

"How's O'Rork?" asked Agent Pyle.

"He's still in intensive care. If he doesn't get an infection from that creature he should fully recover." Colonel Price stirred his coffee with a small plastic stir stick. "How's the leg?"

"I'll live," said Jake.

Colonel Price smiled. He knew Jake's type wouldn't admit if it hurt or not. The colonel's face went somber. "It's too cliché to say it's honorable to die while serving our country. I've lost some good men in the last few days and we're no closer to finding out where that damnable bomb is. We have alerts out but I'm not sure that will be enough, especially if we can't see these monsters."

"Colonel," said Jake. "I promise when we catch up with them, I'll find out where the bomb is and make them pay. These creatures can't hide behind diplomacy or immunity."

Without further comment they all gathered their gear and headed outside as they heard a helicopter. Tank and Sergeant G waited outside. They shook hands with everyone, and Tank gave Agent Williams a huge hug. "Since I won't be there to watch your back, little lady, you be careful."

Agent Williams at first frowned at being called a little lady again then grinned. "The same goes for you."

"I wish we were going with you to finish this, but we don't have the authorization," said Colonel Price.

"We'll make sure it's taken care of, Colonel," said Viktor.

Colonel Price shook the big Russian's hand. "Two days ago, I wasn't sure about having a Russian here but anytime you want a spot on my team you're always welcome."

———

JAKE, Viktor, and the two FBI agents were flown directly to Mexican Hat where they were met by Deputy Sheriff Sergeant Coleman who drove them to the lodge. Sheriff Jefferson waited at the entrance to the hotel and shook hands with everyone. "I heard that you had a rough time in Nevada," said the sheriff.

"We lost a lot of good soldiers back there," said Jake.

"How's Deputy Bridges?" asked Agent Williams.

The sheriff smiled. "He's lucky, the round nicked his neck. Your journalist friend Simpson should have died too but someone professionally applied a tourniquet around his upper arm to stop the bleeding. They're both at the Medical Center over in Shiprock."

"Maybe Deputy Bridges did it and just doesn't remember?" asked Agent Pyle.

Sheriff Jefferson shook his head. "I don't think so. The EMTs said it was expertly done." He turned to Jake. "Your dog's over at Doc Hodge's vet office with some bruised ribs so he should be up and around by now."

Jake allowed himself to smile briefly for the first time since hearing the bad news. He felt Malachy must have bandaged Al and kept Deputy Bridges from bleeding out from the neck wound.

The sheriff led them down the hall to the conference room where crime scene tape crisscrossed the doorway. He ripped down the tape. "Are you sure you want to see inside?"

Jake turned to the others who nodded. Sheriff Jefferson opened the door and stepped aside to allow them to enter. The interior of the room smelled of death, blood, and sulfur. The conference table was broken in half and the chairs were scattered all over the room. There were several large pools of dried blood on the floor along with blood splattered on the walls. At least six piles of ash were scattered around on the floor indicating that demons had been killed during the attack. Sheriff Jefferson pointed to the piles. "From what I've learned about these monsters I'm guessing that these were demons at one time?"

Jake nodded.

"I thought you were the only one that could kill these things?" asked the sheriff.

"I am," answered Jake. "But angels can too."

Sheriff Jefferson raised an eyebrow, didn't respond, but looked around the room with a new perspective. It also confirmed Jake's belief that some heavenly being had been here. He walked around and studied the scene along with the others.

Agent Williams spoke up. "It looks like Simpson was attacked over there, Deputy Bridges was shot here, and the spot by the door is where Lieutenant Begget was killed."

The others nodded in agreement.

"It appears that the women weren't injured or at least not seriously," said Viktor. "But why take them?"

"To use them as leverage?" asked Agent Pyle.

"Perhaps," said Jake. "Demons sometimes do things just to be cruel. They enjoy causing pain."

"But where did they take them?"

"I think I know where we might be able to find out," interjected Sheriff Jefferson. "Deputy Bridges was doing some checking and saved his information on the department's computer server. He'd found a connection between the weapons we confiscated and a German company called Wargwolf." The sheriff motioned for them to step out into the hallway, out of the gruesome scene, and shut the door. "This company has a facility down in Arizona near Kayenta around the Black Mesa area where coal is mined."

"Deputy Bridges emailed me that the weapons belonged to Wargwolf Inc. but in the hands of this private security company," said Agent Pyle. "Also, Agent Robbins from the Flagstaff office said that Flagstaff police ran the license plates on Wargwolf vehicles."

"I wonder where they're getting victims to use to test their experiments," said Viktor.

"I wonder too," said Agent Williams. "We'll have the Flagstaff office contact the police there and find out. I don't know if we have enough for a search warrant."

Jake suddenly had an idea. "I think I might know a way."

CHAPTER NINETEEN

Criminal Investigations Division
Flagstaff Police Department
911 East Sawmill Road
Flagstaff, Arizona

ON HIS DRIVE INTO WORK, Detective Brutten's phone rang, and he noticed it was the dispatcher.

"Warren, this is Trish, I got some crazy woman on the phone saying that another woman's been taken. She gave me a license plate and was insistent that I call you."

Detective Brutten pulled over, stopped, and wrote down the license plate. "Thanks, I'll check it."

"I went ahead and ran a check after she hung up. It's registered to a company called Wargwolf up in Kaytena."

"Wargwolf?"

"Weird sounding company, huh?"

"It sure is, thanks." Detective Brutten hung up.

Upon arriving he noticed a note taped to his phone which requested him to contact the FBI office in Flagstaff. He dialed the number and FBI Agent Robbins answered.

"Good morning, this is Detective Brutten from the Flagstaff Police, I had a note to call you."

"Thank you for calling, Detective," answered Agent Robbins. "We received an alert that you ran the license plates on vehicles that belonged to a company named Wargwolf."

"What's the deal with this company? We've had some suspicion about them abducting women."

"How odd, we have an FBI team in the Kayenta area and southern Utah conducting several death investigations and this company's name keeps coming up."

Detective Brutten sat straight up. "Deaths? Are any of them missing women?"

"Not so far," answered Agent Robbins. "The only woman killed was from out of state visiting with her husband. The rest were men."

"I have numerous missing women from this area, and it seems to occur after they have contact with one of those Wargwolf vehicles."

"I'll notify the agents and if they find out anything they'll contact you," said Agent Robbins before hanging up.

Detective Brutten sat and stared at the missing persons files. He had a feeling that there was more to this than the FBI was giving out.

Navajo Tribal Police Department
Route 7
Chinle, Arizona

SGT. GREYMOUNTAIN CAME to the window of his office when he heard an SUV pull up outside. Jake had called earlier and said they were driving there to talk to him again. He watched as Agent Williams, Agent Pyle, Viktor, and Jake climbed out. Sgt. Greymountain met them at the door. "Welcome back, I wasn't expecting to see you so soon, so I was surprised when you called." He could tell from Jake's slight limp, cuts, and scratches that things hadn't gone well. "Come inside and tell me how I can help."

They sat or stood around the sergeant's small office and filled in Sgt. Greymountain on the events leading up to their arrival. At the end, he picked up his phone and began dialing a number. "I'll call my grandfather."

"Don't bother, Grandson, I'm already here," said a deep voice from the doorway.

They all turned to find Elijah Greymountain grinning. "I saw your truck come in so I knew something might be up." He looked around the room. "Where are the two young ladies? I was looking forward to their company. They didn't make this trip?"

"They've been taken," Jake growled.

The elder Greymountain frowned. "That is unfortunate; do we know who?"

"Yes, we do," said Sgt. Greymountain. "Please sit, Grandfather, and we'll update you."

Twenty minutes later, Elijah Greymountain shook his head. "This is a bad situation. Devil spirits with a nuclear weapon is a bad omen. We leased the land to that Wargwolf Company in exchange for money for tribal improvements, but I feel it's time to evict them."

————

LATER JAKE TOOK a quick shower in his motel room in Kayenta. His leg ached from the wound, he felt frustrated, lonely, and confused. The harder he tried the more people got hurt. Law enforcement officers, soldiers, and innocent civilians were either dead or injured and they were no closer to finding the bomb or stopping them. Ellie and Pam were missing. The journalist kid had lost an arm but was recovering. Roscoe was resting at the vet's office in Utah. He and the FBI were always one step behind, and it was unacceptable.

Jake put on a bath robe and stepped into the room but suddenly realized he was not alone. A giant with golden colored skin stood by the table. Malachy didn't give his normal jovial greeting, so Jake knew things were not going well on his side either. Jake tried to smile. "Evening, Malachy."

The heavenly being stepped over and placed a hand on Jake's shoulder. "Jacob, it's good to see you."

"What happened?"

Malachy turned and sat on the corner of the bed. "We've been in constant battle with the fallen."

Jake sat in one of the chairs. "You know they have a nuclear bomb now."

Malachy nodded. "Yes, I know. They've taken it to Germany with them. As you know while you were in the caverns, we were battling them and that's when they took the opportunity to attack Ellie and Pamela. It was fortunate that Kiara had remained behind and was able to keep them from finishing off Deputy Bridges and Albert, but she wasn't able to keep them from kidnapping your friends."

So, she was the one who treated their wounds "Tell her thanks."

"We are pleased to serve God, but she will be glad to hear that. She's recovering from her injuries."

Jake raised an eyebrow and looked over at him. "I didn't really think about angels being hurt; I mean angels are from heaven. Well, you know what I mean."

Malachy finally smiled. "Yes, I do. And yes, we can be injured or killed as easily as the fallen. She fought bravely and will be well soon enough. We will prevail, Jacob, so you must keep trying."

Jake looked at the heavenly being with hardened eyes. "Nothing's going to keep me from finding Ellie and making them pay for all the pain and suffering they've caused."

————

Federal Bureau of Investigation
Office of Director
935 Pennsylvania Avenue Northwest
Washington, D.C.

DEPUTY DIRECTOR RUIZ and FBI Director Chisom were seated in the FBI director's office on speaker phone with Agent Williams.

She'd emailed Deputy Director Ruiz a complete report of the events in Nevada and the attack in Mexican Hat.

"I'll send Sheriff Jefferson our condolences for the lieutenant's death," said Director Chisom. "The secretary of defense briefed the president on what happened at Nellis. I don't want to harp on the fact that we need to find that weapon and soon."

"Yes, sir," came Agent Williams's voice from the speaker. "Major Taft was told that the weapon is in Germany."

Director Chisom raised both eyebrows. "How does he know that? It wasn't in the report you submitted."

Agent Williams hesitated.

"Agent Williams?" asked Deputy Director Ruiz.

"Sir, Major Taft told me after I'd submitted the report. He said his angel friend, Malachy, told him."

Director Chisom looked over at Deputy Director Ruiz who didn't seem surprised. "What about this Wargwolf facility there? When are you planning to hit it?"

"As soon as a team arrives from Flagstaff with the police detective, we'll hit it after dark."

"Good, I hope Major Taft's two female friends are still there and maybe we can get lucky and find some evidence we can use against these people. Are you sure the warrant's good?"

"Yes, sir," answered Agent Williams. "Based on the information about the weapons and the missing women from Flagstaff we convinced the Navajo Tribal Council to approve the warrant. It's in their jurisdiction and I think they're tired of this mess too."

"Let them stand in line. Keep us informed." The director hung up and turned to Deputy Director Ruiz. "Oscar, I know that these creatures exist because of what we've all seen, but it's going to be hard for the president to sell it to the German authorities that they have demons with a bomb in their country."

Deputy Director Ruiz closed Agent Williams's report and laid it on the table. "I know, sir, but I just hope that they don't wait until it's too late. Any idea when they might use the weapon?"

"Perhaps," said the director, "the logical target would be during the World Economic Summit that's in Berlin in a couple of days. I'll inform the president, but I doubt they'll cancel the conference. I'm sure they'll believe they have more to fear from protesters and terrorists than a group of invisible monsters with a fifty-year-old bomb that we can't even officially admit exists."

Deputy Director Ruiz shook his head. "They have no idea."

"No, they don't, so that's why you have to make sure it doesn't happen."

———

Wargwolf Estate
Highway 160
Kayenta, Arizona

IT WAS WELL after midnight when the Flagstaff FBI team along with Detective Brutten, Jake, Viktor, Agents William and Pyle, Sgt. Greymountain, and four Navajo officers drove several vehicles slowly down the highway. They were fortunate because there was no moon so they hoped their approach would not be noticed but it made it harder for them to drive without their headlights. They parked a hundred yards down from the entrance. A five-man team hustled down the shoulder of the road and surprised the guard in the guard shack who was taken into custody without an incident. The rest drove quickly up to the gate. Agent Robbins motioned Agent Williams over to the shack.

"What's wrong?" she asked.

"The guard has to enter a code to open the gate and he's not talking," explained Agent Robbins. "We don't have time to try to get him to talk."

"Can we blow the gate lock?"

Agent Robbins nodded. "Of course, but that'll make noise. I don't think they can hear it from up at the main facility as far away as it is but there's a chance."

Agent Williams nodded. "We don't have a choice, let's do it."

Agent Robbins walked back and began setting up a small charge on the gate with another agent. Agent Williams walked back to their

SUV. "The gate requires a code so they're going to have to blow the gate."

Sgt. Greymountain walked up from their vehicle and was told the reason for the delay.

"When that gate blows, we need to get to the building as fast as possible," she explained. "As we briefed, you and your men help us with the perimeter and our team will enter."

Sgt. Greymountain nodded and went back to brief his men. A moment later, a flash followed by a small explosion was heard as the gate was blown open. The FBI vehicles and Navajo police vehicles flipped on their lights and raced up the winding road toward the building but when they rounded the last turn, they were met by an unusual sight...Elijah Greymountain. The elder Navajo stood just outside the entrance with other Navajo men with rifles. "Welcome friends, we were wondering when you'd get here," he said with a smile.

The agents shined their lights around and to their amazement they saw fifty or more armed Navajo men surrounding the building. Sgt. Greymountain stepped up. "Grandfather, what's going on?"

"We knew that you'd come up the road, so I decided we'd come the back way and make sure no one left out the back door," explained the elder Navajo. "We have the outside secured but the inside's your job."

Sgt. Greymountain was speechless while the others smiled and chuckled. Agent Williams and Robbins approached the door where a Navajo man had one of the security men tied. "How many men are inside?" asked Agent Robbins. The guard just stared at them defiantly. Agent Robbins shoved the man against the wall. "How many men are inside and are they armed?"

The man sneered at Agent Robbins. "I have diplomatic immunity," said the man in a thick German accent. "I don't have to answer anything you say. I have rights."

Elijah Greymountain stepped up and touched the FBI agent on the shoulder. "Maybe I can be of some help."

Agent Robbins shrugged and stepped back to allow the elder Navajo to approach the man. "Now, can't we be reasonable?"

"American swine," said the man. "You red skinned heathens are even lower than Jews."

Elijah Greymountain smiled. "Yes, you are absolutely right, but you see this is our reservation, our jurisdiction, our rules, and your immunity doesn't work here. We red skinned heathens are a wild group. Do you know that we're experts at skinning a man alive?"

The man glared back.

"Did you know we know exactly how much skin we can peel off of a man while holding him over a bed of coals without killing him?"

The man's face paled slightly.

Elijah Greymountain motioned for one of the Navajo men to come over. "Take this stupid white man and show him our ancient ways. Be sure and save his scalp for me to put on my big woom poom teepee."

The Navajo man sneered, pulled a large knife from his belt, and dragged the guard towards the woods. A few other Navajos followed. The guard kicked and fought but finally screamed, "I'll tell you; I'll tell you!"

They shoved and prodded the man back to the entrance with the point of a knife. "There are only five armed men inside. The rest are lab techs finishing up a few things before leaving."

The Navajo man with the knife grabbed the guard's hair and put the knife to his scalp.

"No, no, it's the truth," whined the man.

Jake stepped up "What about the two women they brought here?"

The guard was visibly shaking. "All the women are down in the lower level and were used as experiments."

Jake closed in on the man until they were nose to nose. "You had better hope that they're alive or I'll do worse to you than these Navajos."

Agent Williams had the guard taken and placed with the other guards behind one of the Navajo police vehicles. Viktor looked over at the elder Greymountain. "Do you really know how to skin a man alive?"

"Of course not," answered Elijah Greymountain with a grin. "I saw it in an old B western movie and figured that he'd believe the stereotype."

The FBI team set up on either side of the door with the handheld battering ram. "Do you think they know we're here?" asked Agent Pyle.

"Probably," said Agent Robbins as she pointed up at a surveillance camera mounted above the door. "We need to be fast but be careful. Look for booby traps."

The FBI entry team indicated they would cover one half of the building while Agent Williams, Agent Pyle, Detective Brutten, Jake, and Viktor would cover the other. They slammed the ram into the door, breaking the lock, and stormed the facility. They carefully searched the upper floors but found no one. "This half is clear," said Agent Robbins. "What about you?"

"We have one room left to clear but so far nothing," responded Agent Williams. They cleared the last room, a small space filled with supplies. "We've cleared the whole upper levels."

"Why would the remaining guards leave it empty?" asked Agent Pyle.

Agent Robbins shook his head. "I don't know but I don't like it. It smells of a trap so watch your back."

"I agree, I don't like it," commented Agent Williams. She remembered the trap in the past the now dead demon Ghazi set for them at one of laboratories on the east coast. It cost the FBI several agents' lives.

They came to an elevator next to a locked metal door. A small window in the door showed a set of stairs descending to a lower level. Both the elevator and the stairway had an entry pad that appeared to be a retina recognition device. Agent Williams called for the same guard as before who was dragged in by two Navajo officers. The man confirmed that it was in fact a retina recognition entry.

"We need him to open the door?" explained Agent Williams.

"What if he won't?" asked Agent Pyle.

"We can have one of the redskin heathens cut his eye out and then use it. We need his eye, not his whole body," suggested Agent Robbins with a snicker.

The guard volunteered to open the door using his eye while still intact. When the reader scanned his retina and confirmed his identity the door clicked open. The team quickly but quietly worked their way down the stairs to another door that led into a lit hallway. The hallway was empty, so the entry team split up and entered the first two rooms alert for any trip wires or traps. Jake and his team entered the room to the right which was dark so using the lights attached to their weapons they scanned a large laboratory and beheld a ghastly sight. The room was littered with bodies all dressed in scrubs, lab coats, and guard uniforms. They had all been shot.

"I guess they outlived their usefulness," said Agent Williams dryly.

Agent Robbins radioed and said they'd found the same thing in the other labs.

"This is why we didn't encounter any resistance," added Viktor.

The groups worked down the hall and came to a T, so they split up and went left or right each ending in a single unpainted metal door.

Agent Williams looked back at Agent Robbins who was posed at the other door. They checked the edges of the doors for any type of explosive trigger mechanism and when they found none, they quickly opened the door and entered. They found another hallway with several large steel doors that were several inches thick. The place reeked of ash, sulfur, and blood. A small metal stairway led up to an empty observation deck. Agent Robbins climbed up to the deck which overlooked empty cells corresponding to the steel doors. The walls were scratched and smeared with blood. "It looks like this is where they kept some of their experiments."

As soon as Agent Robbins's group had entered through the door, Agent Pyle jerked open the other door and they charged in...to an occupied room filled with over thirty different shaped, colored, and sized half demons that immediately growled and took up defensive stances as the entry team leveled their assault rifles.

"Jake, don't shoot," said a familiar feminine voice he immediately recognized as Pam's.

The half demons separated, and Pam was accompanied by a

strangely human looking female half demon who stepped forward. The reddish-purple half demon held Ellie carefully by the shoulders. They were all dumbstruck. Jake stepped up and hugged Ellie who seemed to be dazed. "Are you alright?"

Ellie was wrapped in a blanket, nodded, and smiled weakly. "They drugged me and were going to inject some deadly embryo into me but when I came to, I was here."

Jake and the rest of the team looked on in confusion. "What's happened?"

Before Ellie could explain several women with shaved heads came forward. One woman pointed at the half demons. "They saved us," she said. "The guards were going to kill us, but they stopped them."

"That's right," said the half demon woman. "They were going to inject your friend with that deadly embryo but we...prevented it."

Jake looked at the half demon. She had one blue eye and one yellow eye but other than having no hair she looked human. "Thank you..."

"Eudora," added the half demon woman. "My name is Eudora. The full bloods only referred to us with numbers, but we gave ourselves names. They planned to kill off the women donors first and then our people, but we knew in advance. We removed the guards down by the cells and remained here because your female friends felt that you'd be here eventually."

Detective Brutten stepped forward. "How many women, I mean, human women are here?"

"There are about a hundred," answered Eudora. "We hid them back down in the cells and stood guard up here."

"How many of your...people...are still here?" asked Agent Robbins. After arriving with his group from the other hallway, they'd stood in awe at seeing half demons for the first time.

The half demon woman's face turned sad. "There are only thirty-two of us left here." She turned to Jake. "Your friend said that you went to the tunnel in search of the bomb. How many of us did you find in the tunnel?"

Jake looked at the floor momentarily before he answered sadly.

"I'm sorry, but we didn't find any of your people in the tunnels. The end of the tunnel had been caved in. We only ran into live oversized hogs and killer scorpions."

That comment caused grumbling amongst the half demons. A large hawk faced half demon with huge wings that reminded Jake of a comic book character spoke up. "I am Thessar, those were Degen's pets. He used to make us fight them to entertain him."

"Degen?" asked Agent Williams.

The half demon nodded. "Yes, He's one of Lucifer's princes but not from this area. He's with those Nazi women."

"Priska Getman and her granddaughter," added Ellie. "I met them but only briefly."

"Thank you for telling us," said Eudora. "I'm sure they caved the tunnel in to trap them once our purpose was served. We'll go there and see if any of our people managed to dig out. We need air to breathe but can last longer on less."

"Why do you refer to your kind...I mean species...as your people?" asked Agent Pyle.

Eudora motioned to the group of half demons. "We're all half demons, well, the ones that turned out better. Some died shortly after being born, some were too wild to be allowed to continue to live, and some were killed during Degen's sport. We're all half demons and half human. Demons hate us because we're not full blood and humans will hate us because we're half demon."

"I don't hate you," said Ellie. "You saved our lives. You could've just left us to be killed by the guards, but you didn't."

"Yes, thank you," said one of the women. Soon the rest of the women joined in thanking the remaining half demons that had saved them.

Ellie looked up at Jake with tears in her eyes. "That Degen monster said you were all dead."

Jake smiled and hugged her even harder. "Not hardly, it would take a lot more than a horde of hell's demons to stop me from getting here."

Ellie leaned into Jake. "What about Al and the two deputies?"

"Al and Deputy Bridges are going to be fine, and so is Roscoe," said Jake, "but Lieutenant Beggett didn't make it."

Ellie nodded sadly. "I'm sorry, he was a nice man."

"Do you know where they plan to use the bomb?" asked Agent Williams.

"No, they always kept quiet about their plans for the bomb," replied Eudora.

Jake looked down at Ellie. "Don't worry, we'll find the bomb."

The rest of the entry team broke up and began escorting the women upstairs. At the entrance they sat the women down around on the ground until they could get a school bus from the local school to transport them out. Most were overwhelmed at being free and being out in the fresh air for the first time in weeks and months.

Sgt. Greymountain, Elijah Greymountain, and the Navajo men weren't sure what to make of the large group of creatures that emerged from the building. They'd been briefed about what had been found downstairs but hearing and seeing for oneself is a different matter. They didn't have long to worry as the half demons were determined to find out what happened to their kin in the tunnel, so they immediately disappeared into the darkness obviously heading west to Nevada.

Detective Brutten located Chrisee and Sarah from Flagstaff alive along with many others.

"How did you know to look for us?" asked Sarah.

"Your friend Beth alerted us to it," answered Detective Brutten.

The women smiled. "Tell her thanks for us."

"You can tell her yourself when you get back," said the detective with a smile.

Agent Williams and Agent Pyle stood and watched. "Do you think they'll be alright?" asked Agent Pyle.

Agent Williams shrugged. "I don't know, Terrell. They'll need a lot of counseling and help after what they went through."

"How inhuman," said Agent Pyle, "someone really needs to pay for this."

Viktor had walked up behind them. "And they will, comrade, they will."

Wargwolf Industries Warehouse
Hessingdorf, Germany

AFTER ARRIVING AT A PRIVATE AIRFIELD, Priska Getman and her granddaughter, Gerda, were driven to a nondescript warehouse building in Hessingdorf, outside of Berlin. Once inside they entered an elevator which descended into a large underground complex. The walls were painted plain white but had the Nazis swastika painted at various places along the hall. The doors were all solid looking wooden doors with expensive intricate carvings. They halted at one door and a guard wearing a black Nazi uniform ushered them into a large room. The furniture expensively furnished with overstuffed leather chairs and a couch on Persian rugs. The walls held priceless paintings. A heavy, gaudy, chandelier hung over an oval shaped wooden table in the middle of the room.

Priska Getman and Gerda made themselves comfortable. Gerda sat on one of the overstuffed leather chairs while Priska sat in her wheelchair.

It's good to be back at the *Fuhrerbunker,*" said Priska.

"Yes, *Grossmutter*, it is," answered Gerda, "Now that we have the weapon."

"It's not as nice as the original *Fuhrerbunker* which my mother told me about. Mother said those evil allies destroyed it during the war."

"Now, *Grossmutter*, don't get worked up again. Soon all will be set straight."

A man in a white formal jacket came in with coffee and pastries.

"Is Degen positive that Taft and his horrid people have been disposed of?"

"Why, my dear, Taft and his two agent friends are dead in a cavern along with those expendable military units. The two women are dead as well along with all the donors and extras. Everything has been cleaned up nicely."

Gerda stirred her coffee and smiled. "It was fitting for Taft's little woman to die screaming."

"Which one is that, dear?" asked Priska. "My memory isn't as sharp as it used to be."

"She's the preacher woman from that small trailer church in some dusty little town in Texas."

"Yes," said Priska. "Now I remember her. We spoke to her right before we left."

Gerda still stirred her coffee.

"What's wrong, dear?" asked Priska. "You seem bothered by something?"

Gerda sat her cup down. "I'm concerned about the blast. Will the *Fuhrerbunker* withstand the blast this close to Berlin? Why couldn't we be farther away?"

Priska smiled. "Now don't worry, my child, this facility is far enough underground and shielded with walls four meters thick. With over thirty rooms and the kitchen, we have enough supplies to last six months. We are impregnable. And after the blast and confusion, the new Fuhrer and his minions will rise and take over as was destined, first Europe and then the rest of the world."

———

Navajo Tribal Police Department
Route 7
Chinle, Arizona

SEVERAL SCHOOL BUSES arrived at the Wargwolf facility and took the women back to the police department where they were subsequently sent to Flagstaff or to the regional hospital. Detective Brutten, Agent Robbins, and his group had obtained the names of the women and would make notifications to loved ones and friends as to the women's whereabouts. Sadly, most of the women had been homeless, transients, or prostitutes so chances were nobody knew they were missing.

Agents Williams and Pyle finished typing their reports and emailing them to Deputy Director Ruiz in Washington, while Jake,

Viktor, Ellie, Pam, and the two Greymountains sat around a small table in the department's break room.

"So where do you go from here?" asked the elder Greymountain.

Jake sat back in his chair. "We know that the bomb is somewhere in Germany so that's where we're headed." He looked over at Viktor.

Viktor shrugged. "I still have to recover the stolen item so I'll tag along."

"What item?" asked Sgt. Greymountain.

Jake looked over at Viktor who nodded. "Sergeant, would you believe if I said these demons have Hitler's bones so they can extract DNA and clone him?"

The sergeant shook his head. "A few weeks ago, I wouldn't ever have thought it believable but now I'd never doubt what they could do."

"So how do you plan to find them?" asked the Elijah Greymountain. "Won't they be watching for you?"

Jake rubbed his chin in thought. "They may think we're all dead, but we need to be careful in case they find out we're not. We'll have to be inconspicuous. That means avoiding commercial flights. I'm sure Agent Williams can get someone in Washington to get us a military flight over there. That might help, but first we need to hide Pam and Ellie."

Ellie looked up and frowned. "We're not hiding anywhere. We're going with you. Did this last escapade show you what happens when you leave us behind? We're safer there."

"I agree," said Pam.

"You would be much safer here. We can leave you here with the Greymountains," explained Jake.

Ellie shook her head. "And while you're gone, what if they come again like they did, and someone here gets hurt again or killed like Lieutenant Beggett?"

Jake looked over at Viktor for support, but he just shrugged. "*Da*, they do make a good point, Jacob."

Jake looked over at the two Greymountains who each seemed to have found something interesting to look at on the floor.

"Oh, for Pete's sake," grumbled Jake. "But only if you do what I tell you to do for your safety."

"Of course," said Ellie. "Haven't we always?"

Jake rolled his eyes and grunted.

Viktor had been eating a sandwich from the vending machine and threw the wrapper in the wastebasket. "I have some contacts in Germany that can help us hide. I'll make some calls and see what I can set up."

Agent Williams came in with her laptop and set it on the table. "I'm glad this went off without a hitch. I can't imagine telling Oscar that another operation went bad and cost lives."

"You're right," said Jake. "Maybe this means we're getting lucky."

"Let's hope your luck holds out in Germany," said Elijah Greymountain.

Agent Pyle came in the room and leaned against the counter. "Did I hear someone say Germany? What's next?"

"It's simple, comrade," answered Viktor. "We sneak into Germany; stop a group of crazed Nazis and demons from cloning a new Hitler and setting off a nuclear weapon."

"Oh, I see, and I thought it was going to be difficult," said Agent Pyle sarcastically.

———

Dr. Hodges's Veterinarian Office
213 E 3rd Ave
Mexican Hat, Utah

ON THE WAY to the medical center, Jake, Ellie, Pam, and Viktor stopped at the vet's office to pick up Roscoe. They waited in the small waiting room until Dr. Hodges came out followed by Roscoe. Jake bent down and rubbed his fur. "How are you, buddy?" Roscoe wagged his tail and barked. Ellie rubbed his back. "You had us worried for awhile. No more leaving you behind."

"That's some dog you have there, Mr. Taft," said Dr. Hodges.

"He's fit as a fiddle. His ribs will be sore for a few days. I must say he's got quite a history."

"Jake's a cow dog when he isn't chasing demons, so he's picked up a few cuts and scars," explained Jake. "I'm sorry about the animals that were slaughtered here the other day. I wish we could've anticipated it; we might've prevented it."

Dr. Hodges knelt and rubbed Roscoe. "I too wish we could've prevented it, but we have to keep moving on."

They loaded back into the SUV after saying their thanks again and headed east to New Mexico.

CHAPTER TWENTY

Northern Navajo Medical Center,
US Highway 491
Shiprock, New Mexico

IT WAS late evening when the group drove into the parking lot of the medical center where Al and Deputy Bridges were being treated. They entered Deputy Bridges's room after showing their identification to the deputy guarding the door. Deputy Bridges was sitting up sipping water through a straw. He smiled when they entered. "Well, it's great to see ya'll. I was told about what happened at the Wargwolf building but I wanted to hear it for myself."

They all smiled except for Viktor who simply nodded.

"We were fortunate," said Ellie. "I was so relieved to hear that you and Al are going to be ok."

The left side of the deputy's neck was heavily bandaged.

"You were right about the Wargwolf. If it hadn't been for you, we wouldn't have known where to look. We owe you," said Jake.

Deputy Bridges shrugged then grimaced from the injury in his neck. "I was just doing my job. Now maybe I can get a vacation."

They all laughed and chuckled.

"Yeah, now the lieutenant and I can go fishi…" Deputy Bridges caught himself.

The room got oddly quiet.

"I'm sorry to hear about Lieutenant Beggett," said Viktor. "I was beginning to like him."

"Yes, we're sorry to hear that," added Pam. "It all happened so fast we didn't really get a chance to know for sure."

Deputy Bridges glanced down sadly. "Thanks, he was a good man."

"So, when are they going to let you out of this place?" asked Jake trying not to dwell on the lieutenant's death.

"They said I can go home tomorrow. The bullet went straight through without hitting anything important. What are you going to do next?"

"We're headed to Germany to find them," said Viktor.

"You get some rest," said Pam with a wink, "Agent Williams said she'll come by and visit so you'll need your strength."

Deputy Bridges's face blushed. When they reached the door, Deputy Bridges called out. "Hit 'em a few extra licks for me…and the lieutenant."

"You can count on it, Will," said Jake.

They walked down the hall to Al's room and knocked. A nurse opened the door. "I just finished changing his bandages; you can go in but don't stay too long."

They all nodded and entered. Al was half reclined in the bed with an IV in his right arm. His left arm below the elbow was gone and heavily bandaged. He smiled weakly when they entered. "Jake, Ellie, Pam, Agent Gordya, it's true then, you really are alive and well. It's a miracle." His glasses were on a table to his left and he tried to reach it instinctively with his left arm but stopped. Viktor reached over, picked up his glasses, and handed them to Al.

"Thanks."

Viktor nodded.

"We had a little help from some half demons," said Pam.

Al's eyes widened with surprise. "Half demons helped you?"

Ellie nodded and quickly told him about how the half demons saved the women at the Wargwolf facility.

"Wow, that will make a great addition to my article."

"So how are you?" asked Jake.

"I'm getting better. As you can see, I'm going to need some therapy and a prosthetic arm, but other than that I'm glad to be alive."

"You seem to be taking this better than we thought," said Ellie.

Al shrugged. "The way I see it I've had a run in with demons on three occasions and I'm still alive so it can't be that bad." He then fiddled with his IV nervously. "I'm...I'm sorry I wasn't able to stop them from taking you."

Ellie came over and hugged him. "You were very brave."

Jake laid a big hand on the young man's shoulder. "You did fine, Al. You were unarmed against armed mercenaries and demons. You tried to stop them as best you could. You're a real hero, Al. We're proud and grateful for what you did. Like you said, you've encountered demons three times and are alive to talk about it so that's something."

Al looked up with tears in his eyes. "I didn't faint this time."

Jake smiled. "No, you didn't. Now, get some rest. I think after this they'll be writing articles about you."

Wargwolf Industries Warehouse
Hessingdorf, Germany

GERDA AND PRISKA were in an observation room looking through the glass into the lab area that was processing the DNA sample that was to become the new Hitler when suddenly the door flew open and Degen stomped into the room.

"Idiots," shouted Degen. "Morons...how could that ignorant cowboy and his friends escape from the caverns?"

Priska tried to calm him. "Now, dear, are you positive this is true?"

Degen hissed. "Of course, it is. They were seen leaving the human's base in Nevada and returned to Arizona."

"They have no idea where we are," said Gerda.

Degen glared at her. "Don't be so sure. Every time I think he's out of my way he shows up. The facility in Arizona was raided and his two women friends were rescued along with all the donors. I want all the airports, docks, and entry points covered. If he comes into this country I want to know."

"Yes, dear," said Priska.

The tiger demon stomped back out and slammed the door, almost ripping the door off the hinges.

Priska looked up at her granddaughter. "Make sure we have all the entry ports covered."

"Yes, *Grossmutter*, but what if he does manage to make it here?"

"Then he can die with the rest of them."

———

Airborne over the Continental United States

A C-17 GLOBEMASTER aircraft cruised eastward across the western sky. Before it took off from Luke Air Force Base in Phoenix, AZ, several large containers carrying aircraft parts were loaded on board headed for a base on the east coast. Twenty minutes into the flight the loadmaster unlocked one of the cargo doors and pulled it open. "You can come out now, I think we're good."

Jake, Viktor, Ellie, Pam, the two FBI agents, and Roscoe climbed out of the stuffy metal container.

The loadmaster grinned. "This is a first for me. When the President of the United States orders us to smuggle you to the east coast I do it, but I've never transported FBI agents, a Russian agent, two women and a dog before." He motioned around the interior of the aircraft with his hand and pointed out the latrine, the small galley, and the webbing set up for sleeping. "It's not the Ritz, but under such short notice it's all we could do."

"It's perfect, thank you," said Jake.

The loadmaster looked at Viktor and frowned. "No pictures either or you'll have to walk. The first step's a killer."

Viktor held up his hands in surrender. "No cameras, comrade. I come in peace."

The loadmaster chuckled and went forward leaving them alone. Roscoe jumped up on one of the webbed seats and got comfortable.

Agent Pyle looked around. "I've never been smuggled on a military aircraft before. I guess the president has a little pull?"

Agent Williams snickered. "When you're the commander in chief you can do that."

After returning from New Mexico, they were smuggled in an old Navajo's camper down to the FBI office in Flagstaff. After the FBI director briefed the president, Agent Robbins transported them in a windowless van straight to Luke Air Force Base where they were crammed into a metal container and loaded onto a C-17 Globemaster transport aircraft. The inside of the container had been cramped and hot, but Agent Pyle commented that it was better than the inside of a giant snake.

Agent Williams opened a large file and removed a map of Germany then pointed to several places on the map that had been circled in red ink. "From what the FBI and CIA intel says the Wargwolf Company has several locations across the country. Most of them are active warehouses and store fronts so I doubt they'd be there. There are two locations that belong to the company but don't show to be active. One is in Beidenkopf and the other is in Henningsdorf."

The others gathered around and studied the map. Agent Pyle pointed to Hennigsdorf. "If I was to guess I'd say this one. It's close to Berlin where they're having the economic summit. The others are too far away."

"Why would that matter?" asked Agent Williams.

"It's just a hunch, but I would think that as fanatical as these people are they'd want to be as close to Berlin when things hit the fan."

"True," said Agent Williams. "But wouldn't they also be caught in the blast or fallout?"

Viktor spoke up. "Perhaps they have an underground complex

that wouldn't be damaged by a blast. My understanding is that it wouldn't level Berlin completely."

Agent Williams nodded. "They just want to kill the leaders at the summit would be my guess."

Jake looked at Ellie and Pam. "I don't suppose any of them said where they were going?"

Ellie and Pam shook their heads.

Agent Williams pulled some photos from the file and passed them around. "These satellite photos were taken over the last several days. The warehouse in Beidenkopf is deserted but the one in Henningsdorf appear to have some vehicular traffic coming and going."

"A closed-up warehouse with traffic coming and going? Sounds like we found the place," said Agent Pyle.

"Da," added Viktor.

"Ok, then," said Agent Williams as she folded up the map. "Henningsdorf it is. I'll try to get as much information as I can about that location."

Jake turned to Viktor. "How's it going on your end?"

"I made contact with several of my associates before we left and as soon as we land, I'll call them," said the big Russian. "I must warn you though these men are not upstanding citizens. They owe me and can get us places or supplies that no one else can."

Agent Williams nodded. "I'm sure we can look the other way this time as long as they don't go too far over the line."

During Jake's years in covert ops, he'd met such men and most could be trusted but only to an extent. "I agree with Agent Williams, we welcome their help, but they have to know we aren't going rogue, and the less obvious we are the less chance of being found out by these fanatical people. Demons are everywhere, even listening in at the FBI, so we must be careful. Try to keep information and contact with your folks at the FBI to a minimum." He looked over at the two FBI agents who nodded.

"I'll brief Oscar. I'm sure he understands," said Agent Williams.

After sleeping in uncomfortable web seating and eating warmed up meals, the six of them grumbled as they climbed back into the metal container when the aircraft was on final approach to Wiesbaden AFB, Germany. The aircraft touched down and taxied to a large hangar. Once inside, the doors were shut and the metal containers were unloaded.

The container doors were opened, and they once again climbed out but not before Jake made a visual sweep of the interior of the hangar for any unwanted invisible guests. Once Jake was comfortable that no demons were inside, the other three occupants climbed out. They were escorted to a side office and were met by a young captain. The officer took in the odd group and frowned at Roscoe. "I'm Captain Moore. I was briefed by Wing Commander Colonel Harrelson who sent me to...assist."

"Thank you, Captain...now who all knows we're here?" said Jake.

Captain Moore had been in the military for five years and had been promoted to captain just last year. His job was as an intelligence officer when he received a coded message from the pentagon about the arrival of the visitors. He notified the wing commander's office and was then ordered to assist them with whatever they needed. Captain Moore felt that babysitting these "guests" was a waste of his valuable time, below his rank, and he didn't like being questioned by this obvious redneck cowboy. "I believe that's classified...sir. Now if I can be of..."

"Maybe you didn't understand my friend," interrupted Viktor. "He asked who all knows we are here?"

Captain Moore stared at the Russian who's face looked to be chiseled from granite. "You must be the Russian agent I was told was coming which makes it more important that you don't know. Also, there are the two female civilians."

Agent Williams stepped forward and showed him her badge. "Excuse me, captain, but this is a matter of national security so I'm going to need to know who all knows about our presence. If you need to check on our clearances, we can wait. Please contact the Director of the FBI or the White House and they will advise you. Feel free to ask for the president."

Captain Moore stiffened at the mention of the president. He nodded and disappeared into another office.

"Nice guy," said Agent Williams sarcastically.

"For a jerk," said Pam.

Ellie elbowed Pam. "Shush."

A few moments later, a pale faced Captain Moore came back. "The wing commander, the operations officer, and I are the only three that know of your presence right now except for the crew that brought you here."

Jake smiled. "Thank you, Captain. Did you read the message about our arrival out loud at any time that someone might have overheard?"

"No, sir."

"Good, thank you," said Jake.

Agent Williams looked around the hangar. "This is as far as you can take us, Captain. Since there are no more military bases in Berlin since the wall came down in '91 there'd be no reason for a military van to go there."

"We have the embassy in Berlin but that's it," said the captain.

"Too obvious," said Jake. "They'll be watching for us there."

Viktor took out his cell phone. "I'll see what I can do."

"So, why's it so important if I'd read the message out loud?" asked Captain Moore.

"In case demons overheard it," said Jake bluntly.

"Demons?"

"Yes, Captain, demons," said Agent Williams.

"Big, ugly, invisible demons with sharp teeth that would suddenly appear and happily rip you to shreds," added Agent Pyle with a grin.

Captain Moore's face paled a little more and even though he thought it was a joke he still suddenly felt uncomfortable and glanced nervously around the hangar.

CHAPTER TWENTY-ONE

Unknown Location
Berlin, Germany

A FEW MINUTES after four a.m. a milk delivery truck pulled behind a run-down building on a darkened street in a dilapidated section of old Berlin. The driver of the van flashed the headlights once, then twice and the overhead garage door opened at the side of the building. The van pulled in and the door cranked back down. A minute later, the lights came on in a large loading area and three men approached the van. Two were armed with assault rifles and the third was a short, stocky, older man with a bad combover to cover his bald spot. The driver of the van stepped out, walked to the rear, and opened the rear doors. Instead of racks of milk, four people pointed weapons at the men in the garage. The balding man's face broke into a wide grin showing stain yellow teeth. *"Herzlich willkommen* Viktor, it's been a long time."

Viktor motioned for the other three to lower their weapons and climbed out of the van. *"Da*, it is good to see you too, Wilhelm. It's been too long."

The two men embraced in a bear hug. Viktor introduced the

others. "This is Wilhelm Meier, a good friend. His family has owned a milk producing business for many years."

Jake nodded. "That's why we traveled in a milk delivery van?"

"*Ya*, Herr Taft," said Meier. "Unfortunately, with the economy so bad I've been forced to expand my business…in other areas."

Nobody wanted to know about his other business ventures and didn't ask. "We really appreciate you helping us out," said Agent Williams.

Meier shrugged and smiled. "Nonsense, anything I can do for an old friend. Since we have had to keep it discreet, I imagine it's something that is not to be publicized."

Viktor nodded. "*Da*, and it's a matter of international importance for not only us but for you."

"I see. Whatever I can do to help, all you have to do is ask."

Roscoe began to growl. Meier looked down at the dog. "Does your dog not like Germans?"

"Would gunshots be routine in this area?" asked Jake quickly.

Meier raised an eyebrow and glanced at Viktor who nodded. "*Nein*, this building used to be in the communist area and has never totally recovered even after the unification so random gunfire is often heard and rarely reported."

"Good," said Jake. Before anyone could ask, Jake pulled his .45 handgun, pointed it at one of Meier's men and fired. Meier ducked while the other bodyguard swung his assault rifle around at Jake, but Viktor reached out, grabbed the barrel of the rifle, and pushed it down.

"*Was ist das?*" yelled Meier, "Crazy American cowboy?"

Before Jake answered they suddenly smelled a rotten sulfur smell and looked at the fallen man but instead of a human a large demon laid on the floor. Jake holstered his gun. "Roscoe doesn't like demons, especially unwanted eavesdropping demons."

"*Gott im Himmel*," said Meier. He looked a Jake. "Heinrich has been with me for years, but you knew he was a demon?"

"Yep," nodded Jake. "Even when they take on human form I can tell."

Meier nudged the dead thing with the toe of his shoe which left a gooey residue on the tip. "What a horrible smell."

"They rot incredibly fast," said Agent Pyle.

"But why was he spying on me?"

Jake shrugged. "It's probably been here for years watching and pretending to be a human. Maybe he's been keeping tabs on your other business dealings. This is why we have the need for secrecy, so these demons won't know we're here."

"Do they all look this bad?" asked Meier.

"Nope," said Agent Pyle. "Some look worse."

"They come in all shapes and sizes," explained Ellie.

"We couldn't continue with our mission with it here...alive," said Jake.

Meier still couldn't believe that a member of his staff had been a demon spying on him. "*Nein*, it's no problem, Herr Taft, whatever you need."

"Good," said Jake. "Because we're going to need some equipment and one of your vans."

The *Fuhrerbunker*,
Wargwolf Industries Warehouse
Henningsdorf, Germany

GERDA WAS DRESSED in a close fitting bright red evening gown with her hair up in a twisted bun. She entered an expensively furnished dining room guarded by a soldier in a black Nazi SS uniform. High back chairs were positioned around a large oak table with a large candelabrum in the middle. The dishes were china, and the cloth was silk. Her grandmother was already at the table in a wheelchair. Degen's stench arrived a moment before he did, and he sat at the head of the large table.

No one spoke as a bowl of soup was brought to the table by two men in formal white suits. The two women ate in silence while Degen slurped his meal by picking up the bowl and drinking it.

Degen then belched filling the room with the stench of decayed flesh and sulfur.

"Must you do that?" said Gerda. "I don't care what you think of me but at least have some manners with *Grossmutter*."

Degen slammed a furry clawed fist down on the table which made the dishes rattle. "All this china and pretty things disgusts me. Soon I will be able to have things the way I want them."

"Now, dear," said Priska. "The economic summit is only a day away and then we can start to rebuild."

Degen sat back and roared with laughter. "I don't want to build, I was to destroy, then make it in my image as it should be."

Gerda stiffened visibly. "Don't you mean in the Fuhrer's image?"

Degen glared at the woman. "Your half demon Fuhrer will do my bidding. He will only be half demon while I am a full blood fallen. We will not follow a half-breed."

"This whole plan is for the Fuhrer to return to his full glory," said Gerda.

Degen growled. "The real Hitler was to do my bidding, and all would have worked if he hadn't allowed the Braun woman to distract him. This one will do as he is told."

Gerda's face was red with anger. She was about to say something when Priska put a hand on her arm. "Now, child, calm down. This is for all of our benefit."

Dinner was served before the arguing continued. It was an Austrian favorite, *Wiener Schnitzel,* served with lemon, and cranberry sauce. Gerda was visibly angry and didn't speak during dinner while Priska talked about the Germany of old and how things were going to revert back to the "old days". Degen of course chewed, slobbered, and gulped his food. The two women then talked about how the world was going to be after the bomb had been detonated and the ensuing chaos, while Degen's eyes stared with a darker yellow glow.

———

Industrial Warehouse Section
Henningsdorf, Germany

JAKE AND VIKTOR both lay prone behind some brush across from the warehouses in the dark and watched. It was well past dark, and nothing moved. Both men wore dark camouflage clothing with their faces painted over in blacks and grays. They each wore night vision goggles to recon the area.

The Oder-Havel canal, a tributary of the Elbe River, separated them from the warehouses so they felt confident they couldn't be spotted. Using some of the satellite photos obtained by Agent Williams they'd located the main warehouse and for hours they'd watched closely. Besides the occasional demon that flew over or stomped by, the only thing that gave any indications that it was occupied was a roaming human guard dressed in black.

"What do you think?" whispered Jake.

"I can't see the demons of course but besides the guard I wouldn't think there's enough here to make me believe they have a nuclear weapon inside," answered Viktor.

The earpiece in Jake's ear squelched. "Jake, this is Agent Williams. Anything to report?"

Agent Pyle and Williams were monitoring the area from one of Meier's dairy trucks several blocks on a side street off Henningsdorfer Strausse.

"Nothing really, just a few demons and a lone guard out front?" replied Jake into his small mike. "We're on our way back and then we can decide how we want to proceed."

Despite their precautions a set of yellow eyes watched the dairy truck from a nearby tree.

———

Airborne over the Atlantic Ocean

A PARTICULAR BOEING 747 known as Air Force One cruised over the Atlantic Ocean at 39,000 feet while most of the staff and media inside slept. In the forward cabin on the mid level sat President Campbell dressed in slacks and a blue cotton shirt. He spoke by conference call to FBI Director Chisom who was back in Washington D.C.

"So, as I understand it," said the president, "Taft and your two agents believe that this group has the weapon just outside of Berlin in a warehouse."

"Yes, Mr. President," replied Director Chisom's voice through the speaker. "They narrowed it down to the one owned by Wargwolf Enterprises."

The president sat back in his chair with a coffee cup in one hand. "Do they have any solid proof that I can take to the German government?"

"No, sir."

"That's what I was afraid of, Bill, I can't tell the German Chancellor that the daughter of a female icon of old Germany is in league with demons and has a stolen nuclear weapon, without proof."

"I understand, sir."

President Campbell trusted Jake's word but didn't want to cause an international incident without something to show for it. "Tell Taft that he needs to get us some definite proof so I can use it to persuade the Germans to act."

"Mr. President, I feel obligated to ask you not to attend the economic summit. You know this threat is real."

"I know," replied the president with a sigh. "But I can't hide from this. That damned weapon came from American soil and if it was ever found out that we hid while the rest of the world's leaders were in danger it would be disastrous."

"Yes, sir."

"Keep me updated," said the president and hung up. He sat for several minutes running the options through his head, rubbed his tired eyes, and picked up the direct line to the Pentagon.

———

Meier Milchwerk
Berlin, Germany

THE SMALL GROUP sat in the office area of one of Meier's milk delivery buildings they had arrived at earlier. Agent Pyle sat at a worn wooden desk where he downloaded and printed the photos taken of the Wargwolf warehouse. The rest sat in a few plastic chairs or leaned against a metal file cabinet.

Agent Williams examined the photos. "I see the guard but that's it."

Jake reached over with a marker and drew a circle around a spot on the photo. "There's a demon standing right there."

"It's weird that even in a photo Jake's able to see them," said Pam.

Jake nodded his head. "Sometimes I wish I couldn't."

"So where do we go from here?" asked Agent Pyle.

Agent Williams spoke up. "We know they have a small nuclear device. We also believe they have it in that warehouse and it would make sense that they plan to use it during the economic summit. The question is how do they plan to get it inside with all that security and when?"

"It may not be as difficult as it seems," replied Viktor. "With modern technology they could put it in a suitcase or large briefcase. It could be made small enough to be disguised as a vehicle part such as a car generator."

Jake turned to Pam. "What have you found out about the economic summit?"

Pam sat across from Agent Pyle at the desk in front of her laptop and scanned the screen. "It seems all the major world leaders along with the president will be there. The list is extensive."

"What does it say about the location?" asked Agent Williams.

"The summit's held at the Estrel which is a huge hotel in the suburb of Neu-Koeln near Berlin. This article says it's about 15,000-square meters and that's just the Convention Center. It also says that it's the world's largest hotel complex with over 1,125 rooms."

"*Ja*," said Meier. "It's a giant complex, and you're supposed to find a nuclear device that could be the size of a car generator?"

"A needle in a haystack," said Ellie.

"You Americans never cease to confuse me," said Viktor. "Why would anyone be looking for a needle in a haystack anyway?"

Jake smiled at the Russian's remark. "I think the answer is to make sure that doesn't happen."

"How?" asked Agent Pyle.

"We go visit the warehouse and get it before they take it to the Estrel."

"And how do we plan to do that?"

"Simple, Viktor and I will walk into the complex and take it back."

————

Tegel International Airport
Berlin, Germany

AIR FORCE ONE landed at Berlin's Tegel Airport without incident and President Campbell along with his entourage were transferred to a motorcade. On the drive to the Estrel the president called FBI Director Chisom again but was informed that no new information about the bomb had been obtained. The president hung up and mumbled something under his breath.

"What's the matter, dear?" asked First Lady Trish Campbell from across the seat.

The president shook his head in frustration. "Bill Chisom said there's no news on the damned bomb."

"I see," replied the attractive forty-nine-year-old blonde woman. "Give Major Taft some time. He saved Ann from that monster Ghazi so we both know he has a knack for coming through for us."

"I know, but we're dealing with not just our lives but the lives of other leaders of the world."

Trish Campbell reached over and patted the president's hand. "I know, but Major Taft and his friends have never let us down."

"I know you're right, but I'm concerned his luck may be running out."

The motorcade pulled up in front of the fabulous Estrel complex.

The modern convention center, entertainment, and hotel complex was a marvel of glass, steel, and concrete. One end resembled a giant glass triangle while the main complex was rectangular shaped. The president and first lady entered the centrally located atrium decorated like a main street marketplace and were escorted to the elevators immediately to the left. As they rode up the elevator, the president thought that this beautiful building could easily become a massive coffin for all the world leaders if the FBI and Taft failed.

The *Fuhrerbunker*
Henningsdorf, Germany

DEGEN ENTERED one of the scientific laboratories located in the underground complex where several white-coated men worked. "Is the device ready?" he snarled.

The head technician, a thin, pale-skinned German jumped at the sound of Degen's voice. "*Ya*, Herr Degen, the device is armed and being attached as we speak. It will be ready for tonight's events."

"Wonderful news, so no one will have to lose their head," said Degen as he left the lab.

The head technician breathed a sigh of relief and wiped the perspiration from his forehead that wasn't there a moment ago.

Degen entered the main living quarters where Priska sat. Three aides bustled around the elderly woman styling her hair and applying make up. Degen grunted which caused Priska to look over at him. "What's the matter, dear?"

"Why do you have to spend so much time making yourself look that way?"

Priska cackled. "Why, Degen, my dearest, I want to look my best when I go to the reception and dinner."

A man wearing a Nazi uniform came into the room followed by a small black birdlike demon. "This…thing…has some information for you, Lord Degen."

The little black demon flew over, landed on Degen's shoulder, and whispered in the demon lord's ear. Degen listened for a moment and nodded. "Keep an eye on it. If you see it again then notify me immediately."

The demon flew off without another word.

"What's the matter, my dearest?" asked Priska.

"A milk truck was seen parked near us and didn't appear to be making deliveries."

"Are we being spied on?"

"I don't know," grumbled Degen.

"Could it be those FBI agents and that dreadful man Taft?"

"I haven't heard that they were in Germany but if they are they will never leave alive." The tiger demon looked around. "Where is that brat granddaughter of yours?"

"Gerda is in the spa getting a facial so she can be at her best for our glorious victory."

Degen growled and sat in a darker corner. He hated all the glamour and happiness. "Just make sure you both get there on time."

"Don't worry, my most precious, we won't be late. This will be a night to remember."

"Yes, it will," replied Degen with a grin that showed his canines. "Timing has to be perfect in order for you to get out before the explosion."

"*Ya*, I understand. We'll be back here before the device goes off so we can enjoy the victory together. I just wish mother could've been here to share in the joy."

Degen nodded his shaggy head. "Frieda understood our goals, much more than her spoiled great granddaughter."

"Gerda understands, she's just of a different generation."

"Then she needs to adjust," grumbled Degen.

"She will along with the rest once it's over and you've taken control."

Meier Milchwerk
Berlin, Germany

"I'M NOT AT ALL happy about just the two of you doing this," said Agent Williams. Jake, Viktor, and the two FBI agents sat in the main warehouse cleaning their weapons and doing last minute equipment checks. Jake was cleaning his two Colt 45s. "As I said, you and Agent Pyle will be in the van up the street in case anything goes wrong. Once Viktor and I have the weapon you'll be our means of escaping the area."

"I think one of us should go in Viktor's place."

"Do you speak German?" asked Viktor flatly.

"No," snapped Agent Williams.

"Stephanie," said Jake, "I know you want to be there, and we understand but Viktor is fluent in German in case we need an interpreter and we've worked covert ops together in the past so we can anticipate each other's moves. It will be fine."

"I still don't like it," fumed Agent Williams who scooted her chair out and stomped to the other side of the warehouse.

Jake rubbed his forehead in frustration. Agent Pyle snickered. "She'll be ok but look at me; I'm stuck with her in that milk truck the rest of the time."

"Lucky you."

Agent Williams came back with her cell phone in her hand. "The president and first lady are at the hotel."

The others nodded. Pam and Ellie came over when they overheard Agent Williams.

Jake put down his weapons and motioned for them to a nearby table where a map of the area and satellite photos were spread out. "From what we've seen the warehouse is protected by a guard at the front entrance and one at the back overhead delivery docks. Except for the occasional demon that comes and goes there is nothing. Surveillance cameras are located at the front entrance and rear docks but there are several side doors that's not, but we have to be careful not to be seen." Jake pointed to a side street about two blocks away. "Agent Williams and Pyle will be in the milk van ready to transport us out or give us backup should things go badly." He traced a finger along the map showing the route that he and Viktor would follow along the river to the back of the warehouse.

"We take out the guard and enter through one of the back loading doors."

"But how do you know where to look?" asked Pam.

Jake motioned to Viktor. "That's where Viktor's knowledge of the German language comes into play. There must be some type of lab or work room that they've kept the weapon in, so we just persuade someone to tell us."

"And then?" asked Agent Pyle.

"And then," said Jake, "we grab the weapon and get back to the milk van as fast as we can. You notify Director Chisom and anyone else you want. The sooner someone comes and gets it the better."

"But what about Viktor's mission to get the bones back?" asked Agent Williams.

"As soon as the weapon is safe then the authorities can raid the place and the bones returned to Russia."

"Sounds like a solid plan," commented Agent Pyle.

"That's what I'm afraid of," said Agent Williams. "There is no such thing as a great plan."

"Cynic."

———

Estrel Hotel
Sonnenallee 225, 12057
Berlin, Germany

AGENT MEADOWS ENTERED the president's suite with a note. President Campbell was relaxing on a large sofa reading through some of the latest reports from the Middle East. Without saying a word Agent Meadows handed the president the note who opened and read it then handed it back to the secret service agent. "Tell them good luck," said the president.

Trish Campbell came out of the bedroom at the sound of the president's voice. "Who needs luck?"

Agent Meadows left the room as President Campbell glanced around as if he was looking for anyone, invisible or otherwise, that might be listening. "The FBI and Taft are going to pay a visit to those people tonight and see if the bomb's there."

"Well good, then we have nothing to worry about so you better start getting ready unless you plan to go looking like that," said Trish who walked back into the bedroom.

The president rolled his eyes and got to his feet.

"And don't roll your eyes at me," said Trish from somewhere in the bedroom. "Even if you are the president."

President Campbell chuckled to himself.

———

The *Fuhrerbunker*
Henningsdorf, Germany

GERDA ENTERED her grandmother's room wearing a blue, sleek, satin evening gown with her hair styled and pinned up on the back of her head. At Gerda's entrance, Priska turned her motorized wheelchair around and smiled. "You look absolutely stunning. If only your mother could see you now."

Gerda smiled back. "*Danke, Grossmutter*, I too wish *mutte* was here to see this glorious day." Gerda twirled around so her grandmother could see her.

"You will be the most beautiful one there," said the elderly woman.

"*Nein*, you will be the most beautiful one there," said Gerda.

Priska blushed. "I'm just an old woman, but tonight will be our victory."

"*Ya*, it will be a new beginning for Germany and for us."

"I'm going to puke if you two keep this up," said a gruff voice followed by the stench.

"Why do you have to try to ruin everything?" replied Gerda. "All our plans are finally about to come true, and you can only be rude," said Gerda.

Degen dropped into a large chair. "Just don't screw this up.

After the reception you will find an excuse to leave so you can be back here before the explosion."

"Yes, my dearest," replied Priska. "We have everything planned out. Nothing could go wrong."

One of the Nazis came into the room dressed as a chauffeur. "The limousine is waiting."

Degen stood up and walked with the two women to the elevator. "Don't let me and His Majesty Lucifer down."

As the elevator doors closed, Priska smiled. "I've been waiting decades for this; nothing will stop us."

A minor demon approached Degen and whispered in his ear. "Go find out why?" he replied.

"Is something wrong?" asked Priska.

"Nothing that affects our plan. Just one of my spies watching a small-time thug who runs a dairy hasn't reported in lately. Nothing to worry about."

———

NEARBY TWO MEN in camouflage worked their way through the warehouse area and knelt behind a dumpster. "We're in place, there's a limo parked at the loading dock," said Jake.

"Roger that," replied Agent Williams from the dairy truck parked a quarter of a mile away. Agent Pyle sat on a stack of empty milk crates while Agent Williams paced the interior of the truck. "Now we wait."

The loading dock doors opened, and the limo pulled in and the doors closed. "The limo went inside," said Jake. A few minutes later, the doors opened, the limo drove out and left. "The limo's gone."

"You think someone from Wargwolf is going to the gala for the opening of the summit?" replied Agent Williams.

"If there's going to be a bomb there, I won't think so unless they plan to leave before the bomb detonates but we'll soon find out," said Jake. A guard stepped out from a side door and lit a cigarette. Victor and Jake silently slipped up and incapacitated the guard. Jake removed the man's key card and radio.

"We have a key card from one of the guards," explained Jake.

"Where's the guard now?" asked Agent Williams.

"Sleeping," answered Viktor.

Jake inserted the card in the key reader, and it clicked. They quickly opened the door and entered. Once inside they found several offices that were vacant. A hallway led to the main warehouse which was lit with a few emergency lights and littered with old shipping crates. "We're in the main warehouse but it looks deserted."

"Maybe there's an underground complex?" asked Agent Pyle.

"We'll check around and get back to you," replied Jake.

"Okay but be..." replied Agent Williams when suddenly the doors of the dairy truck were ripped open and three armed men pointed weapons at them while a demon stood at the rear. "Halt, put your hands where we can see them," ordered one of the men.

When the transmission went dead Jake looked over at Viktor who shook his head. They slowly began searching the warehouse looking for a way down. The two men had worked their way through half of the warehouse when an outer door opened and harsh voices could be heard. Jake and Viktor ducked behind a stack of crates and watched.

Agents Pyle and Williams were pushed and prodded by the armed men towards the other side of warehouse. The sound of an elevator door dinged, and they saw light from the interior when it opened for a moment then closed. They carefully worked their way to the elevator and Jake used the key card to call the elevator. After making sure it was unoccupied, they entered. There was only one other button to go down, so they rode the elevator down. When it stopped and opened, they readied their weapons but the corridor was empty.

The hallways were concrete with the Nazi swastika painted periodically down the hall. When they came to a row of windows they carefully looked in and saw a huge laboratory filled with workers.

"I would think the bones you're looking for is in there somewhere," said Jake.

"Da, we need to find the bomb and our agent friends then come back for them," replied Viktor.

The radio taken from the guard squawked in German. Viktor listened. "It says the prisoners have been taken to interrogation room 2."

"Any suggestions as to where we find room 2?" said Jake.

Viktor shrugged. "We ask."

———

Meier Milchwerk
Berlin, Germany

ELLIE, Pam, and Herr Meier were in his office trying to wait patiently. Pam browsed the internet for information on the gala at the hotel while Herr Meier sat at his desk working on business Excel sheets.

"I hate waiting," said Ellie.

Pam looked up from her laptop. "You know Jake? Hurry up and wait."

"Funny," snapped Ellie.

Roscoe was resting on the rug when his head jerked up and growled.

"What's wrong with your dog?" asked Herr Meier.

Before anyone could answer screams and gunfire erupted outside the office. Herr Meier jumped up and headed to the door, but Ellie grabbed his arm. "Don't go out there. Demons."

Screaming, screeching, and gunfire continued then suddenly went silent. Herr Meier grabbed a pistol from his desk drawer.

"It won't do any good," said Ellie.

Herr Meier shoved the gun in his waistband and started shoving his desk towards the door. "Then help me barricade the door."

With Ellie and Pam helping they shoved the heavy desk against the door.

"This will only slow them down," said Ellie.

"And of course, no windows," said Pam sarcastically.

Herr Meier walked over to a bookcase and pulled on it. The

bookcase rotated out like a door revealing a small door. "I use this sometimes when I need to leave without anyone knowing."

The three bent down and went through the door into a small, narrow walkway between the walls. Herr Meier pulled the bookcase back against the wall. He pointed to his left and they quietly worked their way down and around the corner that ended at an air intake cover. He pushed on the cover, and it pivoted out enough for him to see that no one was around. They climbed out as quietly as possible and hid behind a row of milk stands. Bodies were littered across the milk warehouse floor. Demons could be heard in the offices overturning furniture and searching for anyone hiding.

"Any suggestions?" asked Herr Meier.

Pam pointed to his Mercedes. "We can leave in your car."

Herr Meier pointed to the overhead doors that were down.

"Give me your car keys. I'll drive and when you hit the open button, we'll pick you up on our way out."

"But the demons will hear it opening," replied Herr Meier.

"It's our only option. If we stay here, we die," answered Ellie.

Herr Meier nodded and handed the keys to Pam. The two women crept around the milk stands trying to keep Roscoe from barking. When they reached the Mercedes, Pam reached up and pulled on the car handle to fortunately find it unlocked. Ellie and Roscoe climbed in back and Pam slipped in behind the wheel. Herr Meier waited until the second she started the car and hit the green open switch. The heavy metal doors began to rattle and rise slowly as Pam threw the car into drive and raced towards the door. Ellie looked out the back window and saw several demons stomping down the hallway. Pam slammed on the brakes at the open door and Herr Meier threw himself in the front passenger seat. "Go, GO!"

Pam slammed on the accelerator, and they sped out of the parking lot with several demons in hot pursuit.

CHAPTER TWENTY-TWO

The *Fuhrerbunker*
Henningsdorf, Germany

JAKE AND VIKTOR crept along the hallway alert for any hostiles, human or otherwise, when they heard footsteps. The two men flattened themselves against the wall as two men in Nazi uniforms came around the corner. Viktor's hand shot out and clamped over one of the men's mouth while placing a knife to his throat. At the same time, Jake slammed his pistol into the skull of the other. Jake dragged the unconscious man into a nearby empty storage room with Viktor following with his. After a few minutes of questioning, they learned where the interrogation room was. So he was unceremoniously tied up with zip cords Jake had brought in case, and gagged him. Before rendering him unconscious they removed his uniform which barely fit Viktor. The unconscious man's clothes didn't fit Jake much better.

"These uniforms won't fool anyone very long," commented Jake.

"Da, so we need to get to the interrogation room quickly," replied Viktor.

The two men stepped out into the hallway in their ill fitted clothing and tried to look inconspicuous.

———

MEANWHILE IN INTERROGATION ROOM 2, Agent Pyle had been tied to a chair and a Nazi guard had unsuccessfully tried beating any information out of him. The other guard stood by with Agent Williams over in the corner.

"Has he given you the information?" asked Degen as he entered the room.

"Nein," replied the guard.

Degen growled. "Then stand over by the woman then." He looked down at Agent Pyle whose left eye was almost swollen shut and had numerous facial cuts. "Stupid human, where is that moron cowboy at?"

Agent Pyle looked up and smiled through a bloody split lip. "Like I said we came here alone."

Degen backhanded him causing his head to snap back. Agent Williams lashed out and struck one of the guards in the throat and elbowed the other in the nose. She leapt onto Degen's back and tried to choke him. Degen simply reached back and plucked her off like she was a minor annoyance. He glared at the two guards. "Idiots, you let a woman do this?" He threw Agent Williams across the room and into the wall. She slid to the ground, sat up, and glared back defiantly. "Stay there, woman, I will deal with you next. You two get me someone in here that can control her."

Jake and Viktor were rounding the corner and almost to the interrogation room when they heard a request for two guards. Using the radio Viktor volunteered them. When they arrived at the door and entered, the two injured men stumbled out with one holding his nose to stop the bleeding and the other trying to breathe so neither noticed the odd-looking men wearing uniforms too small for them.

"Watch the woman and don't let her hurt you," said Degen without turning around. "Now, human, I will enjoy slicing you open and removing your organs one at a time if you don't tell me where Taft is."

Agent Pyle laughed which angered Degen. "I am really going to enjoy this."

"Wait," said Agent Williams. "I'll tell you where he is."

Degen stared down at him. "If you think it will keep me from killing you, it won't help."

"I think it will," replied Agent Pyle. "He's right behind you."

"How stupid do you think I am, human?" roared Degen. "What kind of fool do you take me for?"

"A really stupid one," said a voice from behind Degen in a slow Texas drawl.

Degen spun around and looked closely at the two guards. The two men were in uniforms that were obviously too small. The tall dark haired one raised his Heckler and Koch G3 assault rifle, pointed it at Degen, and emptied the weapon into the demon. Degen stumbled as the rounds struck him, and for a moment seemed amazed before falling dead to the floor.

Agent Williams and Jake raced over to Agent Pyle and began untying him while Viktor covered the door.

"You're late," said Agent Pyle. When he was released, Agent Williams tried to help him up, but he jerked his arm away. "I can do it myself." He stood up and promptly fell to the floor.

Jake and Agent Williams helped him up. The radios started squawking.

"They are sending men to investigate the gunshots. We need to go now," said Viktor.

Agent Pyle stepped over Degen's rapidly decaying body. "Just a second," he said. He kicked the dead demon.

"Feel better now?" said Agent Williams. "Can you go?"

Viktor and Jake slipped out into the hallway with Agent Williams helping Agent Pyle. Viktor put the radio to his lips and spoke German into it saying the shooting came from the other direction. "Maybe it will delay them long enough," he explained.

———

Estrel Hotel
Sonnenallee 225, 12057
Berlin, Germany

THE GALA for the World Economic Summit had already started when President Campbell and First Lady Trish Campbell entered the huge room decorated as a ballroom. They walked among the delegates greeting them and shaking hands. Secret Service agents along with protective agents from numerous countries discreetly monitored the crowd.

Priska and Gerda Getman arrived in their limo and Priska was helped into an electric wheelchair. They passed through security and entered the party.

"It's such a lovely place, *Grossmutter*, it's a shame we have to destroy it all," comment Gerda.

"Ya, but we can build a bigger and better one as soon as the Third Reich rises from the ashes," replied Priska.

Before Gerda could reply, President Campbell and Trish approached the two women. "Good evening," said the president.

"*Guten Abend*, Herr President," answered Priska. "I am Priska Getman and this is my wonderful granddaughter, Gerda."

Gerda nodded politely.

"It's such a wonderful evening and such a lovely place to have it," commented Trish.

Priska shrugged. "It's just a shell of what it could have been, but at least it's here in Berlin."

President Campbell raised an eyebrow. "We hope that the summit will help all countries improve and be successful."

"My only concern is for my country and the return to glory."

Before the president could reply the woman turned her wheelchair and left.

"What a dreadful woman," whispered Trish. "That's the woman we think has a bomb?"

The president nodded. "I hope Taft and the FBI can find it if it really is here."

"Major Taft will come through for us; he has before. Now, let's enjoy ourselves."

———

East side of Berlin

PAM RACED up and down streets once leaving Meier's dairy building with demons slowly overtaking them.

"Are they still following us?" asked Pam as she slid around a corner narrowly missing two pedestrians.

"Ya, and they are almost on top of us," cried Herr Meier.

As if on cue one demon grabbed onto the side of the Mercedes and began smashing the side windows. The creature reached in only to have Roscoe clamp down on the thing's arm. Pam swerved to the right and sideswiped a car which knocked the demon off as it was sandwiched between the two cars. "No hitchhikers," yelled Pam out of the driver's window. "I hope you have good car insurance," she added.

"I hope so too," replied Herr Meier.

Another demon leaped onto the rear trunk lid tearing holes in the metal.

"Hand me your gun," said Ellie.

Herr Meier gave her the handgun. "But you said it won't do any good."

Ellie aimed the gun towards the back window and fired twice, knocking the demon off the trunk. "It won't kill them but might slow them down." She looked at the gun for a moment. "I have an idea."

"Good, because there's more behind us," yelled Pam as she skidded around a corner and raced west onto Frankfurter Allee.

Ellie grabbed her phone and pulled up a map of Berlin.

"Fraulein, this is not the time for checking your phone," said Herr Meier.

"No, I'm looking for a nearby cemetery. Demons can't go there," snapped Ellie.

"Then let's find one fast," replied Herr Meier.

CHAPTER TWENTY-THREE

The *Fuhrerbunker*
Henningsdorf, Germany

THE GROUP slowly worked their way down the hall but from the sounds on the radio the Nazis were coming closer. They approached the large laboratory.

Jake pointed inside. "Maybe we can hole up here until they pass by."

Viktor nodded and used the key card to unlock the door. The group entered quickly and approached two men in lab coats. Viktor told them that if they cooperated, they wouldn't be hurt. The two scientists stared at the injured Agent Pyle, and the armed group and agreed. The two men led them back towards a rear area when a lab technician came through a door, saw them, and retreated back inside. A second later, the alarm claxons sounded.

"So much for hiding," said Agent Williams.

A group of armed Nazis stormed into the lab and began firing at the group.

"Jake pointed to the door the lab tech had entered from and said, "Go, go, looks like our only avenue."

They raced into the other room to stop in their tracks. The lab tech had already fled out a side door but in the middle of the room was a reinforced glass cage surrounded by electronic monitoring equipment. The cage held a huge hairless humanoid monstrosity. It glared at the group with one yellow eye and one brown eye. The six-foot creature looked like a cross between a human and a Nean-derthal. It was the creature's face that had them staring wide eyed. It was the face of Adolf Hitler.

"Holy Hitler look alike," said Agent Pyle.

"They actually did it," said Jake.

Before anyone else could comment, the door was riddled with bullets. The group split up and took cover behind the equipment. The doors came open and the armed men fired into the room indis-criminately. Jake and the other returned fire but stopped when they heard a loud cracking sound. To their horror the glass cage had several cracks in it from the gunfire. The thing was pushing on the glass causing the cracks to get larger. The armed men then stormed into the room but stopped abruptly when one wall shattered, and the creature leapt out. "I will destroy you all," roared the monster. The armed Nazis hesitated which gave Jake the opportunity and pointed to another door. "Let's get out of here." The group converged on the door and fled the room as the Hitler-faced creature grabbed a large metal cabinet and hurled it at the Nazis. They entered another hallway and ran towards the elevator when a huge hippo like demon blocked their way with numerous Nazi guards behind.

"This could be bad," remarked Agent Pyle.

"Do ya think?" replied Agent Williams.

———

Invlaiddenfriedhof Cemetery
Scharnhorststraße 31, 10115
Berlin, Germany

THEY RACED down Invalidenstrasse as demons climbed onto the car only to have Ellie shoot them off while Roscoe barked, growled, and bit them when they tried to reach in. It delayed them until the slide on the gun locked back.

"Any more ammo?" asked Ellie.

"Nein, I wasn't expecting a war," said Herr Meier.

Pam slammed on the brakes and turned onto Scharnhorstsrasse which dislodged a demon that slammed into a parked car causing the car alarm to sound. "It's got a wall around it."

Ellie pointed to a break in the wall which had a small road going in, except it was closed by an iron gate.

"No, Fraulein, it's a national cemetery, one of the oldest," yelled Herr Meier.

"It's that or get killed by a pack of demons," replied Pam.

She swerved and collided with the iron gate, ripping the hinges loose from the pillar, glanced off the pillar, and drove down the small road only to have smoke pour out from under the hood. Pam swerved onto the grass barely missing a gravestone as the car died. When it stopped the roof was ripped back by two demons.

"Out, out," yelled Ellie.

Roscoe barked and snapped at the demons while the three bailed from the car. One of the heathens jumped off the roof onto the grass beside Pam but screamed as its feet began to sizzle. It flew back onto the roof of the car as Roscoe leapt out.

They ran and hid behind several gravestones.

A demon swooped down and grab at Herr Meier but dodged away when Pam threw a handful of rocks and dirt at the demon, burning it.

"What now? We can't throw dirt and rocks forever," asked Pam.

"I'm not sure," said Ellie as she dodged a flying demon that tried to pluck her off the ground. "Maybe someone will call the police."

A demon tried to grab Ellie, but Roscoe bit down on its leg, but as it flew up, Roscoe held on, lifting him up and off the ground. The creature reached down to grab Roscoe when the demon's head suddenly was removed from its body as a flash of gold and white flew by.

"Is that what I think it is?" asked Herr Meier from behind a large cement statue.

"You mean who?" said Ellie. "She's an angel."

"Of course," he replied. "Demons are here so why not angels."

The angel Kiara grabbed Roscoe and set him to the ground. While Pam, Ellie, and Herr Meier threw rocks and dirt at the demons, Kiara fought with them in the air.

————

The *Fuhrerbunker*
Henningsdorf, Germany

BEFORE JAKE COULD GET a shot off at the demon, more armed guards came up behind them so they had to retreat to doorways, returning fire at both ends of the hallway.

"We're running low on ammo, Jacob," yelled Viktor.

Jake snapped a few rounds at the huge demon which was hard to miss but due to the constant gunfire from the Nazis it wasn't having much effect. The demon was almost upon them when the men behind the large demon abruptly stopped shooting. A large hairy arm suddenly reached around the demon and jerked it backwards and twisting, effectively breaking its neck. The hippo like demon fell to the ground which revealed a giant ape with one yellow eye and one normal. Taking the break in the gunfire to his advantage he stepped out to fire at the creature when a voice rang out from behind the ape.

"Major Taft, hold your fire, he's friendly."

"Colonel Price?" asked Jake.

"Roger."

Then several men in military camo appeared from behind the ape and laid down an overwhelming barrage of gunfire which drove the Nazis back into retreat. Colonel Price stepped around the ape, patted the thing on the shoulder, and approached Jake.

"Are we too late for the fun?"

"No, sir Colonel, I would say your timing is perfect. But how?"

As the sound of gunfire died down Colonel Price explained, "The president called the Pentagon and ordered us to deploy here. Based on the intel sent to us from your FBI friends here we located you."

"But how did he get here?" asked Agent Williams pointing to the ape creature.

"We insisted on coming to help," said a familiar female figure as she approached.

"Eudora?" replied Jake.

Colonel Price nodded. "When we were packing up to come here, they showed up and insisted on helping. No way was I going to say no."

"We found a lot of our own still alive after the cave in. Without your help and information, we never would've been able to save them. We owed you and we want pay back."

"How many are here?" asked Viktor.

"About fifty," answered Colonel Price. "That's all we could cram into the aircraft with us and our gear. Any idea where the bomb is?"

"No, sir, but I know who to ask," replied Jake.

————

Invlaiddenfriedhof Cemetery
Scharnhorststraße 31, 10115
Berlin, Germany

PAM, Ellie, and Herr Meier continued to throw cemetery dirt and rocks in their vain attempt to keep the demons at bay while Kiara dodged and dove, clashing with the demons. Suddenly she was gone.

"Where'd she go?" yelled Pam from behind a headstone.

"No idea," answered Ellie.

With Kiara gone the demons intensified their air assault on them. A demon grabbed Herr Meier by the coat but luckily, he just let the jacket slip off. As the demon tossed the jacket aside a bright light shone on the creature and gunfire erupted. The monster was struck several times and screamed as its body burned. Larger caliber gunfire ensued striking several demons causing them to burn and screech. Sadly, numerous monuments and gravestones were also hit. The demons fled.

"Miss Thompson, are you ok?" yelled a voice from behind the

lights.

The three then realized the lights were headlights from several military vehicles.

"Yes, we're here," replied Ellie from behind a monument.

"I'm Major Wilkins from the U.S. Armed Forces. I think you can come out now. They seemed to have left."

Ellie, Pam, Herr Meier approached the two armored vehicles.

"Are we glad to see you," said Pam. "But how did you know where we were?"

Major Wilkins smiled, "The FBI told us where you were at but when we arrived the milk building was empty except for several dead civilians. We then just followed the path of destruction through the city to you."

Herr Meier pointed at Pam. "Fraulein Demolition is to thank for that."

Pam shrugged. "Hey I was trying to keep the demons off us."

A tall black male came up and shook her hand. "I'm Sergeant George Little, but you can call me G, and I like your style." He then turned to Colonel Price. "But we received info from the colonel. He said they breached the Nazi bunker and found Major Taft and his agent friends alive and well."

Major Wilkins nodded. "Excellent." He turned to the three. "Would you like a ride?"

"Nein," said Herr Meier. "I will return and see what I can do about my people and my warehouse."

Ellie and Pam loaded Roscoe into the back of the Hummer.

————

The *Fuhrerbunker*
Henningsdorf, Germany

JAKE LED them back down to the laboratory where they found several scientists and lab technicians huddled down in a storage room. The three scientists were more than happy to share the information at Viktor's encouragement.

"The bomb is in the old woman's electric wheelchair?" asked Colonel Price.

"Da, that is what he said," replied Viktor who had been asking the questions in German. "He said it's attached to the motor of her electric wheelchair. She can activate it from there."

"But she'll die with the rest," said Agent Williams.

Viktor shook his head. "Nyet, the plan is for the wheelchair to break down and she'll leave it there. When they get far enough away it will detonate."

"Can a bomb be that small?" Agent Pyle asked.

Colonel Price nodded. "Yes, they can make them small enough to fit in a briefcase, but the yield will be less."

"But enough to destroy the building and anyone inside," Jake added.

Colonel Price called the number given to contact the secret service, but the line was constantly busy. He then switched to his radio however all he received was static. "Something is interfering with the radio traffic."

"The Nazis must be jamming the signal at the hotel," said Jake.

"We need to get there ASAP."

Before they left the lab, Jake and Agent Williams checked the back lab area but the creature with the Hitler face was gone.

"We can look for him later," Agent Williams said. "One crisis at a time."

As they were leaving, Viktor came out of the lab with a small, padded envelope which he stuffed under his jacket. Jake glanced at him. "Bones," commented Viktor.

On the ride up the elevator Colonel Price radioed Major Wilkins and advised him to divert to the hotel. He turned to Jake. "Phil has the two women and your dog. They'll meet us at the hotel."

At the entrance to the elevator on the first level the rest of the unit waited. As they loaded into the armored vehicles, the half demons followed. Tank sat in the driver's seat as Agent Williams climbed in. "Missed me," he said with a grin.

"Shut up and drive," growled Agent Williams.

CHAPTER TWENTY-FOUR

Estrel Hotel
Sonnenallee 225, 12057
Berlin, Germany

SECRET SERVICE AGENT MEADOWS approached the president. "Mr. President, we may have a problem." They stepped over the side. "We have no radios, either they've failed or jammed."

"Could it just be failed transmissions?" asked the president.

Agent Meadows shrugged. "It could be, but on a massive scale, I doubt it."

The president nodded. "Any word from Taft?"

Agent Meadows shook his head. "No, sir, but with communications down we wouldn't know."

"Keep me informed and put someone on the Getman woman. I want to know where she is at all times."

———

Downtown Berlin

THE CONVOY of military vehicles raced through Berlin with fifty various types of half demons following which made quite a spectacle as they arrived at the barricades.

A Berlin police officer approached the lead Humvee. "Can I help you?"

Colonel Price leaned out of the window. "I'm Colonel Price of the United States Army. We have information of national security. We need to get to the hotel immediately."

"Nein, Colonel, the radios are down so we have no way of getting clearance." The officer then pointed to the mob of half demons gathered around. "And are these things with you? Is this some sort of costume party joke?"

Colonel Price gritted his teeth. "They are with us. We have information that there is a bomb in the building. Do you want to be personally responsible for this?"

The officer turned and spoke to another Berlin police officer.

Viktor nudged Jake. "My friend, I think we have more problems. Demons."

Jake nodded, "There are always demons about."

"No, I can see them too," Viktor replied and pointed up the street.

"Not good."

Agent Williams yelled, "We have demons incoming!"

At the sound of the commotion the two Berlin officers turned and froze at the sight of dozens of various sized demons hooting, clicking, screeching, flying, and running directly towards them. The officers drew their weapons.

"Your weapons won't work, so get behind our vehicles," yelled Colonel Price. He turned to his unit. "Demons are trying to stop us. Engage and fire at will while we try to get to the hotel."

Tank gunned the engine and rammed through the barricades while the others opened fire on the demons. Using the cemetery-imbedded ammo several demons screamed and started burning where the rounds struck them. The half demons charged the oncoming demons. "It's payback time," they yelled.

The armored vehicles raced down the street a short distance to the hotel while demons clung onto the vehicles fighting with half demons. The news media that was camped out front of the hotel turned their cameras and attention to the nightmare that was approaching. Some fled while others hid behind their TV vans capturing this unreal science fiction looking situation with military units firing at strange creatures who were fighting other strange creatures.

The Humvees pulled up in front of the hotel and the occupants unloaded. Jake ran to Ellie and told her to stay close. Colonel Price ran up to the door and confronted the armed agents at the door. "I need to see President Campbell, NOW."

––––––

INSIDE THE GALA the sound of gunfire could not be heard over the sound of the music and chatter of conversations. Agent Meadows dashed up to the president. "Sir, we have a situation. Major Taft and Colonel Price are here and need to see you immediately."

The president nodded. He and the first lady followed Agent Meadows out of the gala into the hallway. He noticed other protection units and agents from other countries were scrambling into the gala. They met Colonel Price, Jake, Viktor, Ellie, and Pam in the large hallway. Several half demons followed.

Colonel Price saluted the president. "Sir, we know where the bomb is. It's in the Getman woman's wheelchair."

The president turned to Agent Meadows. "Get the woman and ask the German Chancellor to meet us here."

Several Secret Services Agents immediately dashed off in different directions.

"Do we know anything about the bomb?" the president asked.

"The scientists in their lab said that it's big enough to destroy several blocks of the city but we also have to deal with radiation," explained Colonel Price.

German Chancellor Bauer approached with his security people. "What is going on here? You have your military units shooting in front of the hotel and people in costumes rioting. This is unacceptable."

"Chancellor Bauer, we have a serious situation. We have reliable information that a small nuclear weapon is in the building," explained the president.

The German Chancellor's eyes widened. "A nuclear bomb?"

"Yes, and it gets worse. We have information that Priska Getman has the bomb disguised under her wheelchair."

Chancellor Bauer shook his head. "There must be a mistake. She is the daughter of a famous actress and pillar of the community."

At that moment, Priska Getman and her granddaughter arrived under armed escort. "What is meaning of this?" demanded Priska Getman.

The chancellor put his hand on her shoulder. "My dear Priska, I'm so sorry for this. These Americans think you are sitting on a nuclear device."

"That's ridiculous," she replied. "We're not staying here to be accused of such nonsense. We're leaving."

As she turned her wheelchair to leave, Jake reached out and grabbed her.

"Unhand me, you American pig."

Jake had noticed her fiddling with one arm of the wheelchair. He jerked her hand away and exposed a timer that was counting down from five minutes.

Five Minutes

Everyone stood and stared for a brief second. "What have you done, Priska?" the chancellor said.

"What is good for Germany," she said calmly. "Nothing can stop it. Now Germany will be reborn."

Gerda Getman turned and dashed down the hall but came up short when Roscoe grabbed the hem of her dress. A second later, Gerda was hit from behind and driven to the floor. She looked back at a woman holding her down. "You," she screamed, "You half bred, get your hands off me."

"My named is Eudora," said the half demon woman. "And you are finished." Gerda was handcuffed, jerked to her feet, and led away.

Colonel Price looked around in frustration. "Any ideas? All this for nothing."

Jake turned to Agent Meadows. "Get everyone down into the parking garage's lowest level. Being underground might help. I have an idea."

Agent Meadows nodded and started ushering everyone towards the below level parking garage. The chancellor's agent followed and soon a mass exodus was headed below. Ellie came up to Jake. "I'm staying with you."

Jake shook his head. "It's safer for you downstairs. I'll join you."

"I love you," she said.

"I love you too, now go."

4:00 Minutes

Jake turned to Eudora. "Where is your ape friend?"

Eudora dashed around the corner and was soon back with the half demon ape that had helped them at the bunker.

3:00 Minutes

Jake pointed to the elderly Getman woman, "Get her out of the wheelchair so we can remove this thing from the building. It might help."

Agent Pyle and Williams tried to remove the woman who screamed and scratched at them to prevent them. The half demon ape shoved them aside, lifted the wheelchair up with her in it, and lumbered towards the front doors.

2:20 Minutes

The president and first lady were rushed down to their limo and were being loaded into the back when Trish insisted Ellie and Pam join them. The four sat inside with Roscoe on the floor while the secret service agents took cover.

"The vehicle might provide us some protection," the president said sadly.

The first lady reached over and grasped Pam's and Ellie's hands. "Your friends will come through."

Ellie nodded but knew even Jake couldn't stop a nuclear bomb.

Suddenly the heavenly being Kiara appeared in the tight confines of the limo. "Have faith," she said and disappeared as quickly as she appeared.

The president and first lady stared at the spot where she appeared.

"Was that?" asked the obviously wide eyed and surprised president.

Ellie and Pam nodded.

1:30 Minutes

The ape creature reached the door and burst outside with the screaming Getman woman.

Jake, Colonel Price, Viktor, Agent Pyle, and Agent Williams followed. Major Wilkins ran up. "Colonel, what's going on? All the demons have left."

Colonel Price nodded and pointed to the ape. "That's because he has a nuclear bomb set to go off in one minute."

1 Minute

Major Wilkins's eyes widened. "Then we were too late."

"I'm afraid so, Phil," the colonel said sadly. "It's been an honor serving with you."

Major Wilkins nodded. "It's been an honor, sir."

Colonel Price turned to the other sad faces. "When we started this thing in Nevada, I never would have guessed it would end like this. We tried."

Suddenly a voice from above yelled at the ape, "Give her to me."

Without hesitation the ape leapt upon one of the Humvees and held Priska Getman in her wheelchair above his head. She was snatched away as a white and gold flying blur named Malachy flew by and shot up through the sky.

Everyone stood with mouths open gaping at the winged figure as he grew smaller and smaller as he flew up into the atmosphere.

"Well, I'll be," Colonel Price said. "Was that what I thought it was?"

Jake grinned. "Yes, sir, that's a friend of mine."

"Malachy has wings," commented Agent Pyle.

Jake shrugged. "First time I've seen him with wings, but angels never cease to surprise me."

30 Seconds

Malachy flew higher and higher. Priska Getman screamed and wailed but as she got higher with less oxygen and the air became colder, she slowed. "Let...me...go."

15 seconds

"With pleasure," Malachy said and let go of her. The wheelchair turned and Priska, who was seat belted into the wheelchair, tumbled and began to descend along with all her crazy dreams. Malachy turned and disappeared just as the bomb detonated.

Inside the hotel the people on the main level heard a blast and a moment later the electricity blinked out and car alarms sounded outside. Jake turned to Viktor and slapped him on the back. Agent Williams and Pyle high fived everyone.

Down in the parking garage they all waited. They didn't hear the blast, but the electricity went out and they heard the car alarms. The president looked at his watch and then over at Pam, Ellie, and the first lady. "It's past time. They did it. I don't know how they did it, but they did," he said with a huge grin.

Trish smiled. "I told you they wouldn't let us down."

The door to the limo opened and Agent Meadows yelled over the sound of the car alarms. "You can come out, Mr. President."

They all exited the limo and the agents produced flashlights. They looked around at the dignitaries in the garage who were all smiles and cheers. A moment later, Roscoe barked, and Ellie saw Jake walking towards them. She ran, hugged him, and kissed him. "I don't know how you did it but I'm so happy you did."

Jake smiled. "Malachy flew down and took the woman and her wheelchair up into the atmosphere. The detonation was minor. It'll knock out electricity and communications nearby but not much else."

"Malachy flew?" asked Pam.

"He had wings," Jake replied.

"Wings?"

The president approached and heard their conversation. "I'm just glad you have friends in high places, Major."

Jake shook the president's hand. "Me too, sir, me too."

EPILOGUE

J Double T Ranch
Sutton County, Texas

IT'S BEEN over a month since the incident in Berlin. Jake and Roy were in the new barn working while Al was sitting outside on the steps of the house waiting to start the small feast they had planned. Ellie was sitting in one of the rocking chairs with their ghostly friend, Ned, rocking in the other.

"When is the colonel supposed to be here?" Al asked. He glanced over his shoulder at Ellie. He still hadn't quite gotten used to seeing Ned.

"Any minute now," replied Ellie. "How's the new prosthetic arm working out?"

Al held up his state-of-the-art prosthetic arm. "It's awesome. It's the newest and best one yet."

Ellie nodded. "Well, when the President of the United States insisted on you getting the best and most modern, that happens."

Roscoe had been asleep between the two rocking chairs raised his head, looked toward the gate, and barked. They all turned to see an olive-green sedan throwing up a cloud of dust as it approached.

Ellie stood up. "Looks like Colonel Price and Pam are here. Roscoe, go get Jake."

Roscoe trotted off toward the barn while the rest got up and waited as the military vehicle pulled up and stopped. Colonel Price, wearing civilian clothes, climbed out and approached the group. Pam climbed out of the other side and hugged Ellie. He shook hands and introduced himself to Al. "So, you're the courageous journalist that hung out with these crazy people?"

Al blushed. "I was there for some of it, but I'm not sure I was brave."

"Nonsense," said Colonel Price and patted Al on the shoulder. "You lost part of your arm trying to stop a demon so that makes you a hero."

"I just need to finish up my article."

Ellie patted him on the shoulder. "And you will, as soon as Jake gets out of the barn we can eat, and you can get whatever you need. I've heard a lot of magazines want the story. You're about to be famous."

"I just want to tell the story," said a red-faced Al.

Jake and Roy came walking up. Jake shook hands with Colonel Price and introduced him to Roy.

"You had to bring Pam with you?" Jake asked.

Pam frowned. "Funny, Jake, he needed directions to your place from town and I was the girl for the job."

They all went inside and filled their plates with BBQ from the local restaurant that Jake had brought from town. Once they were seated and began eating Al started trying to fill in the gaps.

"So, what happened right after bomb detonated?"

Jake wiped his mouth with a napkin. "Well, since the bomb was a smaller one it only caused an electromagnetic pulse which knocked out the electricity and some minor problems. Once it was clear, as you read in the media the economic summit was postponed until they could restore the electricity."

Al nodded. "What about Gerda Getman?"

"She was arrested and is claiming that she was just a pawn in her grandmother's scheme," explained Colonel Price. "The news seems to be buying her story, but we'll have to see how that pans out."

"And the bunker?"

"It was cleaned out by the German authorities. The data they took from the lab there is being analyzed. Hopefully they'll share with us what they learn."

Jake nodded. "It's a good thing Viktor grabbed Hitler's bones before we left, or he might never have gotten them back."

Al had his laptop open and was typing feverishly. "And speaking of Hitler, did they find the creature?"

Colonel Price and Jake both shook their heads. "No, the Germans are still looking for the creature," replied Colonel Price. "My guess is some of the Nazis were able to sneak the thing out during the confusion."

"So how did the German chancellor take the news about the bomb?"

"The president and the chancellor had a meeting about it," Colonel Price answered. "That's all I can say about it officially."

Al nodded. "I understand. I'm sure it's a sensitive issue."

"But I can tell you that the chancellor told the president that the next time you invade his country illegally, have a shootout with demons, and damage one of Berlin's beloved cemeteries he may not be so forgiving, even if you did save the world's leaders," explained the colonel.

Everyone laughed. "Actually, the chancellor was happy and thankful we were able to stop the threat and avert a possible world-wide issue," he added.

"I heard that the half demons went back to Arizona," said Al.

"Yep," Jake said, "They returned to the reservation area where they can be less conspicuous. Elijah Greymountain has taken it upon himself to help them and is in Washington lobbying for them."

After they finished eating, Colonel Price pulled a small box from his jacket and handed it to Jake. "This is for you."

Jake opened the box which held a pair of silver oak leaf clusters.

Colonel Price smiled broadly. "It's my honor to notify you of your promotion to lieutenant colonel, pending the promotion board's approval. I think with the president's input it shouldn't be a problem. Congratulations, Jake, you've earned it."

Jake smiled. "Thank you, sir, but we all earned it."

Colonel Price nodded. "I agree, but I can't give your group promotion or medals, just a thanks from a grateful nation and president."

"I heard a rumor that a general's star might be in your future," said Jake.

Colonel Price shrugged. "We'll see."

Pam and Ellie teared up and Roy grinned.

"What about Stephanie and Terrel?" asked Al.

"Oscar sent me an email the other day and said they are being honored for their work. Maybe the rest of the FBI will take them a little more serious," said Jake.

They all looked at each other for a moment and burst out laughing.

———

LATER THAT EVENING, after everyone had left, Jake and Ellie were sitting in his living room when a heavenly host suddenly appeared. After the initial shock of him appearing in their living room, Ellie jumped up and gave Malachy a hug. "We are so thankful for your help. You saved the world from major problems if all the leaders had been killed at one time."

"You're welcome," answered the huge heavenly angel. "I am blessed to serve God. And congratulations on your promotion, Colonel."

Jake smiled.

"How is Kiara?" asked Ellie.

"She's fine and will heal. We must always be vigilant. These fallen are always planning something."

Jake nodded. "And when they do, we'll be ready."

"Yes, we will."

A LOOK AT DEMON HUNTER BOOK THREE: THE DEMON ERUPTION

The demons have upped their game by setting off a world-ending chain of volcanic eruption.

Jake and Ellie Taft thought they were in for a nice honeymoon getaway… They couldn't have been more wrong.

When a volcanologist and the owner of an oil drilling company are both kidnapped, the FBI calls in Jake and Ellie for their special "expertise". No one understands the demons — or the way they fight — quite like the Taft dynamic duo.

It also doesn't hurt that they have angels looking over them.

But this time, the demons — led by Tarnac, a fiend more vicious than any the FBI have come across — are targeting dormant volcanoes at the edge of the world. Thankfully, their victims aren't as eager to help as the demons thought they would be. Not even the hybrid clone, succubus Hitler is interested in demonic plans anymore.

Join Jake and Ellie and a whole host of action-packed characters as they fight demons, using half demon hybrids who have switched sides in an effort to save the world from — literally — becoming Hell on Earth. Not all will survive the battle in Antarctica, but who will win?

AVAILABLE OCTOBER 2022

ABOUT THE AUTHOR

Kerry Adcock is a graduate of Angelo State University with a Bachelor of Arts degree. After serving in the U.S. Air Force, he then spent 37 years in law enforcement working in patrol, and as a detective in the Special Victims Section as well as in the Homicide unit.

He has lectured and taught classes on sexual assault and sex offenders to the police academy as well as local and national women's groups. He's received awards such as the Police Medal of Valor and Detective of the Year. He is currently retired and lives in Arlington, Texas.

Kerry is an accomplished artist as well, focusing primarily on painting acrylic on canvas.

www.ingramcontent.com/pod-product-compliance
Lightning Source LLC
Chambersburg PA
CBHW011423010726
47494CB00011B/2468